Wild Court

With very best wishes,
M

Matthew Samuels

ISBN: 9798377565864

FIRST EDITION
www.theabditory.co.uk

For content and trigger warnings for all my books, check theabditory.co.uk/content-trigger-warnings.
In particular, this book contains frequent and graphic swearing, horror elements and unpleasant scenes including torture. If in any doubt, please check the web page or contact me directly to avoid any unnecessary distress.

Part One

The Shamblers

Ben

Friday Night, Somerset House

"You know, for someone who hates people, you sure do care a lot about what they think," the man next to me says slowly. He smells of stale body odour and urine, overlaid with cigarette smoke and cheap alcohol.

We're friends.

I'm sitting on a low wall, somewhere near London's South Bank with a guy who calls himself Jack. He tells me that he's been homeless for about four years, since he lost his job and broke up with his wife. His story terrifies me, but he seems to accept it with pragmatism. It's awful how easy it is to end up on the streets, but I guess that reminder alone is one reason why people avoid the homeless.

I've known Jack for about six months. He begs on my route to work, towards the bottom of the Strand. He sits close enough to the shelter and soup kitchen to get fed when it's open, but not so close as to get crowded up against the other homeless people. He's got a dog, a cute pup called Petra who warmed to me straightaway and pesters me insistently for scraps. I've noticed that a lot of homeless people have dogs these days. Good early warning system for trouble, I suppose.

I got talking to Jack one night after leaving work drinks early. I'd been tossing him pound coins for a while and he knew me by sight, he claims. I was about to walk past and instead found myself sinking down beside him and sharing the late dinner I'd bought from Leon. He smelt a little, but I didn't really mind.

"I don't hate people," I say carefully. Spending time talking to a man with no home has made me slow and thoughtful with my words. "I just don't enjoy spending time with a lot of them at once."

He nods. Jack's got a degree in marine biology and – when he chooses to deploy it – a razor sharp wit. He doesn't deploy it much, mind you; living on the streets tends to erode your sense of humour pretty quickly.

"You don't resent them?"

I pause, turning it over in my head. For some reason, sitting with Jack is entirely a low-pressure conversation. He's happy to wait for an answer and I've learned that he likes to think about his answers to my questions too. Once I'd gotten over the initial oddness of the speed of our discussions, I realised that it made for a pretty relaxing way to talk.

"Well, sometimes," I admit. "But usually when I'm tired out after a long day. You know, like when you've had enough and want to get away from it all for a bit and you're good once you've had some time to yourself. I want to help people, I really do, I just find them difficult."

Jack nods and stays silent. If he disagrees with my argument, he's pretty quick to point it out, but silence usually means he's mulling things over and understands.

I've always been like this. Even when I was a kid, I needed time to myself and that's kind of why I chose to work in a library. I love books and I actually do love helping people to read and learn. My library is pretty slow, except at lunchtimes or before 9am when people drop in on their way to work, and that suits me down to the ground. Course, it pays terribly, despite being in Mayfair. I guess I'm lucky to still have somewhere to work after the politicians cut funding to virtually nothing a few years ago.

And I should add that I like my colleagues too, but work nights out can be exhausting in London. Lunchtime usually sees me finding a quiet space in a park, the corner of a coffee shop or even the stacks, trying to fence off some peace and quiet.

I live on my own. I shared, but then I got a pay rise about a year back and realised that if I moved further out, I could get a studio flat out in the sticks and balance the drop in rent with the more expensive commute. It was no contest, even if it meant I couldn't give as much to Jack and the others as I used to. I used to have all kinds of standing orders set up with charities, but had to cut back as my rent crept up and pay stayed the same. I think it's the same for Londoners everywhere.

"Ben," Jack says carefully. "I've been working with this organisation, and they're looking out for people like you. I've been trying to decide whether or not you'd be interested, or whether I'd really be doing you a favour by introducing you, but they're not going to be recruiting for much longer."

I frown. He's not mentioned this before, and I do already volunteer when I can, and he knows this.

"What, like the shelter or something?" I ask.

"No," he says. "No, it's different. You'd still be helping to fix a problem, but it's a tougher one."

"Cryptic," I say, laughing. "A tougher problem than fixing benefits, housing and homelessness under a conservative government? Really?"

He fixes me with a serious look, and for a moment I forget about the grubby wall that we're sat on, the tourists walking past, the cute dog at our feet. "Absolutely," he says. "But Luke can explain it better than I can. And he'll probably show rather than tell. Look, check it out, but remember that you don't have to help, ok? There's other people doing a lot already."

He levers himself into a standing position, his sleeve catching on brickwork, flashing a shoddy-looking, presumably home-made tattoo on his arm. He stands, leaving me sat on the pavement, as if our positions had been reversed.

I'm still baffled. "Sure," I say, spreading my hands. "I can check it out. Where are they based?"

Jack looks like he's about to grin, but he doesn't, instead flicking me a coin, which I catch awkwardly with both hands.

"You'll figure it out," he says. "And take a friend, that one you're always telling me about, Matt. You're late, but I reckon you'll work out."

"Fine," I say, shaking my head in amusement. "Be cryptic. But get that tattoo looked at, ok? It'll get infected one day."

He laughs, pulling on his pack, bending to sweep up the change from his Starbucks cup and straightening his coat.

"I'll see you again, ok?" he says, and more than anything, that gives me pause, but then he's gone, coat flapping, his stink receding, Petra following dutifully behind. People look at me as I hold the coin and I can feel them evaluating whether they should toss me one as well. I don't have a cup, a sign or a dog, and maybe because of this, no-one gives me anything. I feel acutely uncomfortable for a moment and realise how dirty it is down here. I sigh, pushing myself up and start to walk down towards Waterloo Station, shaking my head at Jack's joke, more than a little confused.

~

Waterloo East station is bright in contrast to the dim glow of the South Bank, white fluorescent lights washing the colour from skin and giving everyone a deathly pallor. I've got fifteen minutes until my train arrives, so I pick up an Evening Standard and flick through the pages, leaning against dirty brickwork.

Celebrity news, scandal, marketing stunts. Another ten British marines killed in Syria, I read, Prime Minister to face Parliamentary enquiry.

I glance up. The platform isn't full but there's plenty of workers and tourists heading back after a busy day and a quick drink that turned into three. There's a tang in the air, concrete after a storm, even though it's not been raining. There's a woman to my right, smartly dressed, staring into space. She looks bored. An old couple are sat on the pair of seats to my left, glaring at a group of guys who are being loud, still gripping lager cans and occasionally bursting into raucous laughter. Nothing out of the ordinary, nothing to be worried about. I get back to the paper and read about the lost marines until my train arrives, swapping one set of strip lighting for another.

I settle into a seat at the end of the carriage and idly pull Jack's coin from my pocket, meaning to put it in my wallet. Funny guy, I think to myself, turning it over and over in my hand.

Only, it's not a coin at all.

It's easy to see why I made the mistake: it's a gold token of some kind, made of metal like a coin. There's a set of numbers on one side, and a bird holding a twig on the other – a dove, I guess?

The text is small, so I bring it up closer to my eye. It looks like a grid reference and what could be a time in the twenty-four-hour clock. I've got decent reception on my phone, so I look them up.

Juggling the token, my phone, a scrap of paper and a pen balanced on the back of my bag, I work it out. Near as I can tell, it's a side street not far from Centre Point. There's a shelter there, I know – maybe it's some kind of commemorative token to get in?

Weird.

The train stops at Greenwich and a horde of tourists and goers-out get on, panting from the exertion of running up the long ramp at the side of the station where the town cut-through drops you off. They're noisy, eating fast food and drinking the last dregs from beer cans or wine bottles. A couple of them have those new face masks on, the pollution ones with the designs on them. I saw a guy with a skull one the other day – almost made a woman faint.

Tearing myself away, I look at the numbers on the coin again. If I put the grid references to one side, the date comes out as tomorrow night at what looks like five past midnight.

I sigh, putting it away and taking out my headphones, plugging into some trance and letting the rest of the noise vanish away. The two sets of sound interfere with each other for a moment, then I turn the volume up a bit more until there's only music.

By the time the train pulls in at Erith, I'm tired but my rough edges have been smoothed off a bit and I'm not so ragged, just ready for a good night's sleep.

It's a quick walk from the station to my flat. The clouds drop a few raindrops here and there, but I'm home without incident, curling up in bed and falling asleep before I even pick up a book.

~

"Four hundred marines and members of the armed forces have now been tragically lost in the Middle East in the last year alone," the news reporter is saying. "The Prime Minister surely faces a difficult time justifying British involvement in a situation which shows few signs of stabilisation."

The anchor thanks the presenter and turns to the weather. I'm curled up in bed with a cup of tea, watching morning television. That's the simultaneous blessing and curse of a studio flat: everything's in reach.

I dreamt vividly, waking and instantly feeling disappointed to be leaving the dream. Not usually a morning person, I make breakfast and watch TV, hoping it'll pass. On days like this, I try to look after myself. I watch films, drink soup, play computer games.

Most people would say that sounds pretty boring. To me, it's complete bliss.

I'd put Jack's token on a shelf when I'd gotten home and for some reason, it keeps catching my eye, silently nagging me. I turn it over and over in my fingers, looking at the numbers on the rim.

I shrug. Fuck it. I'm not doing anything else today. Might as well.

I call Matt. It's not very millennial of me, but nonetheless, he picks up.

"What's up, nerd-brain?"

There are some very important things you should know about Matt. He's loyal, kind, shares my love of books and sci-fi, and always, always buys me coffee when he sees me.

He's also kind of a dick.

"Nerd brain?" I echo, snorting. "That's the best you've got this morning?"

"Yeah, you said it – morning," he retorts. "Matt does not do mornings. Especially when he hung out and got high last night."

"Thought you were cutting back?" I start, then stop. "Look, it doesn't matter. Are you free tonight? There's something I want to check out."

Matt's more of a social than habitual drug user, drinker and smoker. It's complicated.

"Check out? Is this another art thing, Ben? You still owe me from last time."

"Um, yeah, I think it is," I stutter. "Look, I'll buy dinner – it doesn't start until midnight so we can have a quiet drink first and you can tell me about last night."

"Fine, fine," he grunts. "Message me where and I'll meet you. I've got an appointment with a dirty Macca's and then I'm going back to bed. Later."

"Later," I say, and hang up the phone.

I sit back down on the bed.

Art.

Sure, why not?

If it doesn't work out, I'll hear about it for the next few weeks, but it's as good an excuse as any.

Ben
Places Betwixt

I buy Matt dinner in a cheap Thai restaurant that we both like. It's one of the things I love about London – you can get good food, cheaply, if you know where to look. The other week I came across a Nicaraguan restaurant and popped in for an awkward solo dinner. I mean, I had to look up where Nicaragua was when I was browsing the menu, but the food was delicious. Anyway, the staff in this place know me, or at least recognise me because I tend to bring my generally abortive first dates along and order pints of apple juice because otherwise I drink too quickly when I'm nervous. It's decent, affordable, café-style and for some reason the noise doesn't bother me as much as in other places.

That's the thing about familiarity. Once you know a place, everything feels a bit safer.

Matt slurps his way through a noodle soup and some Pad thai, demolishing three beers in the process. The owner, a tiny, elderly, wrinkled matron laughs at him and whispers in my ear at one point when he's in the bathroom.

"Your friend has great energy," she says, eyes glinting. "We like him."

"I'm sorry," I laugh. "I think you're in a minority."

"He is a good man," she insists. "But too big, I think, for this place."

And with that, Matt crashes out of the bathroom proving her point. Despite being in central London, which is usually well-equipped with facilities, this place has a toilet the size of a shoe cupboard and I also usually end up banging my head or my elbows before, during or after peeing. Matt sits down, making the chair creak as the proprietor slips back to the counter.

"What was that, Ben? Is she going to give us free fortune cookies?"

I sigh theatrically. "Matt, fortune cookies are Chinese. We're in a Thai restaurant."

"They're actually American," he says, giving his best Ben Kingsley impression.

I laugh in spite of myself and shake my head, turning back to my spicy beef. Once we've finished up – and after I thank the staff profusely for their general patience and the distinct lack of kicking us out however close it is to their closing time – we find a shitty chain bar for a quick drink. Or rather, we stand in a queue with tourists and students for longer than anyone should, for overpriced craft beers lacking much in the way of 'craft'.

It gets close to midnight and I pull Matt away from

a girl he's bothering, despite him swearing blind that he's 'making progress' and 'they could be soulmates', the latter claim much less serious than the former.

Outside, he shuts up and we head north up Charing Cross Road before reaching the relative quiet of New Oxford Street.

At the risk of sounding pretentious, this part of London has always seemed like a place betwixt to me. The British Museum looms not far away, the law districts of Holborn and Temple to the south and east. Tottenham Court Road, with its bright lights, Soho with the aforementioned food and its bars, both lie to the west, but this part of town is a bit of a limbo. We pass a Travelodge, a family standing outside looking at a paper map. There's a cycling shop, a super-healthy café, some offices, but nothing binds it all together in the way that other parts of London seem to have coherence.

I'm nervous. It's a perennial condition, but I'm more nervous than usual, even with Matt next to me. I have to keep stopping myself from worrying at a hangnail.

I turn the corner, the street lights a bright orange against the stark white strip lighting of the serviced office next to me. The next building is the one I want. A grand reception, high ceilings, polished wooden beams overhead, a variety of fabric chairs and sofas contorted into what I can only imagine to be an awkward and uncomfortable foyer to wait in, unless you're the kind of smoothie-guzzling hipster that these places were built to house,

MacBook and iPhone at the ready.

I have neither, obviously. Not really my vibe.

I hesitate for a moment before pushing on the revolving door.

Nothing happens.

I glance down to the other end of the room where a bored-looking security guard sits at a desk. Spots me. Hits a button.

I push again and this time, get through.

Matt sniggers.

The walk to the front desk is long and awkward. I glance around. There's a small café on the left-hand side, magazines arranged neatly on the tables.

"You lost?"

The guard is middle-aged, male, and has thinning brown hair and a moustache. He's got the logo of a security company emblazoned on his regulation jacket.

"Uh, no," I start, my voice feeling thin and inadequate for the distance still between us. "I'm here to see ... uh ... I was given this?"

I fish the golden token out of my pocket and, closing the distance between us, lay it on the desk. The guy behind the desk looks at it as if I've deposited a small turd there instead of the coin.

"First floor, room 105. You'd better hurry up, you're late."

He jerks his head to one side and I follow his gaze to a sign for stairs, then awkwardly try to retrieve the coin, my sweaty hand unable to prise it off the desk until I give up and sweep it into my other hand.

Without turning to look at Matt, I hurry through the door.

It's barely closed before he guffaws behind me.

"Shit, Ben," he says, too loudly for my liking. "Congratulations. Honestly, I thought you were going to freak out and shit yourself."

It sounds nasty, but actually, that's a compliment coming from Matt and in all honesty, his 'business as usual' behaviour calms me down a bit. If he's ever sensitive, then I know I'm in serious trouble.

Halfway up the regulation office stairs, I turn and give him the finger.

"Wasn't far off," I admit. "I thought he was going to tell me to fuck off and call the police."

"He was going to tell *you* to fuck off and call the police?" Matt screws up his face. "Am I still hungover or something? You usually make more sense than this."

I shake my head and laugh. "Wanker."

"More often than you know."

Yuck. Trying to push that image from my mind, I open the door to the first floor and look around, seeing a door marked '105' just down the hall. It's not a terrible office block; some of them are small and awfully dull, but this is fairly light and looks like someone has actually paid attention to the decor.

I pause outside. Should I knock?

Fortunately, Matt's patience with my high-functioning anxiety expires and he pushes in front of me, powering through the door into the room beyond. I crane my neck to see around him, then hurriedly follow him in.

It's a classroom. Or at least, it seems to be a classroom. There are desks, with a variety of people of different ages and backgrounds sat at them, and an older guy sat behind a table at the front. It reminds me of the one time I took an Open University course and went to a tutorial at the college near my parents' house: awkward. Course was great, mind you. Criminology – would recommend it.

I babble when I'm nervous. You might have noticed that already.

"Good, good," the guy at the front says. He's tall and well-built, with black hair in tight curls. "Welcome. I'm Luke. You must be Jack's friends. Please, have a seat and we'll begin."

Thankfully, everyone has done the decidedly non-British thing and sat at the front, so Matt and I slink in without too much fuss and sit at the back.

"Welcome," Luke begins. "You're all here because you've been chosen for the second stage of a recruitment process. I apologise if some of this seems esoteric and obscure, and some of you will have been told more than others, but I assure you, by the end of this evening, you'll have a good idea if this is the kind of career that you'd be interested in. And trust me – it is not for everyone, so if that's you, thank you for attending, be discreet, and don't take the leaflet."

There's a ripple of laughter, but I'm more confused than ever.

"Two weeks ago," Luke begins without further ado. "A young woman took a wrong turn on the way to meet her Uber driver and ended up in a small park off an alleyway not far from here. She was sexually assaulted and eventually killed."

A collective sound of concern ripples through the room and Matt looks at me. I realise that he still thinks this is an art thing like I told him, then find myself grinning. It'll make up for one of the many times that he's pranked me.

I shrug and try to make out this is all as it should be.

"A team of Gardeners was dispatched three days later and closed the small rift that the act caused. Unfortunately, they missed the Darkling that was left behind. Now, can anyone tell me what a Darkling is?"

A team of what? Did he say Gardeners? A Darkling? This is strange.

A guy at the front in a black jacket puts his hand up. He's really much too pale to wear a jacket like that, especially under these lights, but if I was feeling uncharitable – which I am – I'd guess he thinks it makes him look like a badass.

"Yes, thank you," our teacher says, pointing at him.

"It's a spirit," he says with an accent that I'd place somewhere near Southend.

"Yes, quite right. A spirit that feeds off terror, more

to the point. In self-defence, Darklings release some of that terror, allowing them to flee. They are generally non-corporeal, meaning what?"

"They have no physical body," the pale guy says again.

"Good. So, whatever happens, they cannot touch you, only make you feel afraid. So tonight, as part of your induction, we're going to capture and contain the Darkling. Any questions?"

He doesn't pause for very long. "Good – now, you'll leave the actual capture to me, but please consider this your welcome into a different world."

And with that, he heads out of the door, grabbing his coat. Who is this guy? What is this? And perhaps more importantly, thank you so much Jack for telling me everything I needed to know before coming along to this thing.

We're the last people out of the room as everyone else processes down a fire escape. I get the feeling that we missed a fairly significant part of the seminar, but I swear the coin said five past twelve, and Luke did say it was the start of the session.

Matt catches my arm as we follow behind.

"Ben, this is fucking weird," he says. "I mean, it's like that time you took me to that Gresham thing on witchcraft. If there hadn't been those hilarious lesbians there it would have been so boring."

"Uh, just bear with, ok?" I stammer. "This next bit should be good."

"Sure," he says. "But you owe me again, ok? And if there's one more word out of smug fucking Essex Edward Cullen, I swear to god I'll go team Jacob on his ass."

I think for a moment and habit takes over.

"You mean, become the eventual husband of his child? Matt, I think you should lay off the weed for a bit because that's weird even for you."

Matt sniggers, then I break into a snigger as well and we barely make it down the fire escape stairs behind everyone else because we're shaking with laughter by the bottom, a girl in a fur-lined hood giving us a really, really filthy look as we catch up.

I try and focus as we pad along the side street in pairs, before hitting High Holborn, which is full of people getting lost on their way from Covent Garden to Tottenham Court Road. We cross in front of a church and for a moment I wonder where we're going because we're going to hit Soho soon, and nothing mysterious happens in Soho. Matt would tell you otherwise, but his definition of mystery is pretty different to mine, and usually involves women with no clothes on.

But then Luke heads down a side street and I frown. I don't think I've ever been down here before and I pride myself on a fairly encyclopaedic knowledge of London side streets, at least in zone one. They're good for avoiding crowds, you see.

We all bunch up around an iron gate, which – along with a tall brick wall – bounds a small park. Luke twists a key in the padlock and unwraps the chain from around the gate. He pauses and turns around.

"Now remember," he says in a whisper. "These things feed off terror, project consumed terror at you, and are very good at what they do. But ultimately, terror itself cannot hurt you, it cannot touch you, and within a few seconds, it will be contained. Stay quiet, stay still and everything will be fine."

And with that, he pulls the hood of his coat up and it somehow morphs into something else. I swear he'd had a fairly regulation jacket on, but as he pulls the hood up, the change sweeps up and down the coat, lengthening it, turning it into more of a, well, kind of a cloak. It looks like there's something underneath it, like shoulder pads, only more shaped. Everyone else does a double take, but Luke is already pushing into the park.

"Woah," Matt says, forging ahead. "That was cool! This was worth it after all!"

Dumbass.

Everyone except Matt forms a semi-circle around the edge of the park, and he stands in the middle, basically in front of Luke. I can't help but feel like everyone knows quite a lot more than we do. I have absolutely no idea what's going on, other than it's not an art class. Why on earth did a homeless guy get me into this?

A small part of my brain that I try to keep alive, despite the humdrum of London, is telling me that this is pretty cool.

I hold onto that part. Matt is always telling me I should do new things.

No-one – except Matt, of course – really wants to get too close to Luke as he slowly walks around the park, stopping in front of a cardboard box in the corner. It looks big enough to contain a homeless sleeper. Or a body.

Matt is a couple of metres away from Luke, then glances around and realises that everyone but him is a lot further back. I see him about to give a trademark 'whaddup, dickheads?' shrug, but then pauses and takes two steps back instead.

I kind of miss exactly how the next bit happens because I'm watching Matt, not Luke, but I do see Luke lean towards the box, hand outstretched.

Every single light around us goes out.

There's a wave of swearing, gasping and muffled screams.

Only, it's not just dark. It's disorientating. I don't know if you've ever woken up in the middle of the night, not knowing where you are, because you're still half in a dream. You think you're in a hotel room, but you're in your bed at home; you think you're playing cards at a table with friends, but you're in a hotel room. You feel a rising sense of panic because the geography of what you can see with your eyes doesn't quite match up to what you can see with your mind. It's a lot like that. I know I'm in a park, in zone one, not far from one of my spiritual homes – Forbidden Planet – but I can't see anything. In fact, the only thing I can feel is the paving beneath my feet. I can't breathe.

And then something rises up from the box. I can't explain how I can see it, because it's pitch black, only that whatever the thing is, it cuts a hole in the darkness by somehow being heavier, thicker, more present than the darkness. It's a lengthening diamond of slick ebony, rising into the air above us. Two glowing red slits for eyes, a grim slit below for a mouth.

Two thuds to my left.

Have you ever seen that video where someone boils Coke, and what gets left behind is this black, tar-like ooze? Or that Dorothea Tanning picture, Home Light? That's what it's like, only airborne, spreading like an oil slick in the air.

My chest starts to tighten. A sick feeling rises in my throat and I start to get that sensation like when you're on the verge of falling down the stairs, when you lose your balance and know you're going to break something. Or when you're walking home and see two guys walking towards you and you know you're going to get mugged and there's nothing you can do about it. It was like that, only slower, more awful. Impending disaster and complete powerlessness in the face of it.

Then the thing, the Darkling, roars, its mouth widening to show white fangs, eyes glowing more fiercely. I'm breathing in short, sharp pants and I can't move.

The lights around the park crackle and flicker dimly, an orange haze illuminating the park. A guy and a girl on the ground not far from me push themselves up, gibbering, and run, sprinting as fast as they can, away, almost impaling themselves on the spikes of the gate in their haste. Another figure, I can't make out who, isn't far behind.

The Darkling grows, swells, becoming taller and broader and I feel warm piss running down my leg.

Then the Darkling freezes. There's a sharp gesture from Luke and it suddenly disperses, fading to nothing in a second. All at once the streetlights and the lights of the buildings around us come back on.

I can't believe it's over. I can't speak. I can barely breathe.

I'm glad I wore dark jeans.

"There," Luke says, pushing his hood back; it's a plain old jacket after all, no tricks, no shoulder pads. "The first one is always the worst. Sorry about the lights, I should have mentioned they can do that. Now, who's still here?"

Matt is the first to get his breath back. "Fuck," he breathes. "That was fucking awful. You guys do this for kicks? That is some ill shit."

Luke gives him a smile. "I think you've got some homework to do if you want to come along again," he says, reaching inside his jacket. "Here, have a leaflet though – you made it to the end, so you've passed the first two tests. You'll be contacted again shortly as a matter of procedure."

Wordlessly, Matt takes it. It is actually just a leaflet, a shiny, glossy, printed leaflet like you'd get from a National

Trust place or a tourist information centre in the Lake District.

I look around – it's just us left, along with the pale guy, who is busy wiping vomit off his chin.

"Great," I say, keen to get the hell out of this place. "Uh, right, well I guess we've earned a drink then?"

"Sure," Luke says, handing me and the other guy a leaflet as well. "Whatever helps best. See you around."

And with that, he saunters out of the park and vanishes around the corner. The goth guy glances at me and spits into the flower bed, shrugging and walking out of the park and up the road in the other direction, leaving behind a vague smell of faeces. I wrinkle up my nose.

"Come on," Matt says. "You definitely owe me a drink for that. No more art exhibitions for at least a month, ok? And I want to chain-smoke a little bit before we get into the bar. I need to get Team Edward's shit smell out of my nose."

Jolted back into reality, I nod. "Yeah," I say, stumbling out of the park, trying to regain a vague semblance of poise, wondering how visible my piss-stain is and where I can find an aggressively hot hand drier. "Definitely."

Two shots, three cigarettes and a pint later, Matt's good humour has recovered a bit, and we stagger towards Charing Cross to get the last train. I was thankful that we'd managed to find a relatively quiet cocktail bar. I'm exhausted.

The stark brightness of the station lighting is a sharp contrast to the street, a hen party's raucous screeches startling me. I can see Matt working up to some kind of witticism, but thankfully my train is in the platform already.

"Uh, sorry about that," I start. "Good to see you?"

He's looking into the distance and for a moment I see the boy I became friends with in the first week of secondary school, before he started drinking heavily, smoking and discovering the things you can do with girls. He'd been a bit nerdy, like I still am, loved Dungeons and Dragons, fantasy books, gaming, Warhammer.

"Hey Ben," he says, with what I can only describe as a thousand-yard stare, looking both older and younger at the same time. "That was real, wasn't it?"

I nod, not really sure of how it could possibly have been real, or what it means for almost literally everything I thought I knew about the world and how it operates. "Yeah," I say. "Uh, yeah it was. Let's talk in the morning, ok? I'm wiped out."

"Sure," he says. "Are we fucked?"

I cough and look at the train indicator.

"Usually are," I admit, starting to head off. "Later."

"Yeah, later," he says softly, still a million miles away, then more loudly. "Hey Ben?"

I turn back to him from across the concourse.

"I'm in, ok? You know I've got your back."

I nod and feel my eyes misting up a little. I wish I didn't do this. "Thanks man," I say. "I'll catch you tomorrow."

As my train pulls out of the station, he's still standing

there on the concourse, the eleven-year-old boy somehow staring out of the twenty-four-year-old man that he's become.

Matt
Nerdy Little Kids

When Ben and I were nerdy little kids, we lapped up every single Dungeons and Dragons adventure we could find. We were fanatics. It didn't matter that the only dungeon master we had was this awkward guy from a few years above us; when he started talking about deep chasms filled with undead, princesses needing a good rescuing, or treasure troves guarded by horrifying creatures, we all stopped living in the present.

I even went through the books that went with it, and for some reason, one part keeps hitting me in the brains right now. It's a story that one of the characters told about how they used to have this amazing jewel, prize, mcguffin, whatever, then they lost it. They searched high and low for it but couldn't find it – but they did find something that looked pretty decent and similar, so they took that instead. It was a long time before they realised that actually, the original thing was waiting for them all along, and if they'd looked a bit longer and harder, they would have found it.

As I stare up at the train indicators – ok, ok – as I steal another look at the girl in the hen party whose dress is tucked into her knickers, I feel a bit like that person. I mean, we never stopped playing Dungeons and Dragons, and I never stopped being friends with Ben, but over time, I found girls, cigarettes, booze, the occasional spliff. I'm strong, sporty, not visibly a geek; life got easier for me, and honestly, I think it got easier for Ben too because of that.

But sometimes, usually when I was with him, it was like I'd lost something. Sat on a bridge staring out at the river Thames, in a rooftop bar in a quiet moment, or on the rare occasion that he'd drag me into a second-hand bookshop to search out one of the nerdy books that he'd never gotten around to reading.

And look, I love booze. I love women. I have mixed feelings about cigarettes and joints, but they generally fall into the 'seemed like a good idea at the time' category.

Part of me wants to throw myself back into London, find a club, a girl, a bottle, anything, something to take the edge off, because right now it's like all those suspicions that I'd lost something, that I'd set something to one side, something important – they were all true.

That I could have been doing something meaningful rather than all this mundane shite.

If I'm brutally honest, I don't feel like I've had a destination for a while, and I haven't really – truly – been enjoying the journey much either.

That's enough sincerity. Time to make a decision: more London or home?

Shit, I probably need some downtime, tonight was a head-fuck. I don't really want to join the rest of the straight white sharks circling for blood in overcrowded bars. I don't want to go clubbing. I'm going home. The hen party squeals when their train – also my train – comes up on the indicator, then squeals more when they see that one girl has been walking around with a near-bare ass for a while. I snort and turn away. I've got ten minutes so I grab some McDonald's for the trip back and check that I'm sure as hell not sitting anywhere near them.

It's not a long journey. Ben lives out in the sticks because he refuses to live with anyone else. I live with three friends in Greenwich, which is much nicer and has far more cheap student bars than the shithole where he spends his time. Greenwich is so close to central that I've barely finished the Maccas by the time the train pulls up in the platform. I stuff the bag in the bin and barely register the evil looks that three or four passengers give me.

Jealous pricks, they should get their own fast food.

I light up a cigarette as I walk. What the fuck happened in that little garden? That thing, that fucking ghost. It sure as hell it wasn't a special effect, even counting all the build-up and drama from that teacher guy. I mean, the whole thing can't have lasted more than half an hour, tops and no-one pays money for a theatre thing that short – do they?

Jesus. I pass two students on the street, one bent double and throwing up on the pavement. I give the other one a sympathetic look. Shitty job.

Then I reach the bottom of the hill. It's the worst part of the walk home. I give the fan museum my middle finger as I pass. I mean seriously, I know I was a Dungeons and Dragons nerd, but who wakes up one day and says 'I think I'll open a fan museum'? I'm not going to make the obvious joke right now but are there really that many people who love fans? I can't believe that there are, but there it is, still fucking open.

Obviously not open now, stop being obtuse.

Cursing all the way, I stumble up the hill to the maisonette I live in, fumbling awkwardly with my keys to the multiple sets of doors, the image of the ghost-thing flashing before my eyes. I need another drink. Or my bed. Maybe both.

I've just about worked my way inside at roughly the same time as some guy has done the same with my flatmate Jess, her pre-orgasmic noises permeating every room.

Brilliant.

I drink the best part of a pint of water and lean forwards on the counter staring into space, trying to ignore the sex noise.

Matt, have you wasted ten years of your life when you could have been doing something awesome? I feel old and tired. I tread the worn carpet up the stairs, the soundtrack of humping getting louder before I shut my bedroom door behind me.

There's not a lot in here. A double bed, a stereo with cables connected to my laptop. Cheap vodka for shots, bourbon for drinking. A few packets of cigarettes, a Cohiba I'm saving for a special occasion, a selection of cheap lighters. My Ikea bedside table filled with condoms and other odds and ends.

My books – I still read – are mainly arranged underneath my bed in the drawers that I think most people use for odds and ends, clothes and the like. But, as I learned from Ben, the less you have on display, the fewer questions people ask. It's easier to keep most stuff out of view and make shit up if you need to.

The Darkling flashes in front of my eyes when I blink, like when you stare at a light bulb for too long, only in reverse. Shit. Ben's the eloquent one, not me. I make the jokes.

I strip down to boxers and pull on an old t-shirt, throwing everything else in a laundry basket and lying back on the bed.

I'll know what to do tomorrow. I usually do.

Sex noises or none, I fall asleep almost instantly and somehow, miraculously, don't even dream.

~

I still haven't worked out if it was crappy street theatre or something genuinely fucking weird – I suspect the latter – but normality is at least partially restored by the time I head downstairs and find my flatmate Tim teasing

Jess about the guy from last night. I open the fridge and take out a carton of orange juice that I'm relatively sure is mine while I put the kettle on and calibrate the strength of the coffee I'm making to the strength of my hangover, like they're wrestlers sizing each other up.

Two slices of toast, a bowl of cereal and half a cup of coffee later, it seems that the guy from last night was moderately well-endowed and well-off but a bit of a knob.

"What can I say?" Jess admits. "I like bad boys."

"Being a dick doesn't make you a bad boy," says Tim.

"You guys want to go out and get some proper breakfast?" I cut in, their bickering wearing on my hangover like someone trying to floss my brain cavities.

"Little late for breakfast," Tim says, glancing at the clock on the wall. I follow his gaze – it's noon, so he's not entirely wrong.

"I'm game," Jess says. "What did you have in mind?"

"Gypsy Moth?" I offer. "Something greasy from the market?"

Jess laughs, giving me a knowing look. "Hangover food," she says. "Sure."

"Big night last night?" Tim offers acidly.

"Something like that," I reply evenly, pulling on trainers and grabbing my jacket. "You coming?"

"Nah," he says. "Going to Blackheath to watch the game. Princess of Wales from one thirty – come along after if you want."

"Yeah, maybe. Thanks."

Jess raises her eyebrows at me and we head out. It's a clear, fresh kind of day and I can hear seagulls in the distance. Of course, they're feasting on chips and stuff from tourists, not catching fish in the river. I'm actually not sure if there are any, or if there are, how many heads they have.

The fish, not the tourists. Try to keep up.

I take my time appreciating the normality of everything, the herds of families heading to the Observatory, park and Maritime Museum, people driving badly and parking worse. I stop at a stall to buy coffee number two and offer Jess one; I haven't actually spoken to her since leaving the house ten minutes ago.

"You must have had a bigger night than I thought," she offers with a grin.

"Not too big, just a bit weird you know? Went to this immersive theatre thing with Ben, wasn't really my cup of tea. Think I drank too much."

She laughs, a silvery little tinkle that I've always found sweet. "You have no appreciation for culture, do you? I keep telling you, let me have the tickets next time. Besides, Ben's cute."

I've considered hooking up Ben with Jess a couple of times. On one hand, it'd do him good to get laid more, but on the other hand, Jess has the sexual proclivities of an angry honeybadger and I'm not entirely sure he'd survive the night. They're both decent people, but I don't think they're massively compatible and I also don't want my friend to go through unnecessary pain, however good the sex would be.

There it is, see? Real compassion.

"Yeah maybe," I reply, taking a sip of my coffee to disguise my slow reply. "I'll try and remember that. Burgers? Burritos? Pizza?"

"Hmmm," she muses, distracted by an art stall. "Falafel."

"Come on, I had a big night."

"Fine," she says. "Burritos."

We wander along the river path, spilling rice and kidney beans behind us, the shore completely obscured by the high waterline. The food is hot and good and I'm glad I got extra guacamole because the spicy sauce is doing its best to force my hangover out of every sweaty pore in my body.

Greenwich has changed a fair bit in the last few years since I moved here but the Thames is still the Thames. More flats on both sides, but it's the same old river. Dirty, few boats, remnants of industry on the shoreline, kids throwing bread to, sometimes at, seagulls.

"Hey Jess," I say. "You ever feel like you missed an opportunity in your life, like things could have been really different if you'd done something else, found that thing to do at the right time in the right place?"

We stop as she finishes a mouthful and gracefully wipes a napkin across her mouth, looking out over the river at Island Gardens, which isn't actually an island, and has fairly shitty gardens.

"Of course," she says. "All the time. You know, if my parents had bought me Apple stock when I was a little kid instead of premium bonds, if I'd worked harder at school and got into a decent university, that kind of thing. But I do ok now and I don't regret it. There's not a lot you can do about it, you know? Don't fuck yourself up over it."

"Yeah," I say. "I guess you just have to take the next one when it comes, right?"

"Preferably before," she says, with a wicked grin.

"Dirtbag," I laugh, and that sets us both off, earning an evil look from a woman pushing a small child in a pram.

We get to the Cutty Sark pub and Jess vanishes inside for a wee while I light up a cigarette and lean on the railing. A cold breeze makes me shiver and I tuck my hands in my coat pocket, finding the leaflet from last night. I pull it out and have a quick read, but don't get much further than a line that talks about 'threats of a non-human origin'.

I read that again.

And once more.

Damn.

I really, really want in. I have this weird mental image of chasing after an old-school London bus as it draws away from me. I need to get on. I glance at my phone and see that I've got a message from Ben but Jess chooses that moment to come out of the pub and I thrust the leaflet and my phone back into a pocket.

"What's the plan?" she says. "You going to join Tim later on?"

I absolutely am not. I need to speak to Ben, google the hell out of this thing and sign on whatever dotted line they offer me. But I also need to appear nonchalant about this in case it all comes to nothing. Because, you know, I'm nonchalant.

"Think I need to walk this off a bit more, maybe get to the O2, see a film or something – you want to come with?"

She shakes her head. "Thanks, but no thanks. Got a date in a few hours. Cheers for the burrito."

"Good luck," I offer and she flashes me a quick grin, spins around and heads back down the river path. I watch her go for a moment, admiring her. Then I realise how many times I've told myself not to mix business with pleasure. Flatmates with pleasure. Whatever.

I dial Ben's number.

Alice
A History Lesson

This all started for me back in the summer of 206 BC.

I'm sorry, that's misleading: I'm not two and a half thousand years old.

Sometime in the summer of 206 BC – I would say BCE, except that this all does rather support the idea of the birth of Christ – something spectacular happened.

It's apocryphal. That is to say, it's documented in the Apocrypha. The Deutero-canonical books. 2 Maccabees 8, if you want to look it up. A man named Eleazar Averan reads from a holy book and six thousand men defeat a force of nine thousand in battle somewhere near Jerusalem, before defeating a further twenty thousand in a feat that makes that Gerard Butler film look like an episode of Peppa Pig. The commonly-held view is that this book was the Bible and it supercharged the army, which then defeated almost five times its own weight in other angry, well-equipped men.

Later on, Averan is killed by an elephant shortly after

the Syrians take over the town of Beth Zechariah, led by a guy called Lysias.

My theory, and you'll have to bear with me to hear the rest of it, is that the book wasn't the Bible, but rather it summoned something. After the initial conflict, Lysias heard stories of Averan's book and wanted it, because he was a ravaging conqueror general.

Only Jerusalem resists and he doesn't manage it, despite Averan's death. Nor does Antiochus Epiphanes, Lysias' ruler, being struck down with a 'divinely inflicted disease' according to some sources. His son, Antiochus Eupator was essentially a Roman puppet for the brief tenure of his rule – he was really only a child – but I suspect the Roman senate had wrung all the information they needed from him before Demetrius took over and that part of the world became embroiled in a deeply messy conflict.

Don't worry – you don't need to take notes or actually remember any of this. I'm explaining because the conclusion is rather unusual, and I wouldn't want you to think I'm deluded.

Despite my best efforts, I can't find a clean trail from Epiphanes to the next step, Pompey; largely because the labyrinthine depths of the Roman Senate from 161 to 106 BC were exactly that.

But Pompey does invade Jerusalem, which is a dead giveaway. He's allegedly trying to quell a civil war in 63 BC, but what if he's got another agenda? After all, Pompey gets struck by lightning and incinerated, and that's spectacularly unlikely.

What if Pompey found the book, or whatever it summoned and was found unworthy?

Because then there's a string of Romans all trying to 'sort out' Jerusalem. And of course, I buy the other reasons for doing so, but I still think they had another motivation. The region had some significance to them, but nowhere near the significance that it had to the Jews or Christians.

Anyway, one invasion that is significant is Vespasian in 66 AD, a hundred years later – he's not successful but he finds something out. He flees to Britain. I've done weeks of research on Vespasian, and he was an empire builder. I believe that he left clues for his son, before establishing loads of towns and generally believing that he was becoming a god when he died.

Intense family. More on that to follow.

"Do you have this in blue?" a small voice says, interrupting my train of thought.

Hold on a moment, would you?

I look down and see a young boy looking up at me. He's holding a fluffy battle elephant, and I quickly pretend to scan the gift shop floor.

"Yes – right at the bottom. Have a rummage. I won't tell anyone."

He runs off.

I'm not good with children, but I've learnt that if you mention you won't tell anyone that they're doing something, they generally do it without question ninety nine percent of the time. A moment later, he runs back, looking both naughty and incredibly pleased with himself, proffering two two-pound coins. I run it through the till, offering him a bag – which, nebulously, he accepts – and placing the receipt in the bag with the elephant, I complete the customer transaction.

I'll explain that in a moment. Back to Vespasian. Or rather, his son.

Titus – Vespasian's son, obviously – besieges Jerusalem, but loses his temper in a fit of rage, destroying food supplies, crucifying people, generally throwing a complete hissy-fit. The historian Josephus covered this pretty extensively.

Indeed, he was so furious that he held the Jews responsible for losing the object of his desire and forbade them from entering the city – an edict that held all the way until 614 AD.

Averan's book, if it's anywhere, sounds like it's underground, somewhere in the oldest parts of Jerusalem, the parts that escaped Titus' rage. Titus never found it. I don't believe that it summoned God – in the monotheistic, Judaeo-Christian sense of the word – directly, but that it may have summoned something of immense power. Something that could help six thousand people defeat an army of almost thirty thousand and convince the most powerful rulers in the world that it could make them even more powerful.

And in the absence of Pompey leaving clues about

it – after all, he found it, so why would he – the next best thing I have to go on is Vespasian.

Which leads me here.

Roman Verulamium, to be precise, where the Forum was dedicated to Vespasian in 79 AD, having been rebuilt after its sacking by Boudicca in 61 AD.

I can't say I blame her: it's a lousy little town.

It's now known as St Albans. A well-to-do commuter town that I've grown to resent enormously for no clear or rational reason. Until, of course, it gives me what I'm looking for. Objectively, it's a perfectly nice place. Shops, nice park, very middle class.

And that brings me back to the boy and his elephant. When I'm not out on the dig, looking for clues, when funding dries up – which is fairly frequently – I work in the gift shop at the Roman museum, clean up or give tours to large groups of Americans. It's not exclusively Americans, but they do seem to find all of this stuff disproportionately charming, or so they tell me. Most of the dig staff have second or third jobs, but I find the proximity to the site itself useful – not to mention the security privileges.

I rotate with a couple of the others here, doing whatever needs to be done and generally biding my time, or as my former professors tell me, *wasting* my time. The problem with graduating with a first-class degree in archaeology from Cambridge is that everyone seems to think you're going to achieve great things immediately.

Well, I am. I just don't want to tell anyone about it.

They wouldn't believe me.

I think Hugo suspects. After all, he paid for my degree. And he's smart.

Obviously, it's more than that. People would think I had problems. They'd think I was a religious fanatic, except I'm not religious, but I doubt they'd believe that either.

The rest of the shift passes uneventfully, by which I mean I tolerate a string of inane questions – 'which football team did the Romans support?' is probably the best – and field situations like someone trying to pay for a twenty-pound figurine with an expired American Express card, and a child who wets themselves. I did actually feel sorry for them and fished a spare pair of trousers out of the school cupboard. It's not like me, but it really wasn't that much trouble and his parents did most of the heavy lifting. They were pathetically grateful for the trousers, understandably really.

At half past five, I usher the last of the tourists out of the shop and start to close up. That's one of the fringe benefits of the job: we're open from ten until half past five, and while I have to be there a bit early to open up, it's a long way from a London office job where you'd be lucky to scrape nine six. Of course, you'd earn a lot more than I do, but actually it's not bad.

I lock up, do a round of the museum, a perfunctory clean – the proper cleaners come three times a week, but tonight it's just me – then wave to Dave, the museum manager, and start walking through the park to head home.

Home is a short walk away, a one-bed flat on Mount Pleasant, an overpriced few square metres in an overpriced town. St Albans is prime commuter real estate, green and peaceful enough to be popular, close enough to London to be convenient. Although – looking at the price of rail tickets – the travel is almost as much as the rent in some cases, and it's a dreadful service a lot of the time.

But, despite taking up over half of my salary, living by myself means that I can spread out my real work. Walking to and from my job, especially through the park, is also a bit of a novelty in this day and age.

And the park is lovely, especially in spring and summer. I cross a small bridge over the lake, looking out towards the island where herons keep an eye out for fish. The water is looking a bit murky these days and I don't think the council has much money to maintain it. But the paths are clear, ducks, swans and geese flap about, trees cast shade from the late afternoon sun, and it's generally what most people would call idyllic.

I pass a pub on the river, hurrying slightly – it's popular with the tourists, but on a Friday afternoon it'll fill up with locals and sometimes I get whistles. I know it's universal, but I don't much like it here in the evenings; an ancient market town turns into a laddish, entitled nest of vaping drunks pissing in the alleyways.

Thankfully, the short walk home passes uneventfully, and I throw together a stir fry before sitting down to watch the news, idly twirling noodles on a fork.

"The Middle Eastern conflict has proven especially dangerous this year, with the government blaming new insurgent tactics for the tragic loss of life," the newsreader says. "According to one source, fundamentalist groups are becoming increasingly desperate, using more unpredictable and dangerous tactics, forcing friendly units to be more cautious."

Polishing off the last prawn, I swing into my desk chair, firing up my PC and load up a slew of news pages on one monitor, an excel chart on the other. Idly, I start noting down all the recorded conflicts in the last five years where UK forces have been deployed; all the publicly listed ones, of course. A failed recon mission in Iran here, a conflict in Syria there, jotting down the dates, the loss of life, and where things don't quite tally up.

I comb forums, news pages, official spending reports and before I know it, I'm hip deep in statistics, making notes and deductions. My Excel grid blossoms with comments, notes, annotations, calculations, points where reports differ – barring the expected divergence between the Daily Mail's 'averaging for accessibility' – and the Financial Times' careful sourcing, for example.

Two hours later, I get up and stretch my spine, yawning and seeing the dirty stir-fry bowl still on the armchair where I left it. I head to the bathroom, having also ignored my bladder for a while, then to the kitchen, filling a pint glass with water and taking it back to the lounge.

I feel the need to pace, so I walk to the bedroom and back again.

Oh, wait.

I turn and carefully take the framed prints of Kendrick Lamar and Jason Derulo off the wall, opening my wardrobe and sliding out identically-sized posters of Nicki Minaj and Beyonce. My parents were visiting last weekend and it's easier for them to assume I've got a thing for African American men rather than well-established female singers.

I'll do it one day, I promise, ok? I've got a lot on right now and I'm not good with the people stuff.

Redecorations completed, my flat feels a little more homely than it did, despite the dubious floral wallpaper. Some people just don't understand what 'neutral décor' means, but it doesn't really bother me.

On reflection, I make a cup of tea to sit next to the water as I resume my work. Well, not my work, but it's an interesting distraction.

Another two hours later, I sit back and look at the final figures coming up in my pivot table. According to the publicly available statistics, approximately two and a half thousand soldiers from the British military forces have been killed in combat in the last five years.

I let out a low whistle between my teeth: that's a lot. In fact, it's almost two percent of the total armed forces in the United Kingdom – and that's not counting units from other countries. As Kendrick would say, damn.

I save the research into a folder on my PC and file everything away, palming the remote control that turns the projector on and shows what I do think of as my life's work, now covering most of the wall. It's a large virtual corkboard covered with pins and scraps of paper, printouts of articles, charts and scrawled shortened web links. Right at the top are the biblical verses that started all of this, although 'started' isn't quite accurate.

In my first year of sixth form, our General Studies teacher suggested we read the Qur'an, something that most people ignored. I read it and then tackled the Gita, the Book of Mormon and the entirety of the Bible.

The real beginning came when I quizzed the constant, near-incessant bashing of Jerusalem. Maybe it's my secular mind, but I didn't get it. Overnight, my brain began to make links, idly speculating and drawing connections.

Tonight, I'd really like to tighten the links around Vespasian's activities in Britain – or rather, Agricola's activities in Britain; Vespasian came to Britain in 43 AD, long before he besieged Jerusalem. Agricola tried to distract attention from Verulamium by spending a lot of time pushing north into Scotland, but I've seen tablets of shipping manifests sending goods and plans to the relatively new municipium of Verulamium, which I suspect originated with Agricola, and in turn, Vespasian.

The Romans might have been cunning, but they sure did like a list. Blessed are the administrators, for they shall leave behind meta-data. Of course, I could go back to the dig site and do some solo work, but security is usually tighter on Friday and Saturday nights. It doesn't take much for a couple of drunk guys coming back from town to decide that what their girlfriend would like best is a Roman artefact. Yes, I'm sorry, but it is mostly guys. Anyway, it means that if I want to break into an ancient historical site and spend a few hours dodging the gaps in the security camera patterns, brushing the smallest amount of dirt aside from 'my' room, then I have to do it during the week. Mondays are usually the best.

I flex my spine again and settle back into the desk chair, logging into JANET and bringing up some Tacitus. I'm not a huge fan. For the period I'm interested in, it's essentially a secondary source, but it's also generally more complete than Livy.

I take a sip of tea. It's cold. The flat is silent.

I barely notice either.

Ben
Dirty-ass London

I didn't dream at all last night, and that's not like me. My mind rarely rests properly after a full day's work, let alone after drinks, strangers and nightmarish weirdness. I'll often wake up suddenly, imagining someone else in the room, a dark shape becoming real. My last girlfriend used to say that I snored, and when I didn't snore I talked.

Girlfriend might be an overstatement, but we dated for three or four months.

I take my time getting up, opening all the curtains and making sure that as much light as possible floods into my tiny flat. I message Matt and decide that I need to get out of the house before I lock myself in and never leave. I can't make sense of anything. That thing last night, the calm with which Luke dispatched it, the terror I felt. The memory is both incredibly real and completely unreal at the same time.

I consider going for a run, but I can't quite muster the energy, so instead I grab a jacket and walk out along the river. Erith is on the Thames, but it's not pretty. The footpath is a harsh, industrial concrete thing, with a dirty shoreline on one side and barbed-wire fences on the other. Storage facilities, warehouses and works of various kinds lie dormant, conveyor belts and piers for the loading and unloading of food, aggregates – I don't really know what an aggregate is, I've just seen the signs – stand overhead and all around.

Matt hasn't replied to my message yet.

I head inland to avoid the sewage works. On a good day, I'll get down as far as Woolwich, although I've never really felt comfortable there; the Elizabeth line and gentrification has meant that there's money there, good places to live, but its history is rougher, more dangerous. A lot of people don't pick up on it, but it always feels weirdly tense to me.

Sometimes I just need to get out of my own head, so I put one headphone in and plug into some more trance. Only one, mind you, although my shoulders start to feel a bit less tense as I hit the Green Chain, a well-trodden footpath that leads all the way to Crystal Palace, although I've never been that far.

None of this helps.

I'm not far off a full-blown panic attack.

Well, I am and I'm not. There's a part of me that's loving this. The thrill of finding something secret, something unknown, something other. An exit door from normality. Away from the humdrum, the sheer mundanity of London life. I'd always hoped that there was something more out there, as much as I love books, libraries, cosy places as refuges, escapes from an overwhelming world, but also places where more interesting things can happen. Away from oyster cards, touch in touch out, pints of beer, dirty freesheets and the nine to five. Bankers in suits, rushing around. Surely, I've always thought, surely there's something else.

Maybe this is it.

And yet, it's terrifying. Gut-wrenchingly terrifying.

I find a bench, thankful that I've ended up on the green chain rather than the stinky shoreline. I pull out Luke's leaflet.

It's printed like an army leaflet, in similar colours – you know, the black and green, the 'army soldier: be the best' type stuff. That's probably a few years old now, right? Anyway, it starts with a whole load of warnings, that this material is confidential, that abuse or disclosure of the contents therein will lead to a rising scale of fines and imprisonment etcetera. I open it up and start reading.

"The First Extraordinary Battalion, informally known as the Gardeners, was formed in the 1960s as a military-scientific operation that would collaborate with other military forces around the world to preserve non-traditional, terrestrial borders from threats of a non-human origin. The motto of the First Extraordinary, *Compassion and Dedication*, highlights the qualities needed in a potential recruit, and many new members of this unit are retired members of other squadrons. Rather like codebreakers at Bletchley Park during the war, members of the First Extraordinary are often selected rather than volunteering, largely because of the unusual nature of the work."

I pause, hurriedly tucking the leaflet inside my jacket as a dogwalker goes by. They look at me suspiciously. Sometimes I hate living in London; other than the noise, dirt and general stress, I think everyone looks at you like you're a potential pervert, mugger or drug abuser. Londoners don't interact with other people much – I guess that's the nature of being in a big city, but sometimes a little more faith in humanity wouldn't hurt.

They pass by and I pull out the leaflet again. It starts to rain a little.

"You will already have experienced an unconventional situation, and you will have been selected because of your compassionate or empathetic nature. As a candidate, you have one week from your first contact with the First Extraordinary to decide whether or not to enlist."

Enlist? This is serious.

"If you decide to enlist, you should present your current employer with the F77D form on the back page, which tells them that you have been requisitioned by a government body of significant authority, for an unspecified length of time. You should report to 7, Wild Court, London, where the selection process will continue. You will be assessed for the necessary aptitudes and given physical and supernatural training to meet the needs of the job. Any and all questions should be addressed to staff in person."

And that's it. Virtually nothing. Well, except that I could be joining what sounds like an army unit of ghost hunters.

My phone rings.

"Ben? This is intense. Have you read this thing?" Matt says, sounding incredulous.

"Yeah, literally just finished it."

"It's like, hey, do you want to become a British fucking Obi Wan Kenobi? And what's all that shit about compassion? Are they serious?"

My mind flashes back to Jack, and our conversations over the last six months. "I don't understand any of this," I admit, then have a thought on autopilot. "But you know Alec Guinness *was* actually British, right?"

"Not in Star Wars he wasn't," Matt says slowly, in his best 'talking to a stupid person' voice. "But seriously, me neither. Do you think it pays well?"

There's a long silence.

"You're considering this?"

"Hell yes!"

He's almost shouting down the phone now. "I know I almost shit my pants last night but this is everything we've ever wanted. Do you want to be a fucking librarian all your life, or do you actually want to put some of that Dungeons and Dragons stuff to use?"

"Matt, I am a fucking librarian, not a soldier. Come on, I'm the least likely person to join the army. All that Dungeons and Dragons stuff, it's made up, it's not real."

But I can feel him grinning down the phone at me.

There's another long silence.

"Ben," he says. "Seriously, we got this."

"I need to think about it," I say, trying to cut off him.

"Fine," Matt says. "Let me know. But you know what the right thing to do is."

And he hangs up.

I turn my music back on and head for home. I know Matt's disappointed in me. I'm disappointed in myself.

~

I still haven't made up my mind by the next morning and my head can't work out if there's something comforting or annoying about my daily routine. However early I get up, I'm always hurried in the mornings, showering and cramming breakfast down as quickly as possible to make my train, ending up stressed even when I get a seat and the train's not that full.

I guess that's a good thing about where I live though: it's sufficiently close to the end of the line that I usually do get a seat, although I've recently had to compete with the people moving into the smart-looking newbuilds near the station. Look at you with your fancy double glazing and no damp damage on the walls. Of course, if I lived in Dartford, I'd have more trains to catch and definitely get a seat, so I could look down on them instead. But it wouldn't change my rent and it'd add another ten minutes and twenty quid a month to my commute, both of which are quite painful enough, thank you very much.

Deep down, I know that I'm not thinking about the things I should be thinking about, but I've spent the last 24 hours thinking about nothing else, so I tell myself that I'm taking a break.

I don't usually read the Metro in the morning, but as I walk past the newspaper bin "*Grisly Murders in Hampstead*" catches my eye and I snag one to read on the train. It's definitely grisly. I don't know whether they usually go into this level of detail, but either way, the reporters can't seem to make up their minds whether the victims were scorched in a fire or got some kind of all-over chemical burn. Either way, there's two of them, seemingly dumped in the park somewhere and no-one has any idea who did it. I turn back to the fantasy book I'm partway through and try to switch off a bit until my train gets to London Bridge, where my journey gets really unpleasant because I have to switch to the Jubilee Line to get to Green Park. Sometimes it takes three or four tries just to get on.

Then it's a short walk to the Mayfair Library where I'm lucky enough to work. Lucky that there are still libraries to work at, lucky that I managed to get a job here, lucky that it's in a nice neighbourhood rather than a sad, dying local library trying to make it on the pittance of local authority funding. Instead, I count the Bentleys and Lamborghinis parked next to the hotels and apartments in the ten minutes between the tube and work.

Then I stop, fast, making someone behind me swear as they swerve to avoid walking into me. I thought I saw the thing from last night, but it's just someone in one of those breathing masks that cyclists wear, all in black with some kind of skull design on the front. Crap. Something about the diamond shape made me almost jump out of my skin. I apologise to the woman behind me and hurry on, trying to make like there's nothing wrong.

I'm definitely procrastinating. Was Matt right to jump at this? I mean, I don't think Jack would have set me down this path if he didn't think I was capable of whatever this is. He's a good guy, a smart guy. I trust him. I don't trust a lot of people. But this is a lot.

My mind flits back to my commute, my job, my life. I mean, it's all ok – I love the library, the sense of wonder that people get at all the books, all the worlds to be discovered, the sanctuary it provides. But if there's a chance to do something different, something worthwhile, get out of my ninety-minute commute sharing space with London's finest businesspeople – and by that, I mean wedged into someone's sweaty arm pit – well, I probably should?

It doesn't take me long after that to realise that Matt's right.

I get to work at nine on the dot. It doesn't technically open until eleven today but we have a team meeting first thing, then shelving left over from Saturday. Saturdays are usually a really busy day for us but not many people work it – you have to get 'anti-social hours' pay and not many public authorities can afford that anymore.

My colleagues are pretty nice. Julia is my stern-but-fair boss, and Mike and Lucy are the other seniors on today. I'm perpetually pathetically grateful to work here, so I keep my nose clean and never, ever bring Matt inside.

I drop my bag in a locker, find my team and we chat through the focus activities for the week. Julia has hastily re-arranged the classic detective novel promotion in favour of something a little lighter and frothier, because of the murders, and we've also got a couple of school parties coming around.

There's something incredibly comforting about the library itself, the warm brown wooden shelves, books arranged in a slightly slapdash way. I'd never say that to Julia, of course, but the Dewey Decimal System has no respect for modern aesthetics. I'm not one of those design types who insist on organising their books by colour, but sometimes I want to move a few things slightly out of order to make it look tidier. Still, it's all familiar and comfortable – it's not a big library, and some of the space isn't used, except for weddings, which is a reasonably important source of income for us, and the main reason why Julia is so fanatical about tidiness in otherwise fairly empty areas.

And then I'm face to face with the small collection of horror books and one of the covers makes me jump.

Christ, if I'm this jittery after seeing my first demon, what use am I going to be when I'm supposed to be a proper Ghostbuster?

"Penny for them, Ben?"

And there we go again. I jump about a foot in the air, almost dropping the Stephen King I was about to replace, before turning around to look sheepishly at Lucy. She grins at me.

"Sorry," she says. "You must have been miles away."

"Yeah," I say, flushing crimson, I'm sure. "Sorry – it was a weird weekend."

"Bad?" she offers, taking another book from the cart and slotting it back onto the shelf.

"Not sure," I manage. "I'm still thinking about it."

She pats me on the shoulder but doesn't press me any further. I feel a slight pang of panic – if I want to join the First Extraordinary, I guess I have to resign.

I don't want to resign. I don't like confrontation and I love this job. I turn back to shelving books, the minutes inching past as I finish the horror, the sci-fi and join Lucy doing the non-genre fiction. As the clock hits ten thirty, Mike ambles over from sorting the last of the weekend's returns.

"Ben?" he says quietly. We all speak quietly before hours – somehow it doesn't seem necessary to raise your voice. I look over at the balding man, a former accountant if I remember that right. "Julia wants to see you in her office."

"Thanks," I say, setting my pile of books back on the trolley.

"She's got a visitor," he says as I turn to leave, and a wave of nausea hits me briefly, making me swallow, which is stupid. Julia's lovely and I'm a model member of staff. We all are.

I weave my way through the shelves and past the metal swing gate marked 'staff only', before opening a wood-panelled door to a set of stairs. The small, slightly claustrophobic steps lead up to a short corridor and a door labelled 'Head Librarian'. There's another, larger set of stairs accessible from the main entrance, but it means going almost all the way out of the building again, so we usually go this way instead.

I knock, hearing Julia's voice telling me to come in a moment later. I enter, pushing the door open slowly.

Her office is tidy, but crowded with files, papers and books. Her desk is a large, heavy thing, made of some dark wood that I'm always worried about leaving cup marks on if I sit at it – she's not territorial about the space and is more than happy for us to use it as a quiet lunchtime getaway. There's a laptop and second monitor on it, but they both manage to look small on the impressively solid desk.

Julia is sat behind the desk with her fingers laced in front of her. Sat with his back to the wall, at right-angles to both of us, is a man I don't recognise. He's tall and serious-looking, although his untidy brown hair undermines that. He's in black jeans, a blue shirt and dark trainers, and seems to be scrutinising me as closely as I'm scrutinising him. I'd put him in his late fifties if I had to guess, and he's well-built.

I take another step into the room and close the door behind me.

"Ben," Julia says. "This gentleman is from a government organisation that I'm not sure I understand. He says that you might be needed by them, and is here for the last stage of the interview. Is that right?"

Shit. My face grows warm and I'm certain that I'm about to embarrass myself by stammering or some other Ben-like crap. I take a deep breath, ignoring the rising dread that usually goes with public speaking.

"At the weekend," I admit. "It was a surprise – nothing I'd planned."

That *almost* made sense. Julia looks a little relieved, but also perplexed.

"I'll make this easy," the man says, standing. "Ben, I'm Lincoln, with the First Extraordinary. You're needed, but you've got one more test to pass if you want this. We're kind of in a hurry, so why don't you come with me for the last part of the interview process and you can work out if it's what you want on the way."

I freeze, having absolutely no idea what to do, so I look at Julia. She looks at Lincoln; she's got this seraphic, unmoving calm that I would dearly love to possess.

"Lincoln," she says clearly – unlike me, she's a great public speaker and storyteller. "Could I have a few moments to speak with Ben privately? I do believe this is all a bit new."

He glances at his watch and sighs. "Five. You can have five minutes. I'll be outside, and gone after that."

I step out of his way and as the door closes behind him, I sink into his chair.

"Ben," Julia says gently, the slightest hint of her Scottish accent coming through. "Lincoln's credentials were very much in order, so I have no doubt that what he says is the truth, however brusque he seems. I don't know what you're getting into, but I have to ask – what's this all about?"

"I … I'm not sure," I manage slowly, taking a deep breath and letting it out again. "But do you ever feel like if you don't take an opportunity, you'll regret it for a long time? Like this could be something special, something meaningful?"

There's a long silence.

"Thank you," Julia says softly. "That was very honest. And yes – not often, but a few times. The night I met my wife, almost thirty years ago now, there was a dinner event for, well, it's acceptable to be gay now, but back in the eighties it could still be quite frowned upon. I knew I wanted to go. It was like a hook in my chest pulling me – and almost as uncomfortable – but I also knew that if I didn't go, I'd regret it. I was so nervous!"

She laughs and for an instant, I see her as she was thirty years ago, a shy, nervous girl, pretty with a great giggle.

"I met my dear Emma there, and she was as nervous as me, but we spent almost two hours talking to no-one else, the two of us on a balcony like the entire world didn't exist. We danced until the sun came up and nothing was ever the same again. Ben, if you have that same feeling then I say run after this, run and don't let go. But I will admit that I don't really understand."

I have to agree with her. I'm still reeling slightly from her retrospective and hoping that I don't cry in front of my boss.

"It came from a friend," I say. "Someone that I trust, and things happened afterwards that made me realise that it's not a wind-up, that it's important. I'm sorry – it really did only begin at the weekend."

"Then however nervous you are, however much you'd like to stay here, I don't think that you can," Julia says quietly, quickly. "We'll cope. Take the day off, go with this man, think things through."

"Thank you," I manage.

"Scram," she says, laughing. "I guarantee that you'll feel better once you've stepped outside. Sometimes these shelves can be as suffocating as they are protective."

I push my chair back and stand, incredibly grateful for her kindness and empathy. She gives me a brisk nod and looks meaningfully at the door, raising an eyebrow slightly.

I nod back and turn to go, leaving a sweaty palmprint on the door handle.

Ben
The Spider

I join this stranger, Lincoln, outside the library a minute before his ultimatum is due to expire, raised eyebrows greeting me as I open the door.

"Great," he says, flicking his head onwards. "Come on."

For a few moments I walk beside him, trying to get my questions in order, but as I draw a breath, he pre-empts me.

"Ok, kid," he says. "Look, I know, you've got a zillion questions but I'll be honest: I'm not really a babysitter. Three weeks ago, I was happily retired, but there's something big going on and you're one of the last recruits to be hired. The Gardeners need help, and I wasn't about to tell them no, ok?"

That seems to be a rhetorical question, so I don't say anything. We're walking south, towards Hyde Park Corner and the Hilton, the streets relatively full of smartly-dressed people on their way to work and casually-dressed tourists, not on their way to work.

"You got the dove token, right?" he asks, looking at me. I nod.

"So you've passed the empathy test already," he notes. "And you've seen your first bit of weird shit. What did they do, show you a captive Ravager? A Darkling?"

"The Darkling," I say, wondering what on earth – or not on earth – a Ravager is.

"Well, you've obviously got balls," he says. "But they want to be doubly sure, so I have to show you a bit more of the world behind the curtain. Now it's not going to be quite as weird as the Darkling, but you need to think about whether you really want this to be your world, ok? Thankfully, all you have to do is shut up and nod politely."

"So what are we doing?" I ask, his description not really answering any of my unasked questions.

He sighs as we pause at a crossing. "I don't mean to be an arse, I really don't, but like I said, I've been pulled out of retirement. I lost a friend a week ago, and rather than tracking down the killer, I'm interviewing. So, you and I, we're multitasking, and I get that this all feels important to you, like it's destiny, like it's magical, but it's also the real world and we've got responsibilities. Given that you're not from a military background, that's probably the most important lesson I can teach you right now."

I try to digest all that. "I'm sorry for your loss," I manage, as we walk down past an impressive-looking car dealership and crossing over into Belgravia proper.

"Thank you," he says curtly, falling silent for a moment,

then patting his pockets. "Now, like I said, you're amongst the last to be recruited, so if you do decide to join, go to 7 Wild Court tomorrow morning. Before noon, or don't bother."

He hands me another card, with an address and a postcode. I wonder where the "RG" postcode is and how far away it is.

"Bracknell," Lincoln says. "It's not far. You'll be going there straight after Wild Court if you do join up. Pack for a week."

"A week?"

"Training," he says. "And education."

We round a corner, coming to a set of red-brick flats with white columns guarding their porches.

Lincoln pauses in front of one. "Now," he says. "This may seem a little odd, a bit culty. But there's a perfectly good reason for it, so don't worry."

"And that reason is?" I ask, interrupting him as his finger is poised to ring the doorbell.

Another sigh.

"Because it's a cult," he says slowly.

He rings the doorbell for number eleven as I roll my eyes behind his back and shake my head. Of all the Obi Wan Kenobi's to end up with, I have to get the douchey one. A moment later, a woman in a suit comes to the door, looking him up and down with something resembling disdain.

"Ah, yes," she says. "She's been expecting you."

"Good," Lincoln nods. "Perhaps she's been expecting a few other things as well."

The woman gives him an imperious look, beckoning for us to enter. We follow her down a red and black tiled hallway, stairs seemingly leading to other flats within the complex. She pauses to open the door of a flat with a Yale key, entering and holding the door for us.

Lincoln enters first, and I follow, finding myself in a large lounge, far larger than I'd thought these flats would have. Maybe that's why they're called mansions? The room is tasteful and cosy, bookshelves lining the walls, squashy-looking armchairs with carved wooden tables sat next to them, colourful rugs on the floor. Two shaven-headed, serious-looking men stand on the far side of the room, also in suits and a woman in expensive-looking jeans and a white, floral top sits on a chair facing us. Her look is of close scrutiny, as if she's judging and evaluating us.

"Lincoln," she says, in a quiet voice that instantly speaks of authority. "Welcome back. I'm sorry you had to leave your retirement."

"Hello Chloe," he says evenly. "Thank you. Well, if it's all going to hell then I'd rather be in the field, you know."

She inclines her head and gives a small smile, but doesn't say anything. Lincoln sits down on an armchair opposite her and I do the same. They're really very comfortable.

"This is Ben," he says. "He may or may not be the last new Gardener for a while."

Chloe turns the smile to me. "Welcome," she says, and I pick up on a very faint French accent. "I hope you join. The First Extraordinary needs good people."

I wonder how she knows that I'm 'good people' but I'm interrupted before I can ask, as one of the guys in suits brings tea around. I'm not really a tea drinker, but it feels impolite to ask for anything else.

"So," Chloe says. "What can I do for you?"

Lincoln snorts. "I think you know."

One of the men in suits takes a step forward, but Chloe gestures for him to stand back. "Peace, Brother Carvas," she says. "Peace. Lincoln means no ill."

Reluctantly, he resumes his previous position.

"Yes," she says with a glance at me. "The thing that you think will happen, will happen soon. A week, a month, no longer."

"And the other?" he asks.

She looks at a tablet device on the arm of her chair, tapping it a few times, then looks back up. "It leans towards him," she says. "But I know not where he is, or where he'll be. He's exceptionally talented in subterfuge."

Lincoln leans back, his head hitting the headrest. "Yes, he is, isn't he?"

"I'm sorry," she says quietly. "If I find anything, I will let you know. He's a danger to my people too."

The tall man looks back at her a moment later, composing himself. "Of course, thank you," he says. "And, if it's not too much trouble, I was hoping you'd tell your story to Ben here."

Then she laughs briefly, before stifling it. "You hope to use me as your weird test?"

I see Lincoln's mouth twitch with something that's almost a grin, but it vanishes and he nods instead.

"Very well," she says, sipping her tea. "Are you sitting comfortably?"

I glance at Lincoln, confused, but recalling his advice to stay quiet and be polite, I don't say anything either, instead picking up my tea cup and taking a sip. It's a very delicate Earl Grey, and suddenly makes me feel more refined. Is that weird?

"My name is Sophia Amelia Chloe Webster," the woman says. "My late parents called me Chloe, on account of my maternal and paternal grandmothers – with whom I shared the first two names – still being alive when I was born. Some call me The Spider, on account of, well, you'll understand that quite quickly, I hope."

She glances around, smoothing her hands on her jeans, leaving slight marks on them – is she nervous, and if so, why? A moment later she clasps them together, resuming her tale.

"My parents were lead researchers and academics at ESPCI Paris, which lies in the first arrondissement. They were wealthy, and gave patronage to a number of projects around the world. When I was seven years old, and perhaps more by accident than anything else, both of them being somewhat too busy to check our nannies' schedules, they took me to one of the research sites that they had contributed to both scientifically and financially."

"I shall never forget the romance of the journey; a child, lost in the vastness of travel, smiling sweetly at our attendants until they brought me more treats than I could eat, my parents more wine than they needed. Thence onwards, from King's Cross to a small town outside of Glasgow, the train charging through snowflakes, making them dance like a hundred thousand frozen ballerinas."

She coughs, blushing, but continues a moment later.

"We arrived at the research facility with our three bodyguards, quite engaged by the tour. As a child, I am sure I misbehaved, but my parents were very patient – and our bodyguards were quite accustomed, nay, tolerant of my behaviour. I do not remember how far we had progressed through the tour, but it was in the aerial labs, the large treehouses in the woodland, that disaster struck."

"I learned afterwards that a group of terrorists had placed an incendiary device on a train track not far from our location. It exploded exactly as planned, derailing the train and sending all twelve carriages down the nearby hillside. Every single one of the twelve hundred souls on board was killed within a few seconds, including the intended target, the Countess of Hereford, who was a dear friend of my parents. She was travelling with her brother and sister, both of whom were psychics, and to this day I am unsure whether the end result was intended."

"The malice of the act caused an immediate contortion

in the noosphere, forcing many of the scientists within to mutate in terrible and painful ways, seeking comfort only in ending their own lives. Many changed forms, becoming bestial in nature. I could suddenly feel the possibilities in my head, simultaneously more aware and more able to absorb and process vast quantities of information as my parents shouted at the bodyguards to escort me from the premises. One stayed behind with them, firing shot after shot into a scientist whose body was adding new, rigid tissue to his form at an exponential rate. I could instantly tell that the new tissue was simply absorbing the projectiles, and implored them to flee."

"I was pulled away by two guards, one of whom smashed a window as we fled onto the roof, some way above ground. I don't remember how we travelled to the forest floor, the pagoda-like structure receding into the fog of gunfire and smoke, but somehow, we got away."

She pauses to take a sip of tea, and I do the same. It's cooling down, but I'm enjoying it more than a lot of tea I've drunk in the past, and it's distracting me from the fact that she's describing something straight out of a fantasy book. I mean, what's a noosphere? Psychics? Why does she talk like someone out of a medieval drama? It's all a bit much.

"We reached a bridge, having been unable to requisition a vehicle in the chaos. As we approached, two humanlike forms climbed up from underneath. For a moment, I believed that they were survivors who had simply taken refuge. As they emerged, however, I saw that their arms had been elongated into tentacles, capped with short spikes. Their faces had become more like squid-like, bearded with smaller growths. Even in the midst of their mutation, they seized the two guards, who were unloading their firearms into the beasts."

"I fled. Each creature was occupied with a bodyguard, and after a moment of paralysis, I ran as fast as my legs would carry me, aiming for the main gate past the bridge. Finding it unguarded, a vicious rent torn in it, I ran until I collapsed, then climbed a tree with the last of my strength, managing to sleep for a short span of time until the sound of vehicles on the road nearby woke me. At first, I waved, thinking to flag them down, but what chance did I have of catching their attention? Instead, I hurried down the road, feeling a shapeshifter's guile within me, coupled with an overwhelming absorption of information from sights, sounds and smells. At first, I revelled in the new-found awareness. Then I realised I was unable to stop it. I wept openly until I reached the nearby town. The occupants were still stricken with the burden of aiding the emergency workers who had arrived at the scene of the terrorist incident."

"I was the only survivor."

The silence is complete for a few moments before a low whistle escapes my lips. Lincoln looks at Chloe, draining the last of his tea.

"Thank you," he says, inclining his head then looking

at me. "No time for questions. Shall we?"

Chloe clears her throat, also finishing her tea a second later. "Lincoln?" she says, as he stands, making him turn back towards her.

"If the worst does happen, please do count on our support."

He nods, once. "Thank you," he repeats. "Ben?"

I get up as well, unsure if I should thank her, but she winks at me, and I'm so stunned that before I know it, we're out of the mansions, stood in the sunlight.

"Well," Lincoln says, taking a deep breath. "I hope that was enlightening, and that you've been adding to your list of questions to ask tomorrow, if you're joining. We might not meet again, so best of luck."

"What? That's it?" I manage, and he pivots back to look at me, leaning on a column.

"That's right. Completely up to you whether you join or bring a friend or whatever. Welcome to the real world, kid."

"It's Ben," I say acidly, but it's mostly to his back as his tall frame recedes down the street in front of me. "And you were a shitty Dumbledore."

Alice
The Dig

When you're an archaeologist, people generally assume one of two things. First – usually the more likely scenario – is that you're a British eccentric like Tony Robinson or Phil Harding and spend your time dressing up in period clothes, staging mock-jousting tournaments, making your own mead and occasionally digging something up and finishing in a matter of days.

I don't really have a problem with Time Team. I met Harding once at a lecture, and he was genuinely pleasant and well-read. But in terms of timing, they were lucky not to have compromised half the sites they dug up, trying to find something conclusive in three days.

Seriously. I know there's a lot of old stuff lying around the UK, but treat it with a little care, ok?

The other assumption is Indiana Jones, which is a lot less common these days, thankfully. *Crystal Skull* seems to have made the whole genre a bit less popular. Plus, if you watch all four films, there's relatively little 'real' archaeology, making Harrison Ford's character one of those irritating archaeologists who graduated, studied, went on a few digs and then went straight back into academia, calling a quick trip to some – largely accessible – long-lost tomb, archaeology.

Let me tell you about a real day on site.

St. Albans features a very fine hypocaust, an underfloor heating system that was first uncovered in the 1930s. It is believed to have been part of a large town house, is open to the public, and unlike the museum, is free to enter.

The current dig that I'm part of is a project to excavate an area next to the hypocaust, potentially extending the area on display from a fairly extensive heated floor to a much more impressive full Roman house. If successful, it'll be developed into a second museum, charging people to experience a mixed reality Roman house, complete with actors and virtual currency, faux-denarii, to spend in a new shop.

That's the real reason we've received funding for this stretch, although it's staggered carefully, a protected investment from – of all places – a venture capitalist firm in London. At the risk of sounding flippant, I suspect that capitalising on fashionable historical monuments in a well-off area currently has a higher success rate than the next raft of cryptocurrency start-ups.

Today is spent shoulder-to-shoulder with Mark, a twenty-eight-year-old archaeologist who's been working here since graduating seven years ago, Jamie, a forty-something dig veteran and our dig leader, as well as Amy, also a recent graduate, but from Keele. She seems to think that because we're both relatively new to this, and perhaps more importantly because we're both women, that we should be friends. She's irritating, but I try not to alienate her. It's much easier to get what you want when people like you.

We're currently excavating a ten metre by ten metre plot in what I call the study. It's one of the two sites that I believe may contain a clue left by Vespasian's staff, so I'm absolutely committed to this, however mind-numbingly boring the day is. The other place I consider to be a strong contender is the forum, dedicated to Vespasian, but it's a bit too public. This house – probably the most luxurious house in all of Roman Verulamium – probably belonged to a senior administrator, former military, someone high up in Agricola's command. Someone with no clue that a message to Titus had been left in the decoration of their dwelling.

Here's how the day goes.

We all sit around a table in the morning drinking strong tea, while Jamie splits up the segments of today's plot. The hard work of the dig – breaking up the topsoil after the JCB removed the surface layer – has already been done, so today, tomorrow and the rest of the time we're on-site will be spent digging with hand trowels, sieving, brushing and painstakingly recording everything we find. Because we're so close to an existing site, finds are guaranteed, which is great, but also means that we have to be incredibly careful not to damage anything.

We paused last week to catalogue our finds, and yesterday was a regular day in the shop, but from today we're clear to dig for at least the next fortnight.

It's a beautiful day, sunny and bright, and I spend a moment applying sunscreen. We all do this with the least sticky brand we can find; getting sunburnt is unpleasant, but it can also make people do stupid things, not something you want to risk with artefacts that are centuries old. Plus, archaeology gives your skin a layer of dirt like you wouldn't believe, even without applying a liquid to your skin first.

I've adapted my physical exercise to meet the demands of the job – yoga to stay flexible, since you spend a lot of time on your hands and knees and in strange positions, and resistance training for the more traditional parts, lifting large stones away and repeatedly stabbing the earth with a trowel.

You have to try and avoid getting excited every time something pokes up from underneath the soil. It's generally a rock, unless it's coloured or irregularly shaped. Some of my more squeamish co-workers have voiced concerns about finding skeletons, but that doesn't really bother me. Bone is just softer than rock, so you have to be more careful, but it's not actively harmful.

Knowing all that, you can't blame me when I ignore Amy's first squeal of delight. She once giggled like a child after digging up something she swore was the top of a

Denarius and turned out to be a can of Irn Bru.

Mark goes over. He's done well at disguising his crush on her, but he's always first to help and he has a particular way of looking at her. He's a good, smart digger, so I don't hold it against him. When he calls everyone else over, I carefully pick myself up and head around.

I'm not superstitious, which might surprise you, given that I'm convinced of the existence of an artefact of angelic, if not godly power, but I shiver at the sight of the three colourful tesserae that Amy has uncovered. They're faded and still have a thin patina of dirt over them, but they're laid perfectly rather than being discarded tiles from another mosaic. They're aligned. For a moment, the noise of the park, the general public, the chime of an ice-cream van all dims to a distant murmur and there's a hush where the loudest sound is my own breathing. I suddenly want us to work all night to get this done.

"Amy," Jamie says. "Amazing work. This … this is great."

She glows, standing back and admiring the three tiny squares, beaming at everyone around her.

"Seconded," I add in quickly; a happy team is a motivated team. "This is incredible – how big do you think it is? Brilliant."

It sounds slightly wooden but she gives me a big smile nonetheless. If she wasn't so annoying, she'd be pretty.

"Drinks on me tonight," Mark says. "So long as there's a few more."

Jamie laughs, then takes a deep breath and blows it out, running his hand through his hair. "Ok, let's not crowd this one or risk tamping down the soil too much. Amy, you and Mark keep working on this corner here. Let's not assume that it's quite as big as the one next-door, but Alice, you and I will start from about three metres over this way, ok?"

The 'one next door' is about five metres by three metres and is the largest Roman mosaic that I've ever seen. I bite back a snappy rejoinder, instead fixing a smile to my face and stepping over to his mark.

It's slow going after that. Amy and Mark uncover another twelve tesserae heading in our direction and after two hours, Jamie and I find our first one. He stands up and calls both the support team and the museum's PR people to get down here. Any press will really help the funding efforts, even though we're scheduled to be here for another fortnight.

I'm not given to excitability, but I'm practically quivering, humming with anticipation as we dig, brush and scrape the dirt away from the mosaic. This could be it. This could really be it. I've laughed at the idea of people wetting themselves with excitement in the past, but I feel a pang of sympathy for them now. Or rather, a mild twinge of sympathy, since none of them were about to uncover a map to a religious artefact.

At one forty-five, Jamie drags us all away to eat lunch, which we do under the shade of an oak tree across from the dig. It's tantalising, staring at it, and I can tell that Amy is itching to get back to 'her' find – we all are. But I also respect Jamie's judgment, since a hungry dig team is a bad dig team, and his restraint is admirable, even when the PR team turn up and start asking all kinds of daft questions. Of course this is a significant find. Of course we'd hoped to find something like this. Yes, this is a huge development for Verulamium. It's all very prosaic, so I don't get involved. I guess the worst they could do is misspell something that goes into the local rag tomorrow.

Half an hour later, we're 'allowed' back to the dig. It's painstakingly slow work and the PR team leaves after about ten minutes of watching us brush dirt away from another piece of the mosaic.

I barely notice when the photographer from a local newspaper turns up, and later on we're promised a reporter from an archaeology magazine that I've actually heard of.

At six pm, Jamie calls us to a halt, which is far later than we've dug in the past. I reluctantly obey, stretching and brushing myself down. Mark and Jamie carefully catalogue all of the 'loose' finds, while Amy and I lock up the barriers around the edge of the dig and set up our mobile tent over it, in case it rains. We're done and in the local pub by half past seven, which I have mixed feelings about. On one hand, I'd much rather sneak back to the dig and keep going, but on the other hand, it'd raise suspicions from the team and as I understand it, this kind of camaraderie is expected in most team situations.

I try very hard to tune back into the conversation.

"What about you, Alice?" Mark is saying. "Favourite dig in a film?"

I wrack my brain. I don't watch many films, but something from a magazine surfaces and seems to provide an acceptable answer.

"Journey to the centre of the earth," I say. "It's not exactly archaeology, but you've got to give them kudos for persistence."

Mark laughs and I breathe a sigh of relief as he asks Amy, who goes with something much more predictable: Tomb Raider. As far as I'm concerned, Lara Croft is more or less on the same level as Indiana Jones, but does score a few points for representing women. I can't work out if Angelina gains points for being hot or loses them for over-sexualising them though.

Thankfully, the food arrives and I'm able to avoid too much more conversation by eating heartily. In fact, there's an amiable silence. I suppose everyone must be tired, hungry and sore – I certainly am. I've seen that Jamie takes a while longer to recover than I do, and he seems happy to be in the team lead position rather than front and centre of every dig, which is fine with me.

I finish eating last, and it takes me a moment to realise that no-one has spoken for about fifteen minutes – and another to realise that for most people, that's a little abnormal. Jamie looks at me, then clears his throat.

"Alright everyone," he says. "Finish your drinks and

get yourselves home, have a bath, do some stretches. We pushed it pretty hard today and we've got a good week of this ahead, so take care of yourselves. We start at nine sharp tomorrow."

Mark's gaze paints Amy's body as Jamie mentions taking a bath and I suppress a shudder, disguising it by finishing my drink and standing up. "Thanks Jamie," I say. "See you all tomorrow."

There's a flurry of goodbyes and I almost feel a pang of regret at leaving the group. Maybe we do make a good team, after all.

It's a cool evening, but I barely notice as I mentally inventory the things I need to do, and the things I need to look out for in the dig over the next few days, drawing my most pertinent clues to mind.

I hurry home, taking a bath when I get back, scrubbing under my fingernails and trying to let my aching muscles relax. Despite all of my preparations and discipline, my thoughts are still racing when I get into bed. Ridiculous.

The next two days are amongst the most frustrating and satisfying in my entire life. Our pace is painstakingly but necessarily slow. We can't risk damaging anything. A small error with a brush could obscure a crucial clue. Towards the end of the third day on the dig, I realise what's emerging. The long, rectangular object in the mosaic that Mark bet was the start of a chariot is a wall, terminating at what looks like a tower at one end. A green mark becomes a tree, with kudos going to Amy for correctly predicting it, even if she did so whilst giggling to disguise the fact that she knew she was right. Self-deprecation is so unnecessary.

It's Jerusalem. The mosaic is the city. Or at least, the section of the city that I've been looking for since sixth form.

Mark thinks it's Verulamium. He could still be right, but that theory is then discarded the next day when we uncover that the tower building is absolutely, definitely Herod's Temple, which was destroyed in the invasion in around 70 AD. It's very distinctive. Vespasian would have seen it and then destroyed it – which makes it a stupid landmark to use, but it's possible that he left the area before all the damage had been done.

And below the temple, amidst an emerging number of small buildings – probably residential dwellings – there's some kind of yellow mark. It looks like a halo.

I'm not sure whether I was expecting a big 'x' to mark the spot, but I fully freeze for about a minute as I stare at it. Some of the tiles are quite faded, but it's definitely not a structure.

"Alice?" Jamie says, looking at me. I gesture with my brush, suddenly doubting myself.

"What do you think that is?" I ask.

Jamie looks at it and ponders. "Well, we've got a wall, a tower or temple, a number of smaller buildings and trees, so at first I would have said the sun, but obviously it's in the wrong place. It could be religious – a halo for a figure we haven't uncovered yet, or a chariot wheel?"

"Hmmm," I say, thinking fast. I want to find this, but I don't want to be hasty. I'm going to have to wait until we've uncovered the whole thing before I leap to any conclusions.

I turn back to my brushing.

I'm definitely sneaking back in tonight.

Matt

The WeWork in Narnia

Ben and I had agreed to meet at Charing Cross at half nine in the morning the next day and would you believe I almost make it on time.

Mind you, this whole thing could just be a bit of a ball ache – this Gardener guy had shown up at my office the day before and asked me to come and work in a homeless shelter for the afternoon. I'd almost told him to fuck off, but it broke up the monotony and I figured it might be some kind of test, which was obviously what the Darkling thing was all about, so I went for it. No-one popped up and told me that I'd chosen poorly, so I figured I was nailing it and the goblet of fire was basically mine already.

Of course, all that hard work needed rewarding, so I'd had a few impromptu drinks with my new friends and ended up puking in the Thames. I was feeling a bit ropey after that and had hit snooze on my alarm about five times, but my head was starting to clear. I could definitely do with coffee number three though.

Ben's looking worried and impatient by the time I clear the barriers.

"Hey man, look I'm sorry ok, I ..."

He grins and laughs in a relieved kind of way, like the stress is leaking out of him. "Come on," he says, clapping me on the shoulder. "I'm just glad you're here. Not sure I would have had the guts to go there by myself, so you get a free pass for your usual bullshit."

I'm still spluttering as we leave, but I disguise it by ordering two coffees on my phone from a nearby café. We head down the Strand, deftly dodging all the suitwankers.

Ben looks a bit panicked at the idea of being late when we get to the cafe where the Strand hits Kingsway, but I can see the coffee waiting there for us.

I take large slurps of my overly milky filter coffee as we turn up Aldwych at around ten to nine. Shit, we might even be on time.

I think I've been to a strip club around here, at the top of the road. Ben didn't much like it, but to be honest we were both too drunk to still be on the streets and it'd seemed like a good place to sober up. I'm about to suggest we see if it's still there – never hurts to have a plan B if this magic stuff doesn't work out – when Ben turns down a side street and I skid to a halt, thankfully without spilling my coffee. I guess the caffeine is kicking in already.

It smells like piss down here, despite the first building being a 'business school' and looking relatively fancy. How many of these business and language schools are actually a front for kids to do two hours of tuition and a fuck-tonne of Instagram every week for a year, and give their rich parents a break? Well, who knows – I've never had the patience to ask.

The road becomes a dead end and we clamber past a couple of wheelie bins into a pedestrian alleyway. I wonder what time that strip club opens.

"Ben, this place stinks," I say, coughing, as the smell of bins joins the ripe smell of human waste. He has the good grace to look embarrassed as he awkwardly pushes another wheelie bin back towards the wall of the alley so we can get past.

I try not to touch anything, mind my feet *and* avoid spilling my coffee all at the same time, which is really pushing the limits of my capabilities right now. Honestly, the fucking things I do for my best friend. We could get some really weird diseases from places like this, not to mention that the little park the other night was probably full of junkies' needles and all kinds of nasty shit.

Then the Darkling flashes in front of my eyes again and I shudder. Christ. How common are those things anyway? Why aren't they in the papers?

Oh god. This is going to be like Harry Potter, isn't it? Awkward men with bowler hats and terrible moustaches running around doing memory charms so no-one knows that magic and fairies exist.

And then I really do walk into the back of Ben, because he's stopped in front of a door, smartly labelled

"Seven Wild Court".

"Uh, sorry," I manage, as a splash of my coffee runs down the back of his jacket. I don't think he's noticed. "You know, this looks like a Regus office."

"Hmmm," he says, in a tone that says 'this is something that I'll be embarrassed about for at least eighteen months so I'm considering wimping out'.

"Come on," I say, pushing my way through. "If it's a Regus it's a fucking Regus and you're buying me a Macca's."

Ben sighs loudly and I think I've distracted him. Again, see? I can be a nice guy when I put my mind to it.

The inside of the building smells a lot better than the outside and it's really doing its best to look like a rental office. There's two suited receptionists at a large, white shiny desk, sweeping staircases leading up on either side, colourful chairs with a few copies of the Financial Times and a glossy magazine on the coffee table. Thankfully they haven't gone for the whole artisan hipster vibe – you know, bare wood, pictures of the office dogs, that kind of crap – because that really gives me a headache.

"Hi there," I say, striding up to reception as one of the staff behind it looks up. "We're here to see…"

I don't actually know who we're here to see, so it's just as well that Ben pushes past me, almost at a jog, pushing his leaflet-form-thing at the desk. "We have these," he says breathlessly, looking a bit pale. Poor guy. He's basically socially defunct sometimes.

The guy behind the counter glances at the form and then at his counterpart. "Ah, yes," he says smoothly. "Do you have any identification with you?"

Ben freezes, opening and closing his mouth a few times, but I roll my eyes and pull out my wallet, hunting for my driving license, handing it over.

"Uh…" Ben manages, looking like he's about to shit himself.

"Would a bank card do?" I ask for him. "My friend doesn't drive."

Toby Jones – I can read the name on his ID badge now – barely looks up as he scans my driving license and it starts to appear on the screen in front of him. "Sure," he says. "Anything with your name on it."

I can see a dead fly caught in his ocean of hair product but I don't embarrass him by mentioning it since he's being so helpful.

"Thanks," Ben stammers, producing his bank card and we repeat the process.

"Can you call it in?" Toby says to his female counterpart, and she nods in an efficient, vaguely corporate manner that either slightly offends or nauseates me – I can't work out which. She speaks softly into her desk phone, but all I catch are our names.

"Thank you," he says, handing our cards back to us. "You're expected. Please, have a seat and one of the team will collect you shortly."

"Great," I say, heading over to the most comfortable-looking chair and slumping down into it, stretching my feet out. Honestly, Narnian bureaucracy is not what I thought it would be. There's not a single bit of Turkish Delight, or any sign of that girl from Baywatch play-fighting a minotaur. So disappointing.

Ben looks at me sheepishly and I toast him with my coffee cup, then take a large slurp. It's definitely kicking in, thank fuck.

A moment later, Luke – the guy from the shitty little garden with the ghost thing – pops his head around one of the doors behind us. He's in dark jeans and a jumper over a red checked shirt. He looks more like a stay-at-home dad than an exorcist.

Christ, I really hope we don't actually have to do that. Creepy puking twins in a hotel asking you to lick them or some such shit. Think I'd take a rain check and go back to the suitwankers in central at that point.

"Ben? Matt? Over here," he calls, distracting me from my train of thought.

I lever myself up and head over, shaking his hand.

"Thanks for having us back," Ben says, his voice quavering slightly.

He laughs. "Don't thank me yet. Come on."

I follow the magician-lecturer along another generic office corridor. There's even crappy art on the walls here, black and white photos of London streets.

Luke touches a keycard to a door and it opens onto another short corridor. As the door clicks closed behind us, he slides a panel in the wall upwards to reveal a black palmprint scanner.

"Damn," I breathe. "That is some James Bond shit!"

Luke laughs softly. "Yeah, I hear that a lot."

The hand scanner thing shows a green light and the door ahead clicks. Luke hurries on and speaks into another panel before opening the door properly.

"Come on," he says, grinning. "It's about to get much more Bondy."

For once, Ben is way ahead of me as I stand there blinking and eventually manage to follow him through the doors into whatever the love child of C.S Lewis and Daniel Craig looks like.

It doesn't disappoint. I take four steps along the high walkway that we've emerged onto and gawp like a tourist seeing Trafalgar Square for the first time. We're looking down on a large situation room and there's a huge screen on the opposite wall with a map of the world on it, red dots with little boxes next to them giving information about whatever's being indicated. Desks are neatly laid out with their own screens and boxy PC towers, with an eclectic mix of people in smart-casual clothes talking, working, concentrating intently. It's quiet, but there's a directed buzz of conversation and the whir of fans from the computers in the background. No-one seems to be in a hurry – there's no panic or urgency. Everyone seems to be doing exactly what they should be doing in a quiet, determined way.

"Come on," Luke says, gesturing and moving on. "I expect you want to know the full story behind all this."

And that gets our attention pretty quickly, making both of us scurry after him. I'm not ashamed to admit that I scurried, because this of all got extremely interesting, and that grants you a temporary nonchalance waiver.

We follow Luke through another set of doors and he ushers us into a small conference room. Again, classic Regus set-up, plasma screen on the wall, spider phone on the desk, even a few bottles of water on the side. He follows my eyes and gestures to them. "Help yourselves," he says, seating himself at the table, interlacing his fingers and leaning forwards.

I pour myself a glass of water, slide the bottle over to Ben and sit down, waiting for the fun to start.

"Père Pierre Teilhard de Chardin ," Luke says , tapping his smartphone , causing a black and white image of an old guy to appear on the screen behind him . His face is long and pitted , his eyes dark and intense , a stark contrast to the white dog collar around his neck . "A French priest , geologist , philosopher , branded a heretic by some. Born 1881, died 1955."

I'm not quite sure why we're staring at an old dead Catholic but I'm willing to be patient for a bit.

"In 1941, Chardin submitted his work '*the phenomenon of man*' to the Vatican in Rome. His thesis?" Luke shifts in his seat and leans back a bit, getting into his stride. This feels like a fairly well-worn routine. "Chardin believed that he knew something special about the future of mankind's evolution. Not his physical evolution, but the future of our physical and spiritual evolution – namely, that our thoughts and minds would eventually link with Christ. He called this the 'Omega Point' and referred to the linkage itself as the noosphere."

"The paper was rejected and seen as blasphemous. Chardin was forbidden to teach, his papers withdrawn. Two years later, he made a substantial breakthrough while deep in prayer, leading him to write another book in secret. He realised that the noosphere already existed, something he referred to as an energy net, linking the minds and spirits of all humans, animals, and even plants. Incidentally, it also caused him to abandon eating meat."

This does sound a bit much but I'm bearing with. I take a swig of water and do a double-take; I must have left my coffee in reception. Shame, I could use the buzz right now. Still, I do feel a bit like we're getting the scene-setting speech in a D&D game, which isn't a bad feeling. I'm a bit out of practice, that's all.

"Chardin was able to draw on this energy net, using an insignificant fraction of the noosphere's energy. He healed one of his congregation by laying his hands on them, something he ascribed to God's healing power. He later began to doubt this as he found himself more at peace in the natural world than inside his church. He documented how he made plants grow faster, how he could heal minor injuries. He described himself as becoming increasingly in tune with the music of the earth's spirit, something he kept from the church because of the risk of being excommunicated. After his death in 1955, his writings were left undisturbed for years."

Luke looks up. "You both still with me?"

Ben nods. I raise my eyebrows. "Sure," I say. "I mean, it's a bit much to take in, even having seen all this in action, if you know what I mean."

He grins kindly. "Course," he says. "We'll get to that. Bear with me. You're lucky that it's me and not old Angelo. He'd be going on about how millennials don't have any respect these days and how everything was better in the eighties. You didn't hear that from me, of course."

Which is something else that makes all of this weird. This guy genuinely seems like someone I could have a pint with.

"Chardin established a network of contacts encompassing all kinds of religious and spiritual people around the world, trying to work out if what he'd discovered was unique. A few years before his death, he came across Raphael du Bois, a British descendent – or so he claims – of one of the Knights Templar. That's why we've got this building in central London. Raphael's family joined the Knights Hospitaller after the Templars were dissolved, probably so that they could keep the property and assets, rather than any deep-seated affection for St John's Ambulance."

"Huh," Ben said. "I had no idea they were the same thing."

"Schooled," Luke says, grinning. "Well, if you learn nothing else today..."

That makes him laugh, and I think he relaxes a bit. "I think that's pretty unlikely."

"Anyway, Raphael did manage to emulate Chardin's work in the two years prior to the priest's death. He believed – rightly – that the things Chardin had found were important to protect people from problems outside of the normal. He founded the order that we now call the Gardeners, in a corruption of Chardin's name. Until that point, du Bois had been in the military and looking after his family's estate, so he knew a lot of very competent people."

He pauses to take a drink.

"Raphael developed a close network of friends and associates, developing Chardin's system further and establishing linkages through political and military systems. There was a bit of a honeymoon period where he was very motivated, but his credibility had an issue because no-one knew if there was anything to protect *against*, apart from some details in the lore of the Knights Templar – and that intelligence was essentially on a par with myths and legends."

I think we're getting to the good bit.

"But in the early 1980s, during the Iran – Iraq war, a defending force and an invading force were horrifically wiped out in a mysterious incident. No eyewitnesses, lots of corpses. Backup arrived to find everyone, including the twenty-person military squad and fifteen insurgents, dead, with no gunshot wounds, stab injuries or blast damage. They simply seemed to have bled out through their eyes, mouths and other orifices."

That is some ill shit.

"For a few months, both sides accused each other of testing advanced weaponry until it happened again, both at an army base nearby and a village. One of the higher-ups in the British government knew of Raphael and drafted him and two of his associates in, enlisting them alongside a Special Forces unit."

"Raphael found what he described as a spectral signature, leading him to two non-corporeal beings that – and you'll laugh – he referred to as 'shambling old ladies'. These 'Shamblers', as we now call them, are attracted to life. Raphael and his squad tested this with rats, which exploded when touched by the Shamblers. Using the system of meditation that he'd learned from Chardin, he managed to first confine and then entirely disperse the Shamblers, destroying them."

"Unfortunately, this wasn't the last or only kind of threat that Raphael encountered – and to understand why, you have to understand something else about the universe."

I swap glances with Ben. This is either awesome or a complete crock of shit. Or both. I can't read what he's thinking, but we both turn back and listen to Luke with an intensity of concentration that I can't remember the last time I deployed.

"Our planet exists in a solar system, but the entire universe is sandwiched between a zillion other universes at once. The noosphere forms a natural barrier between them, but where atmospheric conditions are similar, where planets are similar and the noosphere thins, gaps can form and things from other universes can come through."

He pauses and Ben jumps in. "The noosphere is the same thing that Chardin used in his magic, right? But by using it, aren't you thinning the noosphere and making it easier for those things to come in?"

Luke grins. "Smart," he says. "But no – the noosphere is an active force, always rushing between people, animals and plants and constantly being replenished. You'll get a feel for this later. But where something terrible has happened, a murder, a war, torture, that kind of thing – the noosphere thins. It's one of the reasons why people are more likely to see ghosts around graveyards and the like."

"Huh," Ben says, reverting to his previous level of eloquence.

"So," I say, cutting in. My turn to play smartarse. "I still don't really get what these shamble monsters are or how this magic stuff works. And if they're in Iraq, why are we worried about that?"

"I know it's a lot to take in, and it won't all make sense at once. Or maybe Angelo is just a better lecturer than I am. But I'll take your last question first. The Iran-Iraq war was called off, at least privately, when the Shamblers were discovered. Publicly, both sides needed a reason to continue putting armed forces into the area, so we used previous footage to justify the expense. It was relatively quick for us to work out how to close the rifts, and this became a turning point that ended the supposed Iran-Iraq conflict."

"Shit," I blurt. "The entire war was made up?"

"Not at all," Luke says sagely. "The beginning was real enough, and there has been conflict off and on, but all sides agreed to cool things off when rifts opened, and given the bloodshed, there were a large number of Shamblers to deal with. One problem is that there's no rhyme or reason to what comes through, so we're perpetually on the back foot."

"So it's suffering that causes these rifts to open?" I ask.

"That's right. Pain, mental suffering – it doesn't have to be physical," Luke continues. "One of the biggest challenges we've had recently is that the incessant conflicts, appeals for help, terrorism and stress in the world seems to have decreased humanity's ability to feel empathy, so we're seeing smaller rifts open because there's no compassion following a bad act. That means a fair number of our forces have been recalled to the UK rather than deal with incidents abroad. At the same time, the government has invested a large amount in promoting brands that foster kindness and empathy, like certain yoga brands, mindfulness apps, that kind of thing."

"And that actually works?"

"We're monitoring it," he says. "We have a network

of volunteers and paid supporters who can check the density of the noosphere across London, giving us some early warning of any problems, helping us to prevent the issue before it happens. You ever wonder why you see so many people in Starbucks with laptops and tattoos? That's usually us."

"So," I say, managing to yank my mind back to my initial questions. "You have no idea what things may or may not come through the rifts and everything is getting worse."

"That's pretty close to it," Luke admits. "There are a few 'species' that are more common – possibly because their worlds are atmospherically very similar to ours – but otherwise, yes."

Christ. We're getting boned by our own shitness.

"Today, the Gardeners operate on two fronts," Luke says, standing and folding his hands behind his back in a gesture that somehow reminds me of one of my lecturers back at university. "Operations with the military abroad, and operations with the police and other forces domestically. Everyone has to be combat-fit in case you're called for duty overseas – you might be with the regular army, but more likely, Special Forces, although your background will be taken into account for things like HALO jumps if necessary. That said, we do have tactical autonomy, so we can operate on our own without permission from other forces – that came about in ninety-one, in recognition of our work in the Middle East."

"Empathy," Ben says during a pause. "That's why Jack was involved. Because how we treat homeless people is a good measure of empathy."

"That's right," Luke says. "We've been varying the conditions a little recently. Did you notice his dog? People tend to give more money when there's a dog."

Ben laughs, despite everything. "That was an experiment?"

Luke nods and grins, but another thought seems to cross Ben's mind.

"Wait a second," he says quietly. "What do tattoos have to do with this?"

"Ah," Luke says, smiling "Yes. Well, that takes us to the second part of Matt's question. Unfortunately, we don't have the time for everyone to achieve the same level of oneness and unity with the earth as Chardin did – although as you know, we do insist that everyone possesses a certain level of compassion and empathy. Raphael's second discovery was that silver has a certain resonance with the noosphere, making it easier to feel, detect and interact with its power. In a successful, but long-lasting experiment, he permanently tattooed himself with silver, making it much, much easier to work with the noosphere. Fortunately, we have since discovered a fast-fading plant-based compound that means silver can be injected into the skin permanently, but that also fades within a day, leaving you with the ability but not the markings, until they're in use."

"Christ," I say, leaning back. "So, the deal is to get tattoos in Narnia's WeWork, learn magic, fight monsters invading from other universes, potentially bleed from my eyes and arsehole, repair gaps in the fabric of reality and probably still lose a war against terrorists and monsters. Did I miss anything?"

Luke thinks for a moment. "No, that about covers it. Still interested?"

Without any hesitation at all, Ben and I are both nodding like that fucking insurance dog.

Ben

Wild Court, Gardener HQ

This is it.

This is absolutely it.

The dream. What I've been looking for all my life. What I've been *wishing* for all my life.

If anything, I really, really appreciate Matt's presence. I mean, he's my best friend, virtually my brother, but there's normally some vestigial annoyance at whatever he's doing. Today, given that it was all I could do to get on the train without peeing my pants, I was just grateful for his presence. He's like a wall that props me up, that I can lean on, and today, his childish jokes barely register. I'm so glad that he's here, that he believed all this and came along.

Ok, ok, I like his jokes. I do them too sometimes.

I didn't expect that this would all be terrifying and exciting at the same time. I suppose it's because it's real, and not a colossal wind-up, although there's a part of me that can't quite believe it. It makes no sense that they've stayed under the radar, but they somehow have. I guess no-one would believe you if you tried to tell them, even if you had photos. It's too much.

"So," Matt is saying. "How do we get these tattoos and where do we learn magic?"

"Well," Luke says. "First you get a tour while I connect your email accounts to our library system, and then you go and do some reading. If you're still with us after that, you head to our training facility in Bracknell, get your tattoos and learn the staves. That's what we call the 'magic' – you'll see why later on. Now, I've got somewhere else to be, so put your email addresses in my phone and I'll hook you up."

I mouth 'Bracknell?' to Matt, who shrugs. It's full of industrial parks and a newly refurbished shopping centre; worst Hogwarts location ever.

With trembling hands, I take Luke's phone and put my email and phone number into his contacts, leaving big sweaty marks on the back as I hand it to Matt, who – graciously, I might add – doesn't remark on it.

There's a knock at the door and I turn in my seat to see once of the biggest men I've ever seen in my life. He must be about six and a half feet high, not a single inch of which seems to have gone into a neck. He's built like a wrestler and despite his casual dress – smart jeans and a black unmarked hoodie – he radiates strength and capability, like a coiled spring. I'm instantly in awe of him.

"Ah," Luke says, looking up. "Ben, Matt, meet Mack."

"Good to meet you all," he says. He's got an American

accent – Midwest if I had to guess, but I'd honestly be afraid to do so. "Teach, you want me to give them the tour?"

"Please," Luke says pleasantly, seemingly unfazed by this leviathan. "Why don't you introduce yourself and then give them a quick look around? I've got to meet the Third to run over a few details before the briefing."

He gets up from his seat and gestures to Mack, who takes his place, then takes his phone back from Matt. "See you both later," he says with a grin, and vanishes from the room.

"Ok then," Mack says. "Well, you want to know something about me? I served three tours. Green Berets. Iraq, Afghanistan, Syria. I started fighting in the war on terror back in 2001, but I'm finishing my career with the real one. These demons, spirits, monsters, whatever you want to call them, you can't reason with them, you can't negotiate. Maybe one day we'll find friendlies out there like we almost did at Karnak, but until then, I ain't leaving and I don't think many others will either."

He leans back and takes a deep breath, letting it out slowly. Matt and I both lean forwards at exactly the same time, and I flush with embarrassment.

"Uh, sir," Matt says. "Karnak?"

"Sure," Mack says. "Karnak, you won't know about that yet I guess. It's the training facility, and you'll be shipping out there tomorrow or later this week. Some of us call it the Abditory, some call it Karnak on account of the statues.

Closest we've come to meeting something that didn't want to kill us, but looks like the Shamblers did for all of them first."

I clear my throat to jump in – statues? But Mack pushes his chair back and stands before I can speak. "No spoilers now," he grunts. "Come on, I'll show you around."

"This building used to belong to the Saint John's Ambulance," he says, leading us down a wood-panelled corridor. "Raphael – that's our co-founder – claims his family got it from when they were Templars, but I think he's full of bull crap if you ask me. Mind you, I cast spells and just last week put my knife through the skull of a flying velociraptor, so who knows?"

We laugh politely. Should we be laughing politely? This man could crush my windpipe with his finger and thumb.

Also, flying velociraptors?

"What you saw earlier is the situation room," Mack continues, opening a door in front of us. "This here is the comms room, where we keep up with our teams, and the other organisations around the world."

I step through and find myself in an airy atrium, large windows letting sunlight into the large hall from above. LCD screens are set into the walls, and long, curving, natural-looking wooden desks are set at well-spaced intervals, a number of industrious-looking people working at them.

"Ok, let me check something," Mack says, pulling

out his phone and tapping at it. "Don't want to interrupt someone mid-call or in an op. Here we go."

He threads his way through the room. It's strangely calm, and there's a breeze that feels like natural air rather than air conditioning. I glance at a screen – it's got another map on it, currently showing London's zone one. Large parts of it are red, some is amber and a few portions are green.

"Um, Mack," I say, making the big man stop and turn. "What does all the red mean?"

"Huh," he says. "That there is the estimated level of empathy and kindness being recorded by our teams and the likelihood of a breach. Almost one quarter of the homeless people in London are recording for us, plus a load of students and others who only know that they have to run a mindfulness monitoring app on their phones in a local coffee shop after we give them the basic tattoos. They tune into enough of the noosphere to get a feeling for how bad things are, and the app does the rest. It's pretty new."

"Huh, so Jack…" I start, then change tack. "Wait, I thought you said this happened when there was conflict and killing?"

"Yeah, it was," he says, lowering his voice as an analyst looks up from her desk at him. "But it's been getting worse. People just don't give a damn any more. You see that big red spot there?"

He points to a chunk of London right by Cannon Street Station.

"You ever been away for a holiday then walked around the city at rush hour? People barely look at you, let alone help if you need it. Our monitors there have the toughest time getting a bit of cash, even with the dogs – and we gave them the cutest ones to be sure."

He walks around the desks and leads us over to a woman in a wheelchair.

"Seline," he says, making her turn around. "You got a moment?"

"For you Mack, of course," she says, smiling. She's well-spoken, but it's not intimidatingly posh. I'd place her in her late thirties and she's dressed fairly casually in jeans and a roll-neck jumper. "Are these the new recruits?"

"That's right," he says gesturing to us. "This is Ben, and this is Matt."

"It's good to meet you," Seline says. "What can I help you with?"

"I'm giving them the grand tour," Mack replies, sitting on the corner of the desk. "Can you show us a recent communication you've had?"

"Of course," Seline says, swivelling back around to face her screen. "This is an information pack from a shamanic practitioner in Spain, Philip Alvarez."

Four different windows pop up on her computer screen, including text in Spanish, a few charts and an image of a guy in a smart blue shirt.

"That's him," she says, gesturing. "He's been with us for a few years now. He's given us a written report about inner Barcelona, which seems relatively healthy at the moment – compared to London, that is – as well as levels monitoring, an encounter with a minor Darkling he shut down in a back alley of La Ramblas after closing a rift, and a few thoughts on our current situation."

"So you speak Spanish?" I blurt out and instantly regret it. What a stupid thing to say – of course she speaks Spanish. Fortunately, she doesn't remark on it, even though I can see Matt rolling his eyes to my left.

"Spanish, Portuguese and Italian," she says. "Languages are essential for analysts because we talk to people all over the world. I've been in touch with our Milan and Cali teams already today."

Mack grins. "We have people here all hours," he says. "It's not easy work. Thanks Seline."

"Take care," she says, turning back to her screen and bringing up another set of windows. Mack starts to lead us further through the Atrium, between the rows of curving desks. They've got an organic, smooth look to them and I have to stop myself from reaching out to touch them.

"So, Mack," I say, hoping that my next question sounds more intelligent than the last. "Do our people ever go through these rifts?"

Our guide gestures to a door and leads us through into another conference room, seating himself with his back to the wall.

"Yeah," he says. "More so in the early days when we thought there might be friendlies out there. It's much less common nowadays. We'll mostly contain the threat and close it back up again. Rifts lead to entire worlds, so there's no point trying to take that job on."

"What I can't quite get my head around," Matt blurts. "Is how weird this all is because it's not weird. This place is like the SAS fucked Lululemon, you know? Everyone here seems so chill but you're actually wizards. I mean, how do you keep it all secret?"

I think he's intimidated by the big soldier, not that he'd ever admit it.

Mack nods slowly and leans forward on the desk, fixing Matt with a serious look.

"Well," he says. "We're big believers in treating adults like adults. You treat a person like an adult and they act like an adult. Remember what we're facing and where most people have come from? Everyone got selected because they're smart or strong or good at recon or whatever but most importantly because they understand what's going on and are kind, decent people. Luke probably told you that the noosphere is damaged or repaired by empathy, right?"

"The last place we want a rift to open is right here, but that's not really it. There's no heroes here. In the army, there's a bit of space for joking around because you're bringing in young people who are strong and can be made to follow orders and reset how they react to situations. Here, we rely on the armed forces for physical protection but we have a pretty specific job, so we focus on that and don't get distracted. We reckon the noosphere started as a force of creation, because animals don't have a lot of empathy, but they do grow, and so do plants."

"But when people started taking all that down, killing the earth, not even caring for their own kind, well, that's when everything went upside down. As soon as someone starts acting the hero, people get hurt. When someone thinks they're special, that's when people forget about other people and the effect that their actions have on them. If you're showing entitlement rather than humility, then everyone's in trouble. And so everyone who works here, or works with us, understands how serious it all is. That's the first part of keeping it under wraps. The second is – well, try telling someone about the Darkling you saw and see how that goes."

I don't really know what to make of that and neither does Matt, who seems to have been expecting some kind of rebuke, but Mack suddenly grins.

"Look at me now," he says. "If I'd asked that question when I signed up to the forces, my squad leader would be calling me a jackass and I'd have been hitting the deck and giving him twenty."

Matt laughs. "Yeah," he says, clearly relieved. "That's more what I was expecting."

I suddenly feel sweaty and nervous again as something occurs to me.

"How much physical training do we need to do?" I ask, dreading the answer.

He looks at me, sizing me up. "Don't worry," he says. "You likely won't be in the field for a while, and you might even suit analyst and comms work – like Seline – more than being out. But pretty much everyone has to be ready for a decent amount of mental, physical and stave work. You might have skills that mean you're suited for an operation and need to keep up with army, marines or spec ops. There's no 2am starts, but you need to not completely panic when you see something weird – and it's ok to call it weird, because it is. But you also need to be calm enough to deal with the public a moment later if needed."

"Shit," Matt says. "So, kind of like Harry Potter. But kind of like Men in Black as well."

Mack gives a quick snort of laughter. "Sure," he says.

Matt has the grace to look a bit embarrassed, but Mack just fixes me with a steely look.

"You'll get training in the staves, physical workouts and more standard learning stuff – like dealing with the public, a more detailed history of the Gardeners, that kind of thing – all blended into one. You have to pass to a decent standard, but you'll get a week's intensive training, then be on low-level duty, usually with a chaperone, the week after. You'll be expected to study and work out in your own time but you won't do a nine to five when you're on duty, more like a half day, then the rest of the time as your own. After that it's one week on, one week off unless something important comes up. After six months, we look at where to place you more permanently. The only thing you might find uncomfortable is that some ops happen at night to minimize public exposure."

"Ok," I say, embarrassed, but also annoyed at my own embarrassment.

"Alright then," Mack says, tapping at his phone again. "If we move, we can make a briefing kick-off and you can see how operations get planned. Then I think we're pretty much done for the day. You need to read up before you can understand much more. Did your reading lists come through?"

I pull my phone out of my pocket and there's a few notifications from my e-reader app. Apparently I've now got a 'secure library' that requires both a VPN and a fingerprint scanner – fortunately, my phone has both – and that the secure library now has over a hundred new titles in it.

"Yep," I say at the same time as Matt.

Mack pushes his chair back and leads us out of the room, heading down another hallway until we arrive at a large, lecture-style room. Another door opens at the back, and Luke walks in with a group of serious-looking men and women who are dressed in a mixture of combat fatigues and casual clothes. Luke catches my eye and nods as Mack ushers us into the back seats. More people arrive quickly and fill the rows from the front, pulling out laptops and tablets, greeting each other. There's a low buzz of conversation.

"Mack," I say quietly, leaning over Matt to speak to him. "Isn't this all confidential?"

He grins. "Sure is," he says. "But you know what I said about treating adults like adults? Starts from the moment you sign up."

Wow.

Then a woman with short, dark hair, wearing a smart suit, walks into the room and everyone falls silent. I lean back and forget to ask about confidentiality and what we tell our families. Not that mine will really notice if I'm somewhere else for a few weeks at a time; it's not like I live at home.

The woman stops at the front of the room and puts a few files and a laptop down on the front desk, slotting it into a dock. The large flatscreen on the wall behind her comes to life and shows a map of Europe which slowly pans to Antwerp, in Belgium.

"Good morning and welcome to this morning's briefing," she says clearly. "Most of you know me, and for those of you who don't, I'm Amelia Taylor of the First Extraordinary. This morning's briefing concerns suburban Antwerp in Belgium, where we'll be working directly with the Belgian police. Whilst this is a four-star operation – that is to say, containment and dispersal of a non-corporeal, rift closure and management of corporeal entities – we are in a civilian area, so this is a tough one. You will be in civvies for this to avoid undue alarm to the populace."

A murmur of noise comes from the fatigue-wearing contingent with Luke, and Amelia turns slightly to address them.

"You didn't sign up for this because it was easy, right?" she says wryly, causing a ripple of good-natured laughter.

"There will be two SAS teams on this mission, liaising directly with DSU in Belgium. Sigma team will run the perimeter and Gamma team will accompany the Third Group from the First Extraordinary into the mission area."

Amelia taps her laptop and the map zooms in even further, to a residential area on the outskirts of town, with a perimeter marked in a red line around ten or so buildings, one of which is highlighted in the same shade of red.

"At 1800 yesterday, Belgian police discovered that a converted cellar in this house was not only being used to traffic women and children by sea from Russia around the coast, but also to prepare explosive devices. An irregularity in the patrol times and satellite coverage in Antwerp harbour has meant that for the last three years, a forty-five-minute window occurs each week when vessels can come and go as they please. We believe this has been exploited for some time."

"All the assets were seized, the house was secured and it was swept by the bomb squad. There are currently twelve suspects being interrogated by the police and Interpol in Antwerp. However, in the raid, one explosive device was detonated and approximately ten people – nine of them women being held in improvised cells – were killed. Only one was retrieved and is currently in a coma in a nearby hospital. We suspect that this triggered a rift opening, because as the fire department were extinguishing the blaze at approximately 2300, one of them spontaneously bled to death from the nose, mouth, eyes and anus. At the same time, two local police were torn in half by what we believe was a Ravager."

The screen changes again and shows two pencil drawings.

I stare for a few moments. The images slightly defy belief.

The left-hand image shows a stocky, ghostly figure in a cloak, hood up. The right-hand image is more terrifying, but the jury's out. It's a squat, heavy-set, reptilian creature, covered in scales, horns atop its head, with large, dripping fangs. It's about as big as a bear.

"Fortunately, Ravagers do tend to sleep after a meal, so we may be able to catch this one while it's still out. The other being, we suspect, is a Shambler rather than a Lesser Banshee. Shamblers don't tend to go far from their point of origin, but they are hard to detect and do travel in packs. Houses within a half-mile radius have been evacuated, and we hope to wrap this up in the next six hours if possible. As such, squads will ship out in the next sixty minutes after this briefing concludes. We have the full co-operation of local police and DSU. Any questions?"

A woman towards the front of the room puts her hand up, and Amelia gestures to her.

"Sanders, go ahead."

"Do we know if there's more than one Ravager?"

"Good question, and no, we do not," she replies. "Sigma team will patrol the perimeter and immediately radio if they need assistance from the First Extraordinary. Standard rules of engagement apply: stay covered and always assume there are more."

One of the SAS – or at least, I assume they're SAS from their fatigues – raises their hand.

"Go ahead," Amelia says.

"Are we using AP rounds? The last time we did Ravagers their hides were almost too tough for standard rounds."

"Gamma team will be permitted AP rounds," Amelia says. "Because of the proximity to the civilian population, Sigma team will carry conventional ammunition and try to force any Ravagers back towards Gamma team's location."

There aren't any more questions, and after a moment, Amelia dismisses the room.

"SAS teams will be given a designation en route. All teams, convene on the roof in fifteen, one five, minutes. Sarah Rujzeda, you are the designated analyst for this mission, so please join them and sync with SAS mission command. Everyone else, thank you for your time."

I start to rise, but Mack leans forward and stops me for a moment as twelve other people – eight SAS and four Gardeners – leave the room quickly. Once the last Gardener is out, everyone else stands and the buzz of conversation resumes.

"Damn," Matt says. "That was serious."

"Yeah," I echo.

"Well," Mack says. "We want to make sure you know what you're getting into. You already saw a Darkling, which is towards the top end of what we usually expose new recruits to, but you deserve to see what it's like once you're trained and if you're in the field. Today is pretty much your last chance to turn back before you're signed on for two years – and that's a short tour by military standards. I'll take you back out now. Do some reading, some thinking on the train and if you're game, head to the training facility tomorrow."

The room has emptied completely, leaving Mack plenty of room to lead us down another corridor, opening a security door onto an ugly grey corridor, then through a fire exit that leads out to Parker Street.

"Later," Mack says with a grin, then closes the door behind us.

I blink in the sunlight, the sudden normality of the busy Covent Garden street hitting me like a bus. Tourists and businesspeople are wandering along, two taxis stopped opposite. There's some kind of impromptu photoshoot going on with a slim guy up the road a bit.

London sounds, car engines, people talking, pigeons getting in the way. It's all a bit much and the normality is almost overwhelming. I suddenly realise that this is probably what culture shock is like.

After about fifteen seconds of standing and gawping,

I turn to Matt.

"Fuck," I manage, eloquently.

"Yeah," he says, his eyes still wide. "Fuck."

Matt

Greenwich and Bracknell

I roll home and pack up my shit like the elite monster-killing magic machine I'm about to become.

There may be the tiniest bit of doubt bouncing around in my head – well, my stomach – but I scrunch it up tight and push it to one side. This is going to be fucking awesome. Working with the SAS or whatever, taking out badass monsters, riding around in choppers. Modern day dream, no more office job. Incredible.

Prepped and set, I hunker down for some serious reading of the ghostbusters manual, no vacuum cleaner backpacks required.

For a couple of hours, I'm sucking down every single bit of knowledge, poring over the bestiary, reading up on staves, flicking back to the history section. I've not been this into a class since my business studies lecturer started wearing see-through tops.

I dimly register Jess and Tim coming back to the flat, but I ignore them arguing over what to put on TV. Once

I've finished the handbook, I slip out – not really like me but go with it – to grab some food and supplies for tomorrow. Who knows what crap they might serve while I'm doing my training montage?

What if I can't do it?

I try to ignore all the self-doubt stuff. It's not healthy.

When I get back, I check my e-reader again. There was a message about further reading and now that I've skimmed the main text, I can see a subfolder offering me more stuff. Hell yes. Preliminary guide to the staves – yes please. I glance at the others – there's one about ethics, one about general conduct, one about Gardener military relations, the various organisational partnerships around the world but they look a bit blah, so I'll catch up on them later.

I also skip over the introductory bits. Most of it was in the foundation book anyway and I figure that I've heard a lot of it from Luke so there's no point running through it a third time. Ok, chapter two, the principles of the staves, great.

The general gist seems to be this: the noosphere is a force in motion, created as life grows, breathes and endures. Through a deep connection with the world's spiritual side, or through the silver tattoos, Gardeners – as well as priests, shamanic practitioners and wicca – can tap into it. The trick is to harness the flowing energy by channelling and activating it as it passes through you, like notes on a musical stave, hence the name, only the bars of the stave are a rapidly moving energy field. I'm paraphrasing, which is why I sound like a bit of a dick.

Also, musical stave, right. Not staves like a staff. Bloody D&D. I'm not a fucking concert cellist, how should I know about music stuff?

Shut up. I know what musical notation is. I'm not a complete savage, ok?

There's more.

By selectively activating the noosphere and tying it all together into a master symbol, it can be released with different effects. However, the guide says, there are a couple of important caveats. Primarily, new Gardeners should note that the impact of the staves on non-earthly corporeal beings – that is, fleshy – is limited. It's a spiritual force, so it can contain and disperse non-corporeal beings that are not of this world, but has a lesser impact on other beings. It can affect them weakly because they're 'not from around here' and the noosphere has an innate tendency to reject them, but this is usually limited to slowing them down or confusing them.

And the same principle applies to beings from this planet, as demonstrated by Chardin, when he healed things or accelerated their growth. He was essentially transferring energy from the noosphere back to the world, but because the noosphere recognises beings from this world as native, the impact is usually limited to positive stuff, healing, growth and so on. Basically, anything that's reflective of how the noosphere gets recharged or normally works.

Next – and my eyes are getting tired now from about four hours of straight reading – comes a warning to fully inducted Gardeners. In areas of extreme disturbance where the noosphere has been exceptionally thinned and rifts have been opened, it may be damaged to a point where the noosphere can't be harnessed. This means that the staves either can't be cast, or if they can, then they can take energy from the nearest source to compensate, and that's usually the life force of the one casting them. The impact of this can vary from mild tiredness and discomfort to severe confusion and fatigue, depending on the complexity of what you're doing.

Damn. So basically, if you're trying to seal a rift where there's been a mass murder or something, it might not work or if it does work, you'll mess with your head. Thus increasing your chances of being eaten by something that looks like Marilyn Manson fucked the Gruffalo.

Brilliant.

On that note, it's time for some sleep. That's more serious study than I've done for years. I look at travel for tomorrow and send Ben a note – commuter trains to Bracknell are really expensive, but it gets a lot cheaper after half nine, which conveniently fits with my desired sleeping schedule. We can meet at ten, get coffee, have a quick smoke and a sausage roll, then be on top form for hitting up an alien world hidden in a shitty industrial park. Plan.

~

Even at half past nine, Greenwich station is full of manspreading suitwankers. I manage to get the last seat on the train, only to realise why: I'm next to a guy whose knees are so far apart that he's basically trying to mate with me like he's some kind of jellied amoeba made of equal parts bureaucracy and polyester. The guy opposite is almost as bad, slouching right down in his seat and forcing me to sit bolt upright so that I'm not touching him.

I wriggle around a bit, glaring at them and getting the guy next to me to at least close his legs a bit so that any passing drafts don't air-condition the train with the smell of his ballsack, before rolling my eyes at the woman next to the slouncher. She grins and shrugs at me.

Thankfully, Waterloo East isn't too far away and the manspreader gets off at London Bridge. I wander down to the main station and grab a coffee and a sausage roll, ambling over to where Ben is waiting outside a pungent cosmetics store. It's one of my favourite games, getting him to wait in the most inconvenient places possible, although I've had to take a break because he wouldn't speak to me for a week after I left him outside a lingerie store for almost half an hour, giving him various excuses about late trains. In fairness to him, he found a coffee shop after fifteen minutes but it was still hilarious.

He looks slightly pale and has a big rucksack leant up against the side of the store. I wave and he gestures expansively.

"Brilliant Matt, thanks for this."

I laugh. "Hey, at least it smells nice. Could have been worse."

He sighs. You know how there's apparently a hundred words for snow in some languages? I reckon Ben has about that many different sighs, mostly about me. This one roughly translates as 'Matt's pranks at an inappropriate time'. As distinct from the sighs for 'Matt's knob jokes in polite company', 'Matt's bad chat up lines', 'Matt burping or farting in public' and 'Matt being overly vocal about suitwankers or people walking too slowly when he's in a hurry'. One day I'll write it down. You know, for science.

"You good?"

"Yep. Let's do this."

We get tickets and find the next train to Bracknell, standing to one side as another huge wave of commuters flows past us. Who are these people who rock up to the office at ten thirty, how much do they get paid and how can I land such a cushty job if I flunk out of magic school?

The train is basically deserted – there's not many people heading out of London at this time, so I spread myself out on a six-seat section, putting my bag on the seats opposite and taking up half of the space. Courteously, of course, so that Ben can claim the other half. Which he doesn't. He awkwardly fumbles with putting his huge rucksack in the overhead space and then sits with his small rucksack and e-reader on his lap, looking like the gawky awkward librarian that he is. Or was, I guess.

I stretch out my legs and polish off my sausage roll. Damn, those things are good.

"Do we need to get a cab from the station?" Ben says, looking nervous.

I lick my fingers and wipe them on my jeans before pulling out my phone and tapping in the address we've been given.

"Looks like it's not too far from the station. Still in a bit of a shitty industrial estate but it'll be alright to walk."

"Ok," Ben says, sipping his coffee. "You nervous?"

I look around the train. We've almost got the entire carriage to ourselves and if I'm being ruthlessly honest, there's a ball of nerves in my stomach.

"Yeah, little bit," I admit. "It's not every day we do this, is it?"

He laughs nervously and turns back to his book for a bit, looking up around Egham just as we go past Royal Holloway Uni, which is a cracking view. I once slept with a girl from here and she had a tiny room in a concrete tower block looking out over this incredible renaissance-style red-brick building, which must have either been nice or a big slap in the face every day, depending on your outlook on life. She didn't seem too bothered. Can't remember her name, but neighbours complained about the sex noise.

"Sarah," Ben fills in for me.

"Stop the train and let this guy get off already. You're already telekinetic, you don't need magic school."

"Telepathic," he mutters. "Or psychic. Telekinesis is moving things with your mind, dumbass."

I grin at him. "I know that."

I go for a quick piss and by the time I'm back, we're just about pulling into Bracknell station. Ben's looking more relieved than I feel and probably glad that once again, I've not found some way of making his life difficult by forcing us to miss the station.

We're friends, I swear.

Slightly guiltily, I help him with his big rucksack and we get off the train to see the bleakest vista I've seen in long time. A taxi rank, a dual carriageway, a crap-looking pub and a load of dirty grey office blocks. More guys in suits and women in regulation cardigans and skirts of a corporately-appropriate length. I want to curl up inside my own butthole and hide.

"Come on," I say without looking at my phone. "I think it's this way."

Ben doesn't follow me. He's seen this before and it usually doesn't end well. Instead, he pulls out his phone and taps at it for a moment until he finds the address of where we're going, looking at me and eventually nodding.

"Fine."

I guess it was a 50:50 chance.

Still, showing a modicum of respect, I let him lead because I've never been here before and really have no idea where we're going. And aside from the occasional sign or overly large logo on a building, these office blocks all look the fucking same to me.

I might have gotten the gym-to-smoking ratio wrong in my life. My shoulders are starting to ache a bit and I can feel the sweat from carrying a week's worth of my stuff around, but then Ben stops outside a nondescript office building.

"This it?"

He checks his phone again, also looking out of breath.

"Yep, think so."

"Cool. Let's go and ..." I bite off a joke. Take a breath. This is serious, Matt. "Let's do this."

Ben gives me a smile, looking relieved.

The inside of the office building looks exactly like I'd expect it to, and exactly like the one where I came for an interview a few years back, not too far from here but in the other direction. Didn't get offered the job, didn't really want it. Plus, I think they all hated me, which never helps.

There's a counter with a receptionist sat behind it, a light blue carpet showing a few stains. A couple of sofas and chairs surround a chipped table with old copies of glossy magazines. Fairly uninspiring wardrobe experience so far, but maybe that's the trick. Still, better than having to cram into a London telephone box – those things honk of piss. I don't know how Mr Weasley did it every day. Maybe everyone else was pranking him.

"Hi," I say to the receptionist as brightly as I can muster.

Then Ben steps up beside me and unexpectedly does the same.

"Uh, hi," he says. "I'm Ben and this is Matt. We're here to uh…"

"Welcome," the receptionist says brightly. "You're expected. Your induction leader will be Christina. She'll be along momentarily."

"Ok, thanks." I say, and head over to a seat, slouching down and taking a long pull from my water bottle, stretching and trying to air my pits a bit.

I've read the front page of the Financial Times three different ways and still can't get it to make sense when the door to my right opens up and a woman who looks a bit like Ben's boss at the library walks in. We've never met, but I've seen her on his Instagram.

"Hi," she says briskly. "You must be the last ones. I'm Christina, I'll be your trainer here. Please, come with me."

I grab my bag again and follow Ben through the doors out of reception as our Obi Wan takes us into our new incredible life. I'm definitely more of a Luke Skywalker than Ben is. He'd just about make C3PO. Well, I've always seen myself as more of a Han Solo figure, but you know, Jedi powers and all.

I'm dimly aware that Christina is talking. Crap.

"... and then we'll get into Karnak itself. Here we are. Now, we're light on guests at the moment so you lucked out – normally, recruits get bunks, but we might as well put you in the senior staff quarters. Take ten minutes to get settled and meet me in room 10A straight down the hall."

"Right, thanks," Ben says. There are two identical doors in front of us, one labelled '5A' and the other '5B'. He looks at me, then opens the door to 5A.

I take 5B and close the door behind me. There's a key in this side of the door so I pocket it and unpack a few odds and ends. Then I decide to have a quick wash and change my shirt. If I'm going to an alien world, I might as well be fresh.

Matt
Pimp my Hide

For once, I'm not late for the meeting. Or at least, no more than a couple of minutes. Ben and I are the only other people in the large conference room, Christina sitting to one side of the long table with a plasma screen on the wall behind her. I sit down on the opposite side and she slides a pack of papers over to me.

"Here," she says. "Read and sign. Final chance."

I almost scoff. There's no way I'm going back now, so I skim the paperwork as quickly as possible. Danger to life and limb, possible death, nondisclosure of state secrets, blah blah blah. I get to the end and there's an absurdly skinny benefits section on the final page – honestly, you'd think something this dangerous would still have final salary pensions but nope, it's a contributory scheme like everywhere else.

Hey, what can I say? I want to be sure I'm going to be taken care of in my old age, assuming I make it that far.

Still, I sign. I guess doing magic might have some

fringe benefits like immortality or something. Thinking about it, that Raphael guy, if he's still alive, must be pretty old, so surely there's something to that? I file that under 'things to ask once we've been here a few weeks'.

"Great," Christina says, as I slide the pack back to her. "Now, we're not going to waste any time, so if you'll follow me, we'll get the tattoos done and then start on the theory."

"Uh, sure," Ben manages. Which, in fairness, is more syllables than I manage to get out. "Is that ... normal?"

"Believe it or not, yes," she says crisply, leading us out of the conference room and handing our packs of paperwork to the receptionist, who is somehow waiting just outside the door, and passes back two plastic passes on lanyards in return. "We find that when you're learning the theory, it makes more sense if you've already been marked."

She hurries down the hall, through a security door and hands us our passes. Ben puts his over his head like a dork. I pocket mine.

"Now, you won't be able to leave the facility for twenty-four hours while your silver fades," Christina continues. "And we won't take you to Karnak until tomorrow, because we also need to run through basic fitness and aptitude tests. The next few days are going to be busy. It probably goes without saying, but please don't call any friends or family unless it's an emergency. Basic security hygiene."

We pass through two more doors, one standard, one heavy-duty, before Christina turns and ushers us through a door marked 'Silverware'. These Gardeners are pretty fucking funny, right?

And then I freeze. Shit. It's like being at the dentist. Ben steps around me and does exactly the same thing. Christina slips between the two of us and stands on the other side of the room.

The room has four reclining seats in it, exactly like you'd see at the dentist, if they went in for communal appointments – which would be a barrel of laughs wouldn't it? Cream, plasticky-looking recliners are spaced around the room, but without the mirror things that can look into your mouth. Instead, they're flanked by arm restraints that resemble blood pressure monitors, also sporting chunky-looking pen-like things with needles at the end.

"Please, have a seat," Christina says, grinning, obviously enjoying our discomfort. "I understand that this may be a little weird for you, so I'll explain everything first."

We both perch on the sides of separate recliners, keeping our distance from the needles.

"In the past, tattoos were applied by hand. This changed about seven years ago when we realised that minor imperfections meant some staves were slightly less powerful than they should be. Everyone's arms are different, and a slightly wobble can make the pattern less even, giving a correspondingly less even flow of noosphere energy during the stave, altering its power. We worked with a medical firm to develop scanners and automated systems that feed your measurements into a system that then calibrates your markings as precisely as possible, making sure that everything is as it should be."

She pauses briefly. "Once you've been marked, the silver will fade after about 24 hours, which is another reason why we prefer you not to leave the facility unescorted. And to answer your almost certainly unasked questions – yes, it will sting a little, as it's no different to any other tattoo, aside from the composition of the substance being injected into you. Yes, it will take a long time – the machines are fast, but you will still be here for about five hours, and yes, your arms will need to be absolutely still. We give you an injection once one of your arms is restrained, and that will prevent you from moving it, but you do get a break every hour to move around, go to the bathroom and eat. Once you're back in the chair, the system will re-scan your arm and start again precisely where it left off, which is another reason why we prefer using machines rather than people. Any questions?"

"When's lunch?" I ask.

"If we get started now, I'll arrange for it to be brought over in an hour. We can re-inject your arm with a reagent to reverse the paralysis so that you can eat normally. Anything else?"

I'm game. I mean, slightly terrified, but game. This is going to be awesome. Or terrible. I have no idea which. "Let's do it," I say, shrugging then looking at Ben. If anything, he's now whiter than usual but I think he'll be fine.

"Can I have a book or something?" he stammers.

"Actually, we have screens in front of the machines so you can watch TV if you want. Or access the library, depending on how dedicated you are."

He makes a little 'hmm' noise and I can see his shoulders untensing a bit from their usual levels of stress. I wish mine would, and that we could get on with this.

"Now, if you don't have any other questions, please sit and I'll inflict pain on you for the next five hours."

"That's what she said?" I manage, evoking a mere snort from Ben.

"It's so much funnier when you explain them," Christina says wryly. Shit, she's a lively one. I'm a bit speechless as she gestures for me to put my right arm into the blood pressure monitor sleeve thing. She does the same with Ben, then turns back to a laptop on a table behind her.

I try to distract myself by looking for the in-flight entertainment that she mentioned. There's a small pull-up screen by the arm of my chair. Awkwardly, I pull it up with my left hand and find the on-switch, just as the cuff around my right arm tightens, holding me firmly. It makes a similar noise to when a desktop PC boots up, then there's a ray of light that moves up and down the length of my arm like I'm being photocopied or something.

"Ow!" I jump and momentarily lose my cool as a needle pokes the top of my right arm and something cold floods down inside it. I can't seem to move it. The sleeve extends up and down, covering my arm from fingertips almost to my shoulder. Ok, so this is really happening. Might as well man up and deal.

I try to be nonchalant as I pull on a pair of headphones – awkward, I might add, with one hand – and put on a comedy, which is sure as shit going to annoy Ben but whatever.

About ten minutes in, it pauses and I tap the screen trying to un-pause it, but to no effect. I look up and see Christina still standing there.

"We've scanned your arm," she says, turning to look at me, then Ben and back again. "And we're about to start on the actual tattooing. I'll be back in forty-five minutes."

I try to find something to say, a question to ask to postpone the inevitable, but before I can get words out, our mentor's gone. I start to look at Ben, but then I feel a scraping down the top of my arm. Shit. It's like the time my mum's cat scratched me, only without the stinging afterwards. Ben's looking uncomfortable, his left hand gripping the armrest tightly.

Well, if he can bear this, so can I. I try to ignore it, put the comedy back on and focus as best I can. Only I can't. Not really.

How long does this last for, again?

After forty-five long minutes, after the pain turns from cat scratch to some kind of sharpened chisel scraping up and down my arm, the door bangs open and Christina walks in pushing a trolley laden with burgers and chips. The pain suddenly stops and I exhale.

"Everything alright so far?" she asks brightly. "Any problems, blood infections, bleeding?"

I gape at her.

"I'm kidding," she says, completely straight-faced. "The entire process is completely sterile. You're so much more fun than the marines I usually get."

Fucking hell.

"Here," she says, pulling the monitor down to horizontal and placing a plate on top of it. "One-handed food."

"Thanks," I manage, receiving a crisp nod in acknowledgement as she turns to Ben.

"How is it that we can still feel pain if we can't actually move our arms?" he asks.

She grins. "Excellent question. What we injected into you was actually a very specific nerve agent. It stops you from moving your arm, but not from feeling – we haven't done anything to your skin, so the minor nerve bundles can still fire. We could give you local anaesthetics, but we'd have to keep injecting you to cover every part of your arm. They take a while to wear off and there's no counter-agent like this one. This was developed for less than ethical purposes by the military, so it's karma that we're now using it to save the world rather than torture enemies of the state."

Holy shit.

"F … fair enough," Ben manages, then looks down and takes a mouthful of burger. Christina hands us bottles of water, then looks around. "Ok, either of you need the bathroom?"

I shake my head and Ben does the same. "Great," she says. "Then I'll leave you to it. Machines start again in fifteen minutes."

And so continues the longest afternoon of my life, broken up only by a trip to the bathroom on the next rest break and swapping arms at the end of the third session. And that's intensely weird: I'm watching the credits start to roll at the end of the film when the sound cuts out, the machine beeps and I wrestle the headphones off my ears as the sleeve starts to slide back. If we've had a few surprises in the last few days, the shock of seeing my arm sparkling like it's covered in shitty tinsel might just take the biscuit.

It's actually sort of pretty, but I'd never say that out loud. Well, badass pretty. It's a bit like barbed wire, but also kind of like tinsel or snowflakes stretched out or the front of a girly notebook from Paperchase, only there's not really anything girly about it. It sparkles a little bit in the light. The edges are definitely red. I'm basically sore from my elbow to mid-finger.

"Damn," Ben breathes.

"Yeah," I say. "Is this awesome?"

"I … I have no idea," he says, staring down at his left arm.

Once again, the door opens and Christina comes in, inspecting the work expertly. "Very good," she says. "No irregularities as far as I can see. Everything looks normal."

She taps the laptop and there's another painful jab into my arm, then a flood of pins and needles. I give my fingers an experimental waggle. Full motion. That's a relief.

"Take it slowly," she adds, as the restraints loosen and then fall to the sides. "Just flex for a minute but don't make any sudden movements. And please, don't touch the silver until at least nine tonight."

This has better fade because otherwise I've got one hell of a sleeve.

"Once you've regained full use, please place your other arm in the corresponding restraint," she adds mercilessly, and the whole process starts again.

Four hours of pain later – apparently, we have to have a half-hour break in the middle of the process for health and safety reasons – my other arm is also glistening like I'm a Christmas ornament. I can't stop staring. It's all part of getting more awesome, I tell myself, but that's sounding weaker and weaker in my head as this gets more and more real.

"Now," Christina says, doing a final check of our arms. "I'm sure you're buzzing with energy after being sat down for so long, so we're going to do some physical tests before dinner. Please, follow me."

And so we go from being stencilled like a kid's picture book to the most normal gym experience in the world, which just adds to the bizarre nature of the day.

Ben looks a bit drawn out, but he does better on the treadmill than I do. I'm pretty fit but I should really give up smoking. Christina paces between the two of us, peering at the readouts on the treadmills, cross-trainers and rowing machines, nodding and making notes on a tablet from time to time.

The gym looks almost exactly like the one I use back home, like almost every gym looks. But I guess we're only doing this to keep up with the military.

"Ok, that's enough for now," our instructor says. "You're done for the day. I'll send you your results later. Please head back to your room and we'll bring you food – don't get used to this, mind you, it's just a tradition. Assuming that you've passed this modest physical test, you're now apprentice members of the First Extraordinary – congratulations."

I'd high-five Ben but my arm is still pretty sore.

"Once you've washed up, you can use the library if you wish, but I'd recommend taking it easy. Your passes won't let you near the front of the building, so please don't try."

And again, with no more preamble than that, she turns and leaves. I pull myself up and then lean back against the cross-trainer, towelling the sweat off my forehead and exhaling heavily.

"Well, shit," I manage. "That was intense. I think I'm going to call it a night."

"Yeah," Ben says weakly, looking a bit sweaty. "See you in the morning."

And with that anticlimactic finish, I turn in.

Ben
Through the Door

I don't sleep well. I've read a lot of articles about how you never sleep properly in a new place and last night was no exception. Once we'd finished for the day, I wandered around the areas I could access – the library, where I browsed some of the books in the extended reading list, stared into space, kept noticing my new tattoos.

Tattoos. I have magic tattoos.

At first, they were slightly red around the edges. I hear that's pretty normal for regular tattoos, but it faded quickly. Now they're they just silvery swirls, curlicues and jagged edges and despite the fact that I wouldn't have had them if it wasn't part of this job, I actually find myself thinking of them as strangely beautiful.

The silver is starting to fade a bit. Christina said it would, but I couldn't quite believe her. I've been trying to feel more aligned with the world and tune into the noosphere like she was talking about but it hasn't worked. I felt like a bit of a prat doing it, so eventually stopped and looked at books instead.

None of this helps when it comes to sleeping. I read more, but my brain is in high gear, or more accurately, high stress gear, churning over and over the same details and spiralling around the same worries. What if I can't do any of this? What if I get kicked out before we've even started? What if I have to go back to the library tomorrow, tail between my legs, having failed at the thing that's basically all I ever wanted as a kid? What if it's incredibly dangerous and I get horrifically injured or killed on my first mission?

When I'm not worrying, I'm reliving parts of the day, and when I'm not doing that, then I'm back to worrying.

Very occasionally, when my brain pulls away from ever-circling anxieties, I wonder what Christina meant when she called us 'the last ones'. Why aren't there any more people being trained along with us? The year can't be full. And what happened to Matt's friend, the 'Essex Edward Cullen'?

I make a mental note to check with Christina tomorrow, then mid-thought, surprise myself by falling asleep.

I wake up a couple of times, one of them a bad one, not knowing where I am, shapes not resolving properly in the darkness, thinking a wardrobe is the way out and only manage to stop the panic once I've opened the door to the corridor.

My head is pretty fuzzy in the morning when my alarm goes off at 8.30. I stand under the hot shower for a long time, trying to clear my thoughts, craving breakfast and coffee. What do you wear for your first proper day in a magician's school? Christina didn't mention anything about more fitness tests today, thankfully, as I recall her disappointed look when she saw my results. I guess she's used to ex-special forces people taking the tests, not librarians, but I can't quite shake the feeling of failure.

I'm doing it again. I try not think at all, focusing completely on simply dressing and wandering down to the cafeteria, where a cheery-looking guy is standing behind the counter stirring a small vat of baked beans. The sheer normality of it all is incredibly welcome, the smell of frying bacon making my stomach rumble. The guy – who sports a fairly regulation white catering outfit – spots me coming in and waves.

"About time," he calls, grinning at me. "Come on over. It's been pretty quiet for the last hour."

I head across to him and grab a cream-coloured tray from a stack, pushing it down the track to where he's standing.

"Morning," I say, mouth on autopilot. "How you doing?"

"Good, thanks," he says. "Nice to have some company at last. Most folk have been up for an hour, so it's been dead boring. Don't worry, you're not late, they're just early risers. What can I get for you?"

I settle for a bit of everything and sit in a corner with my back to the wall, taking big gulps of coffee. I'm about halfway through it when Matt wanders in, hair tousled and generally looking a bit sleepy. I'm impressed – we've got half an hour until we have to be in the classroom, so this is pretty early for him.

"Morning winner," he calls across the room and I wave. He ambles over to the counter and orders a plate stacked with everything I ordered but in greater quantity, and begs for the biggest coffee they have. When the server pushes a regularly-sized mug over to him, he asks for another. That makes the guy laugh out loud, but he does it nonetheless.

Tray laden with fried food, Matt sits down across from me.

"Alright?"

I nod. "Not bad," I say, finishing a mouthful. "Didn't sleep too well, but I'm ok. You?"

"Good," he says, stuffing his mouth with a large forkful of bacon, sausage and beans. "Slept like a champ, even if these itch like fuck."

He gestures to his bare forearms with his now-empty fork, then does a double take. "Son of a bitch!"

The silver markings have completely faded, leaving Matt's arms as freckled as they ever were – I can see where he's scratched them, but otherwise you wouldn't know. I look down at my own and it's the same, although I haven't scratched them.

"That's so weird," I manage, staring at my arm.

"Yeah," Matt says. "Damn. Well, guess Christina knows her stuff after all."

As if summoned, the door to the cafeteria opens and our instructor walks in. She looks like she's about to take a Tough Mudder course, in sporty leggings and trainers with a gilet over a black t-shirt. Her hair is tied back in an unobtrusive ponytail, the only flashes of colour her white trainers, which have vivid red stripes up the side. She must be wearing contact lenses, because the glasses have gone too. Or maybe she laser-magics her eyes when she goes to alien planets.

That sounds almost like something Matt would say. I need to get a grip.

"Morning gentlemen," she says briskly. "Sleep well?"

I nod politely while Matt greets her noisily through a mouthful of beans and bacon.

"Good," she says. "Wheels up in twenty minutes or sooner if you're ready. I'll be in 10A, the room where you signed your lives away yesterday."

Matt stares for a moment, then bursts into laughter as she turns and heads out through the other door.

"Damn," he says, swallowing. "She's funny."

I can't quite summon a laugh yet, the image of the Ravager we saw at Gardener HQ flashing through my mind. Matt notices and looks at me.

"You sure you're ok?" he says.

I sigh. "Yeah," I manage. "Just waiting for the coffee to kick in I guess."

"Course," he says amiably. "No rush."

By the time I'm finished, he's chomped through

almost all of his vast plate of breakfast, so I don't have to wait long. I pop back to my room to clean my teeth and stuff my bag with a notepad, pens and my e-reader, waiting for Matt outside. He reappears quickly, but then goes back in when he sees my bag, noises of rummaging and soft swearing audible from the corridor.

We finally make it to the room as my nerves are starting to fray, but we're actually right on time.

Christina beckons us in and gestures for us to sit down.

"Come in, come in," she says. "We'll be in here for about an hour, so make yourselves comfortable."

We settle in and she starts the class.

"As you've already been told," she starts. "The staves were discovered by father Teilhard de Chardin, a Catholic priest who achieved unity with the noosphere through sheer empathy, concentration and a deep love for his congregation and the planet. He tapped into the noosphere, the energy net created by living things, which is also a psychic shield that prevents other beings from crossing into our realm. We still don't know how or why it was created, only that life, growth, empathy and nature builds and reinforces it, and that cruelty and a lack of compassion erodes it."

She pauses and I gingerly raise my hand.

"Go on," she says.

"Well, I was thinking," I say, trying to form a coherent sentence. "Isn't nature kind of cruel? Doesn't that erode the noosphere?"

"It's a good question," she says. "But if you think about it, nature is rarely deliberately cruel. A cat might play with a bird, but it's a hunter, killing to eat meat. That's nature. It might occasionally hunt and not eat everything, but in general animals exist in a kind of balance with their prey and their habitats. They eventually reach an equilibrium. Too much hunting and their environment can't sustain them, too little and their prey thrive, harming the environment. Humans are the only creatures to be actively cruel, to kill in vast numbers without the need for it, and to repeatedly neglect and kill each other for pleasure. That's what erodes the noosphere."

"Makes sense," I say.

"No problem," she says, flashing a rare grin. "Keep them coming – makes it stick better. Now, one of the main challenges is that we're all products of a society that cares less and less, so establishing an order of people to try and repair this damage isn't easy. Fortunately, former military often have extremely high levels of empathy because of their exposure to suffering. And in general, we do find that they have two types of response: they either shut down after a tough operation or they become careful, valuing human life much more, because they've seen the opposite end of the spectrum. Of course, it also helps that they're familiar with military procedure and know how to handle themselves."

"Obviously, that's not always enough," she continues.

"Which is why we do actively recruit and why you're here. Few of us have a natural aptitude for the staves, although you'd be surprised who picks it up the fastest. Being aware of the premise of the noosphere is the very first step, and having the silvering is the second. What you might have started to feel, if you try to tune in and be aware of yourself, quieting your thoughts, is a general rushing sensation, like putting your arms into a river, or a wind tunnel. There are eddies, currents, streams within it, and that's exactly what we're going to tap into. Try it now."

She pauses and looks down at the laptop on the desk next to her and I try not to look at Matt. If he's laughing then my chances of doing this will sink to approximately zero. He's my best friend in the world but like everyone else, he can still make me feel incredibly self-conscious.

It's not his fault.

Dammit. Clear your mind, Ben.

I push everything to one side and try to imagine that I'm listening to my white noise app, hearing the light pattering of rain on the roof of the library back in Mayfair, taking a moment to just be. The chair is uncomfortable beneath me, the fan on Christina's laptop loud, the lights buzzing. That said, there is a slight sensation on my forearms, like a breeze only without the physical sensation of an *actual* breeze. I try not to focus too much on it, like I'm trying not to startle a bird or something.

It's strange; regular sensations are either there, or they're not. You're either being touched by something or you're not, smell something, or you don't. This is like discovering a sense, and as I explore it, my awareness of it grows.

It's like a gust of wind in cross section, a stream, parts of it moving at different speeds. It feels odd and normal at the same time, like it's always been there but it also like nothing I've experienced before.

"Shit!" Matt's exclamation jolts me out of my reverie and makes Christina look up.

"Got it?" she says, raising her eyebrows, and he nods.

"Good," she continues. "Then you have some promise. Ben?"

I nod as well. "Uh, yeah," I manage. "Something."

"Excellent. Now, are either of you musical at all?"

I played the piano at school but was terrible at it. I don't think that counts, so we're both shaking our heads.

"No matter," she says, turning on the flatscreen TV behind her. "Now, for our particular application of the staves, a very small amount of the noosphere has to be held and focused into nodal points. Raphael du Bois has always been our principal architect of new staves, but we do have a few researchers who are working on developing new applications. We are underfunded, and our main mission remains containment and dispersal of threats. Consequently, the first and most important stave you'll learn is the containment stave, which looks like this."

She presses a button on her laptop and a simple image appears onscreen: a row of three horizontal lines.

"This is how most staves are shown. It's a lot like musical notation and tells you how to hold parts of the noosphere and focus them, temporarily stopping them, if you like."

A black blob appears on the top stave, stretching to the end. Another appears on the bottom stave a second later, slightly indented from the first.

"Many people think of the 'activated' staves as pressure, almost like an indentation. Once you've held the noosphere for a moment, you then need to focus the calibrated energies into this symbol here."

At the end of the stave, a symbol like an 'X' appears, with a small horizontal bar on the upper right-hand part of the letter.

"Containment staves have no effect on people because they're native to this world. However, staves can be projected 'live' and also embedded into natural materials like wood, then released later. Here, give it a go on these."

She slides two small pieces of wood over to us. They look like they could be coasters or something.

"Do we need to be, like, touching them or anything?" I ask gingerly.

"If it helps," Christina says. "Not everyone needs to; some people project quite naturally. Whatever comes most easily."

I lean across and pick one of them up, hearing an intake of breath from Matt as if he's about to make a crappy joke, but doesn't. I guess he's taking this seriously.

I try to concentrate on the staves, tuning into the rushing feeling, getting it more easily this time, and slightly more powerfully. I feel an odd prickling sensation and see the silvering on my arms showing faintly beneath the skin. Again, it's like I'm rediscovering something, something I've forgotten, a dream I once had.

"It's important that you don't try to hold the noosphere too long," Christina says. "Just stay conscious of it and release when you've got the pattern."

Ok. Easier said than done. I try to simply visualise the stave but nothing happens. There's energy rushing past my arms all the time, so instead I hold one section up, then another, leaving a bit of space below it. There's a sensation of building pressure, then I *push* the energy towards the wood and visualise the almost-X at the same time.

Shit! I drop the wood on the conference room table as it vibrates slightly and a small indentation appears in the shape of the symbol I just visualised.

"Christ!"

I jump in my seat, letting go of the sensations completely. "Sorry," I manage.

Christina grins and walks over, picking up the wood and inspecting it. "Very good," she says, touching it briefly. I feel a dispersal of energy and the symbol vanishes from the wood. "Again."

For the next twenty minutes, Matt and I make symbols in wood. I feel a slight pang of dismay when he gets it almost immediately after I do my first one; is he better at this than I am? Then I feel guilty for feeling that.

I focus on my wood, then snigger and glance at Matt, who winks at me.

Christina sighs loudly.

"Ok, enough," she says, five minutes later. "That's plenty for now. We'll move onto the other main kind of stave: dispersal. Containment staves don't last forever, and eventually your non-corporeals will start moving around again. And for your next question, you get about an hour, unless you double-stave them, in which case it's additive."

The dispersal stave is a lot harder and both Matt and I struggle to pick it up.

"Christina," Matt says, after about ten minutes. "So, if we do this right, does this stave send things back to where they came, or does it kill them?"

"Well," she says. "It's another grey area. We don't really understand non-corporeals. You can trap, inspect, examine a corporeal being, but non-corporeals don't have real bodies or substance that we can analyse in any way; they just react explosively with life, which they seem to be drawn to instinctively. We do know that dispersal doesn't send them back where they came from – that would require a rift – so yes, it's essentially terminating them. But no-one should really have a problem terminating something that leaves a trail of destruction when it meets a living being. Thankfully, none of the creatures we've encountered seem to be able to create rifts – only sapient creatures can do that. And dispersing them doesn't seem to be regarded as cruel by the universe either; otherwise, we'd open a rift every time we dispersed one."

"I'll be honest with you both – there's a lot we don't understand. Both Shamblers and other creatures kill, but Shamblers seem to kill because of something to do with their very existence and composition, unlike other non-corporeals like Banshees, which seem to hunt. But none of them seem sapient, and none of their actions seem to thin the noosphere, however horrific they are. No attempts at communicating have ever succeeded, and Shamblers only seem to react explosively with animals, not plant life."

"Jeez," he says. "That's messed up."

"I know," she says. "But once you've seen their impact for real – if there are any small animals or insects in Karnak, for example – you'll get to see them pop, and that's a real motivator."

She's silent for a moment. I guess she must have seen people killed by these things.

"Sorry," I say, and she brightens.

"Don't worry," she says. "You're new, and it's what I'm here for. Now, again."

Half an hour later, she concedes that our embedded dispersal staves are 'adequate', but I realise that there's something else that I wanted to know.

"Can I ask another question?"

"Go on," Christina says, nodding.

"Well, the first time we met someone from the Gardeners, he did this thing where he looked like he'd transformed his jacket into some kind of cloak and protective gloves or something. Can staves do that?"

"Luke, right? He never loses his penchant for the dramatic. Yes, staves can do more than containment and dispersal – if you think about it, you're playing with the energy net from the world itself. It's a flowing, powerful force, and under the right circumstances, you can even move people – or things – along the waves, in the blink of an eye. You might have read about these in your guides, and it's possible that it can do a lot more than that, but for now, we'll focus on these two and also look at rift repair, because they're the most important parts. Now, let's take you to the Abditory."

"Yes!" Matt breathes quietly, pushing his chair back and standing, but my mind is buzzing. What else could we be doing? Was she talking about teleportation? How do I get magic armour?

"Bring your bags," Christina says. "And follow me closely."

I try to stop thinking about how cool magic armour would be and focus as we're led out of the conference room and down the corridor.

"Now, there's one thing you should know about the Abditory," she says. "The oxygen content in the air is ever so slightly different to ours and the gravity a little lower, so you may feel a bit high when you first step through the rift. Don't rush yourself, take your time and you'll adjust."

She pushes through an office door, then a more

serious-looking door with a fingerprint scanner and some kind of symbol lock.

"This room is generally out of bounds to anyone except qualified instructors or research staff," she says. "Karnak is staffed at all times, but it does also have a resident Shambler population."

My stomach churns and clenches. We're going somewhere that has creatures that can make us bleed from our eyeballs? My hands start to sweat, but there's no time to hold back, because Christina is opening the door and I get my first look at a tear in the fabric of reality.

It's profoundly unsettling, partially because the room is so normal-looking. It's got the regulation off-white walls, a couple of worn chairs around the outside, teas and coffees on a small desk with a laptop on one side. But instead of a big conference room table, it's got an area squared off with police tape, and inside the police tape, there's a window into another world. Or rather, a door.

There's no actual door frame as such, just a space where I should be able to see the wall of the conference room that we're in. Instead, I can see what seems to be a softly-lit basement.

"Shit."

I have to remember to breathe.

"Don't worry," Christina says. "Take your time. I've seen marines who have run undercover operations in the Middle East cry like babies at the sight of this. It helps if you walk around it, get a feel for it."

Legs trembling, I step around it. It's like I'm standing on the edge of a train platform, trying not to fall into the gap. I don't dare get closer than a foot from the police tape, and Matt is also circling at a similar distance. As I walk, I can see other parts of the room on the 'other side'; there's not a lot there, only a laptop and a lamp plugged into some kind of generator.

"Why doesn't it close up?" Matt says, making me jump. "I mean, you guys are pretty kind, right? So shouldn't it eventually close?"

Christina leans back against the wall. "In theory, yes," she says. "But Raphael has given special permission for a stave reversal. Every month, he comes down here to keep the rift open by inverting the process usually used to close rifts."

"That's possible?" I ask.

"Unfortunately, yes," she says in a quiet voice. "It's not really a stave as such, more just a manipulation of the noosphere, but if you're ever nearby when he does it … well, it feels wrong."

Matt exhales loudly. "Ok Dumbledore," he says cockily, but I can hear a quavering in his voice. "Let's get this done, unless there's anymore 'put your tray tables in the upright and locked position' that we need to hear?"

Christina pats herself down. "No beard, no wand, but I am guiding children into mischief. One out of three isn't bad. Where's the smart one though?"

I snigger. Matt doesn't usually make jokes like that

because it leaves him wide open to what's coming.

"You're a wizard, Barry," I laugh, making him glare at me.

"Dammit," he says, glancing at our instructor and looking guilty.

"Matthew Barry Potter," she says, laughing. "Your parents were mean. Come on, let's go to Karnak."

Alice
Verulamium and Beyond

That night and the next night – despite the risk of late-night revellers – I go back to the dig and keep working. Most other people would see this as creepy; working by a dim light to avoid detection, in a tent flapping around in the wind, with drunk passers-by just a few feet away as I brush at centuries-old mosaic tiles.

Thankfully, I'm not 'other people' and I simply find it uncomfortable.

It does speed things up. Jamie forces us all to take a break over the weekend, although I pick up a shift in the shop on Sunday. By Tuesday morning, we've uncovered all of the mosaic, Mark brushing away the dirt on the final corner before we all stand back and admire our work.

It's definitely a cityscape, but my directions haven't gotten any more precise. The yellow halo obscures a few small buildings that nestle at the foot of Herod's temple, which lies relatively close to the top of the mosaic. The rest of the scene is filled with people going about their daily lives, two figures who look like minor deities sprawling languidly at the sides. It's a masterpiece, but I wonder if the occupant of this villa got a reputation for being odd for having it. After all, it's far more traditional to have scenes of Rome in your lounge, and it was certainly a bit déclassé to represent the hoi polloi in what was undoubtedly a very expensive commission.

I take a lot of photographs, which doesn't arouse anyone else's suspicions – we're all doing it. The local newspaper team comes back, and there's two reporters from different archaeology magazines with their respective photographers, demanding that we take down the tent as we arrive on-site in the morning, earning annoyed glares from all of us.

Us. It's strange, but I'm more attached to the group than I have been in months. Everyone has become slightly less annoying.

Of course, I'm not doubting myself. In the evenings, when I'm not breaking back into the dig, I'm making sure my passport is up to date – it is – checking if I need any injections to travel to Jerusalem – I do – and any social conventions I should be aware of – probably none as long as I wear long skirts, cover up and wear something on my head most of the time. Nothing unanticipated. How's my Hebrew? Rusty, but not bad. I load up my Duolingo and grab an old phrase book, then find another, specific to archaeological terms that I found online a while ago. My bag is already packed.

As I'm admiring our handiwork, I'm also thinking about how to leave. I'd always planned to simply walk away without any notice, but I feel a pang of guilt at the prospect. There's also the possibility that I'm wrong, that this isn't what I think it is and that there's another mosaic waiting to be uncovered with the real clue on it.

The possibility that I'm wrong about *all* of this does distantly occur to me, but I'm not. I know I'm right. The mosaic is absolute, concrete proof that my theory isn't just a theory.

That doesn't bear thinking about. I can't wait for this.

On Tuesday night I make up my mind. I'm already annoyed because some idiot bashed into me as I was walking home and then had the temerity to glare at me because I called him out on it.

I call Jamie and tell him that my aunt who lives in Australia – the one I've been patiently cultivating over the last few months, in case I needed her for this exact purpose, telling everyone how much I enjoy going out there, how great the wildlife is – has died suddenly and I need to get on a flight to make the funeral on Thursday. I grovel, I apologise, I tell him I know it's terrible timing.

And he's kind about it, which for some reason makes me uncomfortable.

"Don't worry Alice, you've done the lion's share here," he says. What's wrong with me? Am I coming down with something? "We'll need to get the investors in anyway, show them progress, finish cataloguing everything. It's really no trouble."

"Thank you," I say. "I'll be back as soon as I can."

Then I call Hugo and start to tell him everything. Before I'm halfway through my explanation, a private car arrives and we continue the conversation as I'm driven to his estate in Cambridge, the driver taking my bags without a word.

An hour later, the car draws into Hugo's long driveway, floodlit grassy lawns stretching out on either side of us as large gates swing open. It's eleven at night, so I can only see the parts of the building illuminated by the car's headlights and the floodlights, but I know what I'd see if it was daytime: Baba Yaga's mansion.

Hugo comes from a long line of rich eccentrics with a penchant for the paranormal, and for some reason, his house is entirely elevated. Steel and concrete pilings raise the structure twenty feet above ground, and although there are an abundance of windows and skylights in the building, I know that each and every one of them has a metal shutter that can be manually drawn across it, turning this building into an inaccessible fortress. And it is, indeed, built like a fortress. Architectural magazines have commented on it being a bastardisation of a gothic folly and a prepper's paradise, but Hugo refuses to be drawn in to comment. Which, of course, only deepens the intrigue.

There are two main ways in: a large service lift and an ornate stairway, both of which can be blocked off or retracted. The house is regarded as a marvel in some ways, a colossal waste of money in others.

Hugo first found me when I was at university. Somehow, he knew that I was looking into something unusual, and although he didn't press me for details, he made it clear that he was impressed by my commitment and ability, and insisted on paying for my education, no questions asked. At first, I'd been highly suspicious of what he wanted; I'd read stories about this kind of thing, but as the weeks and months passed, it was clear that the answer was 'almost nothing'.

Six months in, he took me out for dinner at an expensive restaurant and danced around the topic for two hours. At the very end, as he paid the formidable bill, he fixed me with a grim stare and asked how my other focus was going. I'd made progress, I admitted, but needed access to a library in the states for a rare text. He nodded.

The next morning, I received an email from the library offering me unlimited access to whatever I wanted.

Like I've said, I'm not good at the people stuff, so I've never quite been sure what to make of Hugo. I suppose that the word most people would use is 'haunted'. He doesn't seem to enjoy being rich, and doesn't fit any of the upper-class playboy stereotypes, which might be why I maintain his patronage.

I step out of the car and walk around to the front, turning my back on the harsh brightness of the headlights as Hugo steps out from the stairway.

Tonight he's in a designer suit, a crisp dark-blue shirt unbuttoned at the neck. His brogues crunch on the gravel as he regards me quietly. He looks drawn and tired and I can see circles under his eyes. I don't think he sleeps very much.

"Alice," he says. "Welcome."

"Hugo," I reply. "Thanks for the lift."

"Come, come," he says, briefly placing one hand at the small of my back and guiding me towards the stairs. "It's so rare that I receive good news. I was hoping you could tell me more and I thought that you might want the jet."

I sigh. Much as I hate flying, arriving at my destination in a private jet would attract too much attention, even if Hugo's credentials could ensure a relatively anonymous and comfortable journey on some levels. But even at those levels, people talk.

I shake my head as we walk up the impressive staircase and up into the mansion proper, passing an emergency cabinet filled with fire extinguishers, fire axes, glow sticks, rope ladders and survival rations. As far as I know, there isn't a big prepper scene here in the UK, but Hugo's commitment would impress even the most die-hard American survivalist.

There's a hydroponics garden in the East Wing. Each part of the mansion can be locked down into its own isolated zone, separated by steel bulkheads. Thereafter, each zone can then sustain a small population for three months without any support from the outside world.

"Economy is fine," I reply. "It's all booked. Stanstead, tomorrow morning."

"Then at least allow me to take you to the airport."

I nod. It's practical.

"And if you would," he says, ushering me into a functional but still opulently wood-panelled study, gesturing to an executive office chair on one side of a large table. "Talk me through everything again."

I sit, sinking into the faux-leather fabric, and start to run through my findings. Hugo doesn't comment and barely moves, except to pour himself a large tumbler of whisky and offer me one or a drink of my choice. I decline the former, asking for water. At the end, he leans forward, interlacing his fingers and lets out a deep breath. He frowns and picks up the phone, dialling a number and talking quietly. I start when I hear the word 'Jerusalem', but he holds up one finger and mouths the word 'please' to me silently, so I give him the benefit of the doubt.

A moment later, he sets the handset down and rubs his forehead with one hand, mussing his immaculately-styled hair. His shoulders sag a little, and his mouth trembles. I can't quite work out if he looks upset or relieved.

"There's an organisation that I fund," he says. "Which specialises in what most people would call the paranormal. They are well-organised, government-linked and unfortunately, I have no doubt that they are genuine. They've confirmed that for a number of years, they have been keeping tabs on a potential asset in the same area, of the same type that your research has revealed. They have also – reluctantly – admitted that they also have a team travelling to the region shortly to investigate whether or not it can be 'brought in'. Apparently, it's possible that things are coming to a head."

"Things?" I ask.

"Things," he says darkly. "Alice, I'm breaching the Official Secrets Act by telling you this, but this organisation believes that an attack of some kind is imminent."

"An attack?" I say. "Terrorists?"

He slumps back in his chair. "No, not really," he says. "I've said more than I should have. But I do believe that it's very important you go to Jerusalem, and find what you're looking for. If you meet this organisation – The Gardeners, they call themselves – you can probably trust them. And on your return, well, I hope you know that you can trust me and always call on me."

I nod again. This is all rather melodramatic. And what kind of a name is 'The Gardeners' for a government body?

"Good," he says briskly, taking a deep breath. "I have a few more calls to make, so if you don't mind, I've had your usual room made up for you, and James will wake you in time for your flight."

Like I said, I don't really do the people stuff, but even I can feel a door slamming, socially. Nonetheless, mysterious organisation or no, this all serves my purpose, so I thank him for his hospitality, and make my way down to the room where I've slept before. It's immaculately furnished;

a plush four-poster bed is waiting for me, all decorated in tasteful reds and greens. The emergency supplies cupboard is clearly labelled, as is the entrance to the panic room, and there's a half bottle of Sancerre in a wine cooler on the table, alongside a bowl of fresh fruit.

I suppose this has been useful. Another organisation has confirmed the existence of *my* discovery, although there's a part of me that resents the imposition. For a moment I have a fleeting impression of James Bond films, of shadowy worlds operating behind closed doors, then push that from my mind. This isn't cinema, this is the real world.

But then again, I'm tracking down an artefact that Roman emperors who fancied themselves as gods failed to find.

Well, most of them were illiterate and debauched. I'm smarter than Agricola and Vespasian put together, and far less debauched.

Irritatingly, I can't quite shift the sense of unease as I slip between the covers. I don't like sharing my discovery, I tell myself. I feel cheated.

But that's not really it.

Lincoln
Hunting

"Unit six is in position," I say quietly, leaning back against the wall of the modern office building. "Ready when you are, team."

I get why we're here. Raiding the offices of our number one suspect is good mission hygiene. Any operation would be remiss not to.

But we're not going to find him. He's five steps ahead of us, maybe more. Any adversary who launches a pre-emptive strike against a retired asset on the other side is either trying to stir up trouble or already has an extensive gameplan with contingencies mapped out. My team knows this, I know this. Half the MI5 team probably knows this. The perils of accountability.

I'm tired. I'm fifty-eight years old, I'm not dead. I can handle an active mission, but I'd hoped that after three and a half decades of hunting terrorists and things that go bump in the night I could retire to my family home, throw some dinner parties and trust that the world was safe in the hands of the next generation.

I guessed wrong.

"Perimeter is secure," Jack, our MI5 handler, says over the comm. "Units six, seven and twelve, please proceed."

I lever myself back to standing and walk to the main entrance of the office building, arriving at the same time as Celia, one of my long-standing colleagues, and Adaora, one of the highly competent members of the MI5 team that I've been paired with.

We push through the revolving doors into the atrium, Celia keeping position on the inside of the door until we can physically lock the entrances and exits. I make eye contact with the receptionist and stride up to the front desk, holding up my search warrant.

"Morning," I say. "Lincoln James, government taskforce. I'm sorry to say that we're here to search the premises on suspicion of complicity in terrorist activities. I'd ask that you lend every assistance to our efforts until our search is completed, and we'll be out of your way as soon as humanly possible."

The receptionist's face goes from friendly to disbelieving to pale in the course of three sentences.

"Y…yes, of course," he says. Poor guy, he's only in his twenties and shaking already. "Can I call someone to help you?"

"I'd ask that you remain calm, and don't alert anyone to our presence at the moment," Adaora says, next to me. "Members of staff may be complicit without even realising, and we'd rather no-one has a heads-up on our presence until the last moment."

"Of … of course," he stammers, fumbling with a keycard. "Please, whatever you need."

I take the keycard and look for the executive lift that was marked on the building plan, finding it tucked into a discreet corner of the room, gesturing to Adaora.

The doors are just opening as the rest of the taskforce arrives, my earpiece buzzing with destinations, teams dividing the building up into sections, allocating specialists for data retrieval, personnel control, physical security. There's no running around, no-one shouts 'clear' and no-one pulls a gun. It's simply a very tightly-run raid, a large polytunnel quickly erected outside, criss-crossed with the metallic webbing of a faraday cage, staff ushered into it one by one until we're done with them.

As the lift doors start to close, I spare a glance for the receptionist. Probably has no idea who he's really working for. Of course, we only know bits and pieces, which is part of the problem.

Lucas Jackson: an inoffensive name for an incredibly offensive man, and as far as I know, the only person to ever leave the Gardeners without formally resigning. Former SAS, he'd started in fieldwork before becoming one of the few members of staff to contribute to experimenting with the staves themselves, working closely with Raphael. Then he'd been disciplined, which was and still is practically unheard of, and relegated to analyst work for six months.

Three months later he disappeared, re-appearing a year later as the CEO of a firm that invested in organisations which – directly or indirectly – profited from the decline of empathy that we're constantly trying to arrest. While the Gardeners pumped money into mindfulness apps, charities promoting social cohesion and support, Jackson invested in companies that made their money from social separation: delivery firms, teleconferencing companies, online payments and home entertainment businesses. Within a few years, he was one of the richest people in the country.

Then the rumours started. His executive assistant was fired after leaking to a newspaper that none of Jackson's office pets lived for more than a month. A vet was called in and testified that it was all natural causes, but one of our psychics flagged a potential pattern and monitoring was established. A week later, an analyst identified a well-disguised flow of funds from Jackson's company to an animal testing lab on the continent, but the investigation failed to find anything conclusive.

He vanished again. His company continued to run, but no-one saw him in public. Then someone – and I strongly suspect Jackson – sent mercenaries to my retirement home, and it was only thanks to a vanity security measure that the chessboard floor of my ballroom wasn't awash with blood. At least, not mine. We ran probability on the mercs, and although they only had links to shell companies within shell companies, there were patterns, linkages to organisations that he'd used before.

The psy-ops team in the First Extraordinary tell me that I've got the borderline potential to join their team, but I've never been quite strong enough to make it through the formal tests. We don't have many of them, so the pressure was quite intense, but it's not my thing at all, and the Gardeners don't take the unwilling.

Then the murders in Hampstead happened, and both psychic trackers strongly linked the occurrence to Jackson, even if forensic evidence found nothing at all. Unfortunately, even though we're government-backed, psychic testimony doesn't stand up in court on its own, so we still have to find evidence the good old-fashioned way.

I work my way up to the penthouse office, which is positioned to have a view over the countryside rather than the motorway or the industrial estate. I trigger a familiar flow of staves to detect invisible supernatural matter. The room is somehow spiritually *trapped*, and in a multitude of extensive and imaginative ways. I call the team up and we get to work, defusing the unnatural flows, untangling the dark knots of noosphere energy held in abeyance, contorted into strange twists.

It's not something we come across very often, but thankfully fixing it isn't that different to closing rifts. We focus on restoring the natural flow of the noosphere, although we also have to be careful not to trigger the ill-effects of the tangles. I don't really know what the traps would do if triggered; after all, the noosphere doesn't strongly affect people, but none of us really want to find out.

An hour later, I'm happy that we've cleaned it out well enough and there aren't any spiritual or mechanical nasties left.

The search itself takes rather longer, and is almost completely fruitless. Celia reports some interesting metadata from the IT guys, Tristan grumbling about the size of the building, but there's very little of note. Still, we freeze the company assets temporarily, given the links that we've identified previously. I'm sure this bastard's got reserves, and his reserves have reserves, but let's not make his life any easier, shall we?

I pace down the corridor. What would I do in his position? What am I looking for? What do I want? I've got money, power, influence, a reasonable grip of the arcane. What else would I want? Where would I be?

The problem is, he could be anywhere.

Anywhere at all.

Matt
Popping Grandmas

I'm still reeling from the indignity of Ben's Harry Potter joke when I step through the portal into this fucknugget alien world where we're supposed to practice our magic.

Yes, my parents gave me a singularly unfortunate set of names.

No, I don't like to talk about it.

Ben and I had agreed not to make jokes about it after we left school but sometimes he 'forgets'. Like I forget about turning up on time and telling him to wait for me outside underwear shops.

Anyway, I'm here on an alien planet. Parallel universe. Whatever. And Christina was right – it does give you a buzz, but it's a weird high like when you've gone on a run and you've found that spot where you feel like you could just keep running for ages and there's more oxygen going through your lungs than usual. It's pretty glorious. I don't normally get turned on by exercise, so it's probably the oxygen talking.

I can instantly see why this place is called Karnak.

Yeah, I've been to Luxor, I'm not completely uncultured. Went with my parents when I was a kid. Saw the pyramids, the sphinx, the whole nine yards. And obviously, the statues.

There's not a lot else in here. There's a lamp, almost certainly from Ikea, and a laptop, and that's about it. The only other way out is a doorway on the opposite side of the room. The lamp doesn't cast too much light, and that makes the carvings on the walls twice as creepy. They're at roughly head height, and show long, thin humanoid faces, but they're definitely not human. They've got slightly elongated heads, raised cheekbones, small eyes and ears. They're distinguished-looking, somehow, but definitely creepy.

Ben appears next to me and Christina straightens up, turning away from the laptop.

"Good, you made it," she says. "Sometimes that takes longer. Usually with civvies, so you did ok."

I'm not quite sure how to respond to that. My witty rejoinder function seems to be offline.

"There's something else you should know about Karnak," she says. "The previous residents of this place set up a kind of projection system that we can't turn off. We're not sure if this was a museum, a gallery, an archive or what, but sometimes you'll see holograms. They're harmless, but can be a bit spooky."

Her tone of voice leaves no room for doubt that she

doesn't find them spooky, but that a couple of noobs like us will almost certainly piss ourselves.

And right on cue, a blue figure drifts into the room, talking softly to itself, although I can't make out any of the words. It's tall, maybe a shade over six foot, and almost unnaturally thin. Its face looks like one of the carvings on the wall, but it's got slightly more angular features than some of the others. It's in a long robe, a hood draped down over its back, only its head and shoulders really visible. It wafts around the room, chattering quietly to itself.

"We haven't figured out any of their language. Physiologically, they seem similar to us, but we didn't find any bodies when we arrived here. We've assumed that they were the indigenous species, but that could be wrong. Either way, we weren't fated to meet. No-one escapes destiny," she says, her voice taking on a serious, sonorous tone at the end.

I scoff. "Seriously? No way they have that here too. I mean, it's a pretty popular gaming franchise, but I wouldn't say no-one escapes it."

Ben just stares and Christina looks at me like I've trodden dog shit onto her carpet.

Awesome: banter cannons are back online. I let out a burp, shrug and walk over to the hologram, poking it with one finger. "So where does the magic happen?"

I hear twin sighs and grin.

This is going to be fucking brilliant.

"If you pause the impromptu stand-up, I'll show

you," Christina says acidly, walking through the hologram and down the corridor. Ben shakes his head, not making eye contact and follows behind her quickly. I look at the ghostly blue figure, which looks sad for a moment, drifting over to the side of the room and then falls silent before fading away into nothingness.

Shit, Matt, how do you know it was looking sad? It's a fucking alien. It could have been mid-dump for all you know.

Best get on with the tour of Hogwarts, I think to myself, and I hurry after Ben.

The gloomy corridor leads upwards, doorways on either side occasionally showing more rooms, all sparsely furnished with obviously human tables, chairs and laptops. After a few moments, we arrive at a broad entrance hall, which seemingly runs the breadth of the building. It's open to the outside world at the front, lined with carved wooden columns. Bright sunshine dazzles me, and I squint after the gloom of the basement.

Christina pauses halfway across the room and gestures for us to keep following her.

"Come on," she says. "You can explore the labs later. We're heading outside."

Ben catches up with her and I force myself to keep to a nonchalant stroll, making them wait for me.

It's quite a view outside, once my eyes have adjusted to being burnt out of their sockets a little. The building we've just left sits at the bottom of a steep mountain range, and on either side of us, tall peaks stretch upwards, steeper than I've ever seen. It can't possibly be natural. I crane my neck to look up, seeing bare rock and snow further up. They must be tall because it's not really that cold here.

In front of us, down a set of wooden steps as broad as the entrance to the lab, and in the gap between two mountains, is a wooded valley. The trees look a bit like pines or firs and there's an avenue of them up ahead, leaving a gap through the woods, presumably so that aliens could travel to and from this building.

I take a few steps outside and turn to look at the structure we've come out of, but there's not much to go on. It's a large, wooden building with what looks like decking or a terrace on the next floor up, and the rest is plain wooden fronting, like some kind of uber ski chalet.

I look over at Ben, who is gaping wide-eyed like a little kid at Christmas staring at all the presents.

"It's amazing," he says slowly.

"It has that effect on most people," Christina says. "We're still not entirely sure where in the universe we are, or if we're still in our universe, but for reasons that will soon be apparent, we haven't explored much further out, except by drone. Come on, let's practice a little more."

She leads us down the steps to a picnic bench and gestures for us to sit. It's warm, pleasant and the air smells slightly of pine needles. I feel a bit like a little kid again. Less annoyed.

It's not natural, I swear.

"Now," she says. "We're going to run through the staves you just learnt, but instead of projecting them into wood, you're going to project them out into the world. After this, we'll lay the basic containment staves into the trees in the avenue up ahead and then call some Shamblers to activate them."

"Wait a second," I interrupt. "Say that again."

Christina shrugs, and I wonder if she's getting a buzz out of this, but she seems pretty matter-of-fact.

"The staves don't work on humans, so the only way to field test them is on real non-corporeal beings," she says. "And here we have a unique opportunity to do that. The beings that left us this facility also left us a device that has the power to attract packs of Shamblers. We don't really understand it and frankly, we've been reluctant to take it back home to experiment with, for a number of reasons."

"We're going to bring the exploding grandma things here on purpose?"

"In a controlled fashion, yes," she says slowly. "They'll come down between the two sets of trees and activate your staves, which will contain or disperse them away. Those that aren't dispersed, you can do by hand."

Ben looks pale. I have to admit I'm feeling a little less than enthusiastic about this but I guess it's what we signed up for.

"Ok," I manage. Not very inspiring. "Sure."

"Attaboy," Christina says, grinning. "Now, when you focus that stave into the 'X'-like symbol, instead of focusing it tightly, I want you to push it out. As you release it, visualise the symbol becoming larger and larger in waves, like it's growing. Like a ripple."

Hmm. Like a ripple, eh? Well, why not, I think to myself. I hold the pattern in my head and try to feel the noosphere through the tattoos that I have mixed feelings about, then hold the stave marks in my head as well and when I feel the energy build-up, I push it out in front of me like I'm Ken from Street Fighter.

As I do, there's a release of energy and for a moment, all of the hairs on the back of Ben's arms stand up.

"Shit!" I blurt. "I did it! Uh, sorry Ben."

"Very nice," Christina says. "Now, without the gesturing. Both of you."

Ben manages it about the fourth time – I guess it's harder without a gesture – and I manage to make it happen the third time because my second is a complete failure.

Then we do them again and again.

It's a deeply strange sensation when Ben's first stave hits me; something definitely passes through me, but other than the arm hair thing and a shivery feeling, nothing happens.

"That's pretty weird," I say, after Ben's fifth successful go.

"Yes," Christina notes. "And it's one of the fundamental contradictions about the staves. The containment staves have no measurable effect on people, so you shouldn't really be able to feel them – but you can. It might be your natural connection to the noosphere, but we don't really know."

With that, she moves onto a test of our dispersal staves, but to my amazement, it's not long before she looks satisfied and announces that we're ready for our first field test.

Trying not to look at Ben – I mean, I don't want him to realise I'm being a bit of a wimp about this – I follow Christina as she heads down the valley away from the temple, research institute, whatever and along the tree-lined boulevard. It's warm but not hot, and the air feels fresh. I'm more awake than I have been for a while, as if I've never smoked, drunk or been hungover in all my life. It's pretty fucking wonderful if I'm brutally honest.

Maybe I should stop smoking?

Christina leads us down the garden path, so to speak, and Ben is deep in his thoughts. I don't fancy making small talk with this slightly terrifying woman so I pretend to look around breezily and admire the scenery.

Then I notice it. There's a soft ringing sound. I glance around, and spot the source – a little wind chime attached to a nearby tree.

"Is that special?" I ask Christina, breaking my silence.

"Only if rung in a very specific way," she says. "The previous occupants left quite a few of them here, and it took us a long time to discover the pattern. As a side note though, the thing you should have noticed is the markings on the trees. They're active dispersal staves, so if anything happens to me during the Shambler exercise, run deeper into the woods and they'll activate."

Ben's gaze follows her finger and I see a couple of indentations on the trees behind the main treeline. Never unprepared, these Gardeners. Kind of anal really, but I guess if it's between that and having my head explode, then I'll take anal anytime.

I find myself sniggering again, then force myself to stop. We're about to do serious work.

The avenue narrows up ahead, and I start to notice that the trees deeper into the woods have loads of the marks on them. They must be the safety staves in case we fuck up.

Christina pauses and counts trees off, takes a couple of steps forward and then looks at us.

"Ok, we'll start here and work our way up. We usually get between ten and twenty showing up, so take the next ten trees each, and we should have more than enough for you to get some live practice in. Embed your containment staves on each side and they'll trigger as the Shamblers come down. Then you can disperse them one by one."

Neither of us move until she raises her eyebrows at us.

"Yes?"

Chivvied along by her question, I head off towards the nearest tree. I must look like a bit of a plum doing it, but I lay my hand on the trunk and concentrate, feeling the wood imprint as I channel my stave into it. I guess this is the easy bit, while I'm not being pursued by ghosts. I move along the treeline, realising that I shouldn't get into bad habits, and while it might look badass, making gestures is going to attract some criticism from our guide-lecturer-resident-pain-in-the-ass, so I try not to. It's tougher than it looks, but I seem to be ahead of Ben by a couple of trees. I wander back towards him – his stave indentations look a bit deeper than mine. Does that mean they're better?

He looks a bit frustrated, but he finishes a moment later and we wait while Christina checks both sets, nodding as she does.

"Ok," she says. "Both sets look fine to me. Do you want to practice your live containment or dispersal staves before I get us going?"

We both nod, and for a few minutes I practice rippling out both types of stave. I feel like I'm getting into it, although I still mess up one time in three by the end. Ben's staves seem to travel further than mine, so although I'm shaping them more easily, his seem to be more powerful. I do have to pause for a moment though to get my breath back – my tattoos are warm on my arms, and I felt strangely faint briefly. It passes quickly, but I make a mental note to ask Christina whether this is supposed to be so tiring.

"OK, that's enough," Christina says. "It's time for the main event. We'll kick off. Stick together, cover each other and if you get into a situation, either call for my help or run into the trees, ok?"

Jesus. Here we go.

Christina wanders over to the side of the path and strikes one of the wind chimes in a rhythmic pattern.

I suddenly feel cold and find myself stepping backwards towards the trees I've marked. Shit Matt, this is not very badass behaviour. I look over towards the neck of the valley, but there's nothing there.

"How long does it usually take for them to appear?" Ben asks. Christina raises her eyebrows and flicks her head over towards the spot where I'd just been looking.

Drifting down through the narrow valley mouth is the butt-ugliest ghost I've ever seen. Admittedly, that's a list of two now, but seriously – this thing looks so much like someone's grandma that I'm amazed I can't smell that stuffy smell that you get in poorly-cleaned charity shops. It's maybe four and a half feet tall, wide and hunched over, wizened, and I can just about see humanoid features on its wrinkled, vaguely human face. It's kind of like it's wearing an old raincoat and some kind of hat, short arms ending in claw-like hands, reaching out for us.

I can see right through it, which is basically fucking wrong.

It moves pretty slowly, and again, I find myself taking a step back, which is completely unnecessary, because as soon as it nears the first set of trees, one of the staves – Ben's, of course – discharges and the thing freezes completely.

"Bravo," Christina calls. "Matt, you need to work on your range. It usually means that you haven't been feeling the noosphere as deeply as you could be. Really try to feel it, hold it for a moment longer than you were before, then channel it, ok? Now, Ben, you go disperse it. Matt, go with him and cover. If another one appears, do a free containment stave."

I barely hear her. My eyes are locked on the small gap ahead of us where the ghost came from. Slowly, hesitantly, Ben sets off for the grandma thing – the Shambler, I should say – and I force myself to follow him. He stops about two metres from it and stares.

I've got to admit, it's intense. I mean, seeing the Banshee thing and the Ravager on the TV was bad enough, but I'm basically nose to nose with a ghost that could make you explode. Thankfully, it's completely immobile.

I elbow Ben. "Come on, man," I say. "Let's do this and get back."

He glances at me, pale, but then looks back at the Shambler and concentrates for a second. Nothing happens, then there's a faint popping noise and Shambler seems to fade a bit.

I blink and it's gone.

"Damn," I swear softly.

"Yeah," Ben says. "Shit."

"Nice work."

"Thanks – oh, crap!"

I look up and see another two Shamblers approaching us, maybe five metres away and moving slowly, but it's enough to send a wave of panic through me. I feel sick, grabbing Ben and then start moving backwards towards the protection of the other staves until my brain starts working again.

One of my staves activates, then Ben gestures and free-casts a containment stave first time, trapping the other.

"Good," Christina calls from the other end of the run. "Matt, make sure you disperse one of those."

I don't manage it the first time or the second time. I can't focus enough to feel the noosphere and get my tattoos working.

Dammit, get it together. I manage it the third time, hearing that slight pop and watching it fade away. Ben's already managed his.

Shit. I just did real magic in the field.

Christina calls for us to fall back a bit and we wait until two more Shamblers come, obediently freezing in place once they hit our embedded staves further down. We take it in turns to disperse them, gradually getting more confident.

It never stops being weird, and after a while, I realise how tired I am.

After about half an hour, the Shamblers start getting less frequent. Half an hour after that, we haven't seen one for about ten minutes. Christina makes us wait for another ten, then gets us to drag a heavy log across the path and set a series of containment and dispersal staves into it before leading us back towards the lab-temple-facility-thing.

I'm exhausted.

"That was good," she says on the way back to the basement. "You supported each other, didn't entirely panic and managed to contain and disperse everything without help. It's a promising start. Now, if you can pay attention for a few moments longer, I'll show you the basics of rift closure."

We get back to the creepy basement with the gap in reality, and Christina pauses just short of it.

"Ok," she says. "Now, if you try to feel the noosphere again through your silvering, and then extend that awareness towards the rift, you should feel something. Don't take any action – just observe."

Well, that sounds like a pile of crap, but sure, ok. I try to extend my senses, wondering if this is how Luke Skywalker felt when he was taking on the remote drone for the first time.

Like a complete prat, that is.

I tune into the faint rush of the energy field along my arms, and take a step closer to the rift.

Yeah, that's weird. It's like a split in space where the noosphere isn't. Like water running around a rock in a stream. Like hair not growing on a scar.

"You feel that?" Christina says and I look back at her and nod.

"Yeah," says Ben. "It's like a gap?"

"Yes," she says. "Now try to feel the ends of it."

I turn to face the rift again and push my awareness

down, following the line of the rift. At the end, there's the rush of the noosphere beyond the gap. If I wanted to, I could push the two edges together.

"Stop," Christina calls, jarring me out of my reverie. "That's the natural instinct of any Gardener, but we do need that rift to get back home, ok?"

I take a step back. "Sorry," I mumble. What a prat.

"It's ok," she says. "Like I said, very natural, and your instincts were probably right – if you push the edges of the rift together, it will eventually start to close up. That's one way of doing it. Another is to re-empathise the area and cause a gradual rise in the amount of happiness, kindness and collaboration nearby – which is why we try to leave this place as uninhabited as possible so that it doesn't close up by itself suddenly, although there are also trees and plants here which do the same thing over time. Now, let's go."

With that, she powers past us and walks back into the normal world.

"Damn," I say to Ben. "That was intense."

He nods, still looking pale, then turns and hurries through the rift.

"Good," Christina says as I step through. "We'll be coming back tomorrow, but for the rest of today, we'll be alternating between the gym and learning about how to work with your military colleagues from around the world. You've learnt the basics of being an apprentice – now it's time to make it stick."

Shit. So, this is really real then. Somehow, I thought this would feel more glamorous, but as tired as I am, it's kind of like being back at school. Only, I have to remind myself, it's actually a million times more awesome.

Alice
Flying Economy into Mystery

By 10.30am, I'm on a BA flight on my way to find a godly artefact, but I'm irrationally wishing that it'd been in Britain, or even France.

I dislike flying. It's cramped and unpleasant. Other passengers are noisy and smelly, and I'm not in control. I try to tune out, watch films and listen to music as much as possible, and I usually pay extra for an aisle seat so that I can get out and walk around when I want, but this time the only aisle seat left was right over the wing. It's an uncomfortable take-off, an uncomfortable landing, and an uncomfortable few hours as the plane jolts and bumps through every available bit of turbulence between the UK and Israel.

Thankfully, we don't crash and die, and after a five-hour flight, I'm making my way woozily onto the tarmac at Ben Gurion, already refusing the attentions of an American family who think I might be unwell. Apparently, I look pale. If I wanted help, I'd have asked for it.

I splash water on my face in the toilets before baggage reclaim, trying to freshen up, although the smell of the vile chemical soap they use in airports makes me shudder.

That said, the airport is impressive: high ceilings, huge sweeping hallways and columns everywhere. If I was feeling better, I'd stop and take a photo.

The heat hits me as I clear the last passport and customs control gate. I think it's only about 25 degrees, but it's a dry heat. I pause and buy a bottle of water to try and clear my head before getting into a taxi.

"First time in Israel?"

I glance at the taxi driver, a balding guy in glasses. I'm not sure if I can manage a conversation right now.

"Uh, yes. Could you take me to the Halmini hotel in Jerusalem please? I'm sorry, I didn't sleep on the plane at all, do you mind if I nap?"

This isn't my first choice – I don't like napping when I'm in a foreign country, in someone else's car, but I'm not planning on sleeping, just closing my eyes so that I don't have to make conversation.

"Of course, no problem," the taxi driver says happily, after tapping his GPS and seeing a relatively substantial fare come up. "Halmini hotel, coming right up."

There aren't many hotels in the old part of the city, but I've managed to find a relatively inexpensive one. I close my eyes, which is a shame, because the scenery is green, lush and impressive. I'll catch it on the way back.

I open my eyes occasionally to make sure that the

driver isn't taking me to some grubby murder basement, but he seems to be taking the main roads that my phone tells me are the quickest ways to Jerusalem. I nap briefly, waking as we hit the outskirts of the city.

The driver catches me as I open my eyes. I mentally calculate how far I think we've got left to go; probably at least fifteen minutes.

"Feeling better?" he says, glancing in the rear-view mirror.

"Yes, thank you," I manage. "Sorry, it was a difficult flight. Lots of turbulence."

"Ah, that is bad," he says, and before I know it, he's telling me about all the flights he's taken recently, the best, the worst, his favourite airlines. I do actually have a bit of a soft spot for the Israelis I've met in the past – they've all been quite direct, which makes life much easier – and if one wants to talk at me, that's fine too. Saves me the work. I try and pay attention in case there's something useful in amongst the chatter.

"And that," he concludes, turning down another small road. "Is why I always fly premium economy if I can."

"I would definitely do that if I could afford it," I admit. That sounds like a vaguely logical thing to say. "Standard is always cramped, but some airlines are better than others."

"And the luggage…"

There he goes again, and before I know it, we're pulling up to the hotel and he stops suddenly.

"So, here we are," he says. "You have a reservation?"

"Ah, yes, thanks," I manage. "I pre-paid."

"Ok, ok," he says, looking around, stepping out of the car. I fumble awkwardly with the seat belt, trying not to let go of my bag and getting out onto the pavement. The driver hands me my wheelie suitcase from the boot and I rifle through my handbag for the right currency.

"Shekels, dollars or euros?" I ask.

"Shekels, please," he says, looking a bit surprised.

"Thanks," I say, as I pay him and turn back to the hotel, trying to avoid any further talking.

He seems to be about to say something, but instead gets back into the car and drives off. Thankfully, the hotel is right on the road and marked clearly with its name; everything else is a confusing array of brick and stone buildings that I don't know how to interpret. I can see a market in the distance, stands and booths leading into a tunnel filled with more shops, but another wave of dizziness hits me. I really need to get into the hotel, so I turn and slowly walk into the foyer, trying not to fall over.

Again, it's impressive. I'd expected something grimy and low-budget, but this place is incredible. I'm in a large, low-ceilinged foyer, with stained glass windows at one side, comfortable-looking chairs and small tables set around the room. There's a glass cabinet with cigars and leaflets in it, and a few artefacts here and there.

I realise that I'm staring, and head over to the counter, where a guy that I'd put in his early forties, kindly-looking, stands looking at me.

"Hello there," he says. "Miss … Alice?"

I'm expected. "Uh, yes, hi," I stammer. "I made a reservation."

"Welcome, I'm David." he says. "Is it your first time in Israel?"

"Yes," I say. "Um, I'm not feeling too well. Is there much paperwork to sort out?"

"Not at all," he says. "Just two signatures, and a copy of your passport, if you please."

I step over to the counter and scribble my name on the forms, which are thankfully in English. Waves of nausea come and go, and I swallow hard. David files the forms and scans my passport, and before anything horrendous happens, he slides a key across to me.

"Your room is down the hall and up the stairs," he says. "Would you like me to send up some dinner later on?"

My kind of guy.

"Thank you, yes," I manage. "That would be really very kind of you."

"It is no problem," David says. "The flight was bad?"

"Yeah," I say. "I'll feel better in the morning."

"I will knock and leave a tray outside for you."

I'm incredibly appreciative of this man's understanding of my need for solitude right now. If I was religious – not an impossible notion at some point in the future – I'd say prayers of thanks for him.

The cloud of dizziness and sickness grows, and I thank David, hurrying away towards the stairs.

My room isn't far and to my surprise, has marbled floors and a bed with an elaborately carved wooden headboard. There's a surprising number of framed art prints, mostly showing scenes from around the city.

I lock the door behind me, filling a glass from a bottle of water left on the side and sip slowly, focusing on being present. Twenty-four hours ago, I was an archaeologist in a sleepy town in Hertfordshire. Now I'm Alice, about to uncover a vast religious secret.

I don't think I can do this.

Of course I can do this.

Can I?

I lie down on the bed and close my eyes. Sleep hits me in a huge wave, folding over me and taking me away almost immediately. I wake at a knock on the door, sleep melting away slowly. I'm still groggy, but I manage to pull myself up and crack open the door, seeing what looks like a chicken Caesar salad outside. The meal doesn't last long – it's really good. The nausea and light headedness are fading fast, and the food seems to be helping, so I sit on the bed, pull out my laptop and find my notes.

There's not a lot to go on. The mosaic didn't provide a lot of guidance, other than that the artefact is, or was probably somewhere near where Herod's temple used to be. Thankfully, I know exactly where that is.

I lie down and sleep takes me back a moment later.

I drift in and out of slumber the next morning but eventually surface, finding that David has left another tray

– this time, full of fruit and granola – outside my door. Bless him. I shower, dressing demurely, and head down to reception, where I find him in exactly the same place, behind the counter.

"Good morning," he says, nodding to me. "Feeling better?"

"Much better," I say truthfully. "Thank you for the dinner and the breakfast."

"It is no trouble," he says. "Are you a tourist?"

"Yes," I admit. "Do you know of any tours of the temple area that I could take? I'm a history student."

"Of course," he says. "There is one that leaves every hour, just down the road. Outside the monastery, not far from here."

He shows me on a map and I put it into my Google Maps. I've got fifteen minutes to get there and google thinks that it's a ten-minute walk. I thank David and walk out into the sunshine.

Hugo
Despair

Isn't it everyone's bad dream? A door that opens to somewhere else. You think you're walking into a hotel room, your kitchen, the eponymous wardrobe in an unfamiliar house, but it opens somewhere, somewhen else?

New places, new people, new experiences. Would you walk through, never knowing if you'd be able to return, or close it and shudder, your back against the door, hoping, praying that when you opened it again, the natural laws of the universe obeyed?

Only that's it, isn't it? We all spend so long watching the news, commuting, working nine to five, nine to six, going to burger bars, wine bars, church services, that we forget. Forget that our understanding of science is the barest scratching on the surface of the laws of the universe. That the universe cares not a whit for humankind and will behave as and how it chooses. That we are, at best, insignificant and ignored in the grand scheme of the vastness of space.

So when the laws of the universe act in a way that contradicts our petty grasp of science, when something triggers an event in our lives so alien to us that it leaves us sweating and trembling and begging for normality, should we be surprised? In a universe that's millions, billions of years old, why should we be surprised when things happen that we don't understand? When our own science and knowledge goes back three thousand years at best, why do we lie to ourselves and say that everything is ok? Why do we deny that we are tiny, tiny specks of life living on a tiny, tiny speck of rock in the cold, dark expanse of space?

Well, because it'd be too much. It's quite clear why.

And there's precedent. The Voynich Manuscript. The Necronomicon. *Fear and Loathing in Las Vegas.* The works of humans who gazed into the void and knew that there was honestly, openly, too much out there to comprehend, that no matter how many drugs they took, how much they drank, how much they prayed, that the universe would stay silent and cold and dark. That the rules would be out of our grasp for hundreds, if not thousands of years. That if we didn't destroy ourselves by conventional means, there could be an unbelievable number of surprises up the sleeves of the universe, a vast number of eyes that could turn, uncaringly, towards our warm little planet, abundant in life and resources.

And the odds are hopelessly, endlessly, fearfully stacked against us. We might as well sharpen sticks and light torches as prepare our guns and planes against the forces arrayed against us.

You'll have to excuse me.

I grow melancholy with age, the heritage of my family.

My name is Hugo. Baron Hugo Delauncey-Morrison, if you'd like to be completely correct. I'm thirty-two years of age, and my parents – in fact, all of my remaining family – died some years ago in a terrible accident. My family is, or was, a line of secret-keepers. A small, insignificant secret in the grand scheme of things. A vast, terrible secret in the scheme of others.

A secret that could easily have me derided, sectioned, humiliated if I made it public.

A secret this large is a terrible, lonely thing. Especially when you're alone with a small housekeeping team, two cats and a lot of money for company.

It doesn't help, believe me.

Why do I carry on? Someone has to. For a bit longer at least.

But some nights, some long, dark nights, it's harder than others.

I endure.

I hope, I desperately, grimly hope, that it doesn't happen on my watch, however prepared I am.

I don't keep the faith. I drink. I rage. I cry.

Sometimes, I pray.

You would too.

If you knew what I knew.

Ben
Bracknell and Erith

We spend a week in Bracknell, with a couple of hours each day in Karnak, which almost seems normal by the end. Both of us are fitter, better at the staves and understand a lot more about the history of the Gardeners and how they work with local military – and perhaps more significantly, Matt hasn't smoked all week, which must be a sign of how much he's committed to this.

I can't help but feel a pang of regret as we leave, although our last day falls awkwardly on a Thursday, so we've got to report back to Wild Court tomorrow.

Then we're back on the train to London. It's an abrupt, almost violent feeling of dislocation. Time seems to just jump; one minute we were training with Christina, and – despite the fact that really, we'd spent some time packing up and saying goodbyes – the next, we were back on the platform of a grubby commuter station.

I still can't shake the suspicion that at some stage this is all going to vanish. Like when you go into the office after a week on holiday and it feels like it never really happened. You've got sand in your shoes, a bottle of the local wine and some photos, but who's to say you were really gone? If you didn't have your memories, no-one would know.

Only it's worse because I've got this Matrix-y, Alice in Wonderland feeling that I'll turn up at Wild Court tomorrow and find it gone.

I try to get a grip on myself and glance at Matt for a dose of pragmatism, only to see that he's dozed off.

Some things never change.

I pull out my e-reader and log onto the 'intermediate' section of the reading list that Christina had selectively unblocked on our last day. We'd had a very informal 'graduation' where she told us that we'd done well and could now consider ourselves minimally competent apprentices and might move up to journeymen in a few years' time. Then she'd told us to read up, keep our noses clean and be polite. I laughed a bit at Matt's face when she'd said that. He didn't quite know what to make of her.

I part ways with Matt at Waterloo, heading to a shop to grab some food before I get my next train; Erith doesn't have that much in the way of good supermarkets or take-aways, compared to Greenwich. Then I sit on the train back home, the sense of dislocation and loneliness deepening, and although I've joined a group that is perhaps the most incredible group of people I've ever met, I don't really know any of them properly, and am very much 'the new guy'. It's a stark contrast to the library, where I knew and was comfortable with everyone.

I hate starting new jobs, and I try to imagine what Matt must be thinking about right now.

It's probably boobs.

That doesn't help.

~

I do feel a bit better the next day, although it's a shock commuting again. The train is slightly less busy than I remember it being when I commuted for my old job, although that might be because it's Friday, and a lot of people work from home so that they can get away quickly for the weekend. I get a pang of guilt as I pull out a fiction book I've been reading, but have to remind myself that I can't be studious all the time.

It's warm but damp outside. Britain is still pleasantly spring-like, but that means showers. You can see the commuters not really knowing how to dress, sunglasses twinned with light jackets and cautiously furled umbrellas. I pause reading for a moment and watch the industrial estates, residential housing and parks slide by, enjoying the rarity of a window seat. I mean, it's not Karnak, where we were consistently a little high from the oxygen content of the air, but it's not bad.

Matt messages me to say that he's in a coffee shop on Kingsway. Apparently, he went out with his flatmates last night and got drunk. They thought he'd been on holiday and needed a 'coming back party', so he's nursing a hangover. I'm actually glad to have some more time to myself – Karnak was amazing, and we did get a few evenings off, but I'm still feeling a bit oversaturated by all the input and newness.

I put some music on to try and maintain my psychological distance as I walk up the Strand. Self-care, Ben, remember your self-care.

"I'm so fucking hungover," Matt says as I collect him from Starbucks, practically hugging his enormous Americano. He's wearing a black and brown hoodie, and with his mournful look, he looks a bit like a basset hound.

I shake my head at my usually-sturdy friend, wondering how much of this is theatrical.

"Something funny?" he asks, and I try not to laugh. Quite often I'll pick up negative vibes from people, but Matt's hangover is actually making me feel better.

We battle our way back across Kingsway and arrive at Gardener HQ. Despite being proper apprentices, we still have to wait to be collected at the front desk.

Then it hits me: how long are we going to be doing this for? Months? Years? Our initial tour is two years, but it could be longer. Am I going to be behind a desk, or actually in the field? How do they decide?

Then Lincoln arrives and interrupts both my train of thought and my relatively calm vibes.

"Morning," he says between gritted teeth. "How was your week away? Please, don't tell me. I've read the reports."

I get up, Matt following suit a moment later, and we

follow Lincoln down a corridor. We turn a corner and two people hurry past us in the opposite direction, talking in hushed tones. Lincoln scans his pass on a door and ushers us on ahead into the large open-plan atrium.

Instantly I'm struck by the difference in atmosphere. Compared to our last visit, it feels a lot busier, everyone seems a lot more intent, and there's an edge of stress. There are maybe forty people sat at the desks, but almost half of that number again either squatting by the desks or perched on them, mostly talking quickly and quietly. I can see a couple of conference rooms off to the side, most of which are full of people talking or pacing.

"Come on," Lincoln says. "I think I see a free one."

We weave our way through the room, overhearing snatches of conversation. I don't know if I'm overreacting, but it almost feels fraught, like the time that our library was inspected by the local council. Julia had been relatively calm about the whole thing, but everything still needed to be perfect and nerves frayed quickly.

"Yes," a guy is saying into a headset. "That must definitely take priority."

I slow down to listen, but Lincoln beckons for us both to join him in the only remaining free room. I sit down and pour a glass of water.

"Now," he says calmly, but I can tell that he's a bit on edge. "Christina passed on that your records were exemplary, so well done. She's not easy to impress. You've learnt the basics of the staves, which all new recruits are taught, but your induction doesn't end here. Until we figure out where we need you most, and where your natural abilities lie, I'll be mentoring you and showing you around the various jobs that need doing around the site. Some of them will be low-level admin and you may get to assist with basic containment and dispersal or rift closure. Today, we'll be checking in with some of the monitoring sites around London."

He pulls out a map from a bag beside the chair. It's a map of central London, with a few cafes circled. Lincoln looks at them for a moment, then begins to number them.

"We'll go to the Caffe Nero just up the road in a moment, then hop on the tube to Bond Street and check in there. After that, it's a short walk over towards Green Park and Piccadilly. Any questions?"

I shake my head, but Matt's head seems to still be clearing.

"Lincoln, remind me again, these sites are where we monitor…?"

"Empathy," he says patiently. "Our monitors are given laptops and tattoos – slightly different to the ones you've got – and they detect the empathy levels in the area. It's an alternative use of the noosphere but doesn't really require active stave usage, and basically looks like a mindfulness app."

"Shit," Matt says quietly. "Right."

"Ok?" Lincoln says acerbically, pushing his chair back and standing.

And almost as quickly as we arrived, we're leaving,

heading up towards Holborn.

"Lincoln," I say, as we wait by a crossing. "Is everything ok? Wild Court seemed different."

He looks at me and doesn't say anything. The lights change and we cross, but despite the crowds I stick absolutely by his side. He sighs.

"You're fully inducted now, so I'll treat you like adults. Empathy levels have dropped considerably, and we're becoming increasingly concerned about a London-wide event. We've recalled a lot of the team from overseas to monitor and patrol, and many staff who would normally be based in Bracknell are now in Covent Garden. Any assets – like Chloe, or other psychics – are being called in as a preventative measure. It could be nothing, but we're taking it very seriously, especially after what Chloe said. The Prime Minister is being briefed tomorrow, if trends continue."

Matt looks like he's about to puke up his Americano, but thankfully we arrive at the first coffee place, not far from Holborn station.

"You guys want anything?" he says, heading to the counter for another drink.

"No," Lincoln says, his tone reminding me a little of Alan Rickman. "Order quickly."

Matt glances at me and I shake my head. Very quietly, he orders a ginger tea and grabs a packet of ready salted crisps. I'd laugh about his state if Lincoln hadn't just told me we might be near some kind of – well, I don't know, something bad.

"What sort of event?" I ask.

He shakes his head, leading us upstairs. "Not now. Not here."

He sits down at a table opposite a girl with a laptop covered in stickers.

"Hey," he says. "How's it looking?"

She glances up, taking her earphones out and looking at us with eyebrows raised.

"Interns?" she says in a Polish accent.

"New recruits. Ignore them."

She starts to grin, then spins her laptop around, showing a graph with a steadily dropping trend line. "It's not looking good," she says. "Things have declined."

"Hmmm," he says, looking at it, scrolling to one side. "Thank you. Keep syncing the data. We appreciate it."

"Sure," she says. "No problem."

Lincoln looks pointedly at Matt, who gulps down his tea, and we head back out onto the street.

"How much do they know?" I ask.

"Enough," Lincoln says. "We don't lie to them, but we also don't tell them everything about rifts and so on. Hardly any of them come inside Wild Court, although we do recruit from the pool of monitors occasionally. Come on, let's get to Bond St."

I glance at Matt, who is now cramming crisps into his mouth. This isn't really what I expected from our first proper day as professional guardians of the world's magical and spiritual boundaries.

After a short, uncomfortable journey on the tube reading about another unpleasant murder on Hampstead Heath – Matt pointedly averting his gaze – we have a similar trip to a Pret where we have to crowd around a window perch at the front of the café to talk to a dreadlocked Pilates teacher. The graph lines seem a little higher than in Holborn, which Lincoln assures us is normal; tourists are generally a pretty happy bunch, compared to workers nearer to the City of London proper.

My stomach is still churning, my shoulders tense. Something's up. I mean, maybe it's just that I don't know enough – I've only been to Wild Court twice, after all – but it seemed a lot more intense, more stressful than our first visit.

I try not to think about it as we have almost identical interactions with laptop-bearers in the cafes in Green Park, but as we're about to walk into a Starbucks in Piccadilly, Lincoln's phone rings and he steps into a quieter side street next to a cheap-looking steak restaurant.

After answering it, he's silent for almost a full minute.

"If that's the case, I can make preparations tonight," he says. "Although if someone could look after the apprentices?"

There's another silence. "Really?" he says in a level tone. "I know it's a long-shot. Yes. Of course."

"Must I?" he says, grimacing. "Fine. Yes, consider it done once I'm finished here. It'll give us an accurate read if nothing else."

He listens for another moment, then hangs up.

"Come on," he says, turning to us. "Let's finish here and then I'll debrief you. Things have changed."

It takes an almost superhuman effort not to ask questions as he leads us to the last monitoring station where we meet a grey-haired guy in a faded leather jacket. I catch Matt tapping his foot impatiently a couple of times as we look at the same downward trend on the graph that we've seen in the other cafes, and the old guy chatters away. There's something going on. I know it. Lincoln is just too much of a dick to tell us right away.

Then I catch myself. If he's not telling us, it's because it's serious. I have to remember that I'm part of something bigger now and have to trust him, however bad an experience I've had so far. Right?

Finally, he finishes and thanks the guy – Moses – before we head out onto Piccadilly. Lincoln looks around and hurries back down the side street before turning to us.

"Alright," he says. "Things have changed and the data we've received today from these and other monitors has increased the alert level significantly, so much so that we're looking at drawing in all of our assets from around the world. Now, we'd hoped to give you a normal weekend tomorrow, but I'm being sent to investigate a last-ditch lead on an asset and unfortunately, you're being sent with me. Go home now, and meet me at Gatwick Airport at nine tonight. We'll be flying to Jerusalem. Your e-readers will be updated with briefing packs that you should read on the way in. Do you both have passports?"

We both nod, and he dismisses us, stalking back up the street.

What the fuck is going on?

Alice
Frustrating Social Archaeology

I should have known that when you piece together historical clues leading to an artefact of extreme religious significance, uncover ancient evidence, fake the need for compassionate leave and then travel for hours and hours on a crappy little plane, arriving in a completely foreign city, feeling terrible on arrival, they don't just hand you the artefact on a plate as a reward.

Perversely, annoyingly, for all my academic skill, for all my intelligence and qualifications, my dedication and perseverance, it's the one thing I'm not very good at that's hindering me.

I'll start from where we left off, taking a tour of Jerusalem's historic quarter. It's spectacular, and for a day, I allow myself to simply indulge in an incredible historical retrospective. I gape at Mount Zion, the Via Dolorosa, the Church of the Holy Sepulchre – it's incredible. One part of my brain is telling me that playing the enthusiastic tourist is good cover, but actually I'm being very authentic right now and making no effort to disguise my love of all things historical. I ask more questions than I should, but our tour guide takes them all in his stride, even if he struggles with a couple of them.

Of course, it's not all great. It's hot and I have to constantly re-apply sub-standard sunscreen because of the ridiculous liquid prohibition on planes. One of my purses gets stolen; thankfully, the one with the least currency and no cards in it – my main one is tucked safely against my skin and it'd take more than a simple pickpocket to get it.

Jerusalem is absolutely jam-packed full of people. It's constant. There's no end of locals, tourists, tour guides, little noisy scooters, all pushing past you to try and get where they want to go.

It's testament to how much I'm enjoying the tour that I still love it in spite of all this. Sometimes I do have to be chivvied by our tour guide because I'm staring and taking photos. I make vaguely polite conversation with a family of British tourists and the heat doesn't bother me like it did yesterday. I'm feeling much better, presumably due to the power of a good nap and decompression time without anyone else bothering me, as well as David's restorative dinner and breakfast.

We're not allowed into the Dome of the Rock, of course, but that's to be expected. I try to engage in conversation with a few men who look like they might be rabbis, but I'm pulled away by our tour guide. I beg him to allow us a diversion to the section of wall that most closely matches the location of the yellow mark on the mosaic. It's packed with residential buildings and swarming with scooters, but there are a couple of men in robes who are definitely going to be my first port of call for interrogations later on.

By the end of the tour, my reconnaissance is complete, so I don't even object to David's conversational overtures when I get back to the hotel that evening.

"You're feeling better now?"

"Yes, much better, thank you."

The foyer really is stunning; admittedly, the ceilings are a little low, but I've noticed that this is fairly characteristic of Jerusalem across the board. The stained-glass windows don't actually seem to look out on anything, but they're all quite pleasant, if a little floral for my liking. The room smells fresh and clean and it's scrupulously tidy; I'll be giving this place a good review on TripAdvisor at some stage.

"Please, you must eat in my family's restaurant this evening – the food will be better than on a tray."

I remind myself that people are more likely to help you if they like you, so I accept, and after freshening up, I head into the dining area of the hotel, where David ushers me into a seat opposite a beautiful, dark-eyed, dark-haired woman and two small boys.

"My wife, Sarah, my sons, Uri and Yosef."

I greet them awkwardly, but Sarah smiles at me as I glance around at the room. It's a slightly older style than some of the other parts of the hotel, with framed pictures of people – I assume, family members or former proprietors – decorating the white walls, the dark wood of the chairs a stark contrast to the white tablecloths and napkins.

"This is a beautiful place," I say. "Was this room originally part of the hotel?"

Sarah gives me another dazzling smile as her two boys play with the drinking straws in their orange juice.

"No," she says in a low, husky voice. "David and I bought this from another couple who wanted to move to America. We didn't change the style out of respect, but I think we'll do it next year. It's good to have a space like this, but it's not quite the same as the rest of the hotel."

I nod as a waiter puts a menu in my hands. "Thank you. What do you recommend, please?"

Sarah says something to the man that I don't quite catch and he gives us both a sweeping bow, taking the menus back before leaving.

"We will surprise you," she says and I try for a smile.

"Thank you. How old are your sons?"

Sarah takes a moment to run her hand through the hair of the one closest to her. "Uri is five and Yosef is six. We've been very blessed."

The small talk isn't too taxing, but I attempt to steer the conversation towards my areas of interest, telling her all about the tours and the mysterious men I saw. She's charming but unhelpful, simply laughing that there are many religious men in Jerusalem and deftly moves the conversation on to ask me what I'm going to do tomorrow, something I fumble with until I ask for her recommendations.

She helpfully points out a few major things that I've not yet seen, and also recommends a tour outside of the city as well as a few things to see around Tel Aviv, in case I'm thinking of heading that way later in my trip.

David and the waiter bring back plates steaming with salmon fillet and some kind of curry on the side – two things I've never seen combined, but the result is delicious, and the two boys seem to delight in my reaction and tease me about it all night long. Once we've finished, our plates are promptly swept away and replaced by an equally delicious praline mousse, which I would guess is Sarah's favourite dish, from a private glance between her and David.

David joins us shortly afterwards and serves up a sweet white wine to finish the meal off, which I sip gingerly until I realise that it's not that strong.

There are a few other guests in the room but it's not that busy, something I ask about. David shrugs.

"We have two big tour groups arriving tomorrow, so we had to turn away a few smaller bookings – it's a small gap. Business is well."

I nod, unaware if I've breached some unknown social rule asking about money.

"So, Alice," Sarah starts. She's giving me maternal

vibes, but it's crossed with a slightly Nigella Lawson kind of thing, which I find attractive. "Do you have a boyfriend back home?"

I shrink back into my seat and struggle to remember the standard lines I've used with my parents over the years. "Ah, no," I admit. "I don't meet that many guys my age in my line of work."

And that's perfectly true. Most men I meet in archaeology are in their forties and fifties.

I don't really catch her response – it's probably something like 'oh maybe you'll meet a nice boy here' or 'we have a nephew we can introduce you to'. I smile, nod and thank them repeatedly for a wonderful meal, suddenly wanting to go. It's a few more minutes before I can make my excuses and leave whilst complementing the food again.

The next day I approach two rabbis who are standing near the place by the yellow mark on the mosaic. I can't be sure, but I think that one of them was here yesterday. My Hebrew is halting and I'm concerned that I'm not being polite enough. Thankfully, they reply in English, but only to tell me that they are busy and can't help.

I insist, asking to see their leader, or if there is someone of importance I can talk to.

They turn their backs to me.

In desperation, I drop Averan's name, and they stiffen, then one of them turns around.

"Leave here," he says in a thick accent. "And do not come back."

A few younger men are starting to gather at the edges of the square. I should get out of here. In fact, I probably shouldn't press the matter further today, and I apologise gratuitously for any offense I've caused, thank them for their help and hurry away from the square by a different exit, trying to catch a glimpse of something I've not seen before, any clue at all.

I don't, and I'm also a hundred percent sure that I'm followed by at least three other guys from the square. I hurry back to a market, but rather than making it easier for me to lose them, it makes it harder for me to keep track of them in the hubbub.

Ok, think Alice. What to do? I head over towards to the Israel Museum, which turns out to be a very long walk through the city. I have to take a long sit down in the café when I get there, rehydrating myself with two large bottles of mineral water, but I'm also hopeful that some of my pursuers lost interest on the way here, and think that I'm just a tactless tourist.

I can't really concentrate on anything in the museum, stunning though it is, although I do leaf through a lot of books in the gift shop, trying to find anything about the area that I'm concerned with.

It's completely fruitless.

I can't face another evening with Sarah and her family, so I stay out as late as I can, eating alone in a small café where I sit in a corner space poring through a guide book I've bought and trying to think of a way to persuade the rabbis to talk to me.

Nothing comes to mind, and my lack of strategy spectacularly fails to serve me the next day. The rabbis see me coming and simply walk away, closing the door of a house behind them, leaving me alone, but feeling very watched.

I spend the rest of the day in the library, where my inability to read much Hebrew significantly hinders me. There's an English section, but it's small and only takes me about forty-five minutes to comb through the books there.

Futile.

An anxious-looking David is waiting for me at the hotel, hurriedly finishing a conversation with an American tour group leader. He thanks the other man and almost jogs over to me, guiding me into a seat in the corner of the foyer.

"Alice," he says quickly. "Alice, those men you bother, they are very important. You must leave them alone. Please. For your own good."

Not only did they follow me, but they followed me all day yesterday and worked out where I'm staying.

"I need to talk to them," I admit. "David, can you tell them that I need to talk to them?"

The kind proprietor goes a little pale. "No," he says. "No, I only speak to their friends, but they are not people you should bother. Please, if you speak to them, trouble can come here."

I pretend to think about it, nod and apologise to him, heading up to my room trying to pretend that I'm embarrassed and ashamed by all of this.

The next day I leave the square entirely alone and try to focus on innocuous tourist activities, but I'm almost certainly being watched. Paranoia is completely irrational, I tell myself, although another part of my brain tells me that it's not irrational if a couple of people followed you for an entire day and left a message with your hotel in a country where you have no friends, no contacts and have been robbed already.

I try another library, the National Library of Israel, on the other side of the city. It takes half an hour in a cab to get there and eats into my cash reserves much more than I'd like.

And again, it's a wholly fruitless endeavour, but then what was I expecting, a book in a public library to suddenly leap out at me and say 'X marks the spot'?

I resolve to try the square one more time before trying … I don't know, the embassy or something?

Hugo. I'll have to call Hugo and see if he has any connections here. I really don't want to do that but I think he'll know what to do.

It takes a while to get my courage up the next morning, and I kill time pacing around a short distance from the square. It's a beautiful cool day, and I drink tea and eat a light lunch in a café nearby before I summon up the courage to do this. This is ridiculous. I've never had a problem with this kind of thing before. What's wrong with me?

I arrive at the square at the same time as three serious-looking men who I'd wager are British. I'm not quite sure why, but there's something about them.

Two of them clock me, pausing by a table in the square as the other heads over to the rabbis and begins talking to them rapidly in hushed tones.

"Excuse me," I say to the two at the table, hoping that they are actually British and that my social radar isn't completely off. "Could you help me with something?"

One of them looks over at me. "I'm very sorry, but we're a bit busy at the moment," he says firmly.

Then the rabbi and the other guy come back over to us. I swear it's the same rabbi as I've seen the past few days.

"You should all come with me," he says. "There has been a problem. A very serious problem."

Well, finally.

Part Two

A Swift and Terrible Brightness

Hugo
Take the Money and Leave

What would you do, in my position? Being told for years when I was growing up that the apocalypse was coming, that we needed to be prepared, that it was the most important thing in the world.

That no-one would believe us.

As a child, I bought into it. I treated it like a game. I helped my dad with inventorying the food supplies, became an expert in vacuum sealing, learnt how to maintain a generator, fire a shotgun, drive a tractor and tentatively started to understand the hydroponics labs.

Of course, when I was fourteen, I had my rebellious phase. A little later than most, but I had more to lose. Then my parents showed me one of the locked rooms in our folly.

Have you ever been to the Hunterian Museum in London? It's a museum of medical history. Brains in jars, livers in formaldehyde, pickled mice, that kind of thing. Well, it was like that, only full of demons. Winged things too large and bodies too different to be dinosaurs or birds.

Five of them, in total, neatly labelled with incontrovertible evidence that each bone belonged to the common skeleton.

Elongated skulls, teeth, clawed hands. This was the finding that had prompted my great, great, great grandfather to write his prediction and for my whole family to become what they are. My father hinted at another discovery, one we couldn't capture for posterity, that had caused our relatives to build the mansion as it is.

That put an end to both my rebellious phase and to sleeping at night.

We all woke up screaming from time to time. You almost get used to it.

What you don't get used to is car crashes. My parents had taken a holiday in Aviemore and were driving back home when their armoured limo was hit by a truck. The car was bulletproof, impenetrable. It wasn't immune to the huge logistics lorry that drove into them and pushed them down the face of a cliff, the truck landing on top of the car and crushing it, killing them instantly.

The insurance paid out, but I didn't need it.

I was seventeen. Quiet, serious, academic. Studious.

I didn't speak for three weeks. I barely ate for one.

They say you go through five stages of acceptance in these situations. Fifteen years later, I think I'm still at depression, trudging through life like a zombie. Of course, it's not just the loss of my parents. It's the waiting. Wondering if it's going to be today, tomorrow or the next day that it happens, and wondering if I should do anything. Because, with everything going on in the world, sometimes I think we've earned a little Armageddon for our sins.

I have my good days. Tentatively, I've made contact with a few of my parents' friends. I've found researchers and organisations that need funding because their theories are too close to truth for any commercial body to sponsor them. Some offered to take me in, to meet.

But there's a part of me which still doesn't quite believe it, even when I sometimes spend hours staring at the skeletons in the safe room.

I guess I'm a coward. Maybe you would be too. Maybe you'd hole up in this Baba-Yaga mansion and keep the jet fuelled, the supplies stocked up, the Netflix running. Maybe you'd be a joiner, getting involved with gusto, thinking we could make a difference.

I thought that too for a while. Two months after the accident, I had to go through my parents' papers, figure out what to keep funding and what to stop. I was worried about money and quickly learnt that I didn't have to be. Only a small percentage of their investment profits were given out to causes. The rest provided an income for me, kept the mansion running and fed back into itself.

One group was named after an obscure French priest. I met several of them, made it through the pleasantries, asked for an understanding of what they were researching.

While my parents weren't joiners either, it turns out they had pretty high security clearance with this organisation.

They showed me what they were researching and it was like the skeletons all over again.

Some of the things they were looking into didn't even have bodies. After fifteen minutes, I stopped leafing through the file, almost thinking fondly of the bones at home. I stood up, dizzy, and threw up in a bin.

When I'd wiped the bile from my lips with a monogrammed handkerchief, taking a large swig of coffee to remove the taste from my mouth, I turned back to face them.

These things, I asked, these things are leaking into our world and you have the means to stop them?

One of them, a serious-looking woman, nodded.

You can have your money, I told her. But I don't want to see you again.

You see, when things are this dark, this awful, you keep going even though it makes no sense to. You know that the rational choice is to go home, blow your brains out, jump off a bridge, slit your wrists, but you don't. You keep getting up in the morning, eating your cereal, pushing funds to organisations that can help, hoping, praying that they can keep these things away from you.

But I won't ever have a family. I won't delude myself with real hope that they can find a permanent solution.

And I hope to hell that I die before the evil comes here.

Matt
Into the Lair

We've been in Jerusalem for a bit now, and so far it's been quite a lot of fannying around.

We landed at the airport and almost before we'd wrestled our bags off that conveyor belt thing, we were whisked away by one of Lincoln's contacts. I called shotgun, but he still took the front seat and spent most of the trip into town talking to the driver in hushed tones. Occasionally I'd catch a word, but they might as well have been talking in code.

Lincoln made a few calls – I assume, back to London – but otherwise pretty much ignored us the whole way, which is usually fine because he's a moody fucker at the best of times, but a little information sharing wouldn't go amiss now and then.

Ben's quiet and to be honest, I'm worried about him. He doesn't fly well and I reckon this has all gotten a bit serious for him. That said, I can't decide if it's sunk in with me yet either.

We're driven straight to what Lincoln calls a 'field office', which is actually another Regus office, although – and I'm never going to say this out loud – it's a nicer one this time. It's got these enormous Kilner jars full of iced lemon water at reception which I greedily lay into, only pausing as I see Ben waiting behind me. I step to one side and let him at it; he rolls his eyes but doesn't say anything.

Like I said, I'm worried about the guy.

"This way," Lincoln says, beckoning us into a conference room. I shoulder my bag again, ignoring the sweaty patches under my arms. It's not that hot here, and it's a dry heat, but I'm carrying quite a lot. I turn into the conference room and see two almost-identical guys in suits sat at the far end, so I drop my bag, nodding to them and sit on the side waiting for Lincoln and Ben.

"Ben, Matt, this is James and Jacob," Lincoln says, pointing to the guys in turn. "They run the field office here. Guys, as you know, we're here to see if we can pick up the asset."

James, the older, bald one, glances at Jacob and swallows. "You do know," he says nervously, but I think he's trying to sound like a badass. "That it's not the kind of thing we can collect? In theory, it hasn't moved for over a thousand years."

"And it could be a moot point," Jacob says. "There's been a rumour of a disturbance."

"A disturbance?" Lincoln says, leaning forwards. "Why wasn't I notified?"

Jacob sighs heavily. "At best, we maintain a loose perimeter. The asset is guarded by a religious sect, and we haven't had actual eyes on it for some time. Yesterday there was a lot of activity around the area and we've not managed to get anything out of anyone since."

"Couldn't be worse timing," Lincoln says. "Things are coming to a head in London, or so our psychics tell us."

James nods. "We got the briefing. We're praying it doesn't reach the continent and we're readying what support we can lend."

"Thank you," Lincoln says. "It sounds like there's not much more to be done here. We'll go directly."

"I'll come with you," Jacob says, starting to stand, but Lincoln waves him back down.

"Don't worry," Lincoln says. "I've met them before."

Jacob actually looks relieved, and I start to wonder what kind of asset we're talking about. I'd imagined some sort of Bourne Identity assassin, waiting to be activated, but if it's guarded by a religious group? I'm going to keep my eyes open and watch Ben's back, let's leave it at that.

After a quick piss, it's back into the car again and into Jerusalem proper, which is actually pretty impressive. I'd imagined that it'd be all dusty and dry with all those pale brick buildings you see on TV, but it's lush and green instead.

For the last fifteen minutes it's slow going. There's traffic everywhere and our driver, however local he is, can't find a way through that doesn't mean waiting around stuck behind other cars and vans. Eventually he pulls over by this building with a courtyard and Lincoln gets out, beckoning for us to follow.

"Can you wait with the car?" he asks the driver. "In case we need to leave in a hurry?"

The guy inside nods and Lincoln gestures for us to leave our bags and get a move on. Maybe if he actually communicated with us out loud once in a while instead of staying in his own secret world, we'd annoy him less.

Worst Obi Wan ever.

"Now," he says. "The people we're about to meet are the keepers of an asset that's been kept here in secret for thousands of years. They're incredibly easily offended and if I thought you'd stay in the car if I asked you to, I'd do that in a heartbeat. Instead, I'm taking you with me, but I want you to promise not to be arseholes, ok?"

Ben swallows nervously and nods. I shrug. "Sure," I say. "You got it."

He narrows his eyes and looks at me sceptically. I've no idea what his problem is.

Either way, he turns around and heads into the courtyard where two serious-looking rabbis are waiting for us. He gestures for us to wait by a table, so we hang around for a few seconds, but then get interrupted by this girl – she looks like she belongs in a library somewhere – who comes up to us and asks Ben for help. Just as he's apologising to her, like he does for everything, and I'm about to tell her to fuck off because we're here on serious business, Lincoln comes back with one of the rabbis.

"You should all come with me," the rabbi says, seemingly including the random librarian in his invitation, which to me, throws serious doubt on how these guys have kept something secret for a thousand years. "There has been a problem. A very serious problem."

I glance over at Ben, who grimaces and raises his eyebrows. I clap him on the shoulder and we follow Lincoln and the rabbi into a house, past two more serious-looking guys in robes who are holding handguns in a sufficiently casual way to make me believe that they are not to be trifled with, before we go down into what I think is going to be a cellar.

Only it's not a cellar. We go down stairs, but after a moment, the walls turn from pale brick to bare rock. The librarian girl is babbling to the rabbi behind us, and I tune in for a moment, but she's got a fairly annoying voice that makes me want to tune straight out again.

"Yes," the rabbi says in a thick accent. "We know who you are, Alice. We've seen your work."

"My work?" she says, sounding very surprised. "How? Did Hugo tell you?"

"Hugo?" he says. "Ah, the Baron. No, but we keep an eye on him."

That shuts her up for a bit, and then we're down the stairs and into this rock-hewn passageway, lit with actual candles. Suddenly I get the sense of being in a Dungeons and Dragons adventure and I'm playing my least favourite character: the wizard.

Maybe I'm dual-class?

Course I am. Fighter-mage, with an usually high – mostly sexual – charisma.

Lincoln is still talking in hushed tones to the rabbi as we pass through another door into a cave. I can't quite work out if it's man-made or not – it's a fairly regular inverted bowl shape, with niches set around the edges, most of them with candles, crosses and crucifixes set in them, alongside a few religious-looking books and basins of water. It smells like incense in here and it's starting to catch in my throat but I don't want to cough in case that offends these guys.

"In here, please," the rabbi says, ushering us through into another chamber. I shake my head, wondering what on earth could be next.

Turns out, it's nothing.

Other than a gaping hole in the ceiling, this place is emptier than Lincoln's list of matches on Tinder. Or Grindr, I guess, I don't know what the guy's jam is. Whatever the dating network is for grumpy guys who take a perverse delight in communicating poorly.

"It was here?" Lincoln is asking, and the rabbi nods. The librarian girl sinks down onto her heels, looking around before putting her face in her hands. She's muttering something and I'm really starting to wonder why we've picked up this tourist.

I peer through the hole in the ceiling. It looks like it goes up into another room, then another, then I can see blue sky through the gap. I glance around the room again, noticing that it's actually not quite empty and that there's a dark patch on the floor. Looks like ash or something, maybe a ceremonial fire.

Fuck – that's the D&D kicking in. I make a note to try and flush it out of my system at some point. Or maybe it'll be useful in my new line of work.

"Until yesterday?" Lincoln is saying.

The rabbi nods again and Lincoln turns to face us. "Alright, detective time," he says in a clear voice. "Until yesterday, this sanctum was home to an angel known to us in English as Raysiel, where it had resided for – as far as we know – over two thousand years. Approximately twenty-six hours ago, an acolyte was saying the traditional prayers here when the guards outside heard words that they are relatively confident were 'beyond the iniquity of man', saw a bright flash of light that caused retinal damage to both of them, then heard an explosion. At the same time, a streak of light – presumably Raysiel – vanished through the ceiling in that direction. Theories, please."

For once, I'm pretty speechless. Like, an angel? Seriously?

"Alice, is it?" Lincoln says. "This is your speciality, correct? I'd like to hear from you first."

The librarian girl looks up and I think she might have been crying. She stands up and looks around, taking a deep breath. I guess Lincoln doesn't know her but I wonder if there are other demon-hunting organisations around and maybe she's a part of one, like a less cool Anthony Head or something. Or is she genuinely an academic? She doesn't seem that sure of herself. Maybe they'll send actual Buffy next time.

"Looks like this acolyte was disintegrated or something," I offer, in a flash of inspiration. "You know, unworthy like some Indiana Jones Ark of the Covenant shit."

Lincoln winces, shooting an apologetic glance at the rabbi, who shrugs.

"Matt," he says. "What did I say?"

I look away from his laser-beam stare. "Right, polite, got it."

"Nonetheless," he says. "You might be right."

Alice – the new girl – walks around the room and looks up at the hole, then checks her phone, scrolling for a few minutes. I get the impression that she's forgotten we're here.

"So where did it go?" Ben says, making me jump. I'd kind of forgotten that *he* was here for a moment.

"Heaven?" I say, then wince, casting what I hope is an apologetic look at Lincoln. I don't really want to fuck up being a wizard.

Alice does something else with her phone and turns one way, then another. "I've got an idea," she says. "But I need a bigger map."

The rabbi says something to one of the guards outside the door and a moment later, he hands Alice an iPad. She cross-references it with something on her phone and I start to feel a bit bored. There's really nothing else here to look at, apart from the walls, and they're all covered in writing of some kind.

There's actually fainter script behind some of the newer writing, like someone's written on top of it. I glance up and see it on the ceiling as well. Almost every inch of this room is covered in writing. It's a bit disconcerting, and this room is already disconcerting as fuck.

"Well?" Lincoln says, making me start.

"Nordaustlandet," she says, looking up from the iPad. "Svalbard. Due north. In the absence of other theories."

Lincoln sighs, and I open my mouth to ask a question then think better of it. Isn't Svalbard in that Philip Pullman book, the one with the talking polar bears and Nicole Kidman looking weirdly not hot?

"You're sure?"

The girl looks irritated. "No, of course I'm not sure," she says. "I've dedicated years of my life to following the historical and religious breadcrumbs to what I'd imagined was some kind of artefact or holy book, only to find that – if you're to be believed – it's an angel. And not only that, but that the aforementioned angel *flew away* twenty-four hours before I got here. I'm sure of nothing at this point."

Touché, motherfucker. I guess having Giles here isn't so bad after all.

Lincoln looks over at the rabbi, who says something I don't catch, but then Lincoln's phone buzzes. He glances down and winces.

"I'm very sorry – I need to check in. What's the fastest way out?"

The rabbi starts to lead him out, leaving Alice's question unanswered.

"Ah," Ben says, awkwardly. He's always got to fill these gaps in conversation, I don't know why. Something to do with his childhood, maybe? "Look, I don't know how to tell you this without sounding like I'm lying, but it's not a conspiracy, ok?"

"Yeah," I fill in, trying to help him out, but I don't get much further than that. How do you explain all the stuff we've seen?

Alice opens her mouth to reply, but Lincoln puts his head around the door.

"All of you. Outside. Now."

Much as I'd like to give him a witty rejoinder, you probably shouldn't make too many jokes in a room where someone's just been vaporised.

Instead, we all hurry back through the tunnel and up the stone steps back into the courtyard where we wait for Lincoln to make a phone call. I stay ahead of Ben so that he has to fence all of the questions from Alice, which mostly seem to revolve around whether we know someone called Hugo. Don't think I know any people called Hugo. Sounds like a twat's name.

"Alright," Lincoln says, sounding weary. Actually, he usually sounds pretty weary, so this is the next level for him. Wearier.

"Alice, by the powers vested in me by the British government and the First Extraordinary Battalion, I need to commandeer your expertise in a matter of national emergency. Given the nature of the engagement, I will need you to sign documentation referring to the Official Secrets Act and ask you to lend all necessary assistance to our cause. An analyst will talk you through the details."

He hands his phone to a pale-looking Alice, who takes it and tentatively puts it to her ear. She turns away and I don't really catch what she says, but Lincoln's talking again.

"Things are coming to a head," he says. "Our psychics are aiming to meet at Wild Court tomorrow morning, so we've been recalled."

"Recalled?" I say indignantly. "The fuck we have, we just got here."

"Is it bad?" Ben says, completely ignoring me.

"Look," Lincoln says. "If we were following proper procedure, yes, we'd spend the next few days here interviewing everyone in the region, taking chemical samples, calling in a science team and photographing everything. That's procedure. But I don't feel any resonances here, there's no rift in the noosphere and above all that, we've been ordered to return. So, we return."

I open my mouth and close it again. It's probably for the best. A moment later, Alice hands the phone back to Lincoln with a hand that trembles a little. Can't say I blame her, but honestly, if we were going to add another recruit to our little crew, I'd rather have someone a bit fitter and a bit less nerdy and annoying.

"All ok?" Lincoln says to her, taking the phone but not waiting for an answer. "And in answer to your question, Ben, we're not sure. And that makes it very bad. So please, get back in the fucking car already."

I get back in the fucking car and no-one speaks until we get to the airport. A man in a suit meets Lincoln and hands Alice what I guess is her luggage, judging by the shocked look on her face. I can't say I'd mind someone else packing for me, but I guess I'd be pretty pissed at them for going through my stuff.

Lincoln's on the phone most of the way through check-in and departures, tapping away at his laptop throughout. Alice asks me and Ben questions, but neither of us really know how to answer – we're in the middle of a busy airport. I know I'm a bit indiscrete sometimes, but this isn't really the place for this kind of conversation.

Thankfully, it's not all tense, awkward and weird. There's a Burger King right in the airport so at least I'm able to grab some decent food. I even pay for Ben, earning a hard look from Alice, but fuck her, we've just met. It takes a lot to earn that kind of respect from me. She eventually buys her own.

I fall asleep on the plane not long after we take off, although I wake up at one point, seeing a look of disgust on Ben's face. I sniff. Yeah, must have eaten the burger a bit quickly.

All this Bible detective shit is hungry work, I can't help it if that means a few farts here and there.

I put my head back down again and drift off.

The rising sun dazzles me into waking up as we're flying over London; looks like we're a bit east of the Millennium Dome or whatever it's called now. I rub my eyes and admire the view.

London might not be the best city in the world, but it's a decent-looking one. A flash catches my eye, then another, making me squint, looking west into town.

Shit.

A column of smoke rises in the distance and bile rises up my throat as adrenalin courses through me. I nudge Ben sharply, then there's a bigger explosion and the column turns into a cloud. I look around for Lincoln, my sleep-fuddled brain not quite comprehending what's going on – is this a terrorist attack?

I find him in the seat in front, already awake, dialling a number on his phone.

"Stay calm," he says. "All of you."

I sit back down in my seat as the plane banks away from London, but I can still see the smoke. There's an announcement over the speakers and a surge of panicked voices begin to rise. We're being diverted to Stanstead. My palms are sweating and I'm glued to the window.

I peer through it, trying to make out landmarks. I think … I think I can see the Royal Opera House down there and it's not far from the smoke.

Oh, fucking hell.

Ben is rubbing his eyes, asking what's happening. Alice is looking almost grey, having seen most of what's gone on over my shoulder.

There's been an attack, and although I'm trying to bullshit myself about it, I know what's been hit.

Lincoln turns around in his seat a moment later, facing the three of us. A hostess starts to make her way down the plane, looking annoyed at him. I lean in as he talks quickly and quietly.

"Wild Court has been hit by a major RPG attack. It happened just as the last of our psychics were arriving. The building's gone, along with most of our teams, who were arriving to be briefed. The defensive mechanisms kicked in and the base has shifted to its secondary location, but we're looking at a forty-eight-hour window until the bulk of our forces are back, minimum and we have no idea of the damage. It goes without saying that this is a very, very bad situation. We've been played, and worse still, the ripples from the deaths of the psychics have started to open the potential rift sites at hotspots we were tracking across London, spreading out from Wild Court."

"Rifts?" Ben says, looking like he's about to throw up. "Which rifts? How many are we talking about?"

"From what we can tell," Lincoln says. "All of them."

Chloe
Pregnancy

That morning, I wake feeling pregnant.

Not in the biological sense, of course; more a sense of impending fate. Doom. Purpose.

It'll be today, or near enough.

I must prepare.

My mind synthesises courses of action, likelihoods, paths to investigate. There are many unknowns.

Once I have risen, completed my ablutions and breakfasted, I summon my staff and followers together.

"Something terrible will happen very soon," I say to them, as silence falls. "I believe that it will centre on London, and that there is little to no chance of preventing it. I have awarded each of you an extra month's salary, effectively immediately. Until the danger is past, I would wholeheartedly recommend that you gather your families and leave London in a calm but swift fashion. Please, do not panic. There is little time, but there is some. Enough."

Hardly my most eloquent, but it suffices.

"What comes?" Sister Wilmington asks.

"I cannot tell," I say. "But the conjunction of events is almost certainly near-cataclysmic. If I am wrong, please return in one week. Until then, be in sparsely populated areas, arm yourselves and endure."

Half of my assembled followers leave the room immediately, while the true faithful remain.

"What will you do?" Brother Carvas asks.

"I must help the Gardeners," I say. "The travellers who graced our court earlier in the week will return, and I will meet them at the airport. I believe that our enemy will show his hand at this stage and although the cost will be dear, there is also a chance to divine his plans."

"How can we help?" he asks, and I mentally bless his heart.

"Brother Carvas," I say, and I must confess, my own calculations assumed his assistance. "While I must meet the Gardeners at the airport, we may need to travel swiftly thereafter. Could you take the helicopter and await near Stanstead airport? If truth be told, I'm not certain where things will take me after, so please do take the helicopter later on and find safety, should I forget to remind you."

He nods, and picks up his phone. I thank the assembled congregation and turn back to my rooms to pack. A small rucksack, enough to keep me supplied but mobile. I fill it with a change of clothes, a toothbrush and facecloth, a small laptop and a spare phone, physical cash in case of electronic failure, jewellery to trade, a small tranquiliser gun with ammunition. On top of that I place a physical map of London, in case the telecommunications infrastructure drops, imported MREs, a water bottle and purification tablets strong enough to make rainwater potable.

I pace around the house, feeling full of anticipation. Idly, I switch most of my local investments to gold and other conflict-resistant stock. I sweep my new headphones, remaining jewellery and favourite books into a large, fireproof safe set into the back of my bedroom before closing the shutters on the windows. I send a message to the staff in my country home telling them to lock everything down, and call the school that I sponsor, asking them if they can disperse the children safely before the end of the day.

I pause, taking a breath. My energy is not unlimited, so I make a light lunch and eat with Brother Carvas and Sister Wilmington. They seem anxious, but more concerned for my safety than their own. I request that Sister Wilmington contacts her friends at MI5 and MI6 with a number of recommendations, and to re-join them temporarily if they are willing to accept her.

The last of the other brothers and sisters pack up, closing doors and checking the emergency generators. I hug them all a fond farewell, hoping to see them alive and well once this has been completed.

I step outside, savouring the cool spring air, walking lightly down the street to Hyde Park Corner station, sitting on the Piccadilly line until Holborn, where I switch to the dreaded Central Line. It is busy, but with my understanding of the prior loading points of the train, station entrances and exits, and the time of day, I select the least busy carriage and secure a seat on each journey before alighting at Liverpool Street.

The crowd moves strangely at Liverpool Street station; I stand for a moment on the balcony and follow the ebb and flow of the human traffic, watching it rush, coil and flow like a stream. There is a degree of agitation in the air, above the usual levels for this location. It's as if the collective unconscious of humanity somehow knows that the end is coming.

I'd penned a brief missive to the Gardeners and the government on my way here, and it sends as my phone re-connects to the network. The Gardeners have their own psychics, and I know that they're aware of what's going on. Although sharing intelligence may lead to more work in the short-term, in the long-term, it's usually a worthwhile investment.

I slip through the crowd and purchase a ticket at the machine. There's stress and anxiety radiating from the traveller behind me, so I use a little-known glitch to add a small amount of credit to the next trip purchased.

The next train to Stanstead leaves in ten minutes, so I have some time to buy a snack and a drink, taking my time and enjoying the sensation of almost pirouetting through the crowds. There's a skill to moving through large numbers of people; that may sound odd, but I have frequently found it so.

As we pull into the station, I realise that I may be early. My phone rings as I'm deliberating between entering the airport and finding a café or hotel.

"Lincoln," I say, seeing the name on the display. "I hope you're safe."

"The angel's gone," he says quickly. "The psychics are being recalled. Your intelligence came at a good time. Got anything else for us?"

I flinch at the depth of his intensity. He's a good man, but fierce.

"It's coming," I say. "If your aim is to flee, then flee. But if you aim to help, return here as soon as you can."

"Flee?" he snorts. "You know me better than that. Do you have anything concrete?"

I shake my head. "No," I admit. "Only that it'll be here soon. Almost immediately. Everything points to it."

"Fine," he says. "Stay safe."

"When you return," I say. "I'll be here. To assist."

"Directly?" he says, at first sounding distant, as if he were about to hang up.

"Directly," I say. "Perhaps with you, perhaps with your new aides. There's a deeper game."

"Keep me informed," he says quickly. "I'll see you soon."

With that, he hangs up. I earnestly wish that I could add substance to my feelings, but other than suspicions, fear and patterns in the probability matrices, I have little to work with.

I turn, looking over to the Hilton hotel. That should do nicely.

The young gentleman behind the desk regards me neutrally until my details come up in his terminal. I remind myself to purge my electronic details in the next five years; it wouldn't do to have hoteliers asking questions because I don't look 35. Of course, the better hotel chains are famously discrete, but it only takes one member of staff. If they knew the truth about my real date of birth, there would be many, many more questions, and likely from government departments, although it's private pharma that I'm more concerned by.

"Ms Webster," he says. "Welcome back. Will you be staying with us long?"

I shake my head sadly. "Unfortunately, not," I say. "Just one night will suffice."

He taps away at his keyboard. "We have a suite available on the top floor if that would suit you?"

I nod, proffering my card.

"That won't be necessary," he says. "We have you on account."

I grin, making him blink and look confused, but he recovers his composure momentarily.

"Can I help you with anything else?" he offers.

I think for a moment, cocking my head to one side. Yes. Yes, he can.

"An ethernet cable with standard RJ45 adapters," I say. "An additional monitor for the evening, twenty-four inches will suffice. Steak frites and a glass of Malbec served at seven fifteen pm. A bowl of sweet popcorn at nine and a selection of croissants for tomorrow."

He stares for a moment. "Sure," he says, scribbling notes. "Of course, Ms Webster. We'll send those up."

"Thank you," I say, offering a smile. "That's very kind of you."

"No problem," he says, pushing the keycard across the counter at me as if it were poisonous. This does happen sometimes, so I push it from my mind and simply head up to my suite where I watch the planes taking off until the monitor and cables arrive, connecting everything together and accessing my monitoring suite through a highly customised VPN.

I lose myself in patterns for the next two hours, staring at security data, shared intelligence reports, paranormal data, terrorist data, threats from nations – rogue and otherwise – checking and rechecking, trying to feed my abnormal brain with information until it bursts.

Other than potential incursions from the east, I find nothing. Traces here and there point the way to Jackson, but there's precious little that's conclusive. I know in my heart that it's him. He likely knows that as soon as he shows his hand, the combined weight of the UK's armed forces – traditional and otherwise – will be upon him, so it's certain that he'll have a robust plan.

What would I do in his place?

I would strike, firmly and decisively, forcing my enemy to fight another, weakening them sufficiently to accomplish what I needed to do. Then I'd become untraceable.

Untraceable.

Of course.

I call Brother Carvas.

"Brother Carvas," I say. "Are you well?"

"I am, thank you," he says, after a short delay. "Did you arrive safely?"

"Yes, thank you also. Have you arrived?"

"I'm not far from the airport," he says. "In a field. I'll send you GPS co-ordinates."

"We may need to be here the night," I say. "I'll arrange accommodation for you, but be ready. Can you tell me, is there a heliport near the Gardener training facility in Bracknell?"

"Not as such," he says. "But there are plenty of car parks. I'm sure we can find somewhere."

"Excellent."

If I needed a place to flee, somewhere truly untraceable, then I'd flee to another realm, where surveillance was impossible, and there was a safe and well-established area to hide in. The portal in Karnak would easily satisfy such a requirement. Of course, it tells me little of his endgame, but it feels like progress. It is something of a gamble; in theory, he could vanish through any rift at all, and the one in the Gardener building is well-guarded, but it is also safe and familiar. My intuition tugs me towards it.

I arrange a room for Brother Carvas and receive a message from Lincoln informing me of their flight plans. I tell him of my suspicions and pass the details onto Carvas and Gardener HQ as well. I'm watching a plane take off when a knock at my door announces dinner. I eat, then find a suitably relaxing film to watch from my bed. The popcorn and croissants arrive exactly halfway through, precisely to my liking, and I doze off as the credits roll.

Eight hours later, I wake sharply, sitting bolt upright in bed, the hairs on the back of my neck standing up.

It's now.

The adrenalin melts the sleep from my body and I dial Carvas, waking him and telling him to be ready. I shower, dress and eat hurriedly, gathering my bag and rushing from the hotel towards arrivals.

I've just entered the terminal when I feel the first missile strike. I'm not Gardener-trained, but I feel the noosphere itself bend and then fracture as waves of pain and terror flow through me, making me physically stagger. Alec Guinness said it best when he talked about millions of voices crying out; it's a silent scream, felt by every fibre in my body.

I turn to my phone and see the reports come in, Gardener notifications arriving a moment later.

"All assets. Catastrophic event at Gardener HQ. Majority of First Extraordinary now unavailable after contingency measures engaged. We have Shambler presence in Covent Garden Piazza. Ravager sighted on Kingsway, suspected rift. Local police and anti-terror squads are deployed but arcane backup needed urgently. All assets, retired or active, check in on this frequency."

I usually refrain from profanity, but on this occasion, I make an exception, running through my armoury of English, French, German, Spanish, Italian and Latin swearwords, startling several nearby tourists.

Perhaps the most agonising part is that I have to wait. I check in with the secondary dispatcher, offering the location of a weapons cache that has sufficient armour-piercing rounds to dispatch a Ravager, and inform them of my intentions. They're grateful for the former and confused by the latter, although promise to pass it back to whoever is co-ordinating efforts.

Thankfully, Lincoln walks into arrivals a few moments later, talking urgently into a microphone attached to an earpiece. Ben and his friend Matt – I've studied their files – are with him, and at first, I think that's it, but then I see another girl with them. She looks faintly familiar, but I'm certain we've not met.

Lincoln nods to me and I fall in step with him, receiving perplexed looks from Ben and Matt.

"Who the fuck are you?" Matt says. He looks tired.

"Matt," Ben says. "She's the one I told you about. The Spider?"

I certainly like Ben more than the other.

We arrive outside as the address system announces

that all inbound flights will be redirected. All outbound flights will continue for as long as they can and I assume the government has told the airlines to move people as far away as possible.

Two black cars draw up in front of us and Lincoln turns to face us.

"If this were a normal attack," he says, wincing slightly. "You'd all come back with me and run containment, but given my suspicions, and those of the Spider here, we've got new priorities. Ben, you and Alice need to follow up on the asset. I won't bullshit you: it's an outside chance and there is every likelihood that you'll be disintegrated on sight, but if you can recruit it, it can help us. Without Wild Court, we're in serious trouble. Let me make one call and we'll see how near we can get you to Svalbard."

The new girl, Alice, shakes her head.

"I can call Hugo," she says shakily. "He offered me his jet a few days ago."

"Good," Lincoln says, turning to me. "Take the car. Quick as you can."

"You get a jet?" Matt says, looking at Ben in awe. "Fucking-A, man. What do I get?"

"Chloe, I want you to take Matt and see if your suspicions play out," Lincoln says over him. "If he's there, find out what he's up to. But recon *only*, you understand me? He's too dangerous to tackle and I mean that."

"What?" the lout says. "Chloe? Look, who even is she?"

I ignore him for a moment, then realise something.

"Please, don't worry," I offer, attempting to make peace. "We'll be taking a helicopter."

"Boo-ya!" he says, sticking his tongue out at Ben. "I get the chopper … get down!"

Ben rolls his eyes. It looks like a well-practiced routine and in honesty, I rather dread this trip, even if it is for the good of the world, and with supernatural protection – albeit of the amateur variety.

"Stay in touch," Lincoln says, opening the door to the car. "Don't engage without consulting me or HQ. Stay safe. I'm going back to London."

Matt makes to get into the other car, but I hold out a hand to stop him. "It's not far."

He looks at me in surprise, then turns back to look at Ben.

"Alright brother," he says, seemingly serious for the first time, and his energy changes. He has a sentimental side, perhaps. "Don't get dead, ok?"

They embrace, and Ben looks at me, pale.

"Good luck," he says, climbing into the car.

The other girl – Alice – climbs into the car without a word, and they pull away.

"Come on," I say. "We should hurry."

Hoping that the moment of solemnity, or at least, silence, lasts for a while, I lead him over towards the field where the helicopter waits for us.

Ben
The Apocalypse Mansion

I think I'm going to throw up.

I'm not great with travel sickness at the best of times. It's worse when I'm stressed, and it turns out that there's nothing more stressful than travelling with a secret organisation for five hours, only to miss the thing that you're there for by a day, before travelling back pretty much the same day to arrive in London during a paranormal terrorist attack.

I don't want to think about it too much. The thought of rifts opening across London, and those things coming out actually makes me gag with dread. They'd been terrifying in the Abditory, and that was under controlled conditions with an experienced person with us. The thought of more spilling out and no Gardeners, the thought of having to handle them myself, on my own without Lincoln or even Matt around doesn't bear thinking about.

And the idea that someone did this *on purpose*? Lincoln won't say anything about them, but it's clear he knows who they are, and given that a lot of the Middle East conflict was a cover-up, it's almost certainly not your conventional terrorist group. What could they possibly gain from all of this? I guess no-one knows, and that's why Matt and Chloe are doing what they're doing.

My breath is coming in short, shallow gasps. I try to pause and get a grip on myself.

And Wild Court is gone, albeit temporarily, from what Lincoln says, although that's also stretching the limits of my imagination. From what little he said, the inner core of the building could simply teleport – there's no other word for it – riding the flows of the noosphere from one 'anchored' place to another in case of absolute emergency, which defies sense, even in the face of what I've seen and heard. Or maybe it doesn't. It's risky, but something that Raphael had apparently insisted on for a time like this. I'm incredulous. And nauseous.

I wind the window down and take deeper breaths. Alice, the investigator, whatever she is, glares at me. I've not really spoken to her much, and maybe I should try, but it's the last thing I want to do right now.

"You should probably tell me more about your organisation," she says, forcing the issue. "If we're going to stand a good chance of success, we should pool intelligence."

I swallow, wishing that the car would use larger roads and that I could sit in the front seat. Maybe conversation will distract me.

"It's part of the military," I say, trying to marshal my thoughts. "It's called the First Extraordinary Battalion, but most people call it the Gardeners, sort of after its founder Pierre de Chardin . Like, a corruption of his name . He was a priest."

If I'd fumbled the start of a story this badly with Matt, he'd have made at least five jokes at my expense by now, but Alice just sits there, taking it all in. Heartened that she's not going to tear me a new one, I keep going, and eventually make some semblance of sense.

I think.

"All this time," she says, once I've finished. "Hugo was funding this too."

"Hugo?" I say, emboldened but still nauseous.

"Baron Hugo Delauncey-Morrison," she says. "A rich English eccentric. Although, knowing what we know now, perhaps not so eccentric. He funded my education and his family has been funding your organisation for some time. I don't know how his family knows – knew – what they know, but his house is equipped for this exact situation. It's a fortress."

"And he has a plane?"

"Yes, a small jet," she says. "And his house has a runway. I hope we can convince him that we need it. He's a bit of a coward sometimes."

"A coward?" I say, taken aback.

"Yes," she says curtly, with no further explanation, then launching into an overview of her own background.

She's an archaeologist, apparently, but it sounds like she's more of a paranormal investigator. The kind of obsessive I would have immediately discounted in the past if she hadn't been quite so bang on the money.

A moment later, we draw up outside a set of impressive-looking iron gates topped with barbed wire, a large driveway behind them. Alice dials a number on her phone and a camera swivels to look at us from the top of the fence. She speaks quietly into her phone and for a moment I think that we're going to have to turn back and drive away. A part of me really wants that to happen.

Instead, the gates swing open, barely enough to let us through, closing quickly behind us.

'House' doesn't quite cover it.

It's a mansion, if Baba Yaga had featured on Grand Designs in the early noughties instead of being a Slavic witch in medieval times or whatever. The whole thing's on chunky industrial stilts, like you'd expect in a marsh or something, but it all looks pretty dry out here. It's huge, and aside from the vast stilts, it's basically your bog-standard English mansion, all tastefully pale brickwork with long chimneys and elegant balconies.

Well, except that most of the windows are protected by metal shutters, and I can see two guys taking furniture off the balconies and putting it inside the house before more shutters close over the doors.

The car pulls up alongside one of the larger stilts, and Alice hops out as a guy in a suit – I guess this is

Hugo – emerges from a door somewhere. He's got mousy brown hair, slicked back with product, soft features, shifty, nervous-looking eyes and is wearing a red and blue tie that screams public school. I know my own prejudices are coming over, but I'm suddenly glad that Matt's not here – he'd be ten times worse.

I open my door and step out. Hugo looks like he's just thrown up.

"Hugo Delauncey-Morrison," he says, holding his hand out.

"Ben," I say, shaking it. It's a firm shake but a damp one.

"It's here, then?" he says, looking at me. I nod, swallowing and summoning all my available gravitas. It's not much.

"It seems to be spreading outwards from Covent Garden," I say, slightly amazed at my own coherence. "We're not sure how far it'll get. We'd previously been looking into an asset overseas, and got back just as it happened."

Hugo wipes sweat from his forehead nervously. "Alright, quickly then," he says. "Before it gets here, if that's possible. Where are we going?"

He gets even paler when Alice tells him, and ushers us over towards the stilt, which has a lift built into it, tapping at his phone as he presses the button to make us ascend.

"It's about four hours flight time," he says, talking quickly. "If we can get permission to land at Longyearbyen.

One of my relatives raves about it, and the Radisson Blu there is actually half-decent. We might be able to hire a helicopter to take us to Nordaustlandet, but I hope you've got an idea of where we'll need to go after that – from memory, it's about half the size of Wales."

I flinch. All of this is completely theoretical at best. I hope Alice knows.

Still, we'll be better off there than in London during the apocalypse.

A surge of shame washes over me as the thought enters my head; coward, I think. Matt and Lincoln are charging into the front line and you're running away to a snowy wilderness overseas.

Alice nods. "I'll need your maps," she says crisply. "Good ones. And equipment."

"Of course," Hugo says, seemingly mollified by our pretence of organisation. "I'll make ready the equipment with … my apologies, what was your name again?"

"Ben," I repeat.

The lift doors open, and I don't quite know what to make of it all. At first glance, it seems to be a very traditional, wood-panelled mansion corridor, with portraits set at intervals, occasional dressers topped with urns, that kind of thing. It's also heaving with people. They all look terrified, and they're clutching rucksacks, tins of food, framed pictures, stuffed animals. Alice and I both look at Hugo expectantly.

"What would you have had me do?" he says, helplessly.

"When the news broke, I telephoned the local radio station to offer sanctuary to anyone who couldn't get to a safe place. It seemed like the decent thing to do."

Neither of us say anything, and Hugo doesn't seem to be expecting it, instead leading the way down the corridor, clapping various people on the shoulder and answering a few panicked questions – mostly about where the bathrooms are, how to use the internet, and whether he's heard any more news.

He hasn't heard any more news.

I glance at my phone. There's nothing from Lincoln, and only a brief message from Matt with a picture of the view from the helicopter.

"Sir," a guy about my age says as we turn into a large room full of cupboards. He looks pale, and his hand trembles as he reaches out to Hugo. "Sir, are we safe here?"

Hugo turns to face him. "We're as safe as we can be," he offers. "Now please, sit tight, keep an eye on the news, and stay calm."

It sounds like something he's said a lot, but the guy seems to take it, nodding wanly and heading back out into the corridor.

"Ok," Hugo says, closing the door behind him and looking at the various cupboards and drawers. "Arctic gear, arctic gear – yes, here we are."

He pulls out three large rucksacks, all bright orange, then sizes me up for a moment. "We're about the same build," he says. "That's fortunate."

He pauses, taking a moment to check a label on the top of the rucksack and nods. "All in date," he says. "Very good. Ben, could you take these back down the way we came? If people see me hauling rucksacks around, they might panic a little. I'll speak to them directly and be down in a moment. You can see the runway from the other side of the house."

Awkwardly, I pull on one of the packs. It's heavy, but not as back-crushingly bad as I'd imagined, so I start drag-lifting the other two down the corridor, apologising to people as I retrace our steps back to the lift. I have to pause halfway to catch my breath, but also because I'm challenged by an old guy who wants to know where I'm taking the bags. I thank my lucky stars that Lincoln actually got us proper, formal-looking government ID, and flash it at him. That makes him shut up, but I'm a bit shaken by the encounter. Strangely, having to focus on dragging these bloody bags to the lift helps me to take my mind off it.

As usual – but probably completely illogically – I feel better once I'm outside on ground level. I swivel around, trying to see where Hugo might keep his jet, and eventually spot a large hanger through the strut-like feet of the mansion, enlisting our driver's help in carrying the bags. Dave – the driver – very sensibly suggests driving over, and I hop back in the car after stowing the bags in the boot.

It's a little bit of a way to the hanger, and I'm not quite

sure what to do next – is it ok to load bags into someone else's aeroplane without asking? I've never met anyone with their own plane before.

The doors to the hanger are slightly ajar, and without collecting the bags, I slip out of the car and peer inside. It's faintly illuminated with green emergency lighting, and I can see a snub-nosed plane in there. It looks a bit smaller than one I flew to Edinburgh in for a holiday last year, which had about sixty seats. I tend to count things when I'm nervous; it gives me a sense of control, however ridiculous that sounds.

I doubt that this plane has sixty seats. From what I've seen in films, planes like this have about four seats and people who serve you steak and champagne. There's a set of stairs leading inside, so I decide to just bite the bullet and drag the bags up there now.

"Forget something, did you?" Dave says from behind me, making me jump about a foot in the air. I spin around and hold my hand to my heart for a moment.

"Shit!" I yelp. "Sorry."

Once I've recovered, Dave grinning slightly sheepishly, I shoulder one of the bags and take the other out of guilt as we head across the tarmac to the plane. The hanger smells damp, and the steps are steep and slightly slippery, but we make it up ok.

"Damn," I whisper as I step inside. It's amazing how much of a difference it makes to a plane when you take all but eight seats out. It feels almost spacious. There's a set of four seats essentially facing each other – for meetings, I assume, and the others are set facing away from each other. Large, standalone TVs draped with expensive-looking headphones sit in front of each of the more private seats, and cupboards – no overhead lockers in sight anywhere – are set around the plane. I assume some of them must be for luggage, although one of them definitely looks like a drinks cabinet. Everything is upholstered in a tasteful beige.

"How the other half lives, eh?" Dave says, as he steps up behind me, dumping his bag on the floor. I follow suit a moment later.

"Yeah," I breathe.

"That said," he says, glancing around. "You be careful of this one, Ben. He's generous with his money, but when it comes to Gardener business, he's nothing but skittish."

"Skittish?"

"Skittish."

"Look," I say, taking a breath. "I'm sure if you want, you can ride this out in his house, you know. Stay safe?"

Dave shakes his head. He's a short, burly man, and I imagine him as more of a bouncer than a driver. "Not a chance," he says. "I'm a Gardener through and through. Can't do the staves, but I sure as hell ain't cowering up here while other folk suffer."

"Course, course," I say, holding my hands up. "Didn't mean anything by it."

He grins. "Don't you worry," he says. "Your heart's in

the right place, and I figure you've got a few things on your mind right now."

He's not wrong about that.

I turn to leave the plane, taking care not to slip on the steps on my way down. So, we're going to track an angel. I should learn more about how Alice found this thing, and if Hugo knows anything about it. I wonder if my e-reader has any information on it; I'd completely forgotten to check. I lean against the car and pull it out of my other bag, running a general search for angels.

Surprisingly, it has a couple of entries, although none of them are particularly useful. They largely confirm that there is – or rather, was – an angel in Jerusalem, that it was monitored by a cult, and that its capabilities are largely unknown, on account of the fact that it doesn't seem to have moved an inch for thousands of years. It is listed as corporeal, which makes sense given the small trail of devastation it wreaked on its departure, but which isn't tremendously helpful to me as a wielder of magics for the non-corporeal.

I guess we're winging it, then.

I find myself sniggering hysterically at that as Alice, Hugo and another woman trot across the tarmac, trying to control myself as Dave looks at me askance.

"If you'll not be needing me anymore?" he says, spotting the trio approaching us.

I shake my head and take another breath. "No, no, thank you," I say. "Look – good luck, ok?"

"Cheers," he says. "You too."

And with that, he hops into the car and slowly drives off towards the gate. My phone rings, the screen showing an unknown number. I take a chance and answer it.

"Ben?" a voice says. "Sarah Rujzeda, Gardener Analyst. I believe we were in Amelia Taylor's briefing together a week ago."

God. I cast my mind back to the briefing in Wild Court. Despite the horrific subject matter, the memory has a safe, cushioned feeling to it.

"Uh, hi," I say. "What's up?"

"I'm running control from the temporary base at the Greenwich Observatory and understand that you're on your way to Svalbard to find the angelic asset."

"That's … that's right," I say haltingly.

"As you might have discovered, we don't have a lot of intelligence on it, and the woman that you're travelling with may well be your best source of information. However, there are two things that you should bear in mind: one, proceed with extreme caution. If the forensics are to be believed, then it is capable of not only sudden fits of rage, but also the ability to disintegrate people leaving only a minimal amount of particulate residue. Secondly, that it will almost certainly leave a mark in the noosphere, so if you are unable to locate it with your eyes, trust your other senses, ok?"

"Alright," I say. "Got it. What else? Is Wild Court gone? Have more rifts opened?"

"The rifts are still opening across the country, but whatever caused it seems to be getting weaker. According to recent sigint, we've had reports of Shamblers as far north as Harlow, but nothing further yet – so you should be safe for another hour. That said, don't delay if you can help it. They're fewer in number than in central London, but it only takes one. Don't be a hero, Ben – be careful. You know how we operate."

"Thanks," I say. "Anything else?"

"Wrap up warm?"

I roll my eyes and almost laugh. It's like Matt was still here.

"Look, seriously," she continues before I can respond. "And I don't know if this makes you feel any better, but if the rifts weren't opening, there's no chance you'd be given this assignment with your level of experience. Do what you can, but if you can't, it's more important to come back in one piece. You can assist us on the ground, but Lincoln thinks you can make a difference, so you've got all of us rooting for you."

All of us that are left, I hear.

"Appreciate that, Sarah," I say. "Over and out."

"Go get 'em."

Alice looks at me quizzically as I finish my phone conversation.

"Bags are in the plane," I say. "Everything ready?"

Hugo nods, leading the way up to the jet. "Lizzie's our pilot," he says, gesturing at the woman beside him. "I can take over if needs be. We're fully fuelled and permissions have been fast-tracked. That's thanks to your people, I believe. Might as well make ourselves comfortable."

I sit in one of the 'social' seats, much as I'd like to just gather my thoughts in private. As I sit, I notice that there does seem to be a mini-bar between the seat and the window, filled with cold drinks and snacks, all held very securely.

"There's a few pre-flight checks to carry out. Do we have much time?" Hugo asks, a sheen of sweat visible on his brow.

"We should be ok for up to an hour," I say with more gravitas than I'm feeling. "Alice, could you debrief us again? Was there anything you missed the first time?"

Hugo gives me a strange look as Alice fastens her seatbelt and reaches for a bottle of water, taking a drink and leaning forwards.

She starts to recount a few more details in her long and complicated story about what she seemed to think was an artefact in the Bible, but turned out to be an angel, a record of which was kept in a mosaic somewhere in Hertfordshire. It should sound like a Dan Brown book, but she actually makes it sound pretty dull.

I ask the question I've been wanting to ask her for a while, something that always bothers me about quests in fantasy books. "So, what were you planning on doing when you found it?"

She looks at me seriously. "The discovery would have

changed everything," she says. "It would have conclusively proved at least one major world religion."

"Right," I say, scathingly. "Well, once we've enlisted its help in flushing out the ghosts and demons from zone one, you've got official dibs on the first set of joint press interviews, as long as Raysiel doesn't mind, of course."

She frowns. "It's not about *press* interviews," she says, and I guiltily flinch at the rebuke. "Think of the value to theologians, academia. The world."

"Is … well, do you think it's dangerous?" Hugo interjects, as the plane starts to taxi along the runway.

Alice repeats some story about an army defeating a much more powerful army, which I'm grateful for, because I was about to tell him about the guy who got disintegrated, and Hugo might already have lost his breakfast, if not his lunch.

Thinking of that, I root around in the minibar and find a large pack of ready salted crisps, chomping through them to try and alleviate any forthcoming travel sickness. Knowing what little I know about this plane, it's probably got its own drugs cabinet, recreational or otherwise, but I don't really want to be drowsy right now.

The plane ascends, and I watch the ground recede beneath us, temporarily dazzled by the midday sun, but I don't look away. We pass through the cloud layer, the plane vibrating as we do, and then we're safely above it, in that quiet, calm place away from the normal world where everything is somehow muted. It's a temporary limbo, and I know that after another shorter, probably more uncomfortable journey, we'll be trekking into the sub-zero wilderness to try and find our angelic reinforcements.

I pick up my e-reader again, flicking through it for staves to affect corporeal creatures. There's got to be something here.

I focus, trying to find something, anything, barely noticing as we leave England – and the apocalypse – behind.

Lincoln
Shit Creek

There's a Ravager in the John Lewis food hall on Oxford Street, gorging itself on charcuterie and tourists. The Gardeners have only ever tracked one Ravager at a time within a twenty-mile radius, because we suspect that they're apex predators and sparsely distributed in their own world, but right now, I'm aware of six in zone one alone.

There's a flock of fifteen Whistlers spread across Canary Wharf, creatures that make Pteranodons looks like coal tits. They're barely birds – most of their body is made of a strong but lightweight cartilage, their jaws lined with strong teeth made for tearing. Each one has a wingspan as big as a minibus, gaps in the cartilage making an eerie whistling noise when they dive.

These are the least of my worries. These are the current corporeal enemies.

I've had unconfirmed reports of twenty lesser and one Greater Banshee so far, but our main issue is approximately a hundred Shamblers distributed around the Greater London area. I've had sightings from Holland Park to Shadwell and we don't have anything like the manpower to disperse them, let alone close the rifts. My concern is that we're just at the tip of the iceberg where actual, confirmed numbers of creatures are concerned.

People are dying.

More rifts are being found, and more are opening.

The police and armed forces are working on the Ravagers and Whistlers, and we've already got drone support, but at present there are only twenty stave-capable, trained Gardener field agents available in London. We lost our four most powerful psychics and their escort to an RPG attack that also triggered Wild Court's emergency relocation protocol. I don't know if Jackson knew about the deep, old magic, but the lockdown and survival protocols mean that it'll be at least forty-eight hours before we get backup. Raphael cares deeply about the world, but he knew that somewhere down the line, the Gardeners might need to hide and not come out until it was safe.

Of course, in this specific instance, it means that the rest of us are pretty fucked.

That said, at least we've got support, but I'm not far from commandeering the stave-capable administration staff into the field.

As a retired field operative, I'm near the top of the chain of command, along with my old team. We've never dealt with anything on this scale, but my military training is partitioning it, telling me to take it a step at a time, to either look at the big picture and work up strategy, or compartmentalise and deal with the immediate operation. I'm used to dealing with these threats, but the public is seeing them for the first time.

There's little time for press, but we had the information ready.

We didn't expect to need it all at once.

The non-corporeals are horrific. Shamblers are slow, and they don't handle elevation well, so there are non-stop broadcasts on TV, radio, social media, all telling people to get to their upper floors or high ground with cover so that they're not exposed to the Whistlers, but it's not that easy. There's people in hospitals, schools to be evacuated, care homes and absolute panic on the roads.

With good reason.

According to eyewitness reports, the explosion at Wild Court opened three separate rifts, the Shamblers drifting through lazily. Most people were running away from the area after the RPGs hit, and the non-corporeals arrived just as people were running south, down Kingsway, from Holborn station. The first wave of people edged around the Shamblers cautiously, but the people behind them backed up and pushed.

I'm told it was an elderly man who fell first.

We're still not sure exactly how Shamblers work. On one level, they seem vampiric, but it's more likely – I'm told – that they're essentially on another plane of existence, like biological antimatter. When they come into contact with a small creature, it might simply explode, but a fully-grown human will bleed, very rapidly, from everywhere at once.

There are more coming through on an hourly basis, and military analytics tell us that more rifts are opening, like a series of ripples spreading outwards from Covent Garden.

The car I'm in slows. We've come further than I thought we'd get but it had to stop somewhere. There was almost zero chance that we'd reach the new forward base at the Greenwich Observatory, where trees are being felled and imbued with staves while sniper stations are being set up on the roof so that we can operate safely.

"Sir," the driver says, as people begin to run up the road in the other direction. We're about half a mile north of the Blackwall Tunnel.

"Is there a gun in the car?" I ask, and he nods, looking nervous. It's a Gardener car, but not everyone in the First Extraordinary is a field agent, obviously. He takes a key from his pocket and hands it to me with trembling hands, popping the boot open a moment later. I scan the area and slip out of the car, checking around me before pushing the boot fully open and finding the large case with the rifle in it. I load it, slipping the spare magazines into my jacket pocket and leaving my bag next to the empty gun case.

Two women run past me screaming, one of them pausing to throw up on the side of the road. I move to the front of the car and clamber up on the bonnet, my bones complaining. This isn't as easy as it used to be.

There are three Shamblers up ahead and at least four cars with sizeable blood splatters on their windows.

I reject the idea of hopping from car to car; unless they're actually bumper-to-bumper, it doesn't work like it does in the movies. I vault down, slipping the gun over my shoulder and hurry between the cars, dodging men and women as they run past me in the other direction.

"Leave your cars," I shout. "Go north away from the city. Leave your cars!"

A few people obey me. More stay in their cars, and the traffic's not going anywhere.

I glance around again, checking the area. Nothing yet. I can't sense the rift.

The three ghosts drift lazily through another – mercifully empty – car. They're shrunken, wizened creatures, their stubby, claw-like hands always reaching forwards. They really do look like they're wearing raincoats with the hoods drawn up, only they're more or less translucent, so you can never quite see them properly. Even the blood goes straight through them. They can drift through walls, but are seemingly stopped by more than a few feet of matter, although we don't understand why.

Think, Lincoln. What are we working with here? I glance around, seeing Balfron Tower and an impressive array of graffiti on the walls.

Excellent.

It's chaos out here, and the streets are emptying, but there are still far too many civilians in cars. I shout at them to leave, and a few more obey, but it's too slow. I'm not used to working alone. I can hear someone weeping, the sound of distant retching and screaming. Nothing good.

I position myself between Balfron Tower and the Shamblers, then carefully approach the Shamblers.

My first stave immobilises the nearest one, my next dispersing it. It's not best practice. You should immobilise all enemies before attempting to neutralise, largely because dispersal is a more intensive stave, but I've been doing this for a while.

The other two ghosts shiver and buzz slightly, then change direction, accelerating towards me. I back up, trying to keep my distance. My next stave somehow misses, the silver of my tattoos warming with the quickfire channelling of the noosphere. I take a breath and focus, immobilising the next one, but as I take a step backwards, my foot catches on the raised kerb and I trip, losing my footing. I fall heavily onto the concrete, hurriedly trying to twist and push myself up.

The last Shambler glides towards me steadily and I finally get to see its face, a perversion of an elderly human, slitted eyes, drawn cheeks and translucent fangs; fuck knows what they hunt back on their home planet, or if they even eat.

A few feet behind me there's a dirty brick wall covered in East London graffiti. I reach for the noosphere and channel it through the wall, holding the simple – and more importantly, easy – emergency activation pattern in my mind as I let the energy go. It activates when the ghost is a mere metre from me, my arteries starting to tingle with the proximity. There's a *whoosh* as the staves embedded in the graffiti activate, and the Shambler freezes, immobilised.

If I was a real action hero instead of a tired retiree feeling his age, I'm sure I'd sag back for a moment or run off a witty rejoinder, but I can't spare the time. People are dying and I can stop it. Wincing as I push myself up, I hurriedly pick the gravel and London crap out of my hands and disperse both Shamblers, thanking my lucky stars for Raphael's paranoia. The graffiti had been another of his ideas, a spray paint based on something organic laced with silver, allowing us to set long-lasting staves into tags – the perfect magical defence for the urban environment. He'd suggested it when the empathy levels in town dropped precipitously a decade ago, and we've been preparing ever since, employing a host of urban artists to help.

"Three Shamblers dispersed by Balfron Tower," I say into my mic. "Looking for the rift."

"Roger that, Lincoln," a clear voice says a moment later. "Be aware, Lesser Banshee sighted at New Providence Wharf. Local police are attempting to confirm location."

"Understood," I reply. "Will close rift and liaise. Out."

"Safe hunting."

I walk down the street to a bus stop and sit down in

the shelter, stretching out with my senses, trying to feel the rushing of the energy field around me.

There.

I can feel a rip, not far away, the energy speeding past it like a rock in a stream, or cars around a roundabout. I lock it in my mind and open my eyes, getting up and walking towards All Saints DLR station, trying to remember which of the roads in the estate connect with the main route heading west.

This neighbourhood isn't far from Canary Wharf, where the bankers live. The inevitable gentrification and rising prices has started to push out people who have lived here for decades. It's no wonder there's tension and anger, not to mention respiratory issues because of all the fumes from the Blackwall Tunnel approach.

Then I see it, a splinter of reality from another world, bleeding through into ours. I peer at it for a moment, just as another Shambler comes through, but I go straight for a dispersal stave and – feeling slightly dizzy from the energy expenditure – take a grim satisfaction in how quickly it flies apart into nothingness.

I need to pace myself. I'm not as young as I used to be, and all this gallivanting around with the next generation of Gardeners isn't easy.

Next-but-one, more likely.

I'd like to pause, take a breath, but there's no time. I reach out, feeling the tear in the fabric of the universe and slowly redirect the noosphere to the edges, pushing it back together like I'm zipping up a fraying old jacket. It starts to take, and I direct the energy upwards, seeing incrementally more and more of the normal world replacing the bleak wilderness visible through the crack.

It's slow going.

Five agonising minutes later, the last part vanishes and I feel the local noosphere return to normal, energy flowing as it should. I lean back against a wall as an old guy comes out of one of the houses and – looking at the space where the rift used to be – tentatively offers me a bottle of water.

"You are blessed," he says. "Thank you."

I take the water, unscrewing the top and taking a long drink.

"I'm retired," I say. "But thanks."

He grins a toothy smile and has the audacity to pat me on the arm before turning away. "Not so retired, I think."

I roll my eyes. Why do some civilians scream and run in a crisis and others turn into Yoda?

"Hey," I say, making him turn. "It's safer upstairs if you've got the space."

He gives me a nod and his front door closes a moment later.

"Local rift on Ida Street closed," I report into my mic, glancing at a street sign. "What's next?"

"Lesser Banshee has moved to Robin Hood Gardens, south of Woolmore school. Local police are on scene and can provide medical assistance if needed."

"I'm fine," I mutter. "On my way."

"Understood."

I hurry along the street, looking around and recalling the last time I'd been with a team taking down a Banshee. Thankfully, there's a pharmacy just on the other side of the road; this might seem like a non-sequitur, but trust me for a moment. I pop in and quickly locate the earplugs. There's no-one behind the counter, so I leave a five-pound note tucked into the till and take a couple of packs, just in case the local police haven't been briefed.

They'd better be well-armed. Banshees are semi-corporeal, and the big ones phase in and out of reality. Lesser Banshees are about seven feet high, drift about thirty centimetres above the pavement and from a distance, look like your stereotypical slender, sheeted ghosts with scary masks for faces. Unfortunately, that's not all they are.

On closer inspection – and I know, because I've inspected them closely – it's not entirely clear whether the 'sheets' are part of them or not, but we think so, mainly because they're made of some kind of organic material. Their bodies are densely-packed fibres of what look like twigs and metallic rods, their hands ending in sharp, scissor-like claws. They don't have feet. Their faces are smooth and white, like fine kaolin, but they have three rows of needle-like teeth in their mouths, and they have slitted eyes, like cats. They don't – for reasons that may soon be apparent – have any ears, and our scientists don't yet understand how or even if they hear, or how they float above the ground like miniature hovercrafts.

Lesser Banshees would be terrifying enough on their own, but as you might expect from the name, they wail. Or, as our scientists have repeatedly told me, they emit a near-ultrasonic alternating pulse that is almost more than our brains can cope with. Long story short: if you're exposed to a Banshee wail, you'll do anything to make it stop. Holding your hands over your ears isn't enough, and good earplugs aren't always enough either. I've seen people try to puncture their own eardrums and shoot wildly at everything around them to end the noise.

Our history with these creatures is short, brutal and deeply, deeply unpleasant.

I distantly hear the wail for the first time when I'm almost at the school, and fit an earplug where I don't have an earpiece. It deadens the sounds around me instantly, and I have to remind myself to check the roads twice before crossing, although the traffic has dropped to almost nothing. Hopefully everyone is holed up safely or has got the hell out of Dodge.

There are blue flashing lights bouncing off a window nearby, so I circle around the building until I find the police car. It's not looking good. There's a policeman lying across the back seat of the patrol car, bleeding. I open the door and he moans, then looks up at me as a rank smell assails my nostrils – he's pissed himself and is definitely bleeding from a wound to his arm.

"Lincoln James, First Extraordinary Battalion," I say

loudly, flashing my ID at him. I'm not quite sure if he registers it or not, and his eyes look a bit hazy.

Taking a deep breath, I find my multi-tool and cut through his jacket, finding a first aid kit on the shelf and cleaning his wound. Hurriedly tucking the earplugs in his ears, I fold what's left of his jacket underneath his head and try to make him as comfortable as possible.

"Keep pressure on it," I say loudly before leaving, hurrying around into the park, seeing two more police officers as I near the entrance.

"Officers," I call, making them both spin and point their pistols at me briefly, before seeing that I look like a civilian. I hold up my badge and repeat my credentials, which makes them frown.

"Spook squad," I offer tiredly, and they exchange glances.

"Didn't think you were real," one of them says shakily.

"Didn't think these were, either?" I ask, offering the earplugs, which they take gratefully, extracting wads of tissue from their own ears before putting the plugs in. I hear another screech from deeper inside the park, making me wince.

"Any civilians?" I say loudly, and they both shake their heads. "Alright, these things can move quickly, so here's how we work. We go together, one of you on each side of me. I'll do magic that will hold it in place, but we'll only have about fifteen seconds because it's not fully incorporeal. Don't waste your bullets until it's frozen.

Have either of you shot one of these before?"

I gesture to the rifle on my back, and one of them nods. I carefully remove it and hand it to him; surprisingly, he offers me his pistol, which I take and check. He checks the safety and the magazine on the rifle, so I think it's in good hands.

"It'll scream, and it'll fly towards us, but you've got to trust me, ok? Don't fire until it's stationary. It'll look bloody awful, but then it'll be dead. Got it?"

I look each one of them in the eyes until they nod and I'm thankful they don't run through the usual 'what are these things?' routine, but I guess right now they just want to kill it. Then I follow the sound and look down at the tiny park, seeing the Banshee in the corner.

This one is a greyish colour, its ragged skin billowing out around it. Banshees generally have smooth, chalky white skulls, and this one has a few long wisps of white hair still growing from it. When its skin cloak blows in the wind, it exposes the odd, sticks-and-metal body through the gaps, and I shudder. I glance to the side and see that one of the two police officers has lagged behind a bit. I make eye contact and jerk my head forwards. He gets the idea. He can't be more than thirty-five and this is some weird shit, but we need to do this right. Thankfully, the other one is about my age and world-weary enough to manage this stuff a bit better.

Well, I hope, anyway. Everyone reacts differently.

I tune into the noosphere, feeling a distant rift

somewhere to my right. Must be where the Banshee came in. I run through a more powerful immobilisation stave in my head, as well as pushing a little of the earth's energy field through my own muscles, feeling revived and faster almost immediately. It's handy, but takes a bit more time than I'd like. Then again, if things go south, I'll be glad of the extra manoeuvrability.

The Banshee seems to be eating something. They'll generally tear into their prey after making a kill, which is where we often intercept them. I try not to look, or inhale through my nose.

"Hey you," I shout, and despite its lack of ears, it rises up from the body and rotates around slowly. I wince at its horror-movie face, seeing fangs like needles and thin, black eyes in an otherwise white, skinless skull. I don't take my eyes off it but I hope to hell that the police are still with me. I think I can see one of them in my peripheral vision.

The Banshee tips its head back and screeches, making me slow my pace a little. The earplugs protect me from the worst, but it's still god-awful, like nails down a blackboard.

"Let's get this over with," I mutter, moving faster down the hill, and running the stave through my head, feeling the noosphere flowing through the silver on my arms. I hold back from the last note, and on cue, the Banshee dives towards me, as if it's a fish cutting through water. I release the stave, freezing the creature in mid-air. I glance back at the police officers, then open fire with my borrowed pistol, unloading it at the awful thing. A moment later, both of them do the same, filling the air with a cacophony of gunfire.

The creature collapses to the ground long before the stave wears off, and I sigh with relief. Staves won't hold dead creatures, so the fact that it dropped means that we're safe. I turn around, pulling out my earplugs and holding out the borrowed gun, swapping it back for the rifle.

"Nice work, gents," I offer. "Those things are nasty. Thanks for the support."

One of them sits down on the grass heavily while the other vomits into a nearby flower bed.

I've seen and done worse, so they're probably ok.

"Control, Lesser Banshee down at Robin Hood Gardens," I say into my mic. "Local police have one minor injury, and there's an open rift nearby."

"Understood. No other Gardeners in your vicinity, please proceed to rift when able."

I sigh and confirm.

It's long hours in the apocalypse.

Matt

Fucking Bracknell Again

I'm really not that far off shitting myself.

I wouldn't want to admit this to anyone, least of all the snooty girl sat next to me in the helicopter, but I've never been this scared in my life. We're flying over London as what looks like the literal apocalypse is happening around us.

At first it was just smoke, like there'd been a fire, or bombs or something. Then I saw a dinosaur. Well, a Ravager, I guess. It looked like a cross between a T-Rex and a Velociraptor, and it was basically bounding up and down Richmond High Street snapping at people. I stared, until it actually got someone and I puked out the side of the chopper. I know it's basically impossible, but I swear to god I could hear it from up here over the noise. Worst fucking thing I've ever seen.

And this Chloe girl is just sat there like a sphinx, talking to someone on her headset, no idea who, and hasn't said a word to me since we got in.

Fuck this shit, seriously.

If it wasn't the end of the world I'd make like Christian and bail, hard, magic school or none.

"Incoming!"

The guy piloting the helicopter – Brother Carvas, and don't get me started on that – momentarily looks back at us and I try to look out of the window. There's a few birds in the distance coming towards us pretty fast but nothing serious.

They get closer and I take it back. They're pretty serious.

These birds are huge and look like grey, bony eagles. They're diving at some people on a rooftop. One of them has noticed us and is coming towards the chopper, its wings beating in the air. It's got rows of needle-like teeth, but I don't see much more of it because Carvas pulls the chopper over to one side in a move that should really stay in the cinema, making my stomach lurch.

There's this whistling noise, we lurch again and I hear a metallic scraping sound then see the bird's wing in the window briefly. A moment later we're away, and the fucking thing is flapping off in the wrong direction looking for us. Christ, that thing almost hit us.

Five minutes later we're crossing the M25. There's a big pileup below us and I can see bodies. It doesn't seem real. We're going so fast that it's all out of sight a moment later.

Then I remember that this is a posh helicopter with

complementary spring water and use it to rinse the sick out of my mouth.

A moment later, we're descending towards a familiar industrial estate in Bracknell.

"Brother Carvas," Chloe says loudly as we touch down. "I pray you find safety. Please, flee as far as you can."

And fuck knows why she talks like this. I know I'm a closet D&D fan, but time and place, seriously. Carvas nods and thanks her, and we climb out of the chopper with two rucksacks full of gear that were in the back. No idea what's in them. I should have looked when we got in but I didn't actually clock that they were for us until Carvas told us.

"Come on," Chloe says, tugging me away from the helicopter and through the empty car park towards the office building. "Oh!"

She skids to a halt and I stop looking at her and follow her gaze. Right outside the office entrance is a Shambler, one of the lumbering grandma ghost things, and it's drifting towards us. I swallow and slap myself in the face a couple of times, then roll up my sleeves and try to remember the immobilisation stave. Despite feeling what Ben probably feels all the time – generally shit and unconfident – I manage to get a sense of the noosphere and roll the stave through my head, channelling the energy at the Shambler, releasing it with the last note thing.

It freezes, and I disperse it with a Street Fighter flourish, hearing Christina's voice in my head as I do, criticising my form. Chloe gives me a look but doesn't say anything, gesturing for me to take the lead into the training facility.

I guess it makes sense.

I should be swivelling around checking the corners as I burst through the doors, but I can't quite summon the energy. That's mostly because I'm trying not to retch again at the sight of the body behind the reception desk and the dark stains on the floor and walls, but also trying to tune into the noosphere and feel for any further rifts.

"Fuck me," I breathe, swallowing hard again. "That's awful."

"Quickly, please," Chloe says. She's an ice maiden. No idea how she does it but the less time we spend together, the better. "This does not bode well, despite my warning."

"Thank god it wasn't the fit receptionist," I say, clearing my throat and trying to regain some of my former poise, but it sounds weak even to me, and actually seeing a dead person makes me feel like a massive shit saying it.

"Matt," Chloe says coolly. "With the information that we have, there's a ninety percent chance that all of the support staff within the facility are dead. If you must make remarks reflecting your toxic masculinity, please refrain from doing it within earshot."

Somehow, taking crap from someone helps me feel a bit more normal. I scan my ID and push through the next set of doors, glancing around hurriedly. No Shamblers here. Mind you, I'm staying in the middle of the corridor

– those fuckers could drift through a wall anytime.

"You can get off your high horse," I continue, warming up to a good rant. I spot something moving in the distance. Fuck, it's another Shambler, drifting towards us. "Who gives a shit if I like women and call it out, as long as I'm doing the right fucking thing. Actions, words and all that."

I try to summon the stave but it won't come. I try again, but I can't feel the noosphere that well. It's almost thin, sort of like butter scraped thinly over toast when you're trying to avoid finishing an old pack.

"Come on, this way," I say, pulling Chloe down a different corridor. "I'll sort it in a minute."

"You must know that it's degrading," Chloe says, seemingly unfazed by all of this, but I'm starting to struggle to track the discussion. "Objectifying women. And it's intimidating; unless you've been a woman, I don't think that you can quite understand. It'd cost you nothing to refrain from commenting, and it gains you very little."

Christ, it was just one comment. "Look, there's nothing wrong with objectifying people sometimes," I say, feeling a bit pissed off now, but I don't think I'm really paying attention. "Most people are attracted by something physical, are you trying to tell me that's morally wrong?"

She starts to reply.

"Wait, got it," I say, interrupting her reply. I can feel the rushing energy field again, just as the ghost drifts around the corner. I bring the stave to mind and give it an extra *push*, freezing the ghost in mid-air. I disperse it a moment later, a wave of fatigue hitting me as the Shambler dissipates, its weirdly snarling face the last thing to go.

"I think you'll find it's not the same at all," Chloe says as we hurry through the corridors. How is she still going on about this?

"You can experience attraction without being boorish about it. Besides, what were you hoping to achieve with your comment? Did you want me to find the receptionist for you and tell her how attractive you found her?"

Never thought I could be bored and shit-scared at the same time.

"Just making conversation," I say, trying to get out of the discussion and remember where the fuck we're going at the same time. Oh, right, Karnak. We pass into the canteen and down the hallway towards the rift. Shit. That's the last place I want to go right now, unless there's other Gardeners there?

"Please, don't trivialise the issue."

I'm about to tell her that she can bite my arse when I push the door to the Karnak rift open and everything goes out of my head. I stagger to one side, vomiting onto the floor as I see blood and bodies everywhere. There's dismembered limbs, a head – mercifully facing away from us – and blood, so much blood, everywhere.

It smells horrific, like blood and shit and other things that I don't want to think about ever again. One of the arms doesn't seem to have any skin on it, and I turn back towards the corridor, seeing Chloe turning pale, but she pushes past me and walks into the room, somehow managing to fish a scarf from her jacket pocket and tie it around her nose and mouth. I heave until I've got nothing left in my stomach, coughing and trying to clear the awful taste from my mouth, knowing full well that I'll never clear the awful sight from my memory.

"Jesus," I breathe, putting my elbow across my mouth and trying not to inhale.

I notice footprints in the blood, heading through the rift. "Do you think there are people through there?"

"People?" Chloe says, muffled by her scarf. "Hardly people. But we need to follow."

I roll my eyes. Next time I'm going to Angel-hunting with librarian girl. Or Ben. Or Lincoln. Or fucking anyone else in the world.

"Look," I say, still trying not to gag. I've got to get out of here, so I step back out into the corridor. She follows a moment later, letting the door close behind us. "Level with me – who's this guy that we're going after? What's his deal? Did *he* cause all this?"

Chloe tucks her hair behind her ear and looks around before replying. Normally I'd find that cute, but it barely registers as I'm wiping sick from my mouth. I drink the rest of the water from the chopper, rinsing and spitting some of it onto the floor.

"Lucas Jackson," she says. "Was a Gardener, of sorts, but left under mysterious circumstances. Raphael refused to tell even me. He made forays into the world, identifying trends the inverse of the Gardeners' hopes. Where they saw opportunity for unity, he invested in discord, companies that catered to mankind's dwindling empathy and appetite for community. Delivery firms allowing people to live without leaving their homes, avoid social interaction and the like. He grew richer and richer, but we suspected that he was dissatisfied with simple wealth and wanted more. From time to time, I would see patterns in his activity, but he invested in a small private military force and monitoring became increasingly difficult. Then … this."

She cocks her head to one side and looks like she's listening for something.

"There's no time," she says, glancing at the door. "Can you weave more staves, if the need arises?"

"Sure."

"Then mind your footing," she says, pushing the doors open again and I wince as we try to avoid the pools of blood and occasional … well, it looks like a meat tube, but I'm sure there's an actual biological name for it. It's awful, whatever it is, and belongs inside someone, not on the floor of a conference room.

Chloe steps through the portal, and a moment later, I follow her. I feel a strange pang of guilt as I do, realising that I should be leading the way, not her.

Why the fuck do I feel guilty for not protecting her? I barely know her and she's irritating as hell. Shouldn't

I be searching for survivors? Where's Christina? How far have the ripples spread? I suddenly hope my mum is ok, although she's up north at the moment, so the chances are good. A part of me kind of wants to cry, but I push it down.

I look around the basement, not seeing Chloe for a second. She's in a corner, like she's trying to stay away from something. She sees me, and points – there's a Shambler on the far side of this room, and it's occupied with the body of a guy in what looks like a black military outfit. He's lying face down on the floor in a pool of his own blood and still has a slim backpack on, covered with pockets and utility loops and stuff, and also has what looks like a submachine gun on his back, much good it did him.

"Come on," I whisper. "Let's go."

Chloe gives me an icy look and gestures.

Fine.

Casting nervous – no, careful – glances over my shoulder at the dimly-illuminated ghost in the other corner, I hurry up along the winding corridor, wondering how the Shamblers got past the Gardener defences. The trees were lousy with staves the last time Ben and I were here, and it's not been all that long.

As we emerge into the bright sunshine of the tree-lined avenue, I see the answer. There's more dead people, and they're not military, so I reckon they must be Gardeners. There's a lot of blood here as well – the ground is almost black with it – but I can definitely see bullet holes. More to the point, it's a lot less tree-lined than it used to be, and a lot of the ones still standing are ashen and blackened, like they've been on fire.

"Shit," I mutter. "The fuck happened here?"

To my irritation, Chloe takes this as a serious question. "From the bodies in the training facility, I would surmise that a small number of mercenaries, presumably including Jackson, snuck in by stealth, but were detected at some stage. Realising the seriousness of the situation, the Gardeners fled through the rift to Karnak, and closed it behind them."

"Closed it?" I scoff. "We just came through it."

She closes her eyes briefly before continuing. "It was then opened by acts of extreme cruelty, and the mercenaries slew the Gardeners and destroyed the protection of the staves before continuing onwards, presumably to deter anyone from following them, and to allow further Shamblers through the rift, which slew the remainder of the staff in the facility, who were largely administrative and non-field staff."

"That's a Sherlock Cumberbatch thing you've got going on there, you know that? Is that what Lincoln meant about calling you the spider? Like, do you know everything?"

I can see her grit her teeth, holding back some kind of retort, and without replying, she starts walking on ahead of me.

"Hey," I say, catching up with her as we pass through the ranks of charred trees. "Look, forget I asked, ok? Let's not get dead. Maybe we should go back through the rift and get help, or look for survivors. This is some serious shit – we're not even armed and fuck knows how many men this Lucas guy brought with him."

There's silence as we walk – and there's no sign of Chloe turning around and heading back, I notice.

"I see patterns," she says a few moments later. "Data forms into textures and pathways in my mind. I absorb it, breathe it and then draw out likelihoods. And most unfortunately for us, there is no-one else to help. Even the local police are fully occupied with containing the incursions from other worlds."

"Shit the bed."

"Must you?" she says, with a pained expression.

"Look, what do you care?" I ask indignantly. "I'm fucking here, aren't I? I'm backing you up when no-one else is."

I see her mouth open and close, but for once, she stays silent.

About time.

Then I get a twinge of guilt, but I don't say anything.

We follow the winding valley between the two mountains for about half an hour, not seeing anyone or anything. It's slow going, which annoys me, but better safe than dead. Eventually, we emerge from the woods into a broad grassy field, spotted with a few trees and bushes. The grass is pretty long, but it's still short enough to spot a Shambler if there's one nearby. I'm hoping that there aren't any other nasties here, but Christina didn't actually mention anything, and she wouldn't have missed an opportunity to mess with us.

I hope she's not dead. I should have checked the bodies back there, shouldn't I? In the films, the survivors always take time to bury people, but I didn't even think about it. The sick taste rises in my mouth again but I swallow it down, wincing.

There's a group of people on the far side of the fields. I'm about to turn to Chloe with the first good news we've had for a while when I trip over a body and go sprawling onto my hands and knees.

Thankfully, other than the initial shock, there's no harm done; the ground is pretty soft, but as I pick myself up, I realise why – my hands and knees are now covered in blood. There's another guy in military gear right here, dick hanging out of his trousers, blood staining his eyes, ears, mouth and crotch.

"Jesus Christ," I swear, rubbing my hands on the grass. "Must have gone for a piss when it crept up on him."

Chloe offers me a water bottle and a cloth from her pack – I don't really understand why she'd have cloths, but I don't complain – and I try to scrub myself clean as best I can. Then it dawns on me.

"They were laying low, weren't they?"

She cocks her head to one side again.

"Like, if you'd committed an act of god-awful paranormal terrorism, then every man and his dog would be looking for you. What better place to hide out for a bit than somewhere pretty much no-one knows about?"

She gives a small nod. "I do suspect you're half right," she says. "Although I think there is a far more nefarious mission at hand."

"Alright then," I say, dropping the bloody cloth over the dead guy's knob. "Unless you wanted that?"

Chloe shakes her head.

"In that case, time to get serious."

And, trying not to disturb the cloth, I carefully unfasten his belt and take his pistol, leaving the larger gun. It looks heavy, and it's probably more complicated to use, much as I'd like to hose down some of these fuckers.

I swallow awkwardly. I'm actually not sure about that last bit. Having seen more dead people in the last hour than I have in my entire life, I don't really fancy killing, now that we're here.

Fuck it. Cross that bridge when we get to it. Better to have it and not need it than the other way around. And there's plenty of other uses for a gun than shooting people.

"So," I say. "How do we sneak up on these guys?"

Chloe looks at me, regarding me seriously for what I think is probably the first time. "I don't believe that they'll be expecting us," she says. "And because of their losses and the carnage they wreaked, they may not set a rear guard. We should be mindful of them. Stay low, move slowly to the side of the field there, and avoid using anything reflective."

"That is a weirdly specific set of knowledge you've got there."

"Quite the opposite," she says lightly. "As I told you, my knowledge is exceptionally broad."

Shaking my head, I finish fastening the gun belt around my waist and stoop down, staying an inch or so above the top of the grass. Wouldn't do to avoid being shot, only to bump into a Shambler.

What a fucking day.

Alice
Investigations

Our investigation is proceeding well so far, despite the initial set-back. I can neither confirm nor deny this talk of 'rifts' opening, although Lincoln – from the First Extraordinary Battalion – seemed remarkably convinced and I'm inclined to believe him. Either way, it's irrelevant to my immediate circumstances – we will continue, and find the angel by whatever means necessary. Requisitioning Hugo's jet in a time of emergency was an unexpected bonus, but our journey ahead is going to be exceptionally difficult.

Let me explain my new theory.

I still don't have an adequate explanation for why the angel, Raysiel, remained on earth, so I have to assume that he has a sacred binding oath or a duty of some kind. This sounds terribly imprecise, so you must excuse me. Raysiel burst from the ceiling of the chamber in Jerusalem leaving scorch marks heading due north. From all of the biblical literature I've read, Angels are regarded as strict and stringent beings, so during our flight to Svalbard, I've been concentrating on plotting this exact route.

You might imagine that this is straightforward – excuse the pun – but at these distances, the curvature of the earth becomes very relevant, and makes it rather complex to ascertain a precise exit point. This need is compounded not only by my intrinsic need for precision, but also the fact that we are shortly to be searching for the Angel either on foot or by air, and by my calculations, Nordaustlandet is an island just over a hundred miles wide.

Of course, this is further compounded by the fact that we're unable to fly directly to Nordaustlandet, even in a private jet, because it's completely uninhabited. We're flying to Svalbard Airport, in Longyearbyen, which is another hundred miles away, as the crow flies, from Nordaustlandet. I'm hoping that Hugo can make good on his connections – perhaps in conjunction with the 'Gardener' who seems to be escorting us – and that we can find a helicopter to take us there. Hopefully, the weather also remains fine, because the average temperature at present is around minus five degrees, and bad weather will make this a gruelling expedition.

According to Hugo, at this time of year, there is no 'true' darkness, and we will have sun all through the day and night, which will make searching much easier. I'm uncertain what it will do to my sleeping patterns.

The nose of the plane dips, and I glance out of the window. The scenery, it has to be said, is stunning. Snow-streaked mountains curl upwards, and small ice floes bob in the water beneath us. There's a soft yellow glow in the distance which is probably Longyearbyen itself. Everything is exceptionally mountainous, and despite our great assets – by which I mean Hugo's wealth – I'm uncertain of whether it'll be enough.

My head aches from the pressure change, and I swallow repeatedly, hearing a crackle in my ears as I do. We descend, eventually touching down on the runway with a small bump, but I've experienced far worse on commercial airlines.

We draw to a halt outside a miniscule airport building, the whine of the engines gradually quieting.

"Ladies and gentlemen," the pilot says over the speakers. "We have now arrived at Svalbard airport where the local time is twelve noon, just one hour ahead of the United Kingdom. The external temperature is a crisp minus two degrees. In a moment, I will extend the stairs and you will be free to disembark for passport control. Welcome to Norway. I hope you enjoy your stay."

The Gardener – Ben – laughs nervously, and I glance at him. I'm still unsure as to his utility on this trip, but at worst, he can carry the bags again.

The pilot, Lizzie, appears a moment later and operates the door, unfolding the steps. I realise that there's very little left to be done here, so I fold up the maps in a hurry and stuff them into one of the rucksacks leaning against the side of the plane.

"There's a car waiting outside," Hugo says. "It'll take us into town. We've got bookings at a hotel for a few days, but I need to make enquiries about the helicopter."

I bite back a reply, irritated. I was hoping he would have arranged all of the logistics before we arrived. He's had ample time, but I suppose I won't motivate him by berating him in front of a stranger and a member of his staff. Furthermore, I do need his money and support on this trip if we're to be successful.

Carefully, I descend the steps, shivering in the cold. It's noon, but the sky is dark and overcast. The buildings nearby are low, practical structures, warehouses by the looks of things, and are framed by snowy mountains. Flat, wet-looking bog and glacial moraine descends towards a dirty-looking shoreline not too far away.

I hurry across the tarmac to the small, well-lit building. It's tiny for an airport, but as I understand it, the population of Longyearbyen is barely two and a half thousand, although it sees twelve times that number in tourists each year. There's only one baggage reclaim area and four security desks. Glancing back at us, Hugo beckons us onwards, gesturing at them.

The process is brisk but friendly. The crime rate of Svalbard is apparently spectacularly low – it's a long way to come to cause trouble. Other than the scenery and wildlife, which *is* exceptionally noteworthy, there's very little here.

We're through in short order, and are hurried into a

car just outside the terminal. Hugo sits with the driver, leaving Ben and I to take the back seats as the car follows the coastline towards Longyearbyen proper. He's staring out of the window and I'm inclined to do the same. It reminds me a little of the Scottish Highlands, with small roads winding their way through the mountains, although there's a lot more water here, and the buildings that we pass are very colourful. Red, orange and green structures are common, interspersed with small dark sheds raised up on pilings – presumably to safeguard them from snow and snowmelt, although I can't discern the purposes of the sheds themselves from the outside.

It's barely a ten-minute drive from the airport into the town. I'm surprised to see a cinema on the street before we turn away, pulling up on the side of the next road, outside the Radisson Blu hotel that Hugo spoke so highly of. Hugo turns around in the front seat to face us.

"Right," he says, his voice trembling slightly. "Well, we're here. Alice, if you're still set on this, I'll need to go and see about the helicopter and permission to land on Nordaustlandet. I have to say, I've heard some fairly dreadful things about what's happening in London, so we certainly made the right decision in coming here."

I nod. "Thank you," I say. "Yes, please do."

"Ok then," he says, his voice quavering slightly. "In that case, Ben, see if you can find the best GPS unit in the shops around here, and get backup batteries. They don't last long, and it's the only thing we're missing. Don't worry, everyone speaks English, and if they don't, someone nearby will. Alice, can you handle checking us into the hotel? It's all under my name."

"I'll give you a hand with the bags," Ben says, and I shrug. I'm more than capable of lifting them all, thanks to my archaeology workouts, but I don't object.

Hugo nods and hurriedly rifles through one of the bags, taking out a large, puffy jacket and matching hat, both in blue. I don't have the finest understanding of fashion, but I believe that it looks slightly odd with his formal attire. He holds up a hand in farewell, then walks swiftly down the street.

Ben and I lift the bags from the car and head into the warm foyer of the hotel, where I find the front desk and ask about reservations. The foyer is a large, open area with a sloping, angular ceiling that seems to be part of the internal decoration; I can't decide if it makes it feel like a ski lodge or a bit retro and claustrophobic. There are floor-to-ceiling windows on one side, giving an impressive view of the bay and the misty mountains beyond.

I turn to ask Ben for his passport, but he's talking into his phone and facing away from me. I do really need his passport to check us in, so I tap him on the shoulder and gesture. It takes him a moment to dig around in his jacket pocket, but he eventually passes it to me. I apologise to the man behind the reception desk and he hands me keycards for three junior suites.

Tapping Ben on the shoulder again – to my rising

irritation – I take two of the bags, gesturing for him to follow. We're led through the corridors to the first of the three large rooms, which seem to be next to each other. They all have views of the bay, and plenty of room – for our purposes here, it seems unnecessary, but it's not my money. Relieved to be done with the heavy packs, I drop them down beside the sofa in the living area as Ben finishes his phone call and puts his pack down next to mine.

"There's been another situation," he says, looking grave. "I need to go to the Governor's office. Can you come with me?"

"Raysiel?" I ask. I'd really rather have a moment to wash my face and do some more research, but I suppose this is important.

He nods, pacing around the room and looking out of the window briefly. "That was a Gardener contact, Seline. She didn't have a lot of time, but apparently there's an old research station on the island – it's been abandoned for over a decade – but tour groups do go there fairly frequently. One of the groups reported an incredible flash of light passing through it, dazzling them. When they could see again, one of their party had vanished, but on closer inspection, they reckon he'd been turned into a pile of ash. They're still searching for him, but it's looking less likely by the minute."

"Exactly like in Jerusalem," I add, pleased, despite the tragic circumstances. My theory seems to have been correct after all.

Ben's phone beeps again and he glances at it. "Yes,

I think so," he says. "Seline is connecting me to the Governor now. Her office is open for another hour, but we should go soon if you're ok with that? Meet you in the foyer in ten minutes?"

"Sounds good," I say, simultaneously annoyed that I can't have more time without human contact, and relieved to at least have some time and that things are moving forwards. After a quick wash, I unpack the top few layers of the large rucksack, finding a pair of sturdy walking boots in my size, a puffy jacket much like Hugo's, a matching hat and gloves. A little better equipped for the sub-zero temperatures, I briefly survey the room, tapping my pocket to make sure that the keycard is there, and head back down to the reception area.

Ben arrives late, still fumbling with one of his gloves, beckoning me out of the building. I shiver as we leave, despite the warmth of my jacket, and I'm suddenly thankful that it's simply overcast rather than raining or snowing, although the mist over the far mountains concerns me. If rain comes in, it'll make our work here much, much harder.

We'll cross that bridge when we get to it. There's no point worrying.

"We can cut across here," Ben says, gesturing across the short, scrubby grass. He checks his phone one more time before putting it into a pocket and starting out across the rocky gravel.

I'm not really one to be sentimental, but everything

here is incredibly bare and bleak. Svalbard is a small town, threatened by the elements. The mountains and sea surround us on all sides, and I get the sense of being an interloper, intruding on the land's natural state.

That said, the people seem much more friendly than they were in Hertfordshire. Warmly-attired locals greet us with a pleasant 'hallo' or 'hey' – although from my research, I understand that the correct spelling is 'hei' – and Ben generally returns the greetings.

We scrabble up a gravelled bank towards a couple of buildings on stilts, and Ben checks his phone again before leading us towards an off-white building with a logo on the front. He pauses, then opens the door into a reception area.

"Welcome," a man behind the reception counter says in a thick Norwegian accent. It's quite melodic to listen to, his words dipping tonally in the middle before rising again. "How can I help you?"

I let Ben do the talking, and a moment later, we're being ushered into a small office on the second floor, which overlooks the town. A short, friendly-looking woman greets us from behind a table covered in paper and screens.

"Hallo," she says, tucking a strand of brown hair behind one ear. She's got a weatherworn, creased face, and looks a little tired. "I'm Solveig, the Governor of Svalbard. Welcome to the island."

"Thank you," Ben says, sitting down on one of the

hard, plastic chairs in front of the desk. I take the other. "And thank you for seeing us at short notice. I'm sorry that it's not under better circumstances."

"It is what it is," she replies evenly. "We have very few problems here. Most are due to the tourists and the bears. We have not had a death for some time, and I understand that there could be some very unusual circumstances."

He sighs and glances at me. "If you've already spoken to the First Extraordinary in England, I suppose you'll know that this will sound strange, but Alice here can back it up with historical context. There's an angel, who's been in a basement cavern in Jerusalem for the last thousand years. He finally got tired of being there, disintegrated an acolyte, then flew directly north, vaporising your tourist. We're here to investigate and if we can, bring him back to help with the situation in England."

He's given a fairly apposite overview of the situation, so I don't feel a need to say anything.

"This situation," Solveig says evenly. "England is attacked by creatures from another world? Is this true?"

"From what I understand," Ben replies. "Other worlds, plural. Apparently, there have been rifts between worlds for a long time, and it's only because of a dead priest and a network of nice ghostbusters that we haven't had this before."

Solveig stares, then laughs and Ben joins in a moment later, but they both sound slightly hysterical. I stare at him until he regains his composure.

"Nice ghostbusters," Solveig says, after a moment, shaking her head. "How I wish this was all a joke."

"You and me both," Ben says.

"Then I must lend you whatever assistance I can. But tell me, how do you hope to reason with this thing?"

Ben pales and gives me an anxious look. There's an awkward pause.

"We're working on that," he says, with an audible swallow. The Governor of Svalbard looks at him expectantly, but the silence stretches on until the phone on her desk rings. She glances at Ben before picking it up and has a short, quiet conversation in Norwegian before returning the handset to the desk.

"Your friend has secured use of a helicopter, it seems," she says. "I will give you the necessary documentation and permissions to go to Nordaustlandet. You will need a guide and equipment, guns, alarms for your camp and so on. I will arrange someone to help you. Please, return to your hotel and they will contact you."

"Thank you," Ben says, standing and wiping his hands on his trousers. "Thank you."

"Recommend us to your government," Solveig says. "Remember that Norway aided England when it needed help in these times."

"Uh, sure," Ben says. "Of course."

Once we're outside, he fixes me with an acid look. "Thanks for the help there," he says, sounding annoyed, and starts to stomp off towards the hotel. I'm surprised, but catch up a moment later.

"You're the one with the government connections," I say hotly. "I'm just an archaeologist. You didn't need my help."

He splutters for a moment and turns to face me. "That's not the … I mean, you think I did ok?"

Fragile masculinity.

"We got what we needed. So, yes."

He stares for a moment then sighs. "Shit. I guess we did. Sorry. You know, I've only been doing this a couple of weeks? This time last month I was a librarian in Mayfair."

I snort. He does seem a little inexperienced – and that explains why he was accompanied by Lincoln in Jerusalem – but he has been effective so far. I tell him this, and he flushes.

"Thanks," he says. "Sorry."

"Come on," I say. "Let's do some research into what we'll need on this expedition. I haven't even catalogued what's in the bags from Hugo yet. And you should start thinking about a plan for when we do find Raysiel."

If he looked momentarily heartened before, his face falls, but he seems to rally quickly and we set off back through the freezing town.

Lincoln
Losing the Battle

I'm finally forced to go to sleep by one of the analysts who reminds me of our 'no-hero' mantra. A tired operative is a bad, dead operative, he tells me, but I can tell that he's bone-weary too.

He's right, and I carefully work my way over to the remains of the stairs that used to lead to the upper floor, and climb the retractable ladder instead. Instead of offices, the second floor of the Greenwich Observatory now has bunks set up around it for the Gardener forces, and there are snipers on the battlements of the building, turning this into a well-defended fortress. Celia and Tristan, two of my friends out from retirement, have spent most of the day with armed police, embedding containment and dispersal staves into the surrounding trees, so it's predominantly corporeal enemies we need to worry about.

Of course, that's not true for the broader war. There are now at least a hundred and nine rifts that have been reported across the city, and although we've closed approximately thirty in the last day, the sheer size of London and volume of threats is making progress extremely slow. We're also having to be extremely careful; we've already lost five active field agents to a Greater Banshee, a flock of Whistlers, a Ravager and a horrific fleshy, spined, slimy creature that we've not come across before. We've yet to find friendlies on the other sides of rifts, of course.

We all suspect the answer to that, mind you. Tears in the fabric of reality caused by cruelty and loss are unlikely to result in positive circumstances, our metaphysical analysts tell us, but that doesn't help much. We'd planned for smaller incursions, single incidents, and if it hadn't been for the general recall thanks for our intel, you'd be able to count the number of stave-capable Gardeners on the fingers of one hand. Unfortunately, most of the reinforcements were in Gardener HQ when it locked down, but some were in and around the city.

We've requested backup from metaphysical units in France, but they're still planning how to safely carry the specialists across the channel since the skies aren't safe. We've put out a call for shamanic practitioners, priests, ministers, rabbis, anyone tapped into the spiritual world who might be interested in learning how to use the staves. Late this evening, we had five additional volunteers arrive at the centre from nearby Greenwich and Blackheath to try and replace our stave-wielding casualties.

The non-magical casualties don't bear thinking about. We

lost fifteen police and military to the Greater Banshee alone, and the civilian death toll was in three figures. The military are now fully committed, but they're spread thinly, and most of them are completely unprepared for this kind of combat.

I quietly lie down on an empty bunk, hearing heavy breathing and someone mumbling in their sleep on the other side of the room.

Fucking Lucas. I'd like his head on a spike.

Somehow, despite that thought, I sleep.

I'm woken the next morning by sunlight streaming in through the huge windows. Although teams have rigged makeshift curtains, they can't keep out all of the May sunshine. I find a sink in the staff toilets and wash before grabbing a hasty breakfast in what's left of the cafeteria. There's only one member of staff here who lives locally and was convinced to come back, probably because of all the military around. Everyone else is either First Extraordinary, police or military.

There's an air of tension in the Observatory, but it's actually Seline, the current senior analyst, who's holding it all together. You'd think that a woman in a wheelchair would lose her shit when the only safety is being in an elevated position, but she's a force of nature, handling intelligence and giving orders in tandem with whoever the regular military ranking officer is. I'm more than happy to defer to her and take to the field.

"Lincoln," she says, turning to see me. "Morning. You shipshape?"

I nod. "Ready and willing. What's up first?"

"Glad you asked," she says crisply. "Greater Banshee came out of the river by the Greenwich Peninsula ecology park. We need it dealt with and the rift closed. You're the most experienced on-site. There's a lot of people in Greenwich Millennium Village and we can't get to them at all now."

"Support?"

"We can't spare any stave-capable Gardeners," she says. "But I've lined up five local police, ten army reserves and three former SAS for you. It's all we've got, unfortunately."

"It'll do," I say, with more confidence than I feel. "Any vehicles available?"

She shakes her head. "It's two miles, Lincoln, you're safer on foot. Low and slow, remember?"

"All armed?" I ask, ignoring the truism.

She nods, then gestures over to a briefing room that was probably last used for giving lectures about the solar system to schoolchildren. It's still got sepia photos of Greenwich Park in it, alongside modern explanations of how sundials work, a small black rock on a pedestal that I suspect is an asteroid, and a relatively comprehensive diagram of the planets, including distances explained in easy-to-understand terms.

I walk in, heading to the desk at the front to survey the mishmash of people in front of me. The five police are in uniform, armed with pistols. The army reserves all look young apart from one guy – maybe he was their CO?

Thankfully, the three other people in the room – two men, one woman – look more capable, even if they're only wearing stab vests over their civvies, rifles on the desks in front of them.

"I'm Lincoln, of the First Extraordinary," I say loudly, the room instantly quietening. "Until a few weeks ago, I was retired."

The three from the SAS exchange glances and one of them gives me a weak grin. Good. The start of rapport.

"This morning's assignment is a five-star mission, which means containment and disposal of a semi-corporeal, highly dangerous creature that we call a Greater Banshee. Have any of you faced a Lesser Banshee yet?"

Two of the police and three of the army reserves hold up trembling hands.

"For those of you who haven't, a Lesser Banshee is a screaming bundle of what seems to be metal and some unknown ghostly substance. Its cry will penetrate your brain until you will do anything – and I mean anything – to make it stop. That includes killing yourself and others around you. Earplugs are a necessity."

"A Greater Banshee is usually around fifteen feet tall, and looks like your worst nightmares wrapped in a dirty white sheet. They're also semi-corporeal and will flit in and out of existence, which makes containing and destroying them extremely difficult. Unlike Lesser Banshees, their shrieks will simply cause immense, paralysing pain and haemorrhaging from the ears, nose and eyes. They have long, razor-sharp claws and feed on people. They also tend to be accompanied by Lesser Banshees and creatures that look like dogs made of metallic cartilage – informally known as hellhounds."

"Some of you may not have worked with a Gardener task force until recently. My job is to approach the Greater Banshee and use what we call staves – channelling the earth's natural protective field, or if you like, magic – to freeze the Banshee in place so that you can open fire and destroy it. Causing sufficient damage to its corporeal parts will cause it to die, as long as there's enough of it in the material world. These creatures can be destroyed without assistance, but it's far safer to do it this way."

We'd learned that the hard way, in an operation in Germany. We'd frozen the damn thing in place, blown the parts we could see to smithereens and paused for breath. It'd looked dead, but then it'd rippled and the non-corporeal parts phased back into existence, taking out three Gardeners and a marine with a single swipe of its claws.

"Your job is to keep me safe until I can immobilise the Banshee. That means maintaining an outer and inner perimeter, and then closing it to destroy the creature when safe to do so. Banshees are also extremely quick – and I do mean extremely quick – so it's safer to work together. We'll be equipped with earplugs and comm units to stay in touch, and we'll be leaving on foot as soon as we're all ready. Any questions?"

The faces before me are pale, hands sweaty and trembling, but nobody asks a question.

"Good," I say, starting to point at the people in front of me. "You three – former SAS, correct?"

I see nods.

"Alright. I want one of you up front taking the lead, one in rear guard, the other with me at all times. Police? Two of you on each side, then one in front, one at the rear and one with me again. Army reserves? Form up into pairs and follow the same principle, forming a box around us. Any sign of anything strange, one person falls in and updates me. You keep an eye on your side of the box, and check the air from time to time. The creatures we're fighting can often fly, or they might look like ghosts. All of them are lethal."

I glance around one more time. "Let's go."

My irregular force more or less shapes into what I'd hoped for, and I bark a few orders at the stragglers, although I can't really blame the army reserves. They probably didn't ever think they'd be drafted into a conventional war, let alone a paranormal one.

A few minutes later, we're carefully working our way down the long, broad hill from the Observatory, and the woman from the SAS leans in. She's tall, muscular and I'm certain that she's deadly in combat.

"Sir," she says quietly. "I'd be remiss not to mention this. I think you're making a tactical error by blending units."

I look at her evenly. "Because existing units have coherence and rapport already? And they're more likely to stick together and follow orders?"

She nods, taken aback.

"Honestly, trooper," I say, checking her for insignia. I don't see any. "None of these people have fought with the First Extraordinary before. I have to be realistic. Some of them may not even make it to North Greenwich."

There's an awkward silence, and I try to recall what I remember of working with experienced recruits. Ben and Matt had been all wide-eyed and keen to learn, but this is an entirely different situation with entirely different people.

"What's your name?"

"Martha, sir."

"Martha, this is the worst possible situation at the worst possible time," I say quietly. "And we've all got to do what we've all got to do. Understand?"

"Aye sir," she says, but she seems a little more at ease.

We reach the bottom of the park and find our way onto Trafalgar Road, trotting past takeaways, furniture shops, mirror stores. They're all empty, but on the upper floors I can see faces pressed up against windows. Everyone looks scared and tired, and we're only on day two.

One of the vanguard comes jogging back to me, one of the SAS guys, a muscular, tattooed bruiser with clever eyes.

"Sir," he says. "Something ahead. Possibly one of those ghost things you were talking about."

"Alright," I say. "Martha, stay here and wait for us to come back. You, show me."

He introduces himself as Thomas and takes me past a bubble tea shop, gesturing to a small alleyway. Sure enough, there's a Shambler there, seemingly feeding on or just hovering around the body of a dog or a fox or something. Often there won't be enough left when they come into contact with animals, but if it's large enough, there'll be a body. I tap into the noosphere, not sensing a rift nearby and – taking a step forward – release the stave, dispersing it. A brief wave of tiredness hits me, quickly replaced by a rush of satisfaction as the ghostly creature fades into nothingness.

"Damn," Thomas swears next to me, and I catch one of the army reserves grinning from ear to ear.

"Fucking A," he says, and I clap him on the shoulder.

"That's how it's done," I say, showing off. With any luck, it'll be good for morale.

We don't see any more as we pass under the Blackwall tunnel approach. Then we're into the Millennium Village, its flat blocks a hodgepodge of colours, mostly worn and faded now.

Then I hear it and call everyone to a stop, gesturing for them to put in their earpieces and earplugs, checking that everyone can hear me over the comm, but barely out loud. It's a little disorientating, but it's better than dead.

I remember the last time I fought a Greater Banshee and decide on a little more protection, channelling a more complex stave in my head and partially releasing the energy. A moment later, an energy field surrounds my body as what we call spiritual armour slides into place, manifesting itself as a thin, blue metallic sheen that seems to coat my clothing. You can make it showier, but I don't really have the motivation. I check my rifle; the safety's off and the clip is full. All set.

I check the map. I don't really know this part of town that well, but I can hear the wail in the distance, getting louder and already grating on my eardrums. We round the corner where an arcade of shops sits empty, the square in front bereft of shoppers. I call back the advance team as I see the ecology park in the distance, and what I think is the Greater Banshee.

"Alright," I say over the comm. "Point out any Lesser Banshees that you see, and shoot any hellhounds on sight. Do not engage the Greater Banshee until I give the order. You'll piss it off and then we'll have a highly active threat on our hands, rather than a sluggish creature that's probably well fed."

No-one asks any questions, so I ready my rifle and walk down the footpath towards the park.

The first hellhounds almost catch me by surprise, bounding out of the woods in front of us, screeching like angle grinders. They slip on the damp wood of the boardwalk, claws skittering for purchase, giving us precious seconds to open fire, tearing their strangely durable bodies to shreds. They're muscular fuckers, like skeletal Dobermans crossed with sharks. The bullets make pinging noises as they hit the metallic flesh, but do the job well enough. I hold my hand up in a fist, giving the order to cease fire.

Then I see the Banshee, parting the trees with its huge claws, two storeys high and ashen grey, face like a Halloween mask. Its body seems to be made of sticks, metal rods and barbed wire. A long time ago, I saw one grab a marine in its claws and push it into its own torso, brutally impaling them.

It's almost rippling, parts of its body fading in and out of existence.

Half of my force simply stops and stares, as four more hellhounds come screeching out of the alleyway at the side of the ecology park, in front of two Lesser Banshees. To their credit, most of the army reservists open fire at the same time I do, but I lose three of the five police officers before the dogs are down. The SAS team have grouped together and are firing at one of the Lesser Banshees, and I turn, sprinting over to the other, freezing it in place with a containment stave.

"Remaining police, open fire on my position. Frozen Banshee. Army reserves, assist!"

Then something catches me, staggering me and most of the energy from my spiritual armour depletes. I catch myself, holding onto a fence for stability as the Greater Banshee roars; fucker must have been trying to grab me.

The other Lesser Banshee has reached the SAS team

and has its claws into the one I don't know, but I can't think about that right now. If I don't deal with the Greater Banshee, it'll summon more through the rift and then we'll all be dead. I shape a containment stave and fire it off, but either the range is too great or it misses. I need to get closer.

The air is filled with screams and gunfire, the acrid smell of gun smoke, and the sound of dying. The Greater Banshee has an army reserve in each claw now, chewing another in its scarecrow mouth. We have no idea if they actually need to eat, but it scares the shit out of everyone, so maybe that's why they do it.

I close the distance, nearing its torn-sheet body. It smells like dead things. I fire off a containment stave, then another and another, feeling the drain from channelling the noosphere, my aging tattoos growing warm on my arms. The Banshee seems to falter for a moment, then it ripples, other parts of its body warping into the material realm, leaving it free to move somehow. Fuck.

It throws the reserves into the pond nearby, and they crash through the fence with sickening cracks. I roll to one side as another claw makes a grab for me, slower to my feet than I'd like and feeling something twist painfully. As I rise, I see Martha still grappling with the other Lesser Banshee, Thomas on the ground clutching his side.

"Fuck," I mutter, staggering towards them, managing to shape a containment stave, the Lesser Banshee freezing almost instantly. Martha clutches her side and fires indiscriminately until it collapses to the ground, a reserve in fatigues lending her a hand as another one helps Thomas up. He's bleeding heavily from a head wound and there's a dark patch on his hip.

We're getting destroyed.

I spin back towards the Greater Banshee, which is busy impaling the last two police officers with its claws in rapid scooping motions. I limp towards it as it tips its head back and screams, sending a red-hot knife of sound through my head. I need to do something fast, and a very different stave comes into my head. I feel the noosphere channelling through my staves, a beam of bright light issuing from my fingers, sending me to my knees in just a few seconds, but tearing a fist-sized hole through the Banshee's upper body. Raphael's laser beam, I call it, and I usually can't make it work.

The noise stops, and the Banshee pauses for a moment, then floats towards me, slower now, but fixing me with empty eyes. I send containment stave after containment stave towards it, and finally its claw halts mid-descent.

"That's it!" I shout into the comm. "Give it everything you've got."

I roll to one side as the remaining reserves and Martha open fire in a deafening hail of bullets, some ricocheting back into the park, but a moment later, the huge creature topples backwards, crashing through the trees and splashing into the pond.

It doesn't rise.

I tiredly push myself to my feet, just in time to hear the heavy thud of more hellhounds approaching, their screeches echoing around the park. I spin, but something strikes me heavily in the chest. There's a sharp pain in my arm and everything goes black.

Ben:
The Frozen Desert

Our guide to Nordaustlandet is a rangy Norwegian called Anders, who has spent the last hour outside with Hugo assessing his skills with a shotgun. After meeting us and introducing himself in a friendly fashion, he briefly queried our experience with guns, concluding that neither Alice nor myself were good candidates for scaring off polar bears.

Scaring, mind you, not shooting.

According to Anders, the average male polar bear weighs somewhere in the region of four hundred and fifty kilograms, can run at speeds of up to forty kilometres an hour, and will easily shrug off rounds from pistols and handguns. Shotguns – with plenty of ammunition – are better. It can take six to eight rounds in the air before a polar bear (or an isbjørn, literally, ice bear) is scared off, so it's best to be properly equipped.

Of course – Anders has told us – there are many other preparations that we need to take in the icy wilderness.

Sealing all food into containers, setting alarms around the campsite and checking around it to make sure that we're not on a direct path between a bear's regular route and a fishing site, for example. We must take care not to litter, mind the reindeer, and don't approach either the walruses or bears. We need to dress warmly at all times, and stay close to each other.

He regales us with little-known facts about Svalbard, like how there is exactly one cat here, but all others are banned because of risk to the birds. I get the impression it's a traditional, lighter ending to his 'scare the tourists' routine, but it's welcome. Then he disappears outside with Hugo, who seems surprisingly comfortable holding a shotgun.

I pack and re-pack our gear as new equipment is delivered throughout the afternoon and evening, but spend most of the time with my e-reader, plugged into the nearest power socket. It's absolutely incredible what's in the Gardener library.

There are so many different kinds of stave. We were only taught two in an entire week, but I suppose it does make some sense. The Gardeners weren't expecting us to be thrown into a paranormal cataclysm, they were expecting to tutor us, working out if we were going to be analysts or field agents or mid-level managers, for all I know. I can only assume that basic training usually takes months, if not years, so it's not really surprising.

That said – it really is like magic. Obviously, a lot of

attention is focused on the two primary staves, but there are staves for self-protection, staves to directly damage the semi-corporeal, staves to accelerate movement and enhance your own strength, staves to heal the injured.

And seemingly, the Gardeners tend to specialise in a few distinct types. A field agent specialising in containment of threats – like Lincoln – would likely know healing staves, for example, but wouldn't really specialise in the whole gamut of them. In a normal situation, he'd have support from a team containing at least one or two Gardeners with different skills, although from the little I know about the guy, I suspect he has a few tricks up his sleeve. What else is clear is that although staves draw energy from the noosphere, it's also somewhat draining to channel them, as Matt and I found out in Karnak, and some of them need energy to maintain, like protection spells, because you're constantly channelling the noosphere, and that it's generally easier when you're younger, for some reason.

We're due to leave the following morning, so I settle for learning a protection stave properly, which I'm moderately proficient at by the time we're told to go to bed by Anders. I bridle slightly at his mothering of us, but I need to get into the habit of obeying him unquestioningly if we're to stand a good chance of even making it to the angel.

The angel. Even saying it makes me need to stop and take a deep breath, so eventually I watch a comedy on Netflix in my room to distract myself.

Svalbard, strangely, has phenomenal internet.

I message Matt, but it sits in our chat, ominously undelivered, great internet or no.

Shit.

Hope he's ok.

I wake in the morning after an uneasy night's sleep; the hotel room has good curtains, but I'm still conscious of the strange light in the not-quite night. I wash, then eat a breakfast of unfamiliar breads and – to my surprise – fish. I was kind of hoping for regular British food for tourists, but no such luck.

Alice and Hugo join me towards the end, eating silently. Hugo looks pale and tired, Alice flicking through a book on the local area. I don't know what to say to either of them. I miss Matt and his easy banter. I miss England, for that matter, although I'm too chicken to look at the news to see what's going on. I hadn't looked last night either, but my phone proactively beeped as the news incredulously reported on the invasion of nightmarish creatures beyond belief into Greater London. Aid – military and otherwise – is being carefully flown in from other countries, but no-one knows what to make of it and there are still creatures in the skies making it unsafe, so it's slow-going. I guess we're used to terrorists and – seemingly, allegedly – conflict further afield, not supernatural threats from other worlds.

"Nearly ready?" Anders says, arriving at our table in outdoor gear. His winter goggles are pushed up above his eyes, a woollen bobble hat sitting on his head. He looks completely ready for an arctic adventure.

"We'll fetch our bags and be with you in a moment," Hugo says, looking glad to have an excuse to stop pushing smoked fish around his plate. I guess he's not a big fan of the Norwegian breakfast.

I rise, walking through the off-white corridors, passing tourists. For a moment, I wish I could be them, on a holiday, with little or no idea of the paranormal world beyond. Then again, most of them have probably seen the news and have a pretty good idea of what's going on. As I look harder, most of them do have a slightly twitchy look about them, as if they don't really want to go home, or aren't sure if they'll be going home at all.

I retrieve my pack, tucking my e-reader in at the top, struggling with the weight of the new additions – a tent, a small cooking stove and fuel, ready meals. There's a lot of kit, but Anders did say something about being packed for five days and Nordaustlandet is a pretty big island to search in the grand scheme of things.

Hugo is waiting in the foyer when I get back, hands folded behind his back, but he looks nervous. I've been getting nervous vibes from him this whole time and to be honest, I don't really know why he's here. He didn't really need to come with us, unless maybe he was running away from the UK?

Alice arrives a moment later, and Anders nods, then walks out through the front door of the hotel, leading us across the scrubby gravel back towards the governor's office. It's cold – definitely sub-zero – but my newly-acquired winter gear keeps me fairly warm, although I wish I'd brought some kind of balaclava.

There's a few other tourists and locals around, but it's not busy. Sea birds are carving up the air above us, calling to each other and occasionally diving down to the ground for scraps.

Anders leads us behind the governor's office, where a small yellow helicopter is parked. With an easy, practiced manner, he checks around it before opening it up and gesturing for Alice and myself to get in the back, and Hugo to sit up front with him. It's a bit of a squeeze with our packs, and I don't think it's really meant for transporting tourists. There are two headsets on the back of the seats in front of us, and after a quick glance at Alice, I take one.

There's a few more minutes of further checks – seemingly, everything is fine – then Anders starts up the rotors. I'd expected it to be noisy, but even with the chunky headset over my ears, it's incredibly loud. As the rotors reach what seems to be an almost-painful level of noise, the chopper tilts forward alarmingly, then slowly starts to ascend, the town growing smaller and smaller beneath us.

Despite the distraction of the noise, the view is fantastic. Long rows of colourful houses stretch before us, set around the bay. Slowly, we fly over the town and across the water, briefly crossing land before starting across the sea again.

Sea ice floats in ragged chunks, and I can see seals or

maybe walruses on the coastline. There's something large moving in the water a way away, but we're too high up for me to see if it's really a whale. I'm transfixed, and for a few minutes, I forget all about the noise, the vibration and why we're here.

After maybe twenty minutes, Anders turns around briefly, looking at us.

"We're about to fly over Pyramiden," he says. "It used to be a mining town, but it's completely abandoned now. Very popular with urban explorers, but we try to discourage it – they take too many souvenirs."

Lo and behold, an odd settlement stretches before us, a wide main road flanked by long, red buildings, with larger, pale cream buildings on either side, sat amongst the snow. The buildings are pretty blocky and plain, but I get vaguely Soviet Russia vibes from it – there's a small monument in the middle, and the road layout reminds me of something I once saw in a film.

There's a big triangular peak – I'm guessing it's pyramidal from the name of the settlement – to one side, and it all feels a bit eerie, especially because it's completely deserted.

Then we're past it, and the landscape becomes increasingly desolate and beautiful. There's a polar bear climbing up a hill, and I gesture to Alice before pressing my nose up against the window to stare at it. It's truly huge, even at this distance, a powerful, shaggy, clawed thing the size of a jeep. Suddenly our shotguns seem insignificant, but at least the bear isn't actively looking to hunt us, unlike what's waiting for us back in the UK.

After what seems like an age, we're over water again.

"This is Hinlopenstretet," Anders shouts over the noise. "The Hinlopen Strait. It's the channel between Svalbard and Nordaustlandet. We're about ten minutes from Kinnvika."

Then we reach Nordaustlandet.

It's completely bare. I'd expected some kind of life, or at least peaks and scrubby grass, but it's just bare rock and snow. The coast seems to be shingled, and although there are hills and harshly rising cliffs, it's mostly a bare expanse of basically nothing. If I was intimidated by the stark wilderness of Longyearbyen, this is something else.

Slowly, Anders takes us down in the helicopter, not far from a cluster of rickety-looking wooden shacks and outbuildings. It's all been built with bare, bone-grey planks of wood, giving it the feeling of a lost, long-abandoned settlement.

The helicopter lands a short distance away from the buildings, and Anders shuts everything down, gesturing for us to wait until the rotors have stopped moving before allowing us out. My first impression does very little to allay my fears; it's completely empty, completely silent, and we're completely alone. Even if we weren't here to try and reason with an angelic being, it'd be an intimidating place to be. Truly staggering, but intimidating nonetheless. After being in the crush of London for so long, it's bizarre to think that there are no police here, no shops, no rules, no support. We're incredibly alone, with Anders our only lifeline.

"We'll make camp between the buildings here," Anders says as we assemble towards the front of the helicopter. "It's a little sheltered, and we can rig alarms between them."

His assertiveness is somewhat reassuring. With careful ease, he leads us through the eerie town and instructs us in the best places to pitch our tents; not too close together, so as not to create a minefield of guy ropes. I've never really enjoyed camping, but I like the quiet mindfulness of putting up a tent, and before too long, the bright orange geodesic tent that Anders and I will share is up, alongside the one that Alice and Hugo will sleep in.

Anders has already begun to rig tripwires between the houses, and I tuck my pack into the tent and pause to watch him. They seem to be fairly simple lengths of wire, terminating in stubby cylinders or cartridges of some kind. He pauses, seeing me watch him.

"It's an old design, very simple," he explains. "Small explosive shells. More noisy than harmful, to scare away the bears when they trigger them. If they don't scare them, it'll at least give us time to be ready. Better than having a bear sniffing your tent in the night."

I shudder as he goes back to work. As if we weren't dealing with enough.

Half an hour later, we seem to be done.

"So," Anders says, looking around. "The first part is

over. Now you tell me where we're going next."

I glance at Alice, who already has a paper map, clad in a heavy-duty transparent plastic case, waiting. She holds it out in front of her and I can see that it's marked with a very straight line, from south to north, terminating at the north end of the island, seemingly not too far from here.

"Here," she says. "This is where it should be."

She sounds pretty confident, and Anders inspects the map cautiously.

"About eight miles," he says. "There is a flat area, about here, where we could land – safer to take the helicopter again – and you say we're looking for an animal?"

Alice frowns. "An angel," she says, receiving what passes for an incredulous look on our leathery guide's face. "And it might be sensitive to the noise. If it's possible, I'd rather we walk."

"Very well," he says, after a moment. "We'll tuck the food into the cabins and leave in ten minutes. Gather your daypacks."

He doesn't seem best pleased with the choice, but nonetheless takes it stoically. We heft the food boxes around, and before too long, we're setting out from the camp. Anders equips us all with walking poles, and after a brief tutorial in how to use them for stability, we're off.

It's slow going.

The ground is bare, fractured rock, shingly and unstable underfoot. Anders leads us around patches of snow, but as the land rises gently, we angle around a hill before resuming our initial direction. Streams of snowmelt flow freely towards the sea, and Anders inspects each one carefully before allowing us to jump over them. After a time, I feel like I'm getting into a rhythm, and seem to have a struck a balance between expending physical effort and the icy cold, finally achieving a reasonable temperature. I'm thankful that it's still and calm, and although there's a grey layer of cloud above us and mist in the distance, it's not raining or snowing yet.

"So, how long have you been with the First Extraordinary?" Hugo asks, drawing alongside me. He's got a slightly annoying nasal voice, and I'm instinctively irritated by him, despite the fact that he's only done good things for us.

"About two weeks."

"Two weeks?" he says, flatly. "Two weeks? You're serious?"

I'm not entirely sure how to respond, but then I remember the plume of smoke rising over Covent Garden, the fire, the look of grief on Lincoln's face. "There wasn't anybody else," I say, blinking away tears. "Not after the attack."

I swear he makes a quiet scoffing noise and turns away for a moment, but when he turns back, his voice is softer. "I'm sorry," he says, gesturing expansively. "I've been avoiding your people for years. Understandable, really, when you think about all this."

I shake my head. He knew. He knew about this and all

he did was give money to the Gardeners. I have a thought and push my annoyance away for a moment.

"Are there other organisations?" I ask, trying to divert the conversation. "Like mine?"

He looks over and I can feel his opinion of me plummeting further.

"In America," he says, with some distain. "And on the continent. I sponsor some of them. Otherwise, I sometimes hear from priests, shamanic practitioners, faith healers, that kind of thing. It's hard to tell the quacks from the real deal, so I tend to ignore the freelancers."

The freelancers. It seems like an age ago that Seline was talking to us about the information she'd received from a shamanic practitioner in Spain, before all of this became terrifyingly real. I have no idea if I'd make the same decisions knowing then what I know now, but I kind of think I would. This might be the most awful thing I've ever done in my life, but it also feels right – and it definitely feels important.

"Sure," I say, not really wanting to talk more, but keenly aware that we're dependent on his patronage in more ways than one. "And, uh, thanks, by the way."

"Don't mention it," he says, mercifully falling silent. I rather think he means it literally.

We stop for lunch an hour later, fishing sandwiches from our bags, courtesy of the hotel, or in Anders' case, a more generously-filled and clearly home-made affair. I glance at it jealously, but my tuna and sweetcorn sandwich is actually pretty good, and as I shuck off my backpack and sit on a large boulder, I realise how hungry I am. I guess the cold must take its toll.

Anders insists that we pause after we eat, although he paces around – I assume he's checking for bears or tracks or something. I don't see any, but I watch a flock of birds in the distance, rising and gathering before settling down again. I can hear their raucous cries from here, and I wonder if they can smell what we've just eaten.

"Alright," Anders says, rising and stretching again, glancing around at the desolate landscape one more time. "We carry on."

We carry on.

Matt
Up a Tree, Watching Grandmas

We make painstakingly slow progress around the edge of the field as Chloe co-ordinates our movements with her Minority Report trick. I shouldn't complain – we're on an alien planet full of lethal ghosts and mercenaries who wouldn't hesitate to gun us down and leave us to rot, so I'm pretty happy to be guided by this woman.

As it starts to get dim, we arrive at this tree which is basically perfect for climbing. Loads of handholds, broad, dense branches further up, some leaves – we should be able to keep an eye on the mercs and Lucas without too much trouble, and pretty safe and sound from Shamblers. I have a quick slash then keep watch as Chloe does the same, although much more elegantly, I'm sure.

Then we're up into it, and despite a few scratches, it's basically comfortable. Even with the packs, it was an easy climb, and we can see all the way across the plain to the other encampment where they seem to have lit a fire, which seems like a really, really fucking stupid thing to do.

The packs are full of incredibly normal, useful stuff: a toothbrush, water bottles, a change of clothes, dried food. Chloe's been carrying two bags, and I feel a brief flash of guilt, but she didn't complain or ask for help, so she must have been alright.

"So," she says, looking at me from across the tree. "Do you like London?"

I frown, a bit confused by her choice of small talk. I'd expected planning, something about the Gardeners, the apocalypse, but I guess it's been a bit of a heavy day.

"Uh," I manage. "Sure. Food's good, plenty of places to drink. Too many suitwankers for my liking, but comes with the territory."

She pauses, taking a drink from one of the bottles, and I can almost see her restraining herself but she bites anyway.

"Suitwankers?" she says, as if she's been asked to use one of those little baggies to pick up a street full of dogshit, and not the kind from small, convenient dogs either. Humongous turds from a pack of Leonbergers. On her way back from fucking Ascot or something.

"Yeah, you know, suitwankers," I say. "Cunts in suits. Bankers. Consultants. Sales guys. CEOs. You think I'm toxic masculinity, you should spend time with them."

She arches an eyebrow at me. "I would have thought they'd be rather your speed."

I snort. "Fuck that. They're all dressed up like posh twats but they're wankers on the inside. Least with me you know what you're getting."

Chloe pauses and cocks her head to one side, making a slight huffing noise through her nose. "And you've met a lot of these … suitwankers?"

"Course," I say. "You know, some of them are alright I guess, but as a group, I mean, shits, all of them."

She pauses and something about her expression changes.

"What happened?" she says, almost too softly to hear above the rustling of the trees.

The weird thing is that I know exactly what she means, what she's asking. I'm about to tell her to fuck off, to change the subject, to look for a distraction, but no words come out.

Fuck this. I swallow. I don't really want to get into this – I barely know this woman but I find myself talking anyway. Maybe what happens on alien planets stays on alien planets?

"My dad died."

I briefly make eye contact then look back at the camp across the field.

"It wasn't directly them, you know." I say haltingly; I don't tell this story very often, but I guess if she's psychic she might know some of it anyway. "He worked for one of the big four. Mum got made redundant when we were at school and took a job doing odds and ends but never managed to hold anything down long, so it was on him. He did all hours, trying to keep us fed and dry, but then the financial crash happened and the pressure got to everyone. People did intense stuff, trying to stay in a job, trying to make ends meet. He went from working thirteen, fourteen-hour days to basically sleeping in the office. We'd just see him at weekends and he was like … drawn, like one of those ghosts. He wasn't eating enough, definitely wasn't sleeping enough, and one day he fainted at London Bridge station, right as a train went through the platform. Fell onto the tracks."

I take a deep breath, avoiding any further eye contact. "So, you see," I say, clearing my throat. "Suitwankers."

There's a long pause, then I hear Chloe echo my words quietly. "Suitwankers," she says, and somehow, it sounds more sympathetic than I ever thought it could.

Neither of us speak after that, and honestly, I don't think I want to anyway.

The light starts to fade, and I offer to take first watch. Chloe uses one of the packs to rig an impromptu harness, fastening herself to the trunk of the tree, then leans back on it and closes her eyes.

"Night Matt," she says softly.

"Night Chloe," I say, and stare into the dusk, wondering what the fuck I've gotten myself into. I squint, trying to see what the mercenaries are up to, although after the god-awful shit that went down in Bracknell, I don't really want to think about them too much right now. Or ever.

I stare at the mercenaries' fire for a good half hour, shivering copiously before I realise that the wünder-bags might have something useful in them for this exact situation. Needless to say, there's an expensive-looking down jacket and a beanie hat, which I silently thank Brother Carvas for, however ridiculous his name. I mean, who'd sign up to be a monk in a cult? Like, what do they worship? Her?

Shit, maybe they do.

The next three and a half hours are more comfortable, although there are still all kinds of tree branches sticking in my arse however I move. After that, I decide it's probably my time for a bit of sleep.

Chloe wakes up with a small 'oh' noise, and I give her a moment to wake up.

"Your watch," I say quietly. "You've not missed anything."

She nods, gesturing to her seat, and we awkwardly scramble around the tree so I can take her place, adjusting the straps on the makeshift pack-cum-harness – haha, cum – and then try to get some shut-eye.

Which, miraculously, I do, although I wake up a few times when I shift in my sleep, then can't really move because I'm anchored to this tree.

"Matt!"

I wake up to Chloe shaking me, but trying not to really shake me, if you see what I mean. It's light, but I feel like I've barely slept. I could do with a piss and a bacon sarnie, then another sleep. Guess I'll have to make do with one out of three.

Chloe puts her finger to her lips then gestures

downwards.

Fuck me.

There's a whole load of Shamblers underneath us, moving like some kind of herd. Somehow, I don't think they clock our presence; I've no idea how they see or hear, but I'm incredibly relieved that they're not all flocking around the tree baying for our blood like zombies in a horror movie.

"Shit," I whisper. "When did they arrive?"

Chloe shakes her head and we sit and watch as they slowly drift past us. I get a good look at them –they're pretty horrible to look at but I'm fascinated. Some of them are almost bent double in their raincoat-like cloaks or skin or whatever it is, clawed hands outstretched, as if they're searching for something – which, I guess, they are. I can see strands of wispy hair or something beneath their 'hoods', and occasionally, I think I hear a sighing noise, but it might be the wind.

I count fifteen, then thirty, then forty of them, slowly drifting past us. You've got to wonder what they eat or if they even need to eat – how does something like that exist? I guess the Gardeners have been trying to understand that for a while but if they've not worked it out then there's fuck-all chance of me doing the same, although I am here with a near-omniscient woman who might actually be a hundred years old or something. Should have asked her about that instead of gabbing on about my dad last night.

We wait until they pass out of sight, then I unfasten myself from the tree and fish a cereal bar out of my pack, passing Chloe's to her. She takes it and does the same, before glancing around.

"Will you keep watch?" she says delicately, and I nod, rinsing down the cereal bar with some water. She climbs down the tree and disappears in the other direction to the Shamblers, returning a few minutes later. As she climbs back up, I find myself checking her out.

Shit Matt, focus. There's killer mercenaries and deadly ghosts. Besides, it's going to take more than one kind conversation and a great body to win me over, given how annoying she generally is.

OK, ok, who am I kidding? I've put out for less.

Anyway, I go for a quick piss and try to think of a plan. How long is Lucas going to hide out here with his mercenaries? I obviously don't know the guy, but this can't be all of his masterplan – start the apocalypse and then hide out on another planet for a bit? It doesn't seem like a great plan.

Then there's a burst of automatic gunfire, shouts, and the mercenaries make for the trees on the other side of the field. There's one guy – presumably Lucas – gesturing in the air, but it's too hard to make out if he's containing Shamblers or what. There's more shouting, but no more bullets, and after a moment, the guy runs for the trees as well.

He makes it.

Shame.

I glance at Chloe, and she hands me the pair of binoculars she's been using.

Christ, is there anything these packs don't have in them?

I fiddle with the focusing thingy until the picture is sharp, then look over at the Shamblers, which seem to be surrounding the trees where the mercs are sitting. They all look pretty similar – military guys in khaki and black, all utility belts and gadgets, armed to the teeth. Two of them are still struggling with a particularly long bag, and I wonder what kind of ordnance they're packing. The others are mostly making rude gestures at the Shamblers, occasionally chucking stuff at them, which is obviously an exercise in futility.

I pan around, searching for Lucas, and get my first proper look at him. He's in jeans and an expensive-looking shirt, albeit slightly rumpled now, but otherwise he looks like a regular bloke. He's well-built, although it's hard to tell how tall he is. He's got short blonde hair and seems a bit pissed off. Twat. I instantly dislike him, not that I was too keen on him before.

He's throwing staves at the Shamblers, and does seem to be dispersing them, but he takes a break after a while and the ghosts mill around.

"Why'd they crowd around them and not us?" I whisper, handing the binoculars back to Chloe. She takes a quick look through them and then clicks her tongue.

"I believe," she says quietly. "That they're attracted by strong emotion. I bear them no ill will, and you were asleep, so they passed us by. The soldiers were scared of them, shot at them, had seen people killed by them, so they radiated strong emotion. I think that they feed on it."

"Feed on it?" I frown at her, desperate for a coffee, and wondering if Brother Carvas packed us some Red Bull. "Don't they eat people?"

Chloe shakes her head. "They are incorporeal creatures," she says softly. "And to be grotesque, where would it go?"

To my surprise, I laugh. "So, when they touch someone, the fact that they bleed and die is what, accidental?"

"Perhaps evolutionary. There's little more terrifying than seeing another creature die in such a fashion, and thus, more food."

Huh. It's a good point. I rifle around in the pack and do actually find two cans of energy drink, and down one of them, feeling instantly better. I know this shit isn't supposed to take effect straightaway, but I'm happy with the placebo effect until the real thing kicks in. I offer one to Chloe, but she holds up her hand and shakes her head. All the more for me, although who knows how long we'll be here. I should ration it.

"Do you reckon we should get closer or something?" I ask quietly, but she shakes her head again.

"Too dangerous," she says. "The probability matrices would not look kindly on it."

"Fair enough," I say. "But look, seriously, maybe you should level with me about this stuff. Like, Ben told me what you'd said to him and Lincoln that time, but seriously, where did all this shit come from? How old even are you?"

She sighs, and I can almost see her weighing up the options in her head.

I wait, keeping an eye on the far side of the field to see if the mercs move.

"I was born in 1925," she says finally. "It was 1932 when my parents were killed, at a research facility that predates the Gardeners, but I believe may have been affiliated with one of Raphael's close relatives and following a similar course of inquiry. We were caught in the fringes of what the Gardeners now call a transformation rift, a place where two worlds blur, one contorting the other, perverting its residents into something *other*."

"I should have foreseen this course of events. I did not think to include such a plan as Lucas' in my likelihood evaluations. Admittedly, the death of the psychics in my past that triggered the transformation rift did not result in such a powerful effect as we have just experienced, but perhaps the region was less fragile."

Fucking hell. She actually is a hundred years old. Even with everything I've seen, I'm not quite sure if I believe it. I'm stunned, and as a result, find myself asking the stupidest question.

"Fragile?"

"Empathy has been declining in our society for some

time," she says softly. "I know not where it will stop."

I remember the chat from Luke, back in Gardener HQ and nod, wondering if he's still alive.

Suddenly I feel very small. What am I supposed to do about all this? Ghosts I can just about deal with, but that's the military over there. They actually shoot people. They *have* shot people.

"We're quite fucked, aren't we?"

Chloe gives me a tight smile and nods. "The probabilities rather indicate so."

"Shit. Uh, look though, is it weird being almost a hundred years old?"

"The money and this," she delicately taps her head with one finger. "Rather helps me to stay below the radar. I confess, I do have a great fear of private pharmaceutical companies, although the Gardeners and my own actions have helped me to remain unnoticed. I do sponsor a school, but my followers are – as you may have gathered – rather devoted to me in helping to keep my existence a secret."

"And they what, worship you?"

She laughs quietly. She's actually kind of cute when she does that.

"I will not permit prayer," she says firmly. "They are more supportive than obsequious, but they do believe that I am here, as you are, to help protect the planet in a significant way. Of course, our current endeavours rather support this hypothesis."

"Yeah, I don't have a cult though, do I?"

She winces at the c-word, and I find myself apologising. "Sorry. Followers. Supporters. Whatever."

"Please," she says. "It's nothing. And despite our differences, you were right earlier. You have been a stalwart companion so far."

I shrug. "I can definitely be a bit of a twat though, so you know, sorry about that."

"Oftentimes I get lost in my own research, my algorithms, simply watching the world unfold," she says. "I am far from perfect myself, and I have had longer to change."

"Is that why you talk like that?" I blurt, suddenly uncomfortable. "I mean, not that it's bad or anything, it's just…"

"My English tutor was rather fond of Shakespearian plays," she admits, looking down. "And I must admit, so am I. Over time, it simply became who I am. Perhaps one day I'll change. For now, I rather like it."

"You do you," I add, trying to sound encouraging, then wonder if I'm actually patronising someone who's four times older than me, but she just cocks her head to one side and looks at me.

"Thank you," she says. "I shall."

We don't really talk for the rest of the day, and instead spend the time keeping an eye on the mercs and occasionally climbing down from the tree when Chloe says it's safe, to stretch, sit on something that isn't incredibly uncomfortable, or have a piss. We take it in turns to nap, the other looking out for anything ghostly or merc-y – see what I did there – although neither of us really sleep that well. Despite a desperate need for more caffeine, I hold back on the second can of the energy drink. Once it's gone, it's gone, unless Chloe's hiding some in her pack, which – for some reason – I doubt.

The Shamblers around the mercs eventually drift away, and disappear into the forest. I was kind of hoping that they'd get out of the trees straightaway and the ghosts would come back, but instead they play it cool, waiting it out. Bollocks.

I suddenly think about my family, my flatmates, and feel a pang of guilt for not thinking about them earlier. Mum'll be alright, I guess, but Jess and Tim? I hope they got out of Greenwich ok, although it does sound like the Gardeners have set up camp there, so if you've got to be anywhere in town...

I don't really know what else to do, so I turn to doing the only helpful thing I can in this situation – practicing my staves. Who knew – Matt Potter, casting spells on not just one, but two planets.

Intergalactic badass.

Insignificant, terrified, intergalactic badass.

This planet is wringing far too much emotional honesty from me. I need to stop it right now.

The evening eventually draws in, and I'm exhausted. Guess it's pretty tiring being shit-scared and bored at the same time.

We settle in for our second uncomfortable night and

I deliberately avoid any further sad bedtime tales from the childhood of Matthew Potter.

I'm feeling pretty groggy when Chloe wakes me up for my watch. I wipe the sleep from my eyes and let her take the improvised backpack-harness to sleep. She looks pretty wrecked.

The sun eventually rises, and I'm wondering how long we can do this for. I know we're being all heroic and shit, but honestly, it's overrated, and despite the almost-incessant fearing for our lives, I'm quite keen to get back home, even if home has been invaded by monsters. At least I'd be able to sleep on a proper mattress.

I let Chloe sleep for as long as possible, but she wakes herself up with a start, making me jump.

"You ok?"

She glances around, and hurriedly detaches herself from the harness, looking around for the binoculars. I hand them to her and she peers over towards the mercenary camp.

"Chloe, what's up?"

She rubs her eyes sleepily, and in moving, I catch a whiff of my own body odour. Brilliant.

"Something bad," she says, narrowing her eyes at the camp on the far side of the field.

"More specifically?" I ask, cracking open the last can of energy drink. "Bad 'getting shot at', bad 'ghostly grandmas' or bad 'something completely new to make life really awful'?"

Then the screaming starts, and that pretty much

answers my question. Something's happening in the camp, but I can't see well enough to tell what's going on. The mercs are standing together, but that's about all I can tell, apart from the horrendous noise of someone screeching like they're being … oh, wait … yeah, they're torturing someone.

It's fucking awful.

Chloe hands me the binoculars and I take a look for myself. Most of the mercs are on the ground, including that shit Lucas, and they're fishing someone out of the long bag that I thought had a sniper rifle or rocket launcher in it or something. Instead, it's a familiar-looking guy, bound and gagged and generally being kicked around.

I know him. Last time I saw him, he was serving breakfast in the training facility in Bracknell. Nice guy, not stingy with the bacon.

They string him up to a tree and Lucas starts laying into him. Shit. At first, it's kicks and punches, and that's bad enough, but then Lucas starts making long, shallow cuts with some kind of hunting knife. The rest of the mercs sit around watching, pointing and seemingly, offering advice. I swallow as a wave of nausea hits me. How can they do that? Sick bastards.

"We've got to stop them," I say, putting the binoculars down and turning to Chloe. "They're fucking him up."

She takes the binoculars and looks over, her face torn with indecision. "We can't," she says. "We need to know what they're doing. It's too important.

"Too important?" I say, forgetting not to raise my voice. "They're cutting that guy up. They're going to kill him!"

"But *why*?" she says calmly. "To what end? Torture and pain opens rifts, so it's likely they are leaving this place. It's of the utmost importance that we know where they're going and why; I doubt that they're torturing someone simply to torture someone, especially with the Shamblers nearby."

I pause, about to launch into another tirade, but she's actually right. We're not in a movie and charging in will likely get us both killed. But I can't stand by and do nothing, that's just as wrong. God, this is properly crap. I take a deep breath, scratching my head with a shaky hand.

"Not to mention," Chloe says, voicing my fear. "That we'd die if we intervened."

"Oh, come on," I say, feeling a bit desperate. "Haven't you got some secrets up your sleeves? Some all-knowing combat bullshit, anticipating where the bullets will be or something?"

A look crosses her face, but she shakes her head. "Too much data, too little time," she says. "And even if I could, it wouldn't help you."

"Fuck," I swear. "Please, look, can't we get a bit closer? In case, you know, there's a chance or something?"

"Ok," she says, seeming to steel herself. "But if I say we stop, we stop. And you should have your staves – and the gun – ready."

My hands are trembling violently now, and I jam

them in my pockets to hide it. I'm not too far off throwing up, but at least we're doing something.

So it is, that to the sound of a screaming cook being cut up by a psychopath, we carefully climb down the tree and work our way across the field.

Ben
The Long Night of Solitude

Three hours later, we pause at the top of a bare peak. Anders generally seems to know smart ways around the landscape, like how to avoid too much climbing or how to clamber across the deep channels worn in the rock by water, which are often too wide to hop over.

Hugo keeps falling behind, and I can hear him swearing at the bulky shotgun that he's got slung over his shoulder. I want to feel sorry for him, but going directly uphill with a full pack in sub-zero temperatures takes pretty much all of my attention.

Then everything else stops because we arrive.

In front of us, the bare brown rock sweeps down towards the coast but on our left, it rises sharply to a steep cliff. At the high tide waterline, not too far away, there's a large dark crack in the rock. Blackened ashy marks lead into the cave like landing strips, the rock scorched and burned.

This must be it.

Anders swallows and stares as he sees it, and after a moment, Alice turns to face him.

"Ben and I will go in," she says briskly. "If we're not back in two hours, go back to camp. Wait a day for us, then go back to Longyearbyen and let the Gardeners know we're not coming back."

I take in a deep breath of frozen air, my stomach clenching. This is what we're here for, after all, but nonetheless, I really don't want to go down there. I'm thankful for Alice's conviction – I can't imagine having to do this by myself. A part of me still doesn't really believe that we'll find anything in there, but those dark marks definitely weren't made by a penguin.

Hugo starts to stammer in protest. "She's right," I say, my voice trembling. "There's no point either of you coming with us, unless there's a polar bear in that cave. Or an angry walrus."

Neither of them laugh, but I guess Anders has probably seen his fair share of angry walruses.

Walrii.

Whatever.

"Ok," Anders says eventually. "We'll stay here. If the weather starts to turn, you must come back. It's a long walk back to the camp, and important that we stay ahead of it."

Alice nods, although I don't think she really means that she agrees with him. I don't know if she's just keen to find this thing or if she genuinely wants to recruit it to help back home. Hopefully it's both.

Neither of us speak as we carefully work our way down the rocky hill. The chunks of dark rock are streaked with bird shit and are razor sharp, so we're both taking care not to fall. I'm sure there's a first aid kit in these backpacks of ours, but I don't think either of us really want to use it, especially when the rock is covered in crap.

I'm babbling again, aren't I? I'm fixating on the strangest details.

I'm terrified.

As we get closer to the cave, I can see that the rock approaching it is burned and charred in patches, like elongated chevrons scorched into the earth.

"I'll talk to it first," Alice says in a whisper. "But be ready."

I don't know whether I should use my protection stave or not, but I do, tapping into the noosphere, feeling it rushing past me much more powerfully than in London; it's like standing in the middle of a fast-flowing river. I'm almost physically staggered by it. I hurriedly shape the magic in my head and then release it, a small trickle of power continually flowing through me, as a dull sheen seems to coat my skin.

I nod to Alice, wondering whether I should have looked at staves to protect other people as well, but it's too late now. She gives me a swift nod back, and we start to round the mouth of the cave, expecting a dark and gloomy interior.

It's the complete opposite. There's a brightness inside, bizarrely reminding me of the lighting section in John Lewis, a warm, yellowy light that gets more and more intense the further in we get.

Then I see him.

He's sat on a boulder a few metres from us, and he's clearly a man, but clearly, so much more than just a man. Golden, glowing, feathered wings are furled around him, sheathing him in light. He's bare-chested, and his skin is smooth and gleaming, his trousers as white as the snow we left behind outside. He's barefoot, and has dark, tightly curled hair. His features are sharp and chiselled; he'd do great in fashion photography back home.

I wonder if he can hear my thoughts.

Sorry Raysiel, please don't disintegrate us for my flippancy. It's just nerves.

He looks up and I mistakenly make eye contact. It's like looking into a yawning set of parallel mirrors and trying to make sense of what you see. I can almost feel his age and power, barely managing to look away and take a step back before I lose myself in him.

Alice starts saying quiet words in a smooth, flowing language. I'd guess Hebrew or Aramaic, but I really don't know the difference between the two. She stops, and there's a long pause.

Then he speaks. I don't know if I was expecting to understand him, but it's perfectly clear in my head. He's softly spoken, but it's … powerful, somehow, like the slow creep of a glacier, centuries of force concentrated into this incredible, terrifying creature in front of us.

"I am greatly wroth with the iniquity of man," he says slowly, regarding us. I don't want to look at his eyes again, but staring at my feet is probably the wrong message to send. Should I be kneeling?

"In two thousand years, what has man wrought, but strife?"

"Sir," Alice says, in English this time. "We were hoping that you would help us."

"Help you?" he says, and for a moment I have an impression of barely-concealed fury, a fiercely bubbling heat, scalding hot. "What has mankind done to deserve help?"

"Weren't you sent to protect us?" she asks, frowning, her pitch rising. "Like you helped Averan?"

"Averan?" he says, sounding almost wistful. "Averan *was* a good man, perhaps the last good man until John or Christ himself. I have spent two thousand years contemplating holy scripture, seeing the truth about your peoples. You have had ample time to repent, small race that you are, and yet you wilfully choose wrong."

"Is that what happened in Jerusalem?" Alice asks tentatively. "Is that why you left?"

"I will no longer be amongst your people," he booms, standing. His wings spread and I have to turn and close my eyes to avoid being blinded – the golden light is searingly, painfully bright. "They are petty and unworthy."

"Please," I say, butting in, trying not to look at him. "We really need your help. Rifts to other worlds have been opened, and creatures are flooding in. We can't stop them. Shamblers that kill when they touch you, right in central London and all over the place."

Alice looks at me, and I realise that I might have done something really stupid.

"The rifts?" Raysiel says, furling his wings once more. The light dims a little, but it's still dazzling. "Who dares to open the portals to the judgement worlds? The time is not yet right for the day of reckoning."

I glance at Alice, but she gestures for me to go on.

"My organisation," I start, then speaking more quickly as I realise that I might be giving the wrong impression. "My organisation exists to close the rifts when they open and co-ordinate the fight against the creatures on the other side. Our headquarters were attacked in London, just as four of our most powerful psychics were arriving. It did something and there was some kind of wave that re-opened rifts across town. It seems to have slowed, but we don't have enough people to fight back."

"The Gifted," Raysiel says. "The Gifted should be prohibited from gathering, lest their mental anguish breaks the boundaries between worlds. Your elders should know this. Your high priests have been remiss."

"We … uh … we don't really have high priests," I confess. "The world isn't really as religious as it used to be."

"I know," he says, regarding me. "I was testing your

truthfulness. Man has greatly fallen from his dedication to the Lord."

"In fairness," Alice chimes in, sounding irritated. "There isn't a lot of explanation in the Bible. There's a lot of 'do this' but not a lot of why. Is it surprising that people have turned away? Most people don't like being told to do something without any reason other than 'because I am the Lord'."

Raysiel's eyes flash, and he stands again, taking a step towards us. I can feel the heat coming off him. The ice on the floor of the cave beneath his feet hisses and steams, and for a moment I can smell wet feathers, but what's actually going through my mind is whether this is it, the end. What'll it be like? Will it hurt? I imagine Hugo and Anders standing outside, just seeing a flash of bright light, then turning for home. It doesn't feel real. I can't die.

But it doesn't come. Raysiel takes a very deep breath and his radiance seems to dim. He steps backwards and sits down on the boulder again.

"Yes," he says, his voice trembling with the effort of controlling himself. "Yes, I have meditated on this. In the beginning, you were not ready. Your people were unruly and in need of stewardship. Today, they need more, to understand in order to obey the truth. Or perhaps you are being punished for your lack of understanding."

Alice scoffs, seemingly gaining confidence. "And how were we supposed to understand?" she says. "Who was going to teach us these great truths? How are we going to repent and understand if we're all dead? Are you going to help us or not?"

The angel is silent for almost a full minute, and as my pulse slows, I can hear other sounds outside – birdcalls, waves crashing on the shore.

"I must think on this," Raysiel says softly. "Begone and return tomorrow. You may present your case again then."

"Tomorrow?" I say, taking my lead from Alice. "Can't you help today? People are dying."

"Your people are always dying," he says calmly, slowly, terribly. "It is their wont."

I exchange glances with Alice and she shrugs, flicking her head towards the mouth of the cave.

"Thank you for listening to us," I say. "And thank you for not destroying us."

Alice turns to go, and I start to follow.

"What a creature of terror I have become," I hear the angel say quietly. "It was not always thus."

I hurry out of the cave, and neither of us speak until we're halfway to the hilltop where Hugo and Anders are keeping their watch. I suddenly feel the sweat on my back and under my arms, the moisture chilling me in the cold.

I pause, taking a few deep breaths. I might throw up, or cry. I'm not sure which.

I'm incredibly relieved not to be dead, and that it's over – for now, at least.

"I can't believe you called out an angel over Biblical logic," I blurt, swallowing. "What was that?"

"Not just the Bible," she says crisply. "The other Abrahamic texts are the same. And not really logic, either."

I cock my head to one side and look at her.

"I see what you mean though," she capitulates eventually. "I lost my temper. All that power and he'd stayed hidden. The things he could have told us, the differences he could have made to the world and our knowledge!"

"You think he'll help us?" I say, trying to interrupt a lecture. We're getting closer to Anders and Hugo now, and they're both stood up, looking at us expectantly.

"Maybe," she says. "I do wonder why he hasn't flown back to the heavens. What's keeping him here? If he's not watching us, and he's not helping, then what's his purpose? Obtuse people are incredibly frustrating."

We reach Hugo and Anders, and Hugo embraces Alice awkwardly. "You made it!" he says. "Was he there? Is he going to help?"

Alice looks at me and I shrug, suddenly fighting to stop myself grinning as the relief of simply being alive almost overwhelms me. "He's thinking about it," I say, trying to sound nonchalant.

Hugo's face goes from pasty white to bright red.

"He's thinking about it?!" he shrieks. "Thinking about it? We walk for five hours in the freezing cold, then you stroll into a cave with an angel, centuries old, almost get vaporised but instead have a pleasant little chat and you tell me that he's *thinking* about it? Are you *absolutely fucking kidding me right now*?"

I look at Anders, who raises his eyebrows and waits for a moment before speaking. "You are still alive," he says laconically. "Despite talking to a creature from the spirit world. If we have to come back tomorrow, we come back tomorrow."

Between you and me, I'd like to be able to channel a little bit more of Anders' living philosophy.

I nod, and start retracing our steps with our guide. Alice follows, and for a moment I wonder if Hugo is going to stay right there on the beach. A moment later, there's an explosive huff, then footsteps on the rocky ground. I start to giggle, and then all of the tension starts to come out of me. Alice joins in, and for a few seconds, I can barely breathe for laughter, trying to wipe tears from my eyes with my thick winter gloves.

"Sorry Hugo," I manage, when I've composed myself a bit more. "You're right, you're right. That was fucking ridiculous. You should have seen it – I've never, ever seen anything like that before, and after this I hope I never do. It's not, well, it was absolutely terrifying."

As we work our way across the desolate frozen desert, towering rocky hills on either side, columns of fractured rock streaked with bird shit, we recount the conversation, much to the disbelief of our guide and the eccentric aristocrat.

"Shit," Hugo says, when we finish, stumbling and catching himself on the uneven ground. He picks himself back up and looks thoughtful.

"Do you think we can bring the chopper next time?" he says. "We got lucky with the weather and the wildlife today, but who knows if it'll hold tomorrow."

Anders nods, looking concerned and gesturing behind us. "We should outpace that today," he says, indicating a large, dark-looking cloud bank. "But tomorrow will be a different story."

"He seems a little sensitive," Alice says. "I don't want to upset him more than we really have to."

Our guide shakes his head and falls silent. I understand.

The rest of the walk back to Kinnvika is cold and quiet. Hugo occasionally breaches the silence with questions about the angel's intentions, our intentions and our ideas about the angel's intentions. Our replies become increasingly terse before he gives up completely.

I spy an arctic fox running off in the distance, and a vast number of penguins and walruses on a distant beach, but none of us want to stop; it's three in the afternoon, and we've still got a way to go. Everyone's tired. My feet are sore, despite the excellent walking boots.

When we do get back to the tents, Anders insists on keeping us all together while we cook dinner. He turns some tinned beef into a surprisingly tasty chilli con carne, and although he's got a heavy hand with the chilli powder, I don't mind. Alice's eyes stream a little, but she bears it with good humour.

Once we're all finished, Anders grins and hands around large, white chocolate polar bears for pudding, making me laugh – they're cute, unlike the real deal.

Hugo and Alice retreat to their tent, and Anders sits outside, cleaning his gun. I'm suddenly purposeless, pacing around the strange, empty wooden buildings, not wanting to go too far from the camp. It's still quite light, and I have to remind myself that it's going to stay like this for the rest of the day.

I look around at the huts – the bare boards look like they're made of bone rather than wood, or perhaps grubby, dirty ivory. Piles of logs, presumably for burning, sit alongside most of them, next to wooden tables and chairs that remind me of the hand-carved furniture you see in films about the American civil war.

Everything is bare and bleak, and there's only so many wooden huts you can wander around, however alien and odd-looking they are. After a time, I find my way back to the camp, where Anders is writing in a hard-backed paper journal. I take one of the camping stools and sit on the other side of the cooking pot – it looks like he's already washed up and cleaned everything, and I feel a pang of guilt.

"Thanks," I say, gesturing. "Sorry, I should have helped. I forgot."

"No problem," he says, looking up and giving me a small smile. "You've got plenty on your mind."

"Yeah," I say, nodding. "Yeah, I guess I do."

I lean forward, resting my elbows on my knees and sit looking out at the desolate landscape, wondering if the angel is doing this exact same thing at this exact same time.

It's a long, quiet night.

Seline
Doing What We Must

I've got two French Shamanic practitioners and a Catholic priest who arrived on a speedboat in Brighton. I've got four fully fledged, incredibly tired and bloodied field agents, two rabbis, and six administrative support staff who can just about contain and disperse. I've got more support from the conventional armed forces, but we're desperate for help. We're hanging on by our fingernails.

I'm still tracking eighty active rifts, seven of which are extremely high priority, in dense urban areas that can't be evacuated, or which are spawning incredibly dangerous and difficult creatures. We've got at least a hundred and fifty tracked Shamblers, fifteen Lesser Banshees, and a Greater Banshee that we can't shift out of Hyde Park. There are seven nests of Darklings, including two lodged in the underground network and a single Ravager that may or may not be in Harvey Nichols. Packs of hellhounds roam the streets.

Our teams went all out to contain threats and close

rifts, but we've lost so many. We've got a relatively accurate count on the number of rifts now, and only a few more have opened today. The rate of spread has slowed, but we're in real danger of being overwhelmed by what's left.

The majority of the Gardeners who weren't in Wild Court are dead or out of action.

We pulled Lincoln out of a hellhound's jaws, unconscious, just before it bit him through. He probably won't use his left hand again. The civilian casualties are the stuff of nightmares – the latest figure was fifty thousand in the last forty-eight hours. Our conventional forces and air support have helped us to identify, but not close, rifts.

The Shamblers are deadly and awful but at least they're confined to the ground. We've managed to eliminate all of the Whistlers, thankfully, so we're getting better air support now. The drones have been a life-saver more times than I can count, but I'd really like a Perdix swarm. We're still arguing with the US about a loan.

I've been pulled into the field twice. My skills are logistics and coordination, but I have to help how I can. On both occasions, a burly SAS officer called Tom carried me out of my chair into a basement teeming with Darklings so that I could contain and disperse. The first time, he wet himself and left me with intensely painful bruises because he was holding on too tight. But it's war, so we're not counting – not to mention that the first time I saw a Darkling, I threw up on myself. Normal rules just don't apply, but I'd kill for an acupuncture session right now. I also came a hair's breadth from popping my shoulder right out of its joint, but that's business as usual with my EDS. I'm constantly on painkillers.

Some of the rifts don't seem to have anything coming through, and there is significant concern that non-corporeals have slipped past us.

We've had two transformation rifts, more than we've had in a decade. A small part of a housing estate in Peckham, and one in Angel both started to change and warp within minutes of each other. The people grew tentacles and became feral, or changed into large, powerful tiger-like creatures as the surroundings began to sprout purple vines, and toxic mist spread through the entire area. It took over a hundred soldiers from a base near Salisbury twenty-four hours to support two field agents from the First Extraordinary – far, far fewer than we'd normally send – to close the rifts, as a matter of extreme urgency. The media footage continues to be a state secret, but the memory will be burned into all of us for years to come, and there were no civilian survivors.

I've got two missing staff, ironically our newest recruits. One is still in Svalbard, tracking an angelic asset that I think is a waste of time. Anything that spends two thousand years naval gazing isn't going to be much help, but it wasn't my call. The other was tracking the likely ultimate source of all of this, and according to remote footage, is still on the other side of the rift in Karnak with who knows how many Shamblers. In twenty-four hours, we'll presume that he's dead, along with the semi-omniscient asset who has her own cult here in London. I've got three overseas agents still tracking down leads on spiritual artefacts and shrines, but I'm not holding out much hope for that either.

We haven't heard anything from Wild Court. Raphael has been imbuing the walls with staves for years, affixing the building to a location deep in the New Forest, so that in case of emergency, the whole building *shifts*, riding the flows of the noosphere to a large forest clearing. Like all recruits who reach the advanced section of our guides, I remember reading about the stave, baffled by its complexity. I trusted that it'd work if we ever needed it, not for a moment thinking that it might not quite work how we anticipated, leaving us stranded without help.

Of course, I don't know if the RPG attack damaged the spell or if Lucas knew about the incantation and had a counter stave ready, but we haven't heard anything from them. The building is supposed to lock for forty-eight hours to allow forces inside to fully catch their breath and prepare, but it's been more than that.

In twenty-four hours, we'll have to accept that they're probably dead as well, but that's going to put an extreme strain on morale, assuming any of us are left at that point. I don't know what would happen next; I assume there's a plan. The conventional military would just have to do their best, and we'd be at the mercy of the spiritual forces from our ally countries. Until they arrived, the best we could do with the non-corporeals present would be to evacuate southern England.

"Ma'am," Tom says, pulling my attention away from troop deployments. I've got an active assignment, but I need a minute to finish the battle orders. He doesn't bother me for a few moments, and then clears his throat. I find myself smiling tiredly at his dedication and hit send, turning to him.

"Let's go," I say, suddenly keen to get outside. I can feel a headache coming on and I hope it doesn't turn into a migraine. Slowly, I turn my wheelchair around and Tom helps to get me into the back of the jeep as we're cautiously driven down the long road from the Observatory towards Greenwich and Central London, marines watching for anything unusual.

I'm exhausted, but I'm probably good for a few more staves.

It's strange and awful to think about, but London is being evacuated for the first time since the Blitz. Even the seventh of July couldn't shift the population, but now that the Whistlers are cleared out, the drone of helicopters is constant, ferrying civilians to safe havens far from town, where there are fewer rifts. It's slow, but what choice do we have?

Greenwich is a ghost town. The military took early advantage of the Gardener protection and people flocked to the park to be airlifted. Blackheath, with its large houses and wide, open spaces, was less of a priority, but strict evacuation zoning has been applied - if there's one thing we can't have, it's queues. That'd be an immediate death sentence in the event of trouble.

Empty houses and quiet streets stretch around me. On a regular day, the market would be teeming, tourists sprinting across the busy roads towards the falafel stalls, art sellers, clothing stands. They'd be eating in the open areas by the Cutty Sark on the river. Today there's nothing. Just buildings, stalls with awnings flapping in the breeze, soldiers on guard for the slightest hint of threat.

"Alright gentlemen," I say, over my headset. "You know the drill. Lesser Banshees today, so earplugs in now please."

The two jeeps pull over and pause for a moment, soldiers fumbling to put in the hastily retrofitted earplugs with communications leads threaded through them so that they can still hear each other, even if they can't hear anything else. That in itself has led to a few casualties, with marines being brought down by hellhounds, but it's a lower risk than a Banshee's wail.

We resume our journey, but a moment later there's a muted screech, followed by an enormous crash and an explosion, audible even through the earplugs. Soldiers around me stand and look for the threat, but other than a plume of smoke, there's nothing to indicate trouble, although that in itself is more than enough.

My earpiece buzzes. "Greater Banshee through the rift," Hannah says from the Observatory. "We've got a chopper down and casualties at the scene. Seline, do you want to wait for backup?"

I glance around. I've got nine soldiers with me, which is ample for a couple of Lesser Banshees, but stretching things for a Greater. Not to mention the hellhounds, Lesser Banshees and general increase in ordnance flying around while I'm stationary.

We're not supposed to be playing the hero.

"No," I say through the mic. "We'll spring it before reinforcements arrive from the other side of the rift."

"Understood," she replies. "Will send backup when we can. Good hunting."

I glance down at my tablet and check the location. The rift is marked right by Deptford station, in a small but rapidly-gentrifying square. There's a great beer shop there, Hops and something, run by a couple of New Zealanders, if I remember rightly. I don't drink a lot, and I usually use a straw, but I still like a beer.

I can feel my palms sweating, but then I remember something about the development behind the square, on the other side of the arches. There'd been some local backlash against it – in fairness, it's almost all glass, completely out of keeping with the brown brick surrounding it – and there's a graffiti tag right down the central stairway, in the middle of the building facing the square. If I remember rightly, it's also impregnated with staves.

The jeeps turn onto Deptford High St, and I can hear

the terrible screeching now. It's like fingernails down a blackboard, constantly. There's crashing and roaring, and I wonder what else has come through with the Banshee. We'll pull back if we have to. There are no rash actions in the Gardeners.

We pass salons and markets, the soldiers around me checking their guns nervously. Over the last few days, our teams have been stretched to the limit, and they're fighting incredibly unfamiliar enemies on home turf, all of which is enormously unsettling and awful. They've all done more than anyone could have expected. No-one could have anticipated fighting anything hand-to-hand in Central London, over and above the odd brawl.

The jeep passes under the railway bridge, slowing, and as we're emerging on the other side, there's an impact and we veer off to one side. I'm thrown against the side of my chair painfully, almost tumbling out as we hit a parked car on the left. There's a tremendous amount of noise behind us; screeching and crashing, but Tom relies on Jez and Sarah to keep us safe as they jump over the sides and fire at something. I wheel myself towards the back and he lifts me out, turning us towards the square.

It's a mess.

There's a vast Banshee flailing around in the square, its metallic scarecrow body showing through the dirty grey robe that seems to be partly organic. It's trying to grip what's left of a military helicopter, knocking its claws into the nearby buildings and railway bridge, screaming and taking chunks out of whatever's nearby. Parts of it ripple in and out of existence, making it horrifically present and strangely insubstantial at the same time.

It's taller than the railway bridge, reaching several storeys up. Two Lesser Banshees are circling around underneath it. I can hear the snuffling and barking of hellhounds, but other than the initial encounter, I don't think we've got their attention yet.

The other jeep manages to park next to us, the marines taking shelter behind the vehicles. I glance over at the newbuild on the other side of the Banshee, thankful that it's still covered in graffiti. It's faded a bit now – looks like someone tried to pressure-wash it.

It'll do.

I reach for the noosphere tentatively, but I can feel the rift in the way – it's been torn, ripped upwards like an open zip, and I can't channel anything directly behind it. That's a problem.

"Tom," I say into my mic, gesturing. "I need to get up there."

On one side of the courtyard there's a line of trees and a large building. At ground level, it's all shops with the grills pulled down, but up above, it's Deptford station, with the elevated railway line running at ninety degrees to the newbuild and the Banshee.

Tom finishes taking shots at a hellhound and looks at the structure, then at me. To his credit, he doesn't even wince, and issues a set of commands into his microphone.

Three of the marines peel off towards the left-hand side of the square, three to the right. The remaining two stay by the jeeps. Tom gives the signal and they start to advance. Instantly, four hellhounds bound across the square towards the marines, who pause, drop to one knee and fire their rifles at the approaching creatures, giving no ground. They're all hit, although the last one has enough momentum to take it tumbling into a marine, who falls backwards onto the pavement.

At the same time, the Lesser Banshees start gliding towards the two flanking marine units, screaming and flailing their scarecrow arms and claws around. They're slow, but the marines are distracted by the hellhounds, so there's not much impeding their advance.

Then the Greater Banshee loses interest in destroying the buildings and looks down at us. It screams, pain rippling through my head, despite the earplugs. There's a wash of red, and the marine toppled by the hellhound is suddenly gushing blood over the pavement; his earplugs must have been knocked out by the impact. My gorge rises, but I shout to Tom that we should go, and I push myself forwards, behind the marine unit, the wheels of my chair barely skirting the rapidly-spreading pool of blood.

Tom's right beside me, laying down fire at the Lesser Banshees. I've told him that it's a waste of time, but it's instinct. I give myself a push along, then reach behind me for the noosphere, channelling towards a Lesser Banshee and releasing a containment stave. It freezes mid-screech, and Tom focuses his fire on it, shouting into his mic for the others to target it as well. The right-hand group advances, firing into it, but there's a crash as the Greater Banshee flows forward, ignoring conventional physics, picking a soldier up and squeezing it in its barbed wire hand.

I hear bones break and the body goes limp, just as I reach the entrance to the station. Tom doesn't hesitate – he grabs me and the wheelchair and runs up the stairs towards the platform. His breathing is laboured by the time we reach the top – it's four flights of stairs and adrenalin only gets you so far, but he still manages to scan the platform as we arrive before he sets me down.

There's another awful, awful screech, and the Greater Banshee turns to face us. I can feel the weaker noosphere nearby, but there's a flow of energy immediately in front of me, nearer to the building, so I shape the summoning stave, feeling my tattoos warm as I channel more and more. I direct it into all of the staves embedded in the graffiti and then *yank* them forwards as the Greater Banshee moves towards us. There's a rush of energy and I feel it discharge, the creature freezing in place.

I see Tom yell a command into his mic before he raises his rifle and opens fire, hands trembling with fatigue. The Banshee is hit from below, but parts of it ripple back into existence and for a moment I worry that it'll break free. Thankfully, the marines are nothing if not disciplined, and as soon as another part warps into reality, it's hit by a hail of gunfire.

There's a thud-whomp noise and an explosion as one of the soldiers hits it with an RPG, and the Banshee topples backwards, staggering, then crashing backwards into the building behind it.

It twitches, then lies still.

Tom rushes forwards to the railing, and continues firing. I follow, more cautiously. The remaining marines are firing into a Lesser Banshee crouched over the body of a soldier, and I can see two other bodies lying prone; the first marine to fall, and another, crushed against the side of the building, presumably swiped by the Greater Banshee. Feeling a wave of fatigue, I take a deep breath and shape the containment stave, channelling as much of the noosphere as I can before releasing it, freezing the remaining Banshee in place.

I must have blacked out, because I realise that Tom's now carrying me back down the stairs with the help of one of the other marines. Both of them are breathing heavily from the combat, and I've still got another job to do.

"Need anything?" Tom says, and I shake my head as they set me down. I ignore the smell and the bodies in the square, focusing on the rift itself, trying to take it easy, despite the reasonable probability that something else could come through at any moment.

Once again, I reach further out for the noosphere. I can almost feel that it's exhausted by the terror, the pain and the death, and that the rift is in very real danger of unravelling, like threads of a tapestry just coming apart. We've never seen that, and I don't even want to think about how it would look, an irreparable breach formed between our world and theirs.

I feel sick again, and focus on pushing the flow of the noosphere back towards the gap, reaching down into the earth. I've often found – and this is documented in advanced Gardener guides – that the rifts are less likely to spread downwards. Something to do with the way earth's energy flows.

It starts to take, and little by little, it closes. I feel a surge of relief as the bottom part of the rift knits together, and then it gets easier, the edges almost reaching for each other like magnets.

I feel a piercing pain in my head that might be the start of a migraine and I waver for a moment. The rift starts to peel back, the sheer volume of pain and terror incurred around us working against me. I grip the armrests of my wheelchair tightly, feeling my hands bruise and my joints stretching, but I push the noosphere hard, channelling it back towards the rift.

Little by little by little, it closes.

Then it's done, and I sag back, utterly exhausted. I'll need a break before I can go back to directing battlegroups. My throat feels scratchy, and a jagged edge of pain cuts straight into my forehead.

"All clear," I say into my mic. "Perimeter units, return when secure."

A moment later, four tired, bloodied, pale marines

trot back into the square. They lean back against the wall as Tom calls for local ambulances to remove the bodies. Banshees rarely leave wounded, only the dead.

I feel grey and drawn with fatigue as we drive back to the Observatory, Tom and I alone with our driver, the jeep feeling empty without the others that we've left behind. I've taken out my earplugs as my phone rings, and I tiredly push one of the earpieces back in, answering the call.

"All Gardener call," the voice on the other end says. "This is an all-Gardener call from Wild Court. We've sustained damage, and lockdown protocols prevented exit but we are digging our way out and coming home as soon as we can. We have approximately twenty injured. Please, send transport, medical and demolition if you can. Our ETA is approximately forty-eight hours from location at Wilverley Inclosure. I repeat: we're alive and well, but the building has partially collapsed and progress is slow."

Despite the military discipline and advancing years of my remaining colleagues, the line is flooded with cries of relief and questions choked with emotion.

I glance up at Tom, my cheeks wet with tears. He looks concerned, but I manage a wan smile.

"It's alright," I say quietly, my voice barely audible over the noise of the engine. "They're coming home."

Alice
Angelic Persuasion

Despite the fact that Hugo was the only one aware of the existence of the paranormal a month ago, he seems the most perturbed by the events of the day.

Initially, I ignore him as I write down my findings. The tents are small, but there's sufficient space for us to sit apart, huddled in our sleeping bags. I'm trying to document what I saw of the angel, in case he vaporises us tomorrow – physical characteristics, mannerisms and the like. Although I've been pursuing this with what I thought was a purely scientific detachment, I was surprised at how angry I became at the angel's passivity. To be crass, it was rather like chasing a leprechaun's pot of gold, only to find it full of urine.

My life's work, successful but squandered.

Hugo sits and shivers.

"You don't have to come tomorrow," I offer, looking at him. "Anders can guide us."

He shakes his head. "I can't believe it," he says in a

quiet voice, and I have to lean in to hear him. "I really wanted to die before all of this happened, but it's the end, I know it is."

"Die?" I say, surprised. "Hugo, I know this is all very difficult, but there's no reason why we can't come through this."

He doesn't look up, clutching the end of his sleeping bag. "You don't understand," he says. "The angel, the … things back in Britain. There's no going back now. Now they're here, the world's different. It's … bad."

I can't help it. I scoff and he looks like he's about to cry.

"Hugo," I say. "You're incredibly privileged. If anyone can ride this out, it's you. You have an apocalypse-proof mansion. Your family has been preparing for this for generations. Think of all the regular people who aren't so lucky. The world has changed, but you're one of the extremely fortunate ones."

It's dim in the tent, so I can't quite see if he's crying or not, but I think he is. Either way, he doesn't reply, and instead lies down and faces away from me. I go back to my notes, but it's harder to concentrate. A sullen ally, an unwilling angel, and no clear path. At least Ben has proven reliable, although I haven't seen any of these so-called magical powers yet. Mind you, we haven't needed them, and his organisation has facilitated our onward journey well enough.

His question about the implications of the angel ring

in my mind. I suppose that if what I've seen about the state of England is correct, and not some media fabrication, then one more strange thing hardly matters. Mind you, perhaps people will take comfort in 'good' beings as well as those actively trying to dismember us all.

Not to mention the church.

Maybe I should simply accept my smaller role in the drama and sell my story to the media or write my autobiography, assuming we all survive.

I'm not sure what else I'd do, now that I've reached my goal.

After a while, I put my notebook down and try to sleep.

Curiously, it comes quickly, but I wake every few hours, dreaming about flashes of bright light, intense heat, and eyes that blaze like the sun. I try to marshal my subconscious, but it's resistant to my efforts. Ridiculous.

The next morning, I wake to find Hugo climbing out of the tent. I start up but he's already gone before I can say anything.

That's one less problem, although I feel guilty admitting it. I dress, wishing for a shower after the long walk yesterday.

There's a light patter of rain on top of the tent. That's going to make things harder.

After I pull on more clothes and wriggle out of my sleeping bag, I hunt around in my rucksack for dried coffee and breakfast, unzipping the tent to see Anders boiling water in front of the other tent, using a small camping stove, sheltered by an ingenious tent flap held up by slim metal poles.

"Enough for another cup?" I call to him, and he nods, waving for me to come over. Fastening my walking boots, I scuttle across to him, just about able to keep dry.

A moment later, I'm drinking hot coffee and feeling much more human. I know it's a generalisation, but I'm truly starting to enjoy the company of Norwegians. They're helpful, kind, and as far as I've seen, don't feel the need for meaningless small talk.

Anders pours more water from a plastic container into the smaller metallic container on the stove, and as he's pouring it into a second cup and stirring in coffee, the zip behind him opens and Ben's face appears. Anders hands him the cup, and the tent zips up a moment later.

To my surprise, I share a grin with our rangy guide.

Half an hour later, it's still raining, and our party is gathered under the eaves of the largest hut in Kinnvika. Hugo still looks tired and pale; Ben also looks tired, but seems ready to go.

"So," Anders says. "Hugo, you'll stay here at the camp today. This will be a tough hike."

Hugo starts to protest, but his voice trails off.

"Stay within the alarms, and keep your shotgun with you at all times. Don't cook anything."

The aristocrat eventually meets Anders' eyes. "Alright," he says. "I'll stay."

"Good man," Anders says. "Ben, Alice, this will be difficult. We'll stay within arm's reach of each other when we can, and always keep sight of someone else. Are you ready?"

We both nod, and without any additional preamble, we're off.

It's miserable.

The firm sand and shingle dissolves into a squashy mess underfoot, and the rock becomes slippery. Despite their water-proofing, our clothes and packs get wetter and heavier, slowing our progress incrementally but inexorably.

We circle around the bare peaks, the smooth channels we used yesterday now fast-flowing streams. We're forced to walk to the sides or splash through the water where it's not too deep, but Anders inspects the riverbed carefully before he allows us to do so.

After four long hours, we pause for lunch, sitting and digesting for longer than I'd like, listening to the sound of raindrops pattering on our hoods and jackets. All of the wildlife we saw yesterday – the foxes, the birds, the small scurrying rodents – seems to have vanished, taking shelter from the rain.

"The creature, this man you found," Anders says, surprising me. "He is important?"

Ben starts, sitting upright. "We think so," he says, his hands trembling slightly. "Most of our organisation is gone, and from what Lincoln – my trainer – was saying, we're not sure how much support we'll get from the wider world. The creatures that have come through the rifts are horrific, and we need all the help we can get. This angel could be a great help."

"Good," Anders says, sitting back. "Then this is worthwhile."

"Yes," Ben says. "Yes, it is. Thank you."

Perhaps I should be happy with that, that this expedition is worthwhile. I sit and stare at the rain, trying to plan my own future in a world that has changed so radically in the last week.

I fail, and after another ten minutes, Anders gets us on our feet and we continue onwards.

We rope ourselves together when going through snow is unavoidable. It's slushy and treacherous, but Anders seems to know the safe paths, firmly telling us to walk in his footsteps.

We comply without question.

Sweat runs down my back, chilling me; I wonder how cold it would have to be to freeze, but my scientific curiosity is overridden by the overwhelming need to keep putting one foot in front of the other.

I take one step, then another.

Again, and again and again.

I watch each one. If I slip, we only have each other for help. A helicopter from town would take hours.

The low, dark clouds make everything seem more ominous, but I rarely look up. The rain is cold, and despite the clever structure of my hood, it gets into my eyes even when I'm looking down. The icy wind is relentless, and despite my hat, my face feels cold all the time.

No-one should be out in conditions like this.

After two more hours of trudging through the muck, we arrive on the crest of the hill leading down to Raysiel's cave.

Anders sits down on a nearby rock.

"Good luck," he says, not a man to waste words.

He slips off his pack and starts to inspect his shotgun. I hope it still works in the rain, although judging by the quantity of wildlife we've seen so far, the bears are probably hiding from the rain like everything else. Not that that makes sense when I've seen pictures of polar bears swimming in freezing cold water, but – at the risk of sounding romantic – there's something different about today, as if the animals know to stay out of sight.

I shake my head. I'm being ridiculous.

Ben looks at me, and I nod to him. "Come on," I say, removing my pack and putting it at the foot of the rock near Anders. "Let's go."

He does the same, and we slowly make our way down the hill towards the cave.

We both pause at the entrance, but to his credit, Ben recovers and goes in first.

Raysiel is waiting for us.

He's sat on the same boulder; this impossible man, bare-chested in the freezing temperatures, his golden, shining wings shimmering with a kind of heat-haze.

His eyes are closed, but they snap open when we enter, regarding us with an alien expression.

"You return," he notes.

I feel myself growing angry again with this spectacular being. To be so powerful, but so passive? I stay silent, hoping that Ben will fill the silence.

"Have you … have you made a decision?" Ben says, eventually. "About helping us?"

Raysiel makes a deep noise like thunder rumbling distantly, frowning at us.

"I will not," he says, his bassy voice flat. "It is not my duty to assist the unworthy."

Ben's face falls, but I was half expecting this. I take a deep breath to start arguing, but Ben gets there before I can.

"If that's the case," Ben says, his voice trembling. "There might not be a chance for the unworthy to change, to improve, to realise what they're doing wrong. If there's going to be judgment, then you're denying thousands, millions of people the chance to improve themselves, even kids that haven't been born yet. These things are killing us."

Raysiel's head drops and he shakes, muttering to himself.

"No, no, no," he says, more quietly this time. "Judgment is not my calling. If this is the end time, then so it shall be. I cannot interfere."

"But isn't the order of the end time set?" I say, recalling

Revelation. "Shouldn't there be more things happening? The scrolls, the seven signs, all of that? And if everybody dies, then the end times can't proceed as foretold."

"Human destiny is set," Raysiel grates. "It will proceed as it is written."

Ben sighs loudly, then paces back and forth from one side of the cave to the other.

"Alright, look," he says, pushing his hood back. He's looking pale. "I want to explore this unworthy thing, ok? I know that most people wouldn't rate as, you know, classically worthy in a ten commandments kind of way, but there are some pretty good people out there. I mean, our guide, Anders, brought us all the way out here, twice. He's looked after us, he's not been difficult despite the bad weather and all the weird stuff that's been going on. We've been genuinely helped by some amazing people with no guarantee or even mention of anything in return. My order exists purely to keep people safe and be kind. They've been monitoring the levels of empathy around London for years, trying to stop all of this happening."

His speech trails off, but I pick up before Raysiel can say anything.

"Ben makes a good point," I say, and Ben looks at me, surprised. "You judge people as unworthy, but you've not experienced them. People live all over the world. You can't generalise about everyone from your experiences with one person who might have just been having a bad day in Jerusalem. It's not representative."

"I saw man well enough in that moment," Raysiel says. "Petty jealousy, selfishness."

"Kindness, love, self-sacrifice," Ben adds. "Surely you saw enough of that in your thousands of years there? The dedication of the order who protected you, venerated you. Shouldn't that count for something?"

"I am not here to weigh the balance," the angel says softly. "That is not my ascribed place."

"What about experiencing some of the world itself?" I say, trying to think of other angles of attack. "You've spent two thousand years contemplating scripture, spending all your time with a handful of people. Why not go into the world and see it, assuming you can dampen your glow a little?"

Raysiel snorts – not a sound I'd ever have associated with angels before, and I – perhaps recklessly – press my argument.

"You know, see how people act and speak and treat each other? Try our food, see us dance, look at people with their families and children? And then, after, if you think that's worth preserving, then you can make a well-rounded conclusion. I'm not asking you to help us, I'm asking you to understand all the arguments before you make a decision. After all, what's the alternative? Spend another two thousand years in this cave? It's not a great cave."

I exchange a glance with Ben. The angel doesn't speak, and frowns a little.

"Look, there's so much good stuff out there," Ben says, picking up where I left off. "So many different things to do, different types of food. Nando's, fish and chips at the seaside, Thai food in Soho, Nicaraguan food; seriously, you should try it. And see people in their natural habitats, normal people, regular people, just going about their daily lives like Alice says."

There's a long silence, and I shift my weight from foot to foot, sore from the walk. I'd really like to sit down, but I don't want Raysiel to think I'm being disrespectful and vaporise me after all our efforts.

"I shall," he says. I open my mouth to reply with an objection, then realise what he's actually said.

Before I can act, Raysiel launches himself upwards, rocketing straight into the roof of the cave. There's a hissing sound, then a crash and the rocky roof above him rains down on us as black ashy fragments. I grab Ben's hand and we run outside, stopping a short distance from the cave, turning and squinting, both panting with the sudden adrenalin.

"Shit!" Ben swears, hands on his knees, bent over, but he's looking up at the sky. "Is he gone?"

"I … I think so," I admit, not quite sure if we won or not.

"Fuck," Ben says, and for a moment we stand and stare, looking upwards into the rain for any trace of the angel.

"Alice?" Ben says, standing and wiping his forehead.

"Do you think there's a chance we might have made things worse? Like, what if he goes to London and decides everyone's unworthy?"

I swallow, unsure of how to answer that. Knowing London, there's a good chance of it, depending on where he lands. Of course, it depends what's left, if the news is true.

"It's possible," I offer. "But maybe he won't."

Ben doesn't say anything to that, and stares down at the shingly beach for a while.

"I suppose it's what we were sent here for," he says eventually, and I can't disagree.

We stare for a while longer, but then slowly work our way back up to Anders and relay the conversation. With typical stoicism, he shrugs and nods.

"You did what you came to do," he agrees. "You found him, and he is no longer in the cave."

It doesn't really feel like what we came to do, but the horse has well and truly bolted, so I suppose there's nothing more to be done.

"Alright," Ben says, sounding tired, taking a step and staggering slightly before catching himself. "Back to the camp."

It's a long walk back to Kinnvika, even though the rain eases after an hour. It's still slushy and slippery underfoot, and Anders keeps a careful eye on us, forcing us to take regular breaks on damp boulders. One of my toes is starting to rub against my walking boot, and despite my rigorous exercise regime, my calves are definitely going to cramp at some stage.

I stretch out when we next stop, and to my surprise, Anders joins me. A moment later, Ben, looking awkward, does the same, and I take them through a few yoga poses before we carry on.

Interminable hours later, we spot Kinnvika in the distance, and I'm unreasonably glad of something to break up the incessantly bleak scenery. I can see Hugo in the distance, keeping watch. He spots us, and starts to run in our direction.

"Well?" he says, as he skids to a halt in front of us.

I don't quite know how to sum up where we are.

"It's done," Anders says. "Let's get back to Svalbard."

"Done?" Hugo says, his voice rising. "Done? You mean, it'll help? Where is it?"

Ben takes a deep breath, then lets it out slowly. "We'll explain on the way," he says. "Let's go home."

Matt

Too Tired to be Funny Right Now

We edge around the field towards the group of mercenaries, and I shudder every time the poor guy screams.

I run through a million different scenarios in my head. We can't just charge in. These guys are armed to the teeth and have actually done this kind of thing before.

I've never felt so helpless, or so shit.

Fucking hell. This couldn't get much worse.

It gets worse.

Chloe stops and gestures for us to lie down in the dip between two hillocks, the grass tickling my arms and neck, but I try to do it as slowly and carefully as possible. She nudges me, and I look over in the direction she's indicating. The Shamblers are coming back, and the mercs have seen them. Some of them are heading for the trees, while others are making a line in front of the guy they're beating the shit out of.

We're close enough to see properly now. Lucas has handed his hunting knife to one of the mercs, and is walking through their ranks towards the Shamblers. There's not too many of them yet, but I'm sure he remembers how many there were yesterday.

Ok, so the guy's got balls, even if he is a fucking psycho. He's dispersing the ghosts, laying into them with an enthusiasm that borders on gymnastic. He's sliding around, pivoting as the mercs call out new Shamblers coming out of the woods, occasionally containing one while he disperses another before turning back to disperse. I don't know how he has the energy for it – Ben and I were pretty knackered after doing twenty or so back at Karnak, and he's up to about half of that in a tenth of the time.

Meanwhile, one of his men seems to have lost patience with the cook and stabs him right in the arm, making him scream before he falls silent, passing out and sagging against the ropes.

There's a weird sensation, like an abrupt tearing in space, like a cut, and Chloe seems to pick up on it as well, turning away from Lucas and looking over at the cook. Lucas gives a last flourish and jogs back towards the campfire, making an abrupt gesture at the area in front of the cook, and space *rips*. I swear to god, my bones or insides judder, like I've had my own personal earthquake. If I wasn't already lying down, I'd have staggered – as it is, I shudder like I've taken a shot of tequila or something. I can feel the wrongness of it, like a crude oil spillage at a kid's petting zoo.

Lucas shouts at the mercs, who start to run through

the gap, vanishing one by one. To their credit, not a single one of them seems to hesitate at the idea of the inter-dimensional trip, but I guess they've done this before. The last one disappears through and then Lucas himself raises his eyebrows at the cook, shrugs and jumps.

"Fuck!" I breathe, pushing myself up to standing. "Come on!"

Chloe's already on her feet and pounding towards the rift, but more Shamblers are coming out of the trees. "Help him," I say, trying to keep my voice down in case Lucas hears us. "I'll hold them off."

I'm nowhere near as artful as Lucas was, but I manage, pushing through the fog of tiredness and shaping stave after stave. I remember to keep my distance from the rift where the noosphere is thinner but without getting too far away from Chloe. I glance back at her; she's cut the guy down and is tying a bandage around his arm tightly, before dabbing at his other wounds with some kind of antiseptic, which wakes him up. He inhales as if to scream, then looks around groggily at her.

"Matt!" Chloe calls urgently, as Shamblers begin to come out of the woods on the other side. I jog back over to her, containing and dispersing the newcomers, but it's much more tiring. It's like I've already run a few miles and someone's just told me to start sprinting.

Chloe's draped the cook's arm around her shoulders, and I do likewise on the other side. Awkwardly, we stumble through the rift to fuck-knows-where.

Fuck-knows-where turns out to be almost walking into a brick wall, which I graze my hands on to avoid faceplanting into the thing. Once we're all through, we lower the cook to the ground, and I glance around for a sign of Lucas. He doesn't seem to have left a rear guard, thankfully. I guess when you're being chased by ghosts, you keep going.

I can feel the raw edges of the tear in space, and, reaching for the noosphere, I start to push them together. It's instinctive, and like the other tear at Karnak, I can somehow *shove* the energy of the noosphere into the empty space that the rift occupies, and little by little, it starts to close. It's agonising, and I feel sick rising in my throat as I see a Shambler on the other side drifting closer. Fuck. I give it another huge shove and the rift springs closed like a jammed zip suddenly freed.

Then I actually do stagger against the wall and look around again. Chloe's checking the cook's wounds. He murmurs something and leans his head back against the bricks. I'm about to step closer, but Chloe gestures sharply.

I know this place.

We're in a narrow alleyway between two sandy brown buildings, and I can see an Urban Outfitters in the distance. I'm ninety percent sure we're in Bath, but quite how we walked for a few hours and got from Bracknell to Bath I've no idea.

More important things to think about.

It's really, really bright, which isn't unusual for this

time of year, but there's a weird quality to the light. It's almost white, like the really intense white that you usually see in road tunnels. I stumble along behind Chloe as she hurries onwards towards Urban Outfitters, and we stop at the corner of the alleyway; there's a shopping plaza here, a broad, open space that'd normally have seating and that fake grass stuff in the middle – I can still see the remnants of it – before the other shops start again on the other side.

I say remnants, because in a small crater in the fake grass, seemingly not only content but also merry, sits a very large bearded man. Like, absurdly large. He's about eight feet tall and four feet wide, with greying hair and a white beard, and he's dressed in a loose-fitting orange robe and sandals. He's drinking from what seems to be an animal horn, and somehow, there's a barrel next to him, open at the top. Occasionally – between deep, Father Christmassy belly laughs – he refills his horn from it.

There's a big crowd of people in a circle around him, and he occasionally beckons one of them to join him, but as yet, no-one has.

"What manner of thing is this?" Chloe whispers next to me.

I shake my head in disbelief. "It's like Hagrid fucked Brian Blessed or something."

The Gardener guy behind us groans, and Chloe fishes her phone out and dials an ambulance. I look around, wondering where this guy came from, who he is and what kind of apocalypse came to Bath. Is he, like, the first friendly alien we've seen? No-one seems to be dying or fighting, which is nice.

I had to say it, didn't I?

I spot Lucas.

On the far side of the square, there's another alleyway, slightly concealed by a red telephone box, and I can see him leaning around the corner of it, mouthing something. Two of his goons flank him, looking imposing, but they've put their guns away. I glance to my left and right – there are other mercenaries dotted around, and if you didn't know better, you'd think they were private security for the shopping precinct.

"Chloe," I whisper, and she holds up her hand briefly, then hangs up the phone. I point out Lucas, and she squints at him.

There's something strange missing. I could feel the rift behind us before I closed it, and I could feel the one at Karnak, but I can't feel one here – it's like this guy fell out of the sky, or crawled out from underground. I guess that matches up with the crater, but something's not right.

As I'm watching, the big guy snaps his fingers and another barrel appears beside him, along with a table and a few more glasses. He gestures, and three giggling women, one of whom has a pink hen party sash across her chest, sit down and start helping themselves to drinks, much to his merriment. He gestures expansively, spilling wine down himself from his horn, but it doesn't seem to dampen his spirits.

"It's Bacchus," Chloe says quietly. "Dionysus. What's he doing here? I didn't know he was real."

"Bacchus?" I say. "The wine guy?"

"The Greco-Roman deity of fruitfulness, wine and jollity," she says seriously. "Son of Zeus, holder of festal orgies."

Fucking hell.

"Well, that'd be great if it wasn't the apocalypse right now," I say, pretty pissed off about all this. "On any other day I'd love a guy who conjures wine out of nothing and gets it on with as many people as possible, but that doesn't really help us that much."

It obviously helps Lucas though, because he seems to finish his observations and something changes in the air. This time, I really do stagger with the strength of his magic. Even though I'm not actively trying to tune into the noosphere, I can feel it, like barbed wire being dragged up my tattoos. It's like a river stopping and flowing back on itself, like tugging off a scab that's not ready yet, like something *wrong*.

Something flows from Bacchus to Lucas, tendrils of energy that I can't see but can sense distantly, my tattoos tickling slightly, which is fucking weird but there you are. The big man pales, putting one hand on the fractured concrete to steady himself. He drops his drinking horn and looks around, trying to see where this new assailant is coming from.

"Fuck!" I say urgently. "Chloe, he's … fuck, I don't

know what he's doing, but this is bad."

I drop my pack on the ground and fish around for the gun, pulling it out and actually having the presence of mind to thumb the safety off, although it takes two tries. A girl nearby sees it and screams, starting to run away, and before I can think too much about what I'm doing, I raise it up and fire it into the air.

Guns are really, really loud.

That probably sounds incredibly stupid to anyone in a country where guns are legal, but until you've actually fired one, I don't think you appreciate just how noisy they are, and how much they kick back. I almost drop the thing after one shot, but it's enough to get everyone in the square running in different directions.

It's also enough to get Lucas' mercenaries all looking straight at me, so I duck down and try to run around the square to one side, blending in with the crowd, which is kind of hard when you're holding a bulky handgun and are the one that caused all of this in the first place.

I actually run into one of the mercs, literally colliding with him, staggering both of us. I almost fall over, but he grabs me from behind. I try to pivot and run away, but he pins my arms to my sides and lifts me up off the ground. I kick back, missing, but then feeling a satisfying crunch as I get his shin the second time. He doesn't drop me, and instead, shouts for help and tries to knee me in the bollocks.

We spin around and I'm now facing Bacchus and

Lucas, and I can still feel the flow of energy from one to the other. Bacchus is starting to look grey, and Lucas is glowing white. I look back towards Chloe, and for a moment I can't see her for the crowd. Then it clears and I catch sight of her, and it's like she's steeling herself for something. I pause my thrashing around, which seems to confuse the merc a bit.

Suddenly Chloe's entire body shudders, and there's this heat haze around her. A second later, she's gone, and in her place is this large, tiger-like creature with long teeth stretching down from its mouth. It's a dun brown colour, marked with black stripes that curl around its body, not unlike the tattoos on my arms. It's about seven feet long, well-muscled and powerfully built.

The merc drops me and stares.

I stare too.

With a deafening roar, the thing bounds across the square, springing between people and leaps at Lucas, knocking him down. The Chloe-creature rebounds off the side of the building and comes around again, snarling at Lucas, who is hurriedly pushing himself to his feet, a dark stain spreading on his shoulder.

The mercs get their act together. One of them fires at the creature, missing but drawing its attention. It – she – bounds over and pounces on the shooter, knocking him to the ground and roaring in his face. It's enough time for four others, including the one who grabbed me, to run over to Lucas, pulling him into an alleyway and out of sight, as another three regroup and pull their guns out.

One of them snaps off a volley, striking the creature, making it fall and skid across the paving with the impact, knocking its head against the front of Uniqlo. There's another shimmering in the air, and I blink; then there's just Chloe lying on the pavement, blood staining her jacket.

I realise that I'm stood there like an idiot, so I hurriedly raise my gun and – after a moment's hesitation about whether to aim lower down – fire it twice into the air again. One of the soldiers gestures to the others and they run after Lucas.

I hear sirens in the distance, and, sparing a glance at the big guy in the centre of the square – he's looking a bit rosier already – I sprint back to our packs, then over to Chloe. She's dazed but conscious. My mind is completely blank, but I pull her up and lean her back against the shop window, peeling off her jacket as carefully as I can.

It's fucking awful.

There's literally a hole in her arm where the bullet went through and there's so much blood everywhere. My hands slip in it as it pulses from her body in waves. I find what water I've got left and rinse her arm off, mindless of splashing her, then hurriedly rifle through the packs, spilling stuff over the pavement, leaving bloody prints over the fabric, my hands shaking as I find the first aid kit. It takes me two attempts to open it, and I drop plasters all over the place before I find a strip of gauze big enough to stick over both sides.

Both sides.

Sick rises in my throat, but swallow it down hard, winding a length of bandage over the wound tightly. I remember my brief foray in the Scouts – before I got kicked out for farting in the leader's face on a camping trip, waking him up – and gently elevate her arm above her head. She shivers, her eyes unfocused.

"Chloe," I say, blurting out the first thing that comes into my head. "I don't know what the fuck that was, but I got to get me one, ok?"

Then I surprise myself by bursting into tears.

I try to get my shit together, hurriedly wiping my eyes and nose with my sleeve, taking a deep breath and reminding myself that we are not out of the bloody woods yet. I peel off my jacket and put it over her. You're supposed to keep people warm when they're in shock, right?

Chloe's eyes focus briefly, and she smiles wanly, then leans back against the building and holds her arm up with her other hand. She's white as a sheet.

There's a hand on my shoulder and I turn, seeing two paramedics behind me.

"We'll take it from here," one of them says, and I nod, relieved as they kneel down next to her and start to change her already-soaked bandage. I don't know when they arrived, or if they saw me with a gun, or her as a … leopard … but fuck it, they seem competent.

Before they can notice, I hurriedly tuck the gun back in the bag and cover it with the remnants of the first aid kit, then pour water over my hands to try to rinse off the blood before standing up and surveying the scene.

The square is almost completely empty now. Shoppers cower in stores, and there's a row of policemen advancing towards me with rifles.

I guess *they* saw me.

Bacchus is still in his crater, now facing towards me, and he's regained some of his colour. He refills his horn from the barrel and raises it in my direction.

"Bacchus, god of wine, at your service," he bellows at me merrily. "Thank you kindly for your help, good gentleman and lady."

I'm totally lost, and the adrenalin rush is starting to fade. I'm shaking, but am saved the indignity of whatever shit was about to come out of my mouth by two Shamblers drifting out of the alleyway across from us, slowly starting to make their way towards the line of police. The police raise their guns, but back away.

"Ugh!" Bacchus exclaims, seeing them. "Begone, little demons."

He snaps his fingers and the ghosts vanish into thin air, leaving behind thin trails of mist in the air. Brilliant. The large man laughs, holding his belly as he does.

I start to walk over towards him and the police line, holding up my hands, feeling a pang of anxiety about Chloe. She'll be alright, right? She's got secrets coming out of her arsehole, but she looked horrendous. Then again, she just turned into a fucking tiger or something, and people survive worse, don't they? The medics will help her. I need to get people looking for Lucas – I guess now that the police are here, he won't be coming back anytime soon.

I try to focus on the task in hand and take charge.

"Matt Potter, First Extraordinary Battalion. I'm going to need another ambulance right now," I call over at them, then pause. Should I be doing this? I should be checking on Chloe, shouldn't I?

I take a breath and try to rally a bit of my old swagger. "I've got an injured man in the alleyway, and that woman has been shot in the arm. Secure the area, please. We have a highly dangerous threat still at large, so proceed with extreme caution. I'm also going to need someone to update the First Extraordinary Battalion in London immediately."

I clear my throat and glance at Bacchus. "Remove all members of the public from the vicinity and let me know any signs of the unusual or dangerous. And I'm … I'm going to have a pint with this guy."

But I don't think I quite pull it off. It's hard to be nonchalant when you're trembling like a leaf.

Part Three

When the Gods Awake

Lucas
Advancing Mankind's Progress

There are creatures outside this world that do not obey the conventional laws of physics.

Immaterial beings, beings that shift in and out of reality like a playground. A game board, to be upended when it does not suit them, or reset when it does.

They say that approximately a quarter of modern medicines are derived from plants found in the rainforests. What miracles could we derive from creatures that so obviously flout the rules of the material realm as we know it?

This is the why.

Despite this, the Gardeners work to keep the rifts closed – not open, not controlled, but simply closed, also closing their minds and removing our chance to study these new worlds. Savage and bestial they may be, but also miraculous.

Of course, if someone could expose this secret, then the public demand for the study of these realms would be a clamour, undeniable. Military, medical, scientific research would proceed unabated.

I am not irresponsible.

I know that there is a near-infinite energy source on our very doorstep that stops all of the realms neighbouring us from opening at once, holding back the predators. It could be tapped. It should not be taxed. Weakened, yes. Removed, no.

And yes; I have selfish reasons for doing all of this. In my early years as a member of the First Extraordinary, I came across a text, an ancient book, suggesting that the noosphere was but one of the defence mechanisms protecting the earth.

Another was formed more slowly. As the world aged, the power of human belief resulted in a kind of metaphysical accretion, knitting together creations made purely of reverence, habitual worship, myths and legends, and that these creations would lay dormant, gathering power over the centuries, rudely awoken if the noosphere fractured.

A hundred tales tell of heroes awakening at the time of our greatest need. Truth, hidden in folklore, stranger than fiction and based on a science we don't yet understand. I had a suspicion of where the first would manifest, based on this theory of accretion.

On one hand, these beings *are* a defence mechanism, but on the other, they are batteries. Charged by human belief, converted into raw supernatural power. Power can be transferred: I learned that in my first week as a

Gardener, taking power from the planet's energy field and transforming it into a weapon. Staves are minor shavings, splinters of the power available to us, and I understand its importance.

A god, on the other hand?

I won't lie. I'm no saint. My early experiments took lives. Science rarely makes progress without a cost. The energy that powers our homes also kills us. Heroin and morphine share a common ancestry, one reviled, the other depended on by hospitals everywhere. But when one person, and one person alone, sees the potential of new worlds kept secret by another organisation, does that person not have a responsibility, a duty, to take action?

I've worked hard for my progress.

I gambled, I risked, I ventured. I studied the same trends that the Gardeners sought to prevent, and I harnessed them to fund my research. The Gardeners have government support, I have nothing but my own sweat and my own mind.

Over time, my work gathered pace. I hired help, developed plans, became successful. I monitored my rivals, tapping into their systems monitoring the decline of empathy. Predictably, every single one of their scouts connected to cafe Wi-Fi. Their laptop security was ironclad, the Wi-Fi, less so.

They monitored empathy levels, I nudged them. I funded start-ups delivering goods to homes, making it ever-easier to avoid seeing other people, to avoid building community. The UK has sixty-six million people, nine of which live in London. The ratio of casualties was acceptable, given the potential gains. We are a small island nation, threats easily contained and neutralised in the scheme of the world. The nation has been conquered and re-conquered before.

It would recover.

I experimented upon myself, taking the bulk of the risks. The Gardeners proved impossible to recruit from – I was an aberration, defecting from their cause, the only one to see how narrow their vision was. It proved easy to recruit commercial, logistical, business support, but my singular failure was to create a coterie of the supernaturally skilled. The Gardeners, it seemed, were too good at recruiting, and the world, it seemed, was too good at rooting people's minds in the mundane.

Despite this, I succeeded alone, subverting the principles of the Gardener staves and eventually I was able to draw energy from animals and humans into myself, becoming stronger, faster, better than I was before. I could feel the energy coursing through my veins, but I resisted the urge to spend it, instead using it to cleanse my body of impurities, making me healthier, more powerful. If this was the power I could draw from simple creatures, imagine what I could take from a mythic creation made of pure belief and worship.

The prospect delighted and intimidated me in equal measure, and I experimented with how to handle such power within the confines of my own body, managing it, creating buffers to avoid being overwhelmed, making my own spiritual batteries to charge, eventually manifesting supernatural organs to handle the power.

They are not infallible. I still tire, but my plans have worked well. As the empathy levels of London declined beyond critical points, I set the wheels in motion. I knew the Gardeners and the government would freeze my assets and raid my offices within hours, so for years I siphoned funds to safe havens through shell companies. I knew that the dropping empathy levels would precipitate a panic in the Gardener leadership, and a drawing together of their forces, especially the psychic aberrations who claim to foretell the future, so I hired mercenaries and killers to use this to trigger the disaster that I needed.

I knew that no place on this earth would be safe when disaster was triggered, so I planned to leave.

I did not plan, or know, that I would be followed.

Damn them.

I knew of the existence of this Spider, this Chloe, but she has eluded me. I hoped that she would be one of the first assets to be recalled to Wild Court, given her proximity, but she chose not to return. She chose to follow me through the gate, with someone else, someone I know nothing of. It seemed to be of no consequence.

It was of consequence.

They expect me to retreat, to find another battery to tap, to be coy and keep to the shadows.

And yes, I have another target, a reserve battery, but I shall not be coy. The time for coyness has passed.

"Boss?"

I look over at the closest thing I have to a lieutenant, Maria d'Souza, a gifted logistician and former SAS operative. We've hired the site of Prior Park College during half term, and are using it to gather ourselves after our work. I knew we – or rather, my forces – would need a place to gather themselves, and be assured of their payment after their experiences of the supernatural. Maria, and the group of hackers we've paid to be here, have been distributing funds to my mercenaries, assuring them of our proximity to the end of our work, also bringing fresh blood in.

"Boss, the snipers have arrived."

"Excellent. And our transportation?"

"A37 and A38 are looking clear," she says crisply. "The trucks and the Lambo are good to go. Choppers are waiting for us."

"Remarkable. Morale?"

She swallows, looking nervous.

I understand.

"They're spooked, sir," she says. "We all are."

"These are the birth pangs of a better age, Maria," I say. "We have revealed a bigger universe, and soon we shall reap its rewards."

"Aye sir," she says. "We're ready."

I stand. It's time for Plan A.

Ben

Landings, Brothers and Exotic Dumps

Leaving Svalbard is a hurried, rag-tag, tumbled blur.

Soon after hearing about our experience with the angel, Hugo falls into a downcast silence, which is a small mercy, but a concerning one. We still need his plane and his goodwill to get back to the UK, although I chide myself for seeing the man as a resource. He's dealing with a lot.

We all are.

We're met at the perimeter of town by a cacophony of beeps as our phones regain signal, receiving a slew of updates from news apps, family, the remaining Gardeners – even Matt – threatening to overwhelm us after so little input out in the wilds. We swap news with each other, Hugo momentarily reviving on hearing about the ancient deity that seems to have taken up residence in Bath, but removing himself almost immediately afterwards. Everything else is grim.

We throw our clothes into bags, hurriedly packing at the hotel before being met by a minibus sent and occupied by Solveig, the Governor. I give Anders a hug before climbing in, and he surprises me with a broad grin.

"Good luck," he says. "I'll be praying for you."

"Thank you," I manage. "Seriously, thank you. We couldn't have done it without you."

He inclines his head, then waves to Alice and Hugo, heading back towards town, stamping the snow from his boots.

Alice and I debrief Solveig on the way to the airport. She mostly listens, only asking a few questions here and there, taking the angel's existence in a matter-of-fact way. I suppose that when an entire country has been invaded by creatures best described as supernatural, one unearthly being by itself pales into insignificance, even if it's on *your* island.

"Do you think it'll come back?" she asks, towards the end of the account.

"It's unlikely," Alice replies, shaking her head. "It came here because it was literally the last place on earth. We don't know what it'll do next. If we're lucky, it'll judge mankind as worthy and help against the … the things. If we're not …"

She shrugs, presumably implying that things in the UK can't get much worse than they already are. I don't quite think that's true, but don't voice it.

"Then I must thank you," Solveig says quietly, her voice barely audible over the thrum of the minibus engine. "You've kept our islands safe."

I hadn't really thought about it like that – and it's not

really what we set out to do – but we accept her words.

I'm lost in thought for the rest of the short trip, and after a few formalities at the airport and an open invitation to return whenever we like, we bid Svalbard goodbye. Hugo's pilot Lizzie takes the plane upwards in a smooth take-off, which I barely notice – surprising, for me.

It's only when we get above the clouds that the full weight of the situation hits me. We're heading back to a demon-infested nation with no guarantee of additional help or support for the next two days. According to Seline's report, we don't even know how many Gardeners are still alive in the strangely-displaced Wild Court, and although Matt and Chloe have an idea of Lucas' plans, we're completely under-resourced. There's an ongoing argument between Matt and Seline about what to do next. Matt is all for charging after this guy, which seems like a stereotypically Matt thing to do. Seline wants us back in London helping to close rifts and do containment, which seems like a much more sensible idea. As the ranking officer, she's got inestimably more pull than he does, not to mention a direct line to the Prime Minister, who is currently camped out on a ship somewhere in the channel.

That said, sensible or not, there's a part of my brain that knows Matt's right. Something still doesn't add up. The fact that Lucas doesn't seem fazed by unleashing the apocalypse, and his strange actions with the wine deity make me wonder if there's worse yet to come.

Worse. God damn.

I huddle up in a comfy seat, drawing my knees up to my chest and hugging them. You know, in all the books and films I've seen, the hero is supposed to start off as this novice, this inexperienced blundering nobody, and steadily ascend to greatness. I've got to tell you right now, that's not how it feels *at all.* I suppose that yes, I've learned magic, which is pretty awesome, but I don't feel any stronger, less prone to meltdowns or honestly, any more confident. I'm a hair's breadth away from climbing under my seat and bursting into tears.

Fuck. What to do?

Then I realise, and grin like an idiot. What would my role-model magic-user do? I might not know what Lincoln would do, or Seline, or any of the other Gardeners that I've spent a bit of time with, but there is someone I know that I can take advice from. Someone with nerves of steel, always ahead of the situation.

What would Hermione Granger do?

I bury myself in books.

It's a four-and-a-half-hour journey back to the UK, and for four of those, I barely pause to eat, drink or use the toilet.

I power through the novice-level staves again that we – presumably – would have been taught had we passed our extended 'probation' as Gardeners. I read up on politics, the organisation itself, magical theory. I plunge into intermediate lessons, but dive back into theory again, because there's a whisper of something there, something that seems important, relevant. It's like the smallest hint of intuition, a thread I need to tease out and follow.

It's hard work. Although the texts are written as clearly and pragmatically as possible, it's also new to me – I've barely had a week of formal magical education. It's like mist that gradually clears as I push it to one side. I still don't quite understand how shaping the staves in my mind translates to the effect, but I do start to understand the noosphere as a rushing, busy force, like a river, there to be channelled, or to act as a barrier.

That's why we can shape this force to do something with similar effects, stopping the Shamblers in their tracks, for example, or simply placing them in the centre of a force designed to bar them from this planet, dispersing them. It's a force, but it's also a conduit.

I start to read about stave reversals, which form the basis of 'evil' magic, although so far, it's basically only Lucas that has used them, discounting Raphael's reversal to keep the portal to Karnak open. If staves are the magic of the earth, then staves that can keep rifts open might have been where Lucas started his thinking. Unfortunately, there's next to nothing on them – no walkthrough instructions, just a brief discussion. I suppose that more detailed explanations are likely to be in whatever the Gardener equivalent of the 'restricted section' is, and I'm not getting to that anytime soon.

I practice a new stave, which would seem virtually useless in most situations, but for a beginner like me trying grasp theory, I think it'll help with more advanced techniques – it lets you 'see' the noosphere more clearly. The guide tells me that it's for repairing rips and the like, although from my experience in Karnak, seeing the rip or even feeling it wasn't a problem. I channel the stave, miraculously getting it right first time, and a sort of overlay appears in front of me, a rushing flow of particles weaving a kind of mesh. I glance around, and see the same particles rising up from Alice, less so from Hugo. The archaeologist says something to me, and there's a swell of activity. I cancel the spell and ask her to repeat herself.

"I said, did you need something?" she says. "You looked confused."

"No," I stammer. "No, thank you. Just trying something new."

Alice turns back to her book, and it clicks in my head. The noosphere is fuelled by kindness and good acts, so her offer of help literally contributed to the protective field around the planet, compared to Hugo's self-isolation, which gives nothing back. The effect was microscopically small, but I could still *see* it somehow. Although, in fairness, we are riding in his plane, so that's something – presumably why he was radiating a little.

Then I have to take a moment and try not to think of anything at all. This is all a lot.

This is important, Ben, I tell myself. Get a grip.

I dive back in.

I re-read the section about the theory of the staves

and look back at the protection stave I learnt in Svalbard. It's longer than the basic containment and dispersal staves and has some kind of 'rest' in the middle, which I'd not really noticed before. I have a thought and flick back to the more advanced versions, which are even longer and more specific. They seem – although it doesn't explicitly say this – to be telling the energy *where* to go, as well as what to do, which explains the mild energy drain from the protection spell. After all, the noosphere wants to keep moving, and if you're trying to keep it in one place, it's going to take some of your energy to do so.

The important thing – as far as I can tell – is that the second part of the stave tells the energy how far to go, or where to go, but I can't figure out why that's the case.

I glance out of the window, seeing the east coast of England, and feel the nose of the plane dip a little.

Wait a second.

We shouldn't be descending just yet.

I put my e-reader to one side and glance over at Alice, who looks up a moment later and clocks it as well.

"Hey, Hugo," I call across at the millionaire. "We going down?"

Although he's immaculately dressed in what I imagine are hideously expensive clothes, Hugo still manages to look scruffy, and not in a particularly 'tousled and attractive' way. He looks tired and dejected, and barely meets my eyes as he looks up. Should I be more sympathetic? I'm not his bloody babysitter.

"Yes," he says. "We're going back to the mansion."

"Uh-uh," I say, shaking my head. "We either need to go to London or Bristol airport if we're going to Bath. It's too far to get from your place to town or Bath."

"Look," he says petulantly, sitting up, his aristocratic demeanour suddenly restored. "That's not my problem. This is my plane, and we're landing back at the mansion and you can handle things from there."

I exchange a look with Alice, and she starts to complain at him about being selfish and petty. I tug the phone from the arm of the chair and dial Seline's number. She picks up a moment later.

"We're almost over England," I report. "And honestly, I can't help but feel like there's something important about stopping this Lucas guy. From what Matt's said, it sounds like opening the rifts was part of his plan, not all of his plan. It's got to be something to do with this Bacchus guy."

There's a pause, and I get the sense that Seline has just been talking to Matt.

"I don't need to tell you that this is a risk, do I?" Seline says, her voice crackly over the phone. "But operational procedure agrees with you: unknown risks tend to multiply. I'm not going to say we'll manage because we're in serious trouble, and I've got fewer resources every hour, let alone every day. We'll lend you what assistance we can, but that's essentially nothing beyond the goodwill of the British government. You have full operational autonomy. You're a Gardener, a member of the First Extraordinary.

Compassion and Dedication, ok?"

Suddenly humbled by her faith, I tell her I understand and ask her to do one more thing, then wish her luck and hang up.

"Hugo?" I say, standing. He looks over, his eyes narrowing. "I'm sorry, but we're going to Bristol airport. We're going to investigate what this Lucas guy is doing, and we're going to stop him. I'm sorry that this means we need your plane, but – and I know this sounds stupid – this is *really* important."

His mouth is still open as the nose of the plane rises.

"You're hijacking my plane?!" he says, incredulously. "You're fucking hijacking my plane?"

"I'm sorry," I say. "But we really need this. It'll save lives."

"You don't know that," he scoffs. "You don't know anything. You've been a Gardener for a month. There's fuck-all you can do."

"Hugo," Alice cuts in. "Think about this. Your runway could be swarming with Shamblers. If we go to Bristol, there'll be at least one Gardener making sure that the space is clear. Can you imagine what it'd be like going through a herd of Shamblers at a hundred miles an hour?"

I gesture around at the plane's interior. "A little less beige," I say acidly. "A little more Jackson Pollock."

Hugo pales and there's a long, uncomfortable pause.

"Fine," he says, pursing his lips. "Fucking fine. We'll divert. But once we're there I'm coming with you and you'll get me back to the mansion as safely as possible, ok?"

I try not to laugh at how ridiculous that is. "Look," I say. "Once all of this is back under control, and all the weird shit is back in the right places, and this guy Lucas is sorted out, then absolutely yes. I'll take you back myself if needs be, ok? Good enough?"

He looks like he's about to snap back at me, then takes a deep breath and nods quickly.

"Fine," he says. "I suppose I should have known what I was getting myself in for when I signed up for this."

I try to take some of the sting out of commandeering his plane. "None of us did," I offer. "I'd be doing the same thing in your place if I'd known what you knew."

He shakes his head and laughs bitterly. "No," he says. "No, you wouldn't."

Alice rolls her eyes, but thankfully he doesn't see, and any further conversation is interrupted by Lizzie's voice over the intercom.

"I'm guessing you already know this, boss, but we're going to Bristol airport," she says. "We've been cleared for landing and there's a military escort on the way. Ben's buddy is going to clear the runway for us, but we might have to circle if there's issues."

And we do. Twice. Matt calls Lizzie apologetically – they're taking the opportunity of a new plane to ferry a load of refugees to the airport, and had to divert because of a Ravager sighting. Then they almost ran into a herd of Shamblers outside the airport, which took Matt some time to disperse. I'm expecting him to relate the story in a slightly more colourful way, portraying himself as some kind of expletive-laden action hero, but he's a bit muted. I want to ask him if he's alright, but I hold back. I tell him to take care, then put my finger to my lips and gesture to Hugo, and Lizzie understands.

We descend, and once again, Lizzie lands the plane very smoothly, for which I'm thankful. Flying is not my forte, even when it's in luxury. I do wonder how many of these extravagantly large seats will survive the plane's impending requisitioning by the British government, but that's not really my problem.

The plane taxis around to the bay, and then suddenly there's Matt, a small figure on the tarmac, standing in front of a bus full of people and an open-topped jeep. He looks tired.

Lizzie parks the plane, finishing whatever post-landing checks she needs to do, and skilfully opens the door at the back whilst simultaneously lowering the steps down onto the runway.

"Hey, brother!" Matt shouts up. "You're not dead!"

I find myself grinning and – in all honesty – getting slightly tearful, but I use the short descent to blink furiously and regain control of myself before I give my doofus friend an enormous man hug, complete with back-slapping.

"Not yet," I manage, pulling away and only just

avoiding bumping into Alice, as she comes down the stairs behind me. "But with no offer of protection."

Matt sniggers, putting an arm around my shoulders. "It's bloody good to have you back," he says ruefully. "Not many of these fuckers have a decent sense of humour, although after what they've been through, you can't really blame them."

The door to the bus opens, four police officers getting out first, just as Hugo and Lizzie emerge from the plane.

"Mr Delauncey-Morrison?"

Hugo looks up, sees them and starts to shake his head.

"Oh no," he says. "No, no, no. And it's fucking Baron Delauncey-Morrison, I'll have you know."

"I'm Constable Jamieson," the first one says. "And I'm sorry to say that we need to requisition your plane to get these people to safety."

Hugo crumples down onto the concrete and begins to sob into his hands. I start towards him, but pause; that'd be weird, right?

"Unfortunately, as you can understand, this is a rather pressing need, and we do need to take advantage of the clear runway and your pilot."

Constable Jamieson ignores the weeping aristocrat and a stream of people emerge from the bus behind him. If Matt looks tired, these people are haggard, their eyes red from crying, clutching whatever possessions they've managed to grab, bags, duffels, single hardback books or a laptop. A small girl clings onto her father's leg, weeping piteously. I stand and stare. It's horrible.

Matt dials a number on his phone. "Seline?" he says. "We've loaded up the refugees. Want me to do a sweep?"

He hangs up a moment later, and looks at me. "Come on," he says. "We need to do another inspection of the runway. You might like this bit."

Turns out I do.

A marine with a rifle sits in the front seat, keeping a watchful eye out, while we climb into the back of the jeep, and stand up, clinging to the sport bar on top as the driver slowly starts a tour of the runway, mapping the route of the plane.

We probably aren't going more than twenty miles an hour, but it's pretty exhilarating, driving around this huge open space, the wind in my hair, Matt scanning the perimeter with a pair of binoculars as I keep an eye on the spaces closer to us, ready to cast a stave if needed.

I have to remind myself that this is serious, but Matt seems pretty content to let out a huge whoop every so often, grinning at me.

"Hey," he says, noticing my puzzled look. "If we're doing a good job then who gives a shit how else we act?"

I've got to admit he might have a point.

"Everything go ok with the librarian?" he asks lightly, and I shrug.

"She's alright. We fucked up a bit by not really winning it over, but at least it left the cave and might help. Any word on Chloe?"

"Stable," he says. "They're worried about contamination from whatever the fuck is up with her, but I reckon if she's been living in Mayfair for the last decade or so, then there's probably nothing to fret about."

"And you still don't know how she …?"

"Turned into a leopard?" he says, raising his eyebrows. "Not a clue. Shame, because it was a great party trick. The whole trip was fucking awful though. If I never see another dead body, it'll be too soon."

I swallow, not knowing how to handle that. It makes my trip look like a walk in the park.

Then he clears his throat and puts the binoculars down for a moment.

"Ben?" he says, barely audible over the engine noise and wind. "Do you think I'm toxic masculinity?"

That completely blindsides me.

"What?" I manage. "What do you mean?"

He doesn't reply for a moment, instead, scanning the horizon with the binoculars again.

"I mean, like, maybe?" I stammer. "Aren't we all? It's not like you're homophobic or transphobic or anything, and we're having a serious discussion about emotions and stuff, so it's not all bad."

I'm babbling but for some reason I don't stop.

"Obviously, you're not backwards in coming forwards about women, and you do love booze and smoking. Shit, Matt, I don't know, where's this all coming from?"

Matt opens his mouth to reply, then closes it again,

then seems to marshal his thoughts.

"Chloe," he says. "We talked about it. Well, she talked at me, but she kind of had a point, you know? Despite pissing me off, I kind of found myself respecting her for bringing it up. She's basically a badass, despite her weird way of talking."

"Pfft," I snort, trying to make light of it. "What does she know? Apart from, everything, obviously?"

"Pretty much everything," Matt says. "I actually think I fancy her a bit."

"Jeez, Matt. All I did was fly across the world to find an angel. You chased a villain, shot a gun, dispersed a boatload of ghosts, met a girl you like, rescued a cook and did some serious soul searching. Haven't we got enough on already?"

He sniggers. "Yeah," he says. "Yeah we do. But I might work on some things, you know?"

Then he falls silent, and already I'm overthinking whether I've upset my friend or not, and whether I was truthful enough, but we're interrupted by finishing the tour of the airport, which is thankfully monster-free. The jeep heads back around the main building where the bus, now filled with a few airport staff, also waits for our return.

"They mostly came up with us," Matt says. "There hasn't been much air traffic in the last day – we haven't had enough manpower to clear the runways safely until now, although there were a few people hiding out in the control tower."

"Shit," I manage. "They all came up for just us?"

"Yeah," he says, seeming to rally his former charming self. "Everything's a fucking faff in the apocalypse. You should see some of the places I've had to take a dump."

On that bombshell, we lead the convoy back to Bath.

Matt
Figuring Shit Out

In the movies, it looks fucking badass when your regulation action hero is hyper-vigilant all the time, snapping to attention when the tiniest thing – which usually turns out to be the enemy – rears its ugly head so that they can completely annihilate it.

I'm telling you now, it's a crock of shite.

Staying alert is ridiculously tiring, and ninety nine percent of the time, there's fuck-all out there. But you've got to stay awake for the one percent, because there's every chance that that one little percent is going to cut you up worse than sticking your dick in a blender.

Anyway, thankfully I can spot with Ben, although he's tired from the flight. I'm tired from being the only functional Gardener for a hundred miles and although the military have generally been amazing, they're not much use against the non-corporeal. I'm also tired because every time I close my eyes I see dead people, or worse yet, parts of dead people, and that's so intensely horrible that I've kind of been avoiding it.

We stay awake. The soldiers have these cosy little thermos flasks with military-grade coffee in them, and they're not shy about sharing. I'd have thought that they'd have government-approved drugs or something, but apparently not. I guess you can't win the war on drugs after all.

Still, the coffee's pretty good.

And that's handy, because it takes a really long time to get back to Bath. According to Google Maps, on a good day, it's about half an hour by car.

It takes us almost three.

I swear we don't go above thirty miles an hour for the whole trip. But we arrive safely at the other end, so that's something. The only trouble we have is a couple of Shamblers not far from the airport, and this awful, slimy, spiky thing about the size of an ambulance that the soldiers take care of with what I can only describe as extreme prejudice. They haven't even named the slug things yet, but they're nasty and smell like jalapeno roadkill. I don't really want to unpack that, so you'll just have to trust me.

I'm basically preoccupied with being vigilant the whole time, but as soon as we pass into town, Chloe starts to creep into my head. We didn't really get any time to talk before I had to come over to the airport, and although I shouldn't be surprised that a hundred-year-old omniscient woman can turn into a sabre-toothed tiger given this brave new world that we live in, it totally came at me sideways.

I also didn't expect to be so concerned about a full-time Matt-annoyer and massive pain in the arse, but there you go.

Look, I'm not a total dick, alright? She got shot.

We drive right along the pedestrianised street into the centre of Bath – fringe benefits of the apocalypse and a military escort – and I'm simultaneously relieved and worried to see Chloe sat on what looks like a picnic chair next to Bacchus, talking to him seriously, which is kind of her only speed from what I've seen so far. There's a load of police and soldiers standing around, and she's wired up to a portable drip with a fairly hefty bandage around her arm, and what I assume is a doctor or nurse in a green and white outfit next to her, trying to get a word in edgeways. She keeps shushing him, which makes me laugh. What a badass.

Someone high up in the military insists that Ben and I do a supernatural sweep of the area, which is much less exciting than the supermarket alternative where you at least get some kind of prize that isn't just your own continued existence.

Eventually we're done with all the administration and I finally get to check in on Chloe as Ben and Alice talk to the police.

"Hey," I manage. "You ok?"

I'm usually a bit more eloquent than that, but she smiles and looks at me in a way that gives me a bit of emotional wood. Thankfully, Bacchus conjures up a foaming pint and

I take a long pull, grateful for the distraction and nodding my thanks to the god … demigod … magical bartender?

"I'm ok," Chloe says, turning, then winces. She's obviously not ok.

"Look, can we talk about what happened back there?" I say haltingly but she shakes her head.

"Not now," she says quietly. "I was in a transformation rift. It's fine. This is more important."

"It's not really fine," I say. "Like, are you alright from it? Do you control it or does it happen a lot?"

"Ms Webster, please," the doctor guy says, interrupting us. "You should be resting."

I'm desperate to know more, but she just sighs. "We don't have much time. Please, give me a moment with my friends."

He retreats, and I introduce Ben and Alice to Bacchus. He seems to have taken the opportunity to turn what was a crater of fractured concrete and astroturf into some kind of countryside bower, trees sprouting through the pavement, grass and flowers pushing up, and a few comfier-looking benches around the place. Of course, the police won't let anyone through, despite Bacchus' protestations to allow the 'comelier maidens and stout gentlemen' to come and hang out with him.

"Alright," Chloe says, seeming to muster her strength, taking the coffee cup out of my hand and having a quick sip. "I've been talking to Bacchus, and apparently he and his kind are essentially here as a fail-safe mechanism, triggered by the mass rupturing of the noosphere."

"We return during mankind's greatest need," Bacchus booms, in between quaffing what smells like mead. Half of it ends up down his beard, but he doesn't seem that fussed and it vanishes before it goes anywhere else.

"Great," I say, taking another swig of my pint. It tastes a bit sweet, which is weird, but I go with it. It's free after all. "Isn't that, like, King Arthur's beat? With all due respect and all, we're a bit up the creek here for boozing and orgies. When's the cavalry arriving?"

"Uther Pendragon," Bacchus muses. "Dull man but yes, I expect he'll be on his way with the others. I suppose we all help as we can."

Wait, he's serious.

I turn and pull out my phone, calling Seline. She's disbelieving at first, but agrees to send a small number of local police to Tintagel to keep an eye on things, particularly if Lucas Shithead's going to be around. If it works out well, we could use places like that for refugees.

I put the phone on speaker so that she can listen in to the rest of the conversation. Ben and Alice seem to have acquired tall glasses with pink cocktail umbrellas in them, and the police nearby keep having to put down pint glasses and tankards when they magically appear in their hands.

"So," Alice says. "We may get reinforcements before too long, but to sum up the other pertinent information: we don't know where the angel's gone, we don't know where Lucas is, why he's doing what he's doing or how he's doing what he's doing."

"Well," I start, suddenly feeling a bit uncomfortable under the librarian's scrutiny. "When wankstain was here, it was like he was feeding off Bacchus or something. He was glowing and the big man here was looking like the shitters at Inferno's on a Monday morning."

Ben shudders and gives me serious side-eye. It's so good to have him back.

"I mean, right?" I add, looking over at the wine god, who's still trying to get police officers to join him for a cheeky pint. He gives a small sigh – which, for him, sounds a bit like a train pulling out from a station – and turns back to us.

"It was very wrong," he says gruffly. "As though the life and colour was being pulled from my being."

"There we go," I say, feeling pretty pleased with myself for that deduction. "Lucas is some kind of vampire, or using vampire magic or something."

"He *was* a Gardener," Ben says, quietly.

"Gardener magic?" Chloe says, thoughtfully. "No, surely not. Subverted Gardener magic."

"Yeah," Ben chimes in. "There's been nothing in the books I've read about feeding off other people, but people's energies feed the noosphere, right? And you can invert staves, so if you can heal people, in theory you could un-heal them as well. But what's the link to Bacchus and his kind, if there's more of them?"

He trails off but Bacchus laughs. "This one is wise! A

top-up for the wise!"

Ben's glass refills, spilling the cocktail umbrella onto the street.

"From my conversations with Bacchus, I believe that these deities and heroes are the aggregate product of people's beliefs," Chloe says, filling in for Ben. "Kindness empowers the noosphere, but strong beliefs result in a kind of build-up. Over time, this gains greater form and substance."

"Well, now we know why Bacchus appeared *here*," Alice says acidly. "God of British binge-drinking."

"All are blessed," Bacchus intones. "For one pint or the many. Better to have many."

Chloe clears her throat, and I think she's looking a bit paler. I step towards her, concerned, but she waves me away. "And therefore, a hunting ground for Lucas," she says. "A concentrated source of noosphere energy would be a goldmine to him. It explains the triggering of the rifts; it was a provocation, a trigger for the gods to awaken."

"Look," Ben says, interrupting. "Why can't we just find him wherever there's a god appearing – like Tintagel or wherever – and when he starts absorbing the energy, we absorb it right back from him?"

"I don't know about you," I say. "But I don't know that one. And I'm guessing the Gardeners don't either."

Ben looks chagrined and I put my hand on his shoulder, about to apologise, but Seline chimes in from the phone, making him jump.

"Don't worry," she says, slightly crackly. "As far as I know, there isn't such a stave, and I've read the sections on stave reversals relatively recently as well. We can check with Raphael when the rest of the Gardeners return, but we have to assume that Chloe is right, and that Lucas is the only one who knows how to do this."

I basically see the idea enter Ben's head, and I'm not happy about it at all. "No, no, no," I say. "Ben, that's a stupid idea. That's beyond being a stupid idea. Besides, how would we even do that?"

"Ok, look, best case scenario is that we track him down and kill or capture him by conventional means, right?" Ben says. "But if he does manage to absorb godly powers, then we need a plan B. We're plan B. We need to understand how he's doing it."

I open my mouth to continue telling him what a stupid idea this is, but Seline's there again.

"It's not a terrible idea," she says, picking up his thread. "From what I know about Lucas, he would have loved the idea of preserving his own unique staves for posterity. He'd have a record of it."

"That could be literally anywhere," I interrupt. "It could be on a server in Belize for all we know."

There's a brief laugh from the speakerphone. "He's got a love of the grandiose," Seline says. "I suspect he's got a spell book somewhere."

"A spell book?" I laugh. "That's so lame."

Alice's quiet scoffing cuts across me and I frown at

her. "This doesn't help us," she says. "Where would it be?"

"The Gardeners raided his offices, correct?" Chloe says.

"Correct," Seline says. "But we didn't find anything."

"Can I see?"

"No problem," she says. "Can you get a tablet from the military team?"

I lean over to the nearest police officer, who jogs back to a support trailer and comes back with a hefty ruggedised tablet.

"Matt, can you hold it for me?" Chloe says, gesturing at her bandaged arm. "I'll have to do this one-handed."

"That's what she said," I find myself saying before I can clamp my mouth shut, but I swear to god that a silvery little giggle leaks out of her mouth, and she gives me a grin before starting to tap away at the tablet.

"So," I try to summarise after another pull at my pint. "In the absence of actually knowing where twat features has gotten to, we're going to try and find his spell book, learn his magic, then track him down when we get news of him popping up and *then* drain the magic that he drains from the god in question, right? And then what? Give it back to the god? Take him out?"

Ben looks a bit uncertain. "I … I can experiment," he says. "Empowering yourself or someone else should be relatively straightforward, right? Even if you're using borrowed energy. There's a stave for healing, so this might not be too different."

"Ben," Seline says. "It goes without saying that this is incredibly dangerous. Learning and performing staves is one matter, but understanding them on a fundamental level and creating new ones is something else. Even if you can just learn his stave and drain some of the god energy from him until someone can take him down, that'd be worthwhile. But don't put yourself in danger."

"It's alright," he says. "I read a lot on the plane. I think I get this."

He gets this? Really?

"Don't be a hero," Seline says quietly. "But if you can, do it."

She suggests a number of different staves that he can read about, most of which are in the advanced section of the guide, but it doesn't sound like there's anything that's an exact fit. Ben seems happy to improvise, which surprises me – where's my awkward friend filled with self-doubt? Maybe Svalbard was good for him? I thought he just needed to get laid a bit more, but obviously it was a trip to the middle of fucking nowhere in the freezing cold with an archaeologist and a rich kid to find an angel.

Christ, some people's things are really specific, aren't they? I'm glad I'm not that complicated.

"Got it," Chloe says, tapping at the screen one more time. "Shell company's shell company ordered a gazebo to this address, and a third shell company funded a small, non-corporate construction project in the same place. All heavily encrypted and obfuscated, but nothing I haven't seen before. Looks like a house on the fringes of the Chilterns, not from Pangbourne, near Reading. Extensive grounds, but satellites don't show any substantial conventional defences."

"Unconventional defences?" I ask, but I already know the answer.

Chloe shakes her head, looking almost grey, and I regret asking.

"Reading?" Ben says. "Closer to London, then?"

"Correct," Seline says. "You'll need military support."

"How far is it?" Ben asks.

"Normally, about an hour and a half," Chloe says. "Being careful, maybe three or four on the roads. Faster in the air."

"That's doable," he says. "When do we go?"

She starts to reply and I cut across her. "You don't look good, Chloe," I say. "Look, Ben, Alice and I got this, alright?"

"If I can get a helicopter or a car," Alice says. "I want to look for Raysiel. We may need a plan C."

Christ, I'd forgotten about that and it's a decent idea. "Good one," I agree. "Seline, do we have any backup for Alice? Like, anything?"

There's a long pause. "I can give you one field-trained protestant minister," she says finally. "If you can swing by London. And there's a chopper that MI5 can lend you, although one of them might need to come along."

"Fine," Alice says.

"Then we're good?"

Chloe starts to get up from her chair, and then slumps back down into it, the doctor crowding around her looking concerned. She waves him away one more time.

"Just be careful," she says. "I'll be scanning for any sign of his whereabouts."

"From your bed," the doctor says, and she nods weakly.

"Seline, are you sure you don't need us back in London?" Ben asks.

"I do," she says. "If Wild Court wasn't already on the way back, you'd be here, no question, and realistically I need you urgently and desperately. But this is more important, if only because we can't have this man at large, let alone the possibility of some kind of endgame where he becomes a god. He's already shown a complete disregard for people's lives, and who knows what would become possible for him if he absorbed godly power. Get it done and get back here. You'll have a military escort at all times where we can spare it, but be careful."

"You got it," I say, looking at Ben. Surprisingly, he doesn't look like he's about to throw up, which is weird, because that's exactly how I feel.

"Let's go."

Alice

Hunting Angels Instead

Being away from the hubbub is a welcome relief.

I don't work well with others. The trip to Svalbard went well enough, Ben being pleasant and effective company, but I'd much rather be on my own.

There's a frustrating wait for the helicopter, despite being an honorary member of the First Extraordinary, and until I speak to Seline, things move slowly. There's a note of impatience in her voice, and I make an effort to keep my requests concise. She is, I suppose, co-ordinating a war.

Thankfully, after a short discussion, the MI5 liaison – a small, serious man who doesn't give me his name – seems content to let me go in search of the angel without further supervision. I get the impression that although flying transportation is in short supply, he's more than happy to stay out of harm's way.

It's warm today, heat coming off the tarmac, and on any other day, this might be pleasant. As it is, nervous-looking police stand around, glancing from place to place, watching and listening for any sign of trouble.

The only person who seems calm – other than me, of course – is the helicopter pilot, a cheery-looking woman who introduces herself as Siu-Hing.

"Greenwich first?" she says, holding out her hand for shaking. I take it and nod, climbing up and putting on the ear mufflers and headset.

"You look like you've done this before," Siu-Hing says over the comm. "I'll keep the safety briefing quick, in that case."

"I just got back from Svalbard," I say. "Ranger's helicopter across the islands."

"Can't say I've heard anything about that officially," my pilot says. "Unofficially, well, you've got guts, that's all I'll say."

I can't think of a suitable response, but she doesn't seem to need one, instead giving me a short overview of the features of the helicopter and what to do if we get into trouble. Apparently, the skies have been clear since the last of the Whistlers were cleared out and their rifts closed, but the military isn't taking any chances.

With an uncomfortable lurch, we take off and I'm instantly glad of the protective headgear. It's incredibly loud. We buzz over some beautiful countryside, but my attention is taken up watching for threats. I see a herd of Shamblers as we're passing over Reading, and what look like large, spiky slugs somewhere around the M25, but we're past them before I've really had a chance to look properly.

I've only been to Greenwich Park once, but it's been extensively modified during the invasion. Trees that may have been hundreds of years old have been cut down and fashioned into spiked barriers.

You'll have to excuse me for being slightly sentimental – preserving old things comes naturally to an archaeologist.

Half of the Observatory is rubble, the interior brutally modified to remove stairs. Rope ladders hang from upper floors, and I can see hastily curtained-off areas, presumably for sleeping. The once-lush grass is now scrubby and brown if it grows at all.

We land on a section of road just north of the building itself. As the rotor blades slow, I jump out of the helicopter to see an attractive woman in a wheelchair, flanked by two soldiers with rifles, and a scared-looking woman in a black robe and clerical collar.

"Alice?" the first woman says. "Seline."

Surviving *and* co-ordinating the resistance to the invasions from a wheelchair? She goes up several notches in my estimation. I nod, not trusting myself to shout over the noise of the rotor blades.

"Here's your minister," Seline says loudly. "Jane Mulvaney, meet Alice. Alice was part of the team that tracked down the angel in Israel and subsequently traced it to Svalbard in Norway. We're hoping that the third time's the charm."

Jane holds out her hand and I shake it, her limp,

clammy grip doing nothing for my confidence, but as long as she can shape a stave, I don't mind.

"Need anything else?" Seline says, and I take the opportunity to use the bathroom, but assure her that there's nothing else. On my return, a soldier hands me a rucksack of supplies, telling me to return here if we need somewhere safe to stay this evening. A van finishes refuelling the helicopter, my pilot supervising carefully.

"Where first, boss?" Siu-Hing shouts, once we're all packed in. There are two sites I think we should check out, and the first is the most obvious, but the one I hold the least hope for.

"St Paul's," I shout. "Can you get us to Paternoster Square, or a rooftop in town nearby?"

"I reckon so," she says. "But you'll have to be quick, it's still monster central down there."

My stomach lurches again as we take off, but it's a much quicker ride. Jane spends most of her time practicing magic and either muttering to herself or praying. Either way, she doesn't disturb me much. Siu-Hing has to divert after the report of a Ravager in Bermondsey, and a few lesser Banshees near Bank – we're not directly at risk, but if they spot us, they're likely to follow.

Thankfully, it's not too long before we're touching down in Paternoster Square. It's completely empty, and if it wasn't for the noise of the helicopter, it'd be completely silent. I keep glancing around for Shamblers, shivering at the thought of them gliding in from all the entrances, surrounding us, gradually getting closer and closer.

These flights of fancy don't help. I wrench my attention away and look around properly.

At first, I only notice the deck chairs, mostly upright, some strewn around chaotically, but then I see the bodies. I have to swallow hard and try not to look at them, but Jane bends double, retching onto the pavement. I take a step away as the smell of ripe vomit hits my nostrils, and I fish around for a tissue to pass to her.

She gets up a moment later, apologising profusely.

"Look," I say. "It's horrible. I understand. But I also need you to be vigilant for non-corporeals, ok? If we see something bigger, we'll run, but if there's a Shambler, I'm reliant on you. Are we clear?"

Jane looks ashamed for a moment, then nods crisply. "Yes," she says quietly. "I understand."

The helicopter takes off behind us, hovering above the roof line, and I gesture to Jane. Together, we work our way around to the front of the cathedral, finding the doors wide open.

The impressive interior of St Paul's is spoiled by dark spatters and the stink of bodily fluids. Sweat, vomit, urine and faeces all combine, and I cough and gag as we enter.

Somehow, the power is still on, and there are more bodies on the seats up ahead. I imagine that a lot of people decided to seek God in the apocalypse, but it doesn't look like it did them any good.

Then I spot something else, a shape just beyond the

first section of nave. I gesture to Jane and, trembling, she squints into the distance. I'm suddenly thankful for the wide, open spaces here – being stuck in tight corridors would be a recipe for disaster.

"Is that it?" Jane whispers, but I shake my head – I don't know. Together, glancing around every few paces, our steps uncomfortably loud on the tiled floor, we work our way up the nave.

As we near the figure, it's obvious that it's not the angel. It's a Shambler. I touch Jane's shoulder and she looks over at me. I shake my head and indicate back the way we've come. She nods, her hands trembling, and I pretend not to notice as she wipes her palms on her robes.

We break into a jog as we clear the doors, and Siu-Hing quickly brings the helicopter back down, barely giving us time to clamber in before she rockets us back up again.

"Sorry," she apologises. "Bit twitchy. The waiting's the worst. No luck?"

I swallow, trying to think of where to go next, planning the route, anything to displace the memory of the dead bodies in my mind. "Nothing," I say. "Can you get us to Canterbury next?"

"Half an hour, tops," she says, and I sit back, wondering if we're doing the right thing. St Paul's is obviously the best-known cathedral in the UK, but Canterbury is actually the oldest by some margin. The London site was built after the great fire, making it relatively new; Canterbury

Cathedral was built in 1070, almost seven hundred years prior to that. In fact, the original site dates back to around 597, although it's suspected that it had been a religious area of some kind for hundreds of years even before that. I did toy with the idea of exploring St Peter-upon-Cornhill in London, which is both the highest point in central London and the first church established by the first Christian King of Britain, Lucius. But it's rather small, and I just couldn't see Raysiel going there.

Canterbury is a complete waste of time and fuel, and Jane almost gets us killed by fumbling her staves. We come across two Shamblers behind a carved column, and while she's trying to summon the staves to get rid of them, a third starts to cut us off.

I trip over a kneeler on the floor and crack my head on the stonework, lying dazed for a moment before there's a shout from Jane, and she manages to disperse all three in quick succession. I push myself back up, clutching the back of my head. Thankfully, it's not bleeding, but I'm going to have a decent-sized bump there.

"Let's go," I say, giving the interior a final look. "He's not here."

Looking pale but pleased with herself, Jane offers me her arm – which I gratefully take – and I hobble back out to the car park, where Siu-Hing is waiting for us.

Once we're safely back in the air, I call Seline and tell her the bad news.

"Don't worry," she says. "I'll tell you as soon as we have

any possible leads. Do you have anywhere else to search? You're welcome to come back here – we could always use your insight into the creatures you've seen, and Jane's abilities."

"I'm going to go back to Bacchus, if I can keep Jane a little longer," I say. My mind is buzzing, trying to figure out where to go next, how to approach Bacchus. Think, Alice, think. Where might the angel have gone? "He might know more."

"Please do," Seline says. "The police and the military haven't gotten anywhere with him. He seems to want drinking partners more than anything."

"That's not really my forte," I admit. "But I'll see what I can do."

"Best of luck," she replies, signing off.

I wrack my brain for clues, considering what I know about the origins of angels and what that might mean for Raysiel's destination. I re-read passages of the Bible, occasionally even asking Jane questions about them but although she's got a reasonably good knowledge of biblical verse, she's not an academic specialist. I do google a couple of the better researchers I came across during my studies and extended research, but none of them answer the phone numbers listed on their websites. I send emails, but I'm not holding out hope.

We arrive back in Bath, and I work my way through the cordon to the wine deity, who seems perfectly happy to just sit, drink and laugh merrily. It's more or less the last thing that I want to do after my pointless trip, but I tell myself that it's only temporary, and that he might know something important. I've done worse in the past.

The police have – reluctantly – allowed a few more people through to sit and drink with him, and they're all quaffing flagons of beer, which seem to refill themselves magically. It's a little disconcerting to watch.

"Greetings!" Bacchus calls to me, sounding jolly. "Alice, isn't it? Did you come back for a drink with old Bacchus?"

I take a deep breath, recalling Seline's advice. "Yes, please," I say. "Could you make me one like you did before?"

"One Ambrosial cocktail, coming right up," Bacchus booms, the woman on the far side of the bench looking over inquisitively. "It's not as honest as a good flagon of ale, but each to their own."

Just as I'm reaching for it, there's a distant 'crack' and I turn around, trying to locate the source of the sound. There's another one, and I realise that it's gunfire. The police and military look around nervously, a contingent of soldiers hurrying off from one corner of the square towards the shot. I turn, but there's a splashing sound, and I spin back to see Bacchus dropping my cocktail on the floor, the glass smashing and vanishing a moment later.

He suddenly looks less hearty than usual.

"Oh, no you don't," he says, sounding grim and rallying, rising up from his bower. At the risk of sounding like an idiot, if he's larger than life sprawled out, he's absolutely huge standing up. He must be eight feet tall and almost three or four feet wide.

I stand in his shadow, hoping he doesn't fall over and crush me, trying to follow his gaze. Across the square, I see three men on a rooftop, one of whom is gesturing at Bacchus.

"Ha-ha!" Bacchus grunts, flicking his hand towards the men, and they fly backwards out of view. There's a distant 'thud', presumably as they hit something, and the sound of yelling and swearing. "Don't try the same trick with me twice, younglings."

Two police officers near me hurriedly speak into their walkie-talkies, and I can see the squad of soldiers closing in on the building. Before they can reach it, there's the sound of revving motorcycle engines, and tyres squealing on the road. If that was Lucas, he's making a hasty getaway.

I ignore the subsequent debriefing, although one senior military officer does try – again – to get Bacchus to move to another location.

"I'm stronger than I look, laddie," he says jovially, seemingly unfazed by the attack. "You see, a lot of the other deities depend on actual worship. Me, well, every time someone raises a toast, that's venerating old Dionysus. And with this country's bacchanalia and revels, it's kept me strong for hundreds of years. I thought the Romans liked orgies, but here? Wonderful!"

The military guy looks confused and backs away, shaking his head.

"So," I start. "How about that drink?"

Bacchus is surprisingly good company, even for me. My opening conversational gambit is drinks – I don't drink a lot, but I have drunk and been drunk, so I ask him about his favourite beverages through the ages. He answers with a hearty passion, and although I'm desperate to find out how he was conscious through the years when he wasn't manifesting physically, I suspect that getting too serious in this conversation won't aid my ultimate goal.

Instead, I mention a few cocktails I've had or heard of recently, which he seems intrigued by. He manages to make some of them materialise, but they don't quite taste like I remember them tasting. I suspect that he's tinkered with them – he seems to lean towards sweet, slightly watery ales, which I'm thankful for. I'm not really here to get drunk.

As it starts to get dark, flaming torches appear around the perimeter of the square, and lute music starts to come from somewhere. The soldiers all look puzzled, but after a few minutes realise that it's Bacchus' doing and that it's likely harmless enough.

To my relief, Bacchus seems perfectly happy not talking as talking. He quaffs pints, downs flagons and chuckles merrily, even tempting a few police officers – presumably at the end of their shifts – to have a drink with him, at one stage filling their helmets with mead, much to their distress and his amusement.

I'm not quite sure what's in this drink, which is already flashing warning lights in my head, but I don't start feeling tipsy until I've had three, after which I decide that I do need to broach the subject of business with the big guy.

"Bacchus, sir," I start, but he holds up a hand and interrupts me.

"Please, Alice," he booms. "We're all drinking friends here. Bacchus will do, or Dionysus. Big B, if you fancy it."

He laughs at that, and so do the police officers and others on the benches nearby. I have to admit, it does seem funny.

"Well, Big B, then," I say haltingly, causing another wave of laughter through the group. "What do you think of my friends? Do you think they'll come through?"

Until I say it, I hadn't really thought of them as my friends, but perhaps they are. I don't have many friends, and I'm not quite sure if Hugo will still be speaking to me after what happened with his plane. None of it was my doing, so I don't really see why he wouldn't be, but he did seem quite upset by the whole thing.

"All good folk," Bacchus says merrily. "Of course, they'd do better drinking here than gallivanting across the country looking for spell books. Spell books, I ask you!"

There's more laughter and spilled drinks, and I take a long sip of my own. It is really quite good, even for a non-drinker.

"You don't think they'll find it?" I ask, pressing the issue.

The god of wine shakes his head, spraying foam and beer everywhere from his beard. "Oh ho ho!" he laughs.

"They may well, but human bodies are not meant for the power of gods. I don't know how that intruder was going to do it, but your friends would burn themselves out like moths to a flame without the right preparations. They'd be better off staying here for a drink."

"I don't think that's an option for them," I admit. "Lucas has probably got a plan for what to do with the power, and if he's not afraid to open up the rifts, then I don't think he has any kind of moral compass at all. I'm sorry Big B, but I think they're right."

"Hmmm," the god grumbles, sounding a bit like one of those giant trees from Lord of the Rings.

"Look, if there's anything you can do to help, we'd toast you every night for a year," I say, gambling. "Even if it's just with locating the angel or Lucas. Can you detect them at all?"

"Pah!" Bacchus spits. "There's too many souls to pick out a single one, but as one of my brothers said, sometimes logic can prevail where merriment fails. Not often, mind you, but perhaps you should cast your mind back to your last conversation with Raysiel. Angels are tremendously literal creatures from what I remember of your account, and if he said he's going to do something he'll likely do exactly that."

I curse myself for not applying the same logic to our current situation as I did to the situation in Jerusalem, then try to remember what happened before the angel burst through the roof of the Norwegian cave. Thankfully, my memory is almost photographic.

"Food," I say, standing up. "Ben was telling him to see what people were like, and he was talking about food. Fish and chips, Thai food, Nicaraguan and Nando's."

"Well then!" Bacchus laughs. "That's where I'd go! But have a drink first, fortify yourself."

Against my better judgment, I do take a drink and then look at Google Maps, recalling the way that Raysiel had burst out of the roof of the cave back in Svalbard, then trace a direct route to the UK from there.

The line intersects with King's Lynn, and I zoom in. Almost to the centimetre, the line goes through a branch of Nando's on the High Street.

"Shit," I swear, suddenly feeling faint from fatigue and light-headed from the drink. It's been a long time since I slept, but nonetheless I call over one of the police officers.

"Is that helicopter refuelled yet?"

Matt
Bad Manors

Despite the hurry, Seline insists that we get some sleep before taking on Lucas' mansion. I do almost exactly the right amount of protesting so that I can maintain my image, but then catch myself and stop, hearing Chloe's voice in my head, if not in my ears.

Honestly, I'm actually glad. I'm exhausted.

I help Chloe and her doctor back to the private clinic around the corner, but then we're escorted to the upper floors of a fairly nice hotel nearby. It's less nice now because the lower floors have essentially been destroyed to make it Shambler-proof.

Seline mentions that the preparations will take a bit of time, so I accept the offer of a ham and cheese toastie from the hotel staff and then lie back on the bed. I'm not going to sleep. I'm much too wired.

The insistent buzzing of my phone wakes me after what I think is a few seconds, but looking at it, I've been asleep for six hours already. It's 3.30am. Shit.

"Yeah?" I grunt, answering the phone.

"Helicopter's here," Ben says, sounding groggy. "They're refuelling and loading up the supplies. We're supposed to be outside in fifteen minutes."

"Got it," I groan. "See you then."

I roll out of bed and run a hand through my hair. Fucking hell. Wonder if I can doze in the chopper? This boy needs his beauty sleep.

The shower helps, and I finish off the last of the toastie from earlier on. I don't have much to pack, and I'm on my last pair of clean boxers; that is to say, they're the same boxers, but inside out and back to front, so, technically the clean bits are against my bits.

Some absolute legend hands me a breakfast bagel and a coffee in a travel cup as I get to the bottom of the rope ladder between the first and ground floors. Mentally, I promise to name something after them once I'm knighted.

It's dark outside, but I find Ben and he does that impatient head flicking thing he does when he's trying to look casual about where we're going but he's actually really stressed about it. I nod and follow him. The caffeine's not kicked in yet so the bantersaurus is still sleeping.

Two guys in military uniform fall in on either side of us, leading us up some emergency stairs on the side of the building. They creak alarmingly. Is this how it ends? Plummeting to my death not from being eaten or exploded or impaled but because some idiot let their stairs rust?

Christ, I'm cranky today. I'll get over it.

Despite the shit stairs, we reach the roof. There's one of those huge chinook helicopters on it, you know, the long chunky ones with two rotors. I stop for a moment, and a guy in a suit almost walks into me, dodging around at the last moment and heading into the chopper. I didn't even hear him behind me. Better wise up, Matt, or you're going to get dead from that.

I take a deep breath.

"You ok?" Ben asks quietly, and I nod.

"Sure, sure," I say breezily. "Just need a bit more beauty sleep or caffeine."

He blinks, and I glance over at him. Poor fucker looks like I feel.

"Come on," I manage. "Let's go."

I stumble as I'm getting up into the chopper, but the guy in the suit catches my arm and stops me from completely stacking it.

"Hey, thanks," I say. "Bit higher than I'm used to."

He laughs quietly. "You're Matt, right? I'm Mario, MI5 liaison. I'll be coming with you to the house."

"Good to have you with us," I say, actually wondering what use a spy will be, but maybe he can pick locks and hack computers and stuff. I'd have thought we'd have a tonne of commandos, armed to the absolute teeth to take out Banshees and Ravagers, but I suppose – recalling my D&D days – that you need a good mix of skills in a party to win.

As I blink, taking in the dark interior of the helicopter, I realise that we do actually have a load of commandos with us, or at least, pretty solid military types. There's about fifteen sturdy-looking men and women sitting on the benches that are bolted to the side of the helicopter, all wearing fatigues, holding helmets, guns, checking khaki backpacks and generally looking pretty efficient. There's a few trembling hands here and there, and I can't decide if that makes me feel better or worse.

One of the military people does a quick headcount, then slides the large side door closed, and we're off.

Chloe's helicopter was noisy, but this puts it to shame. Everything judders. The dual rotors are a constant roar, and it's like being in a tumble drier or something. I'll probably get out and vibrate like a cartoon rabbit.

Someone passes me a pair of large headphones, which I accept gratefully, stuffing the last of the breakfast bagel in my mouth.

Mario gets up and taps the side of his head, and everyone stops what they're doing to look at him. He's also wearing a headset, although it's slightly more ergonomic than mine. Probably custom-made by M or Q or whoever. I can never remember with Bond, I'm usually too busy skipping to the fighting bits or the sex scenes.

"Good morning," he says clearly. "Thank you all for coming. This is a joint mission between the British Army, MI5, the SAS and the First Extraordinary. I'd like to start with a few introductions, notably our two primary assets in this mission, Ben and Matt. These gentlemen are from the First Extraordinary Battalion, and will be dealing with any non-corporeal threats – that is to say, things that we can't touch or shoot."

I wave, getting a couple of friendly grins. Someone sniggers, and I hastily realise what's up, wiping ketchup off my chin.

"The person responsible for triggering the opening of the rifts that allowed the Ravagers, Shamblers and other creatures into the country has not yet been apprehended," he continues. "However, we have come into intelligence showing us the location of his main residence. While it's unlikely that he'll be there, given his current tactics, we do believe that there is an artefact there that will help us to negate his ultimate strategy. Army units will maintain a perimeter where possible, and along with the SAS unit, Ben, Matt and myself will infiltrate the grounds, find the artefact and exfiltrate as quickly as possible. We are heading to a location close to London, so we do expect substantial corporeal and non-corporeal threats. Satellites have shown at least two Lesser Banshees, a number of hellhounds and what seems to be a nest of Darklings. I won't lie to you – this is going to be a difficult engagement. Questions?"

A burly woman raises her hand, and Mario points to her. "This artefact," she says with an Essex accent. "What's it look like?"

Mario sighs. "It's a repository of information about

Lucas' methods," he says. "It could be a laptop, a tablet device or even a large book. Likely to be ornate and showy. Our opponent has a penchant for the dramatic."

"A spell book," the woman says quietly, although I can hear it through the headphones.

Mario nods, and I wait for the laughter, but instead there's a low grumbling, and one of the soldiers puts his head into his hands.

Turns out that when you confront people with the supernatural, and it can tear you limb from limb, it's not that comical and nerdy anymore.

On that cheery thought, I ignore the other questions and lean back, trying to get some more shuteye before the chopper lands.

I'm woken by an elbow to the ribs from Ben, and I turn to glare at him woozily.

"Matt," he says, sounding stressed, flicking the mic of his headphones out of the way. "Can I try this new stave out on you?"

I frown, and look around for my coffee, feeling a surge of relief as I find it and take a big gulp. "Sure," I manage. "Whaddya need?"

"I want to try giving you my energy," he says. "I think I've found out how to do it, but I'm not sure. I've … I've kind of made this up."

"Sure," I say. "You got it. Reverse vampire me."

A thought occurs to me. "You don't have to like, bite me or anything, do you?"

He rolls his eyes and I snigger, but I'm secretly relieved. That'd be a bit weird, but I guess I'd do it in the line of duty, being a hero and all.

Ben seems to be either concentrating or holding in a fart. There's something happening with the noosphere, but I don't really know what, and I don't feel any different.

Then I do. My wooziness lifts a little, and my head clears.

"Hey," I say. "That was kind of awesome. If we make it through this, you could sell that as a hangover cure. You ok?"

He nods, cancelling the stave. "Tired. I could feel something coming out of me, but it didn't hurt or anything."

I'm about to make another 'that's what she said' joke, but I don't want to ruin my gravitas further with all the military types. I think Ben knows it anyway, and he kind of snorts and shakes his head. He tries to talk me through how he's done it, but I can't grasp it. I make a few failed attempts, but by the time we start to descend, I haven't got it, and I can see that he's frustrated.

Still, the guy either invented a whole new stave or modified the healing stave to deal with lack of sleep. Excellent.

The helicopter touches down, and the burlier men and women – I'm guessing, SAS rather than conventional military – jump out first, beckoning for us to follow. I snap off my seat belt and get out, Ben close behind me.

We're on a broad gravelled drive, a few metres up from a set of ornate metal gates. It's still dim, but there's the large shape of what I assume is the mansion further up the drive. It's grassy on either side, with dark woodland in the distance.

Famous last words, but it looks clear.

I hear a screeching in the distance, and Mario starts handing out earpieces and earplugs. The SAS – who are padding around the chinook in a broad circle – seem to have their own, but I accept a pair from Mario gratefully; if there's Banshees, we'll need them.

"Alright," he says, his voice coming through my earpiece. "No time like the present. Turner, Hughes, Capelin, you're with us. Everyone else, stay with the chopper. Any sign of non-corporeal trouble, take off and wait for us if it's safe to do so. Matt, Ben, let's go."

Ben and I flank Mario and start towards the mansion, as the woman with the Essex accent and two large men keep a loose perimeter around us.

"Now," Mario says. "The grounds around us are quite extensive, and there seem to be a couple of structures around that look like they're worth investigating. There's one at the top of the lake on the eastern side over that way, then another, smaller one over on the far side of the house. There's gardens and woodland between us, and obviously the house to search as well. Where do you want to start? Can you detect anything?"

He sounds a bit awkward saying it; I guess he's not

quite as comfortable with the paranormal as I thought he might be.

"We can usually detect rips in the noosphere," Ben says, getting there first. "But not creatures or other stuff."

Mario sucks air in through his teeth and kisses them. "That's going to make things harder."

The mansion looks like somewhere you'd go with a National Trust pass, not the lair of a super-villain; it's all in light brown stone, with those annoying, single-glazed sash windows divided into little squares. I had some in a flat once and they made it fucking freezing and damp to boot. The building's got wings on either side of the front part, which juts out a bit – I assume that the bay windows have a great view of the long drive that we've just walked up, reminding people what a big dick Lucas has, or as I suspect is more likely, what a big drive he has, in the absence of externally visible genitalia.

It's kind of impressive – his house, not his penis, obviously, try to keep up – and there's a fountain with an angel or cherub or something that we have to skirt round as we get closer.

"We'll start at the back of the house," Ben says, surprising me. I turn to look at him, wondering where this decisiveness came from.

"It's a hunch," he continues. "Lucas is a diva, right? I don't think he'd have his most valuable stuff in the house where anyone could find it, because he's got to be entertaining the rich and famous sometimes. He'd have a place on the grounds where he could access it, but where it'd be out of the way. And the top of the lake is probably also for entertaining because of the views, but something tucked near to the house and through a wood? Sounds about right for a lair."

Mario nods in agreement. "Sounds fair," he says, and we change direction to start skirting the house.

My headset crackles.

"This is Clarkson," a male voice says. "Satellites are definitely showing motion north of your position. Do you want more support?"

"Negative, but be ready to send backup," Mario says.

"Understood."

We cautiously edge around the house, navigating a small ornamental garden, complete with fishpond. There's some fairly large, expensive-looking fish in there, but I try not to get distracted. I can distantly hear the screeching getting louder, the SAS team gripping their weapons in a way that I imagine constitutes nervousness amongst the highly-trained military elite.

As we round the back of the house, we see them. There's a paved area at the back with expensive-looking sun-loungers and recliners, then a set of stone steps that descend to a large gravelled area with a tree and some flowers in the middle, and another pond. I'm not really doing it justice but there's also two Banshees by the tree, and they are absolutely hideous. If I didn't know better, I'd say that someone had stuck some really nasty Halloween masks on top of a bunch of metal rods and barbed wire contorted into the rough shape of a person, with jagged, scissor-like limbs protruding from the sides where their arms should be. Their faces are basically white ovals of flesh or something, with narrow slits for eyes and a mouth.

One of them sees us and screeches, making everyone take a step back. Its mouth is filled with glinting metal teeth, and despite the lack of human features, it looks really, really pissed off.

Turner, Hughes and Capelin open fire immediately, but Mario's already shouting for them to stop. Four hellhounds, which look a bit like dogs – if big dogs were made of bare metallic cartilage, all tarnished muscle and bone – burst from the flower beds, and start sprinting towards us. Mario shouts at the soldiers to direct their fire at the dogs, also reaching for a sidearm. I suddenly feel very naked, but new routines kick in, and against all my better instincts, I start working my way towards the Banshees, trying not to cross the line of fire.

Of course, the line of fire doesn't stay a line of fire very long. One of the hellhounds falls, leaking white fluid on the immaculate garden, but the other two reach the three troopers, springing at them and knocking one of them – Turner, I think – down onto the ground. The woman, Capelin, grapples with another, Mario beating at it with a truncheon, as Hughes tries to kick off the other one and shoot at it at the same time.

I shape a stave and fire it off at the first Banshee, but

I'm too far away. It screeches at me, and starts to drift towards us quickly, the other one close behind. I break into a jog and run at it, shaping and firing stave after stave. It freezes, and I look at the other one, finding it already frozen by Ben's magic.

I spin around, seeing Hughes on the ground with Turner assisting him and Capelin and Mario covering them.

"Guys!" I yell. "A little help?"

Ben and I back away, and there's a hail of fire as the two SAS let rip with their rifles, taking the Lesser Banshees down in a matter of seconds.

It's suddenly very quiet and I glance around hurriedly, trying to spy out or hear another Banshee, but there's nothing. I can hear the leaves rustling in the breeze, Ben's ragged breathing – fuck, my ragged breathing as well – but other than that, there's nothing.

We hurry back to the soldiers, our footsteps sounding way too loud, seeing Turner binding Hughes' leg and arm, the bandages almost soaked through already.

"I need to evacuate him,"Turner says, and Mario nods.

"Can you manage on your own?"

Turner nods, wrapping another bandage around the soldier's leg before helping the man up.

"Come on," Mario says. "Capelin, you're with us."

The woman crisply changes the magazine on her rifle, then nods. She checks herself with a well-practised ease, tightening bag straps, loosening a pistol in its holster and re-fastening a pocket before standing at ease, waiting for us. She doesn't look fazed by the prospect of riding with us solo, which I suspect makes exactly one of us.

The woods up ahead loom ominously. I get a sick feeling in my throat, but with Capelin and Ben in front, I can't wimp out now. I exchange a glance with Mario, and then we're in.

Despite the light from the rising sun, it's dim in here, the woodland thick and dense, almost as if the trees were pushing themselves together to obscure the light.

Seriously Matt, sort your shit out. You've been through worse than this.

Then I spot something moving up ahead and almost piss myself. I get a grip and stop, hissing at the others to hold on. Capelin instantly aims her rifle, spinning around and checking the area. I don't see anything, but I can definitely feel something up ahead, a wrongness.

"I think there's a rift here, guys," I whisper, and Ben nods.

"Agreed," he says. "Let's take it really slowly."

I catch up with him and Capelin, trusting Mario to keep an eye out behind us, and then I see them. Four or five Shamblers are drifting between the trees, occasionally dipping down to something on the ground.

Then Mario does the absolute worst and most predictable thing in the world and steps on a twig, which breaks with an almost comedic snap.

There's an excruciating moment, and all of the

Shamblers start to glide towards us.

Capelin and Mario stare at them, transfixed, and I do the same. I can't move.

Then I do. Other than Ben, no-one else is going to do fuck all. So somehow I start shaping and casting staves, containing and dispersing the Shamblers just like we did in Karnak. Ben joins me, and we get the last one when it's still a couple of metres away, feeling pretty damn proud of ourselves, even under these godforsaken circumstances.

I turn back to Capelin and Mario, and it all goes south in the most fucking awful way possible.

Blood fountains from their noses, a look of incredulity on both their faces as Mario reaches up to try and stave the flow, but it starts to gush from his eyes, his ears, his mouth. Both of them fall awkwardly, Mario half-catching himself on a tree as he does, and I see two more Shamblers behind them, moving *through* them.

My entire body is shaking. My hands are trembling like motherfuckers as I try to shape a stave. I can't do it.

Ben does it, Mario's Shambler dispersing without being contained, and I grit my teeth, forcing the noosphere through my tattoos and projecting a stave that shatters the other Shambler into nothing.

"Fuck," I manage, surging forwards, and catching Mario as he loses his grip on the tree branch, gushing blood from everywhere. There's so much of it, all over my hands, the ground and his clothes. I don't know what to do, but a second later he lets out a sigh and goes completely limp. He slips out of my hands onto the gravelled path and I kneel down beside him, trying to find a pulse, but there's nothing at all, only a smartly-dressed guy lying in a pool of blood washing over my shoes.

I stagger away, leaning against a tree and looking back at Ben, who's kneeling beside Capelin, but he shakes his head. Bile rises in my throat and I vomit onto the earth, coughing and spluttering, trying to find a tissue to wipe myself with, and eventually managing with a sleeve.

"Shit."

It takes me a moment to get myself together, and I look at Ben, whose face is almost grey.

"Do we go back?"

He shakes his head. "No way," he says.

"What about them?"

Ben presses his headset. "Guys, we've lost Mario and Capelin," he says tearfully, snorting back what I imagine is probably a mixture of snot and vomit. "We're continuing the search. It's not safe yet, but we'll bring them back if we can."

I don't really see how we can carry two fully grown adults whilst defending ourselves from Shamblers and fuck-knows-what, but I don't say anything. We're not going to get out of this wood, are we? I'm suddenly cold, even though it was pretty warm a minute ago.

I take a deep breath, ignoring the taste of sick in my mouth and reach down, taking Mario's handgun. Ben arms himself with Capelin's bloodied pistol and small backpack, wiping the gun awkwardly and tucking it into a pocket.

We hurry on through the woods, glancing around every few paces, trying not to trip over. I'm trembling all over. I don't think I've ever been this scared in my entire life.

The forest path curves one way, then another, and the gloom seems to lift a bit, even as the feeling of wrongness deepens. The path takes a sharp turn and suddenly we're out, looking across a grassy avenue, flanked by trees, towards a tower made of what looks like grey slate. The wizard's tower, I presume. Wanker's tower, more like.

Then I realise something's not quite right about the view; if I step to one side, it changes slightly. There's a rift, showing a grassy vista, about six feet in front of me.

"Ben," I hiss, pointing at it, and I start to feel for the edges, trying to push it back together again. It gets easier as Ben helps, and before too long, it's done, and the sense of wrongness dissipates.

Suddenly a whole other sense of wrongness hits me and I hear a Banshee screeching way too loudly. I spin around, seeing it right up in my face. I fall backwards, trying to cast a containment stave, but I hit the ground painfully, the Banshee stabbing a claw down towards me. There's a white-hot pain as I see its jagged limb pierce my leg, the white metal somehow emerging unnaturally from the other side, and then I completely lose my grip on consciousness.

Ben
Alone

I've been feeling faint since the first of the SAS guys was injured, and now the world is spinning like I'm drunk. But somehow, when I see the Banshee, my instincts kick in and I fire off a containment stave, just as it pulls back from Matt.

He's bleeding, but I can't move. The Banshee is towering a foot above me, its wail hurting my head despite the earplugs. I need to do something to stop this thing, and I swallow, shaping another stave and launch it, panicking – what if there are more? What if there are those dog things, or Shamblers?

The Banshee freezes. I pull the gun from my back pocket, my hands shaking so much that I almost let it drop. I push back the safety catch and try to brace myself before aiming, holding it with both hands, firing at it point-blank.

It's incredibly loud, the bang hurting my ears more than the Banshee's wail, and I feel a sharp pain between my thumb and first finger, but I force myself to fire again and again until the creature simply comes apart, dissolving down onto the ground.

I look around, but don't see anything else nearby. There's a smear of blood on my hand; the gun must have caught the skin next to my thumb somehow, but that's the least of my worries.

"Matt," I say, shaking him, then pull off the light backpack that I took from Capelin, finding a length of bandage in there.

Shit. I can't just bandage him up. He's fallen down and there's dirt on his leg. He's bleeding freely onto the ground right in front of me.

It takes a couple of tries to open the backpack. My fingers won't do what they're told, and I have to take a moment to retch, because it's that or faint, but eventually I find a bottle of water and some antiseptic. I have to cut through his trousers and peel them off him so that the fabric doesn't work its way into his cut, and I marvel that my brain is somehow providing me with this helpful information. Matt watches me woozily, still bleeding. I wash his cut with bottled water, then dab it with antiseptic, which makes him jolt upright. He yells out, then looks at me, propping himself up on his elbows as I wrap the bandage around his bloody leg and fasten it with a safety pin. That alone takes about five tries.

"Fuck, Ben," he says quietly, looking pale. "Thought that was it."

I swallow. "Might still be," I admit.

"Christ," he says, sounding drunk. "Never thought I'd die a virgin."

Then I'm laughing hysterically, and he's smirking, and I think I cry a little bit but eventually we just sit there on the grass, sniggering.

"Can you stand?" I say eventually.

He doesn't even try. "We're almost there," he says. "You go. I'll be right here."

"Matt," I say, welling up, and blinking furiously. "I am not leaving my best friend to bleed here on some twunt's murder lawn."

"Seriously," he says. "Don't be a fucking hero. Get the book and get out of here. You can airlift me once you're sorted."

No way. Absolutely no way. I sit back down, resting my hands on the grass behind me.

"Honestly Matt," I say, not managing to keep the tears at bay. "The Gardeners can go and fuck themselves for all I care."

"Now you sound like me," he says weakly. "So I know you're being a twat."

I stand up and grab his arm shakily, stammering and crying when I speak, but there is absolutely one thing that I'm certain of. I'm not leaving Matt here.

"Get up, you mouldy shitbag. You're coming to that tower if I have to drag your motherfucking weed-smoking dad-joke-making shitting, cunting arse every inch of the way."

I'm shaking and weeping, but incredibly, he does start

to lever himself up, eventually coming to an unstable standing position with most of the weight on his other leg. He drapes an arm around me, and together, me crying, him wincing with every step, we limp unevenly towards the tower. The first time I take his weight my legs almost buckle. I catch myself and recover, leaning into it after that. Metre by metre, we slowly cover ground.

"You're such a tit," he mutters between gritted teeth. "And you said shit twice."

"Shut up."

We're into a rhythm, but as we get near to the tower, Matt looks around and stiffens.

"Better hurry," he says. "Company."

"Banshee?"

"Shamblers. Two of them."

"One each," I say. I don't even know why.

He keeps glancing back as we limp towards the tower, and we almost stumble as we get to the door, which is mercifully – and strangely – unlocked.

Inside is a rich man's man cave. It's full of large plasma screens and expensive-looking laptops, bookshelves filled with both obscure-looking tomes and modern management books. There's a glass-fronted cabinet filled with whisky bottles, fancy-looking glasses on one shelf. There's a leather sofa with a matching footrest, and, perhaps in advance of the apocalypse that he's now caused, a rope ladder dangling from a hatch in the roof.

Matt glances upwards.

"I guess he knew about the Shamblers then?"

I nod, and look around. "Come on," I say. "Up."

"You don't think it's here?"

"On the ground floor, in easy reach? Unlikely."

"Fine," Matt says, and starts to pull himself up the ladder. It's slow going. Sweat rolls down my sides as I wait. I glance back out through the door, seeing the two granny ghosts slowly drifting up towards us, their faces contorted with what I imagine is a hungry rage.

Finally, Matt makes it to the top and I hurry upwards, pulling the ladder up after me. This level seems to be some kind of prepping room; tins of food and large boxes filled with pasta and long-life meals sit on shelves all around. There's a little kitchenette to one side and with shaking hands I grab two glasses and fill them from the tap, giving one to Matt. He takes a drink, then sets it down on the floor beside him, slopping a reasonable amount of it over the side.

There's a fairly standard set of stairs curving upwards to the next level.

"Think I'll just take five here," Matt says, looking pale and breathing heavily. "If that's ok? If you can wait a bit, I can come with."

I shake my head. He needs more than five. "Hold on," I say. I'm an idiot. I know a stave for healing. What was I thinking? I try to remember the details and curse myself for not thinking about it earlier. I flick through my e-reader and try to hold the details in my head, channelling it, but I don't think I quite get it right and have to try again.

Matt looks a bit less pale, and the bloody stain on his leg seems to have stopped growing, but he still looks like hell.

"Nice," he says weakly. "Thanks man, you've picked up some tricks. You be ok up there?"

"I'll be fine," I say. I might throw up. "You hang out, I'll check upstairs. Once you feel like it, see if there's anything we could eat around here."

"Eat?" he says. "You hungry?"

I shrug. I'm really not, but he's lost a lot of blood.

"Just take it easy for now, ok?"

He nods and sags back against the wall. Steeling myself, I climb the stairs to the next level.

Once I'm out of sight, I have to wait a few moments for the world to stop moving because I'm intensely light-headed. I try to breathe normally, but I can't quite seem to catch my breath. I don't know if I'm hungry or thirsty. I don't feel right.

I don't have long; Matt could be bleeding again. The helicopter could be surrounded by Shamblers. Lucas could have found someone else to drain and be becoming a deity right now, and then what?

The next floor is filled with cages of guns and weapons. All of the cages look locked, so I don't even pause. I could barely fire a pistol, so there's no chance anything more heavy-duty would help anyway.

I'm out of breath by the time I get to the top floor,

which has a panoramic view of the gardens and a glass roof showing the morning sky. I can see something dark moving through the trees a way away, possibly a Darkling, and more Shamblers by the lake, but that's not important right now.

What is important is the impressive-looking wooden desk in the centre of the room, with a regal-looking chair in front of it.

On top of the desk is a large, closed book underneath a glass display case. It looks leather-bound, and is almost certainly the spell book I'm looking for, unless Lucas has pulled an Indiana Jones Holy Grail trick, which – from what little I know about him – seems unlikely. I hurry over to it and try to open the glass case.

It doesn't budge.

I try sliding it up and down, pulling it out, looking for a switch on or under the desk, but there's nothing.

I swear under my breath and then smack the case as hard as I can with the butt of the gun, but it doesn't even crack.

I try again.

Nothing.

We can't have come this far to fall at the final hurdle.

I put both hands on the case and try to tune into the noosphere to see if there's any clues there, but suddenly the case shifts. As if by magic, the glass starts to retract, and I hastily move away a step. Just before it fully sinks into the almost-invisible slots in the desk, I spot a smear of blood on the glass and I realise what's happened.

Seriously, Lucas? Blood sacrifice to release your book of spells?

Prick.

Indiana Jones comes into my head again, and wary of any more bullshit, I snatch the book from the desk and run back down the stairs. Thankfully, nothing happens – I guess Lucas was confident in his own cleverness with the blood thing.

Matt's looking terrible when I reach him. His face is grey, and he's looking pretty out of it. He hears me coming down the stairs and looks up.

"You got it," he says, sounding faint. "Legend."

I kneel down beside him and check his bandages. They're wet through, but he's not bleeding anymore.

"Hey," I say into my microphone. "We've got the artefact, but Matt's hurt. Any chance of an airlift from the tower past the house?"

"On our way," a voice says. "We have Turner and Hughes. With you in a few minutes."

I glance down past the rope ladder and see two spectral shapes gliding around beneath me. I swear softly under my breath again. I don't know if I can muster the power for more staves, so with a flash of inspiration I turn back upstairs and stand looking up at the top floor.

Wincing slightly, I draw the gun and fire at the glass ceiling.

There's a deafening bang and my ears ring painfully.

When I look up at the ceiling, I can see a small hole in the glass.

Brilliant.

If I can just replicate that like a million times, we might get out of here.

I head back downstairs to the weapons room and find the only weapon not locked up in a cage, an ornate shotgun mounted on a board on the wall. It's got some kind of metal plaque on it, but I don't bother to read it, instead taking it upstairs, hoping that Lucas is stupid enough to leave his weapons loaded.

He is, and not only does the shot from the gun shatter two window panels, but the gun cracks against my collarbone and gives me a proper slap in the face for good measure. Bracing myself for more of the same, I hold it as firmly as I can and fire at the two adjacent panels, glass raining down on the ornate desk.

Fuck you, Lucas, I think to myself. Fuck you and your man cave. If I was here for longer, I'd piss in your whisky cabinet.

I snigger at that one slightly hysterically. I must be channelling Matt, and speaking of which, I should go. I hurry back downstairs, discarding the shotgun and telling the chopper pilot about the plan.

Matt's sitting up on the floor, and I can distantly hear the helicopter coming, so I pull him up to his feet and slowly we work our way up to the top floor, arriving as two harnesses fall out of the chinook, landing on the desk in front of us. I get Matt into his first before attending to mine.

Being hauled up into the air is one of the least dignified and most uncomfortable experiences of my life, and I hate every second of it, but I'm also too wired and relieved at the same time to care. We're pulled into the helicopter by the army guys, and I sag down against the wall of the vehicle as two of them lay Matt out on a stretcher, unbinding and re-dressing his wound.

Then I'm shaking uncontrollably, and I have to sit with my knees up against my chest, hugging myself, shivering and trying not to cry again. One of the soldiers comes over with a blanket and a bar of chocolate, and sits down next to me.

"It's the post-adrenalin rush," he says calmly. "You been in combat before?"

I shake my head, my lower lip trembling, blinking rapidly. I really don't want to cry in front of this guy.

"It'll pass," he says. "You've been through an intense experience. Just take your time, stay warm, and eat the chocolate for sugar. Like those ghosts in Harry Potter, remember?"

I almost manage a weak grin.

"And I'm sorry to ask, but we do need a destination. Greenwich, or back to Bath?"

"Fuck," I say quietly. "Hold on."

I take a few deep breaths, then pull my phone out of my pocket and dial Seline, conferencing in Alice a moment later.

"Guys," I shout, trying to make myself heard above the rotor blades until the shaven-headed soldier next to me connects my phone to my headset. "We've got Lucas' book. And ideas where we need to go next?"

"I'm sorry, Ben," Seline says. "I've got my hands full right now. Alice?"

"Um," Alice says, and I have to press the earbud into my ear because she's a bit faint and also a bit, well, she's slurring a bit. "I've been pretty busy here too."

"Any ideas at all? Alice, I know you were working to track down Raysiel, but I'll take anything you've got."

"Well," she says, definitely sounding drunk. "I'm on my way to meet him right now. But give me a moment and I'll pull up some options."

"Alice?" I ask. "Have you been with Bacchus again?"

"I have," she says, her voice uneven. "And he said that human bodies aren't made to absorb divine energies, so you just take care when you meet Lucas, ok?"

Fucking hell. We're boned.

"Is Chloe conscious yet?" I ask.

"I'm sorry, Ben," Seline says. "She's still out and her doctor won't permit us to disturb her again. Look, I'm going to have to go, I'm needed in the field. Keep me informed, alright?"

"Got it. Good luck."

"Alice," I say once Seline has gone. "Look, do you have any coffee nearby or anything? Matt's injured, Chloe's out and it's just you and me right now, so please can you sober up a bit? I need you really badly because I've got nothing else and everything's really really fucked."

"Alright," she says, taking a deep breath. "Sorry. Give me a moment."

I keep the line open for the next ten minutes, and I'm sure I can hear rotor blades in the background of her call, but maybe it's an echo or something.

"Ok," she says, sounding a bit more present. "I've got a feed of all the possible deity sightings from Seline's team in Greenwich. I've scored them all based on likelihood, danger for Lucas – that is to say, proximity to large settlements and police forces – and violence. I imagine that he's unlikely to take on gods who are known to be extremely aggressive."

"Can you send it to me?" I say, interrupting her.

"I will," she says. "But Ben, I think there's only one that it can be. Any stationary god will require Lucas to be stealthy, and that's not an ideal situation for him, because it's risky. I don't know if Seline told you, but there was another attempt on Bacchus, and he almost crushed Lucas like a bug."

"What does that leave us?"

"The Wild Hunt," she says breathlessly. "Inherently mobile. Lucas could set up and wait for it to come to him."

"The Wild Hunt?" I say incredulously. "Stags and hunters and stuff?"

"It's primarily a Norse and Germanic legend," Alice

says, sounding more like herself. "There's a possible Welsh site, but there have been far more sightings in Grimspound, in Dartmoor. It's a traditional spectral hunt, led by Woden or sometimes Gabriel or even the devil. I'll send you the location now."

"Woden? I don't know that one. What did he do?"

"Well, it's Woden in Saxon," Alice says. "But in Norse, he's Odin."

"Shit," I say, leaning back and hitting my head against the wall of the chinook, images of Antony Hopkins floating into my mind.

"Ben," Alice says. "I need to go, ok? I'll send you what I've got. Good luck, and I'll be with you as soon as I can."

She hangs up, and my phone beeps as it downloads an email from her with a load of attachments. I pass the information onto the soldier next to me, whose name is David, and then check on Matt. He's sleeping, but the medic tells me that he's stable, whatever that means. Apparently, although I shouldn't have moved him so much, I did a decent job of looking after him, which I assume is partially thanks to the healing stave.

I get up and check on Hughes, casting the stave on his leg and arm, feeling guilty that I didn't think of that the first time around. It's easier this time, and after a moment, Hughes tries flexing his arm and leg, thanking me profusely as he does.

One of the soldiers takes the spell book and starts to photograph the pages, sharing it with the Gardeners and intelligence services, so I'm off the hook for a bit while that happens.

I lean back against the side of the helicopter and ask how long it'll take to get to Grimspound. Apparently, Chinooks are pretty fast, so it'll only be about ninety minutes. I ask David to give me a shake in half an hour if I'm asleep, and close my eyes, not really expecting to sleep.

But I do.

Ben

Before the Hunt

David wakes me half an hour later, and for a moment, I can't work out where I am. It's noisy, it smells of too many people in too small a space, and I could really do with washing my face and cleaning my teeth.

Thankfully, David offers me a mint, and a sip of coffee from his thermos, which actually works out better than I'd expected, so I'm grateful.

Then it's to business.

I've got one hour to digest Lucas' spell book and work out how he's sapping energy from the gods.

Books.

I can do books.

I got this.

There's a flowery bookplate at the start, but then the book starts, and although it's hand-written, Lucas has surprisingly clear handwriting. I skim the preamble; it's mostly self-justification about how the world deserves to know about the other worlds out there, how the government has been keeping things from us and how there are unimaginable sources of power out there that could help people.

Yeah, you really helped people, douchebag.

I'm surprised that rather than being a straightforward spell book, it's sort of a diary. It recounts how Lucas became disgruntled with the Gardeners for not sharing their knowledge, for keeping everything to themselves and denying people the truth. He started to plan how to start his own order that would reveal this to people, and began to consider both the social and financial ways of doing it, planning a long-term campaign, rather than just rage-quitting the organisation.

Smart guy. There's been nothing hasty about this.

He tells of how he started to experiment with the staves. There must be other uses for the noosphere, he writes, more than protecting and containing. He quickly succeeds in doing what Chardin did, healing people and animals, but then tries to research the reverse, empowering himself.

I skip over his accounts of the frustration he feels as he fails to do this again and again and again, even after studying Raphael's primary work on stave reversal. Some of his methods are pretty grim, injuring and then sacrificing animals, and even a human murder. He constantly justifies himself by saying that it'll all be worth it in the end, the lives that will be saved, blah blah blah. It's bullshit and I think even he knows it, but he's so wrapped up in his company dealings – investing in services that are actively taking advantage of and promoting the decline in empathy – that I don't think he pays it much attention. He mentions how difficult and stressful it all is, how the person he killed wasn't anyone that'd be missed, that he made a huge donation to charity because of it, but ultimately, he still killed a guy.

Then he succeeds.

At first, it's on a rat, then a stray dog, then another person. He describes how he first absorbs power from the noosphere, then uses that power to tune into and rip another being's energy from them. You start slowly and gradually, like inching up the corner on a roll of sticky tape, then connect and don't let go, taking more and more and more.

I don't want to do this. It's wrong.

I ask David for a pen and paper, and start making notes. Maybe I could modify this so that it's not quite so horrific.

I'll still have to do the initial rip, but what I want to do is fashion a conduit for the noosphere using the staves, rather than absorbing it directly. I look at the stave for healing again, and the modification I shaped earlier giving away my energy to Matt, then work up a schematic for linking the two. I think it should work – I know which part of the stave notation tells the noosphere energy where to go, and that's the important part.

Of course, I haven't got anyone to check this with

because I'm essentially the only Gardener here, but I do send a picture to Seline on the off-chance that she's around.

"David?" I say, and the soldier looks up from his tablet. "Can I borrow you for a moment? And someone else?"

He nods, introducing me to Sam, the woman on the other side of me. I really should have gotten to know the people who might be laying down their lives for me, but, well, this has all been a lot.

"Ok," I say. "I need to try taking a bit of your energy, and giving it to Sam, alright? I'm not going to take very much, but I need to do it without your assistance, because this is what I'll need to do when we find Lucas."

"Will it hurt?" David asks.

"I don't know," I admit. "But we'll take it slowly and if it does, let me know and we'll stop, ok?"

He nods, and I shape the stave to help me see the noosphere, gradually perceiving the stream of particles or whatever they are buzzing around us. I see the slow rise of energy from David; he's helping humankind, so I guess that gives him empathy and kindness points. I shape my new concept stave and start to direct it away from David and into me, channelling it and then locating Sam, passing it onto her.

At first, it's just a little, and nothing seems to happen. Then I realise I can latch on, dig in, and go deeper, like Lucas' diary says. I'm starting to see beneath his skin, into his very being, which is surreal. There's all kinds of particles zipping around, and I start to siphon them through my conduit into Sam. It's almost addictive, and suddenly I realise, coming back to the physical world, that something's changed, that David's stiffened next to me, and I abruptly stop the process, dissolving the chain.

He sags back down onto the bench and pants.

"Damn," he swears. "Sorry Ben, I should have said something. That felt like getting flu in twenty seconds."

"David, I'm so sorry," I say, shame washing over me. "Is it bad? Will you be ok?"

"Yeah," he says. "It's fading now, but …"

I turn to Sam. She bites her lip and looks down at the floor.

"It felt amazing," she says. "Like I could sprint for a mile with a full pack. Like great coffee. But if that was from David, I don't want it."

"Sorry," I say, feeling intensely guilty. "Thank you. We won't need to do that again. I'm sorry you had to go through that."

David puts a hand on my shoulder. "Ben," he says, fixing me with a hard look. He's greying, and I can see it in his stubble as well. He's got wise eyes and I'm reminded momentarily of my dad. "Ben, if you need to do this to stop this guy, then you do it as many times as you have to, ok?"

I look away for a moment to blink back the sudden wave of emotion.

"Alright," I say, clenching my fists. "But Sam, if you're

ok with this, we'll alternate and do it the other way around. I could do with trying this more than once before we arrive."

Sam nods, and we go again.

The second time I fail entirely and I'm not quite sure whether it's me losing my nerve, or that I just can't tap into the noosphere as well. The third time I do get some kind of control over it and manage to control the flow from Sam to David, but it leaves me starting to feel hot and sweaty all over from the effort.

I feel us start to descend, and Turner stands up, calling for attention.

"Alright, listen up," he says gruffly. "This is an important one. We have solid intelligence that Lucas will be arriving at Grimspound, a Bronze Age settlement, sometime before dusk, in anticipation of another supernatural being that he will be attempting to destroy. We are here to apprehend him, but we expect extremely strong resistance. Lucas has hired mercenaries who are well-armed, and although we do not expect any rift activity or supernatural creatures, he has shown no hesitation in committing criminal acts to get what he wants. Although we have Ben from the First Extraordinary, his primary mission is to mitigate Lucas' supernatural attacks if he engages with the other being."

Turner pauses, and other than the constant noise of the rotors and the engine, it's silent. Ten men and women in military fatigues all sit, looking at Turner with expressions ranging from mild disbelief to grim determination.

"The supernatural entity we are expecting is the Wild Hunt," he continues, sounding uncomfortable. "Ghostly horses, huntsmen and the like. Historical records and local lore suggest that it passes through Grimspound at dusk more often than any other site. Lucas is likely to set up around the site itself, which occupies a bowl-shaped depression, and to fortify heavily. Local police are meeting us on Woden's Way, the nearest road, where two paths lead directly to the site. Unfortunately, given Lucas' prior activities, we anticipate that he will have left traps or teams near to these locations to intercept pursuit. We'll approach from the north, travelling through heavy woodland to Hookney Tor, a hill adjacent to Grimspound. From there, we'll recon the site and plan further. Questions?"

"Numbers, sir?" David asks.

"Ten to fifteen mercenaries with body armour and automatic weapons, as well as Lucas himself, who is a former member of the First Extraordinary," he says. "Possible long-ranged capabilities, but explosive ordnance is unlikely, except as traps, so take care. Shoot to kill, and without hesitation. This man and his forces are directly responsible for the release of all of these creatures and the deaths of thousands of people across the country."

There aren't any further questions.

The chopper gets down pretty low, and I brace myself for landing, but instead it stays close to the ground and starts to sweep along beneath the line of the hills. For stealth, I assume, although if Lucas has satellite support, he might be able to see us coming. Not a lot we can do about that, although I hope someone else has thought about all this.

My phone buzzes.

"Ben," Seline says, at the other end. "I don't have long, but I've had an analyst in America look over Alice's analysis and they do agree that this is the most likely site for Lucas' intervention. We're monitoring a number of other sites, so if we have sight of Lucas at any stage, you'll need to pull out quickly, ok? We've got a relatively stable site with King Arthur at Tintagel, which is also acting as a guaranteed safe refuge for high value individuals, and it's not too far from you. It's relatively safe from rift activity. In addition to Bacchus, we've also got eyes on Frigge or Aphrodite – we're not sure which – in Soho, which is incredibly useful, and we're trying to make better use of her, but we keep losing military staff to … well, you can probably guess."

"So Bacchus isn't the only one?" I ask. "Have any of them said anything useful? Have you been able to talk to them properly?"

"Not really," Seline admits. "They all seem very absorbed with their own agendas. We've also had unconfirmed sightings of the Green Man in the Chilterns, and potentially a battle between Ares and a Greater Banshee in Watford, but we've been unable to confirm. Intelligence doesn't believe that any of these are likely targets for Lucas, and none of them have added anything useful to our collective intelligence."

I struggle to take all of that in.

"I've got to go, Ben," she says. "Listen, stay in touch, and good luck, ok? We're all thinking of you, and if all else fails, the other Gardeners should be back in twenty-four hours. Once they start to come back, we should get more reinforcements from abroad as well. We're almost there, but we need to make sure Lucas is secured, ok? Trust the military, and take care."

I thank her and hang up as a wave of dizziness sweeps over me. David sees me falter and claps me on the shoulder.

"We'll be fine," he says. "This is a regular anti-terrorist operation. There's some ghoulies and ghosties in the mix, but nothing like that manor, right?"

I nod slowly, remembering Mario and Capelin.

"Right," I say, not feeling certain at all. From what Matt has said, Lucas could create a rift by doing something really awful to someone, but I suspect that'd interfere with whatever vampirism he's planning – it's not like the Shamblers would discriminate between us and them.

And then we land and I don't have time to think about anything anymore. I barely have time to check on Matt, who's just about conscious. He gives me a weak-looking thumbs-up and then sags back down onto the stretcher before Turner ushers me out, and I hear the rotor blades of the chinook slowing then stopping altogether.

We've landed on a closed-off section of country road, at what looks like a passing place. The local police have coned off access ahead and behind us, and the large helicopter takes up the majority of the road, the rotors almost touching the high hedges on either side. Our pilot must be a bit of a genius.

The burly SAS officer waves to a man in police uniform, beckoning him over.

"Mike Turner, SAS," he says. "This is Ben, First Extraordinary, and I've got a mixed unit of police, army and anti-terror. You're the ranking police officer?"

The slim guy pales and nods. He's maybe thirty, and I suspect that he's more used to lost tourists and the occasional pub brawl around here.

"Inspector Simon Morris," the guy says. "We're here to support however we can. You're looking to get to Hookney Tor?"

"That's right," Turner says. "You know this area well?"

Morris gives us a nervous grin. "Like the back of my hand," he says. "I grew up in Batworthy, about three miles from here."

"Then you're our man," Turner says, clapping him on the shoulder. "I'll be at your side every step of the way, and once we get within visual range of the Tor, we go low and slow, ok? The man we're looking for will likely have gone straight to Grimspound, but he's tricksy, so we need to keep our eyes open."

Morris gestures to a couple of the other police officers, making introductions that wash over me a bit.

"MacIntyre," Turner says. "You're with Ben. I'll lead with Morris. Then I want a three-metre gap, then Ben and MacIntyre, then the rest of you. First sign of trouble I'll call out if I want munitions and anti-terror, or the ghostbusters."

A nervous ripple of laughter goes through the crowd. "If you need to eat or piss, now's your chance," he continues. "I'm sure local police won't frown on us for using the field there. We'll do a final weapons check before we go – if anyone needs more ammunition or a vest, don't be shy. You've got four minutes."

I join the line of men pissing into the right-hand hedge, as the women clamber through a gap into the left-hand field and do the same thing, less visibly. My hands are shaking a little, but once I've finished, I attune the protection stave, then try to take some deep breaths. I don't know if it'll stop a speeding bullet, but it's better than nothing.

Turner does a quick headcount and passes out chunky vests to the local police, handing one to me.

"It's a stab vest," he says quietly, out of earshot of everyone else. "It won't stop bullets, but it'll protect you if someone gets up close and personal. Not too bulky. As I understand it, you're more or less a civilian, so I'm not going to arm you unless you want a truncheon or something?"

"No, thank you," I manage. He's absolutely right. Given my performance in the tower and complete lack of experience, that'd likely be a disaster. "I'll just take the vest."

David – who turns out to be David MacIntyre, to my relief, and not some stranger – helps me to fasten the vest on over my jacket, then pushes a cereal bar into my hand. I've barely finished eating it when Turner clears his throat.

"Alright," he says quietly, but I don't doubt that everyone can hear him. "Let's go."

Morris – the police guy – leads us slightly down the road, and through a gap into the right-hand hedge. I carefully duck through, taking care not to catch myself on thorns.

On the other side I have to blink and check around me, because it feels like we've just stepped through a rift into another world.

Ben
Into the Woods

The image that comes into my head is Dagobah in Star Wars, and if someone played that trilling noise from R2-D2 I'd almost believe that I'd stepped onto the set.

Everything here is covered in moss. The trees are almost completely engulfed by it, their branches contorted into strange, clutching shapes as if they're trying to beg for help. Where they do have bare patches, the bark is spotty with a pale lichen, making them look diseased. Fallen branches and moss-covered rocks make our progress difficult, and thick bracken makes everything smell rich and deep. I didn't realise that bracken could grow in trees, but fronds of it droop down from branches, brushing my hair as I stoop underneath the low-hanging limbs. If Morris wasn't so at ease with our surroundings, I'd swear that we'd gone through to another place, like Karnak, but thankfully we don't have that to deal with as well.

It's dim, and mist is starting to roll in from somewhere. At first, Turner curses it for making it harder to keep track of the whole party, until Morris mentions that it could also shroud our approach.

It's slow going. There are relatively clear patches where leaf litter and soft earth makes for a comfortable step, but for every foot of that, there's ten feet of cluttered branches and roots, thorns, brackens and grasses obscuring each step, and no clear path anywhere.

I try to imagine coming here on holiday, but it'd be incredibly easy to get lost. I think I know which direction we've come in – made easier by the fact that I'm in the middle of our group – and it feels like we've been going in a straight line, but I'm having to step over and around so many things that we could easily be going in circles.

It is strangely beautiful, but it really does look like another world, especially when we pass through woodland where this pale moss hangs off the trees like cobwebs or snow. It's almost ethereal.

I clamber over another fallen tree and have a flashback to Matt and I doing something similar one summer holiday. He'd described it as 'some real Duke of Edinburgh shit' and I feel a pang of concern for him. What if he can't walk properly again? I hope he'll be ok, but that sounds pretty weak and pathetic compared to what he must be feeling, in the helicopter, waiting for us all.

Then, as quickly as we entered, we're out, stumbling onto a hilly moorland, ponies grazing on grasses not far from us. It's still misty, but there's a slate wall up ahead on the nearby hill, with a gap in the middle. I feel a surge of gratitude for Morris' sense of direction, because there's even a path a few metres from us that heads up the hill. I glance over at him, and he finishes conferring with Turner, beckoning us on. It looks like we're exactly where he thought we'd be.

Carefully, our small band gets about halfway up before Turner holds up a hand for everyone to stop. He points to a soldier at the back of the pack, and together, they carefully work their way to the top, crawling on their stomachs as they near the summit.

There's a long, agonising wait.

Finally, Turner heads back down, carefully choosing his steps to avoid making any unnecessary noise. I strain to hear anything that might indicate Lucas' arrival. All I can hear are the nearby ponies making soft chuntering and chewing noises as they crop the grass and occasionally glance at us, presumably wondering if we've got horse-friendly snacks. Occasionally, someone shifts nervously, or tightens the straps on their pack, but otherwise there's nothing.

Turner beckons us in.

"It doesn't look like he's here yet," he whispers, holding out a paper map. "So we're going to split up. One group will skirt the hills to the left, the other to the right. The right-hand, westerly force will be traversing forest, but I want you to stop halfway to this path here; although Lucas hasn't arrived yet, it's more likely to be guarded or trapped by advance teams. The left-hand, easterly force will keep going until you're halfway to this stream or river. Find a viewpoint where you can stay out of sight easily, and hold position."

The burly officer divides the forces, keeping me and David with him, as well as another soldier and the local police officer, sending the others away.

"Now we wait," he says, hunkering down and sitting on a rock. "We'll take it in turns to relieve Nowak."

The time goes by incredibly slowly, but I don't seem to be expected to relieve Nowak, so I lose myself in my books again. I even take a short nap, until I get woken up by the quiet sound of one of the team marvelling at a few highland cows that have wandered over to us. They're pretty spectacular, with their shaggy coats and long horns, but after a while they drift off in search of greener, or maybe less crowded, pastures.

Everyone tries to eat as quietly as possible, retreating into the trees to muffle the sound.

At around seven 'o' clock, I hear the sound of rotor blades, and everyone looks up at Turner on the Tor. He places a finger to his lips and gestures for us all to find cover. Along with Morris and the others, we head back into the woodland, crouching down in the bracken. It's not long since I last went, but I get the sudden urge to pee.

The sound fades, then there's silence. Above the rustling of bracken, I think I can hear distant voices, but I could easily be imagining it.

We wait.

Fifteen minutes later, Turner wriggles his way down the hill, inch by inch, and joins us.

"He's here. I reckon they're going to send people this way," he whispers. "I saw them gesturing over here. I'll stay here with MacIntyre. Morris, you take the others a short way east, and stay out of sight, ok? The other two squads have eyes on Lucas, and are digging in. I'll signal once the lookouts arrive here. We'll incapacitate them, then all three squads will move in on Lucas' position before he fortifies too much."

I don't want to leave both Turner and David behind, but I have to trust that they know what they're doing. Morris leads us deeper into the woods, then abruptly changes direction. Our path is less direct this time, and he seems to be picking the clearest route, which is a relief, although I'm sure he's doing it to avoid making noise. Eventually, we reach a spot where we can just about see the edge of the woods, and we wait.

We don't have to wait long. My phone flashes up with a message, and I see everyone else checking theirs. It's Turner, and simply says "Moving in. Be ready."

My palms are sweating. The stab vest is suddenly heavy, and I can't quite seem to get enough air.

My phone flashes again. "Spotters down," it says. "All teams check in."

Morris sends a brief reply, and we see replies from the other two groups, before Turner sends "Move in. Stay low and concealed for as long as you can. Fire at will after my shot."

Morris pales, biting his lip, hands trembling as he puts his phone away, and carefully, he leads us through the woodland onto the moor. Bent double, we advance cautiously to what seems to be another low slate wall, and peer over.

Lucas hasn't wasted any time. There's about fifteen men and women in khaki down there, a load of boxes and crates surrounding two large helicopters. Grimspound seems to be a ruin, rocks set out in rectangular formations in a bowl-shaped dip in the land. I assume the rocks mean that there were some kind of dwellings here, and around two-thirds of the military guys are crouched amongst them, keeping a watch on the slopes for any sign of activity. The other five or so are ferrying boxes to and fro, and I assume that they're full of ammunition and supplies. I can see Lucas in the centre, directing the action. He's wearing what looks like a much beefier version of the vest I've got on, and has a helmet to match.

Shouldn't I have a helmet too?

Then I see one of the other soldiers looking distracted, and I follow his gaze across the moorland to the north. At first, I think it's the highland cows again, but then I realise that it's much lighter than it should be over there.

Shit.

I thought they'd come at dusk, but there it is.

The Wild Hunt.

There's horses, complete with huntsmen decked out in gear from all eras, men in reddish jackets with wide-brimmed hats riding next to others in brownish tunics and what I can only describe as Robin Hood-style hats, cloaks billowing out behind them. Women in white dresses wield short bows alongside bare-chested men with winged helmets, all riding large horses that – as they draw nearer – seem to ripple in and out of existence. There's a cloud of something all around them, ebbing and surging forward, and as I stare at it, I can see individual shapes. It's dogs, hunting hounds, their eyes shining yellow, their teeth bared and dripping, charging forwards, darting around the horses, under them, the horses rearing and neighing wildly, the dogs barking and snapping in return.

And in the lead is Woden – or Odin, I suppose – but he doesn't look anything like the Norse legend I was expecting. He's large, larger than the others in the pack, and his horse is a massive grey charger. His beard streams out behind him, at least three feet long, and he clutches a spear that crackles with electricity, a winged eagle on his helmet. There's a fiercely intense look about him, as if he's deep in concentration, focusing on leading this band of hunters across the moor.

I can make out individual colours on each of the huntsmen, but they've all got a slightly bluish cast to them, and if I squint, I can pretty much see through them.

Behind Odin, dark clouds boil, following the hunt and darkening the sky, despite the blue glow. It's a few hours until sunset, but as the cloud roll across the sun, it almost becomes twilight.

"Turner," I say. "The hunt's here."

"Acknowledged," he replies, and although I don't hear or see it, it must be him that fires, a single shot that staggers Lucas, sending him to one knee, before another fells the guy next to him.

Then all hell really does break loose.

There's another shot to Lucas' chest, but there's something gold crackling around him, and he rises slowly, directing his men towards the direction of the shot. At the same time, two other squads come from the east and the south-west of our position, hurrying from their concealed positions and finding cover behind boulders, low walls or hummocks of grassy cover, snapping off shots at the mercenaries.

"Ben, hold position. We need you alive as our backup plan." Turner says in my ear. "Morris, advance. Weapons free."

With a fearful glance at me, Morris, the other policeman and the two soldiers draw their weapons and begin to advance down the slope towards Grimspound. The soldiers snap off single shots with their rifles, and another mercenary falls at Lucas' side. It's painfully loud, the shots echoing around the basin.

I have a terrible premonition of Lucas' fallback plan, and I'm about to call out for Turner again but Lucas vanishes into cover between the two helicopters.

Then the Wild Hunt crests the ridge of Grimspound, pausing as if to survey the scene. Dark storm clouds sweep across the sky, moving faster now, lightning striking the far side of the moor and illuminating the battle, thunder cracking almost simultaneously.

I look up, expecting it to rain, but there's nothing.

Two of our soldiers are cut down by a hail of fire from the mercenaries crouched amongst the rocks, and I catch a brief glimpse of Lucas. He's glowing gold, and despite the gunfire, he's standing with both arms held aloft, like he's reaching towards the hunt. Woden – his horse rearing – starts to charge down the hill, then staggers, slowing to a walk. The large god seems to pale, his bluish tinge fading to a greyish colour, and as I shape the stave to let me see the noosphere, a gushing stream of particles appears between Lucas and Woden, flowing towards Lucas.

I swallow and kneel on the soft earth, the damp seeping into my jeans. I've got an idea, but I'm not sure if it's the right time to be trying something new. I tap into the noosphere and form the staves in my mind, channelling them towards the flow of energy between Woden and Lucas. If I can intercept the flow before it reaches Lucas, then that's better, right?

Nothing happens, and the hunt around Woden comes to a complete stop on the hillside, horses pacing impatiently, hounds pausing and staring down at the scene. A couple of the mercenaries stop and stare as well, quickly being picked off by our shooters, but a couple of our guys do the same and get hit by Lucas' mercs in return. One of the squads is completely down now, or at least, I can't see anyone on that side. I hope they're not dead.

Focus, you idiot.

I re-gather the staves, then work my way around the walls slowly to get a better line of sight on Lucas, trying not to expose myself to gunfire. Lucas shifts and suddenly I see him, the two heavily-armed bodyguards next to him laying down fire towards two of our groups, discouraging anyone from trying to take a shot at him.

I shape the stave, seeing the particles of the noosphere as they energise Lucas. He's already holding so much, and he seems to be weaving the energies into himself. I can odd golden shapes that are inside him, almost like organs, and he's folding and flowing the noosphere energy into them, making them glow more brightly by the second. I grab the flows and hook in, slowly taking a little energy from him, deepening my connection then *rip*, tearing more and more away from him, channelling it back towards myself.

It's awful. I almost hear the noosphere wail, like metal nails being dragged down a blackboard, like someone in the worst pain, like breaking a limb, several limbs, all at once. It's like the stream of particles that bursts towards me is darker somehow. It knows it doesn't belong to me, and I dread it arriving, but when it does it's like someone's infused every cell of my body with caffeine.

It doesn't stop, and it's a lot.

It's too much.

I've forgotten the other part of the stave. I try to maintain the first flow as I weave the second, sending my energy over to Woden, who – after a moment – looks brighter and bluer. The feeling diminishes a little, but I start to feel warm all over, like I'm taking a bath, then like I'm in bright sunshine on a hot summer's day.

The Hunt stays stationary, and Lucas glances over at my position, saying something to his bodyguards. Bullets smack into the slate all around me, one shot sending splinters into my hand, blood spurting from a deep cut. It heals almost instantaneously, knitted together with noosphere energy, and I almost lose my concentration as I watch it.

There's a hail of bullets on the bodyguards' position and they duck back down, one behind a boulder, one behind the helicopter. I try to increase the flow from Lucas to Woden, but I go from uncomfortably warm to sunburn hot in seconds, and have to drop it back down, although the temperature is still rising alarmingly.

There are three flows of noosphere energy now, from Woden to Lucas, Lucas to me and me to Woden, three streams of gold, strong and vibrant in the gloom of the dark sky. There's another hail of bullets on my location and I fall back down onto the ground, keeping hold of the flows like a spiritual cat's cradle.

It's getting hotter. I push myself back up, and to my horror the skin on my arms is reddening with sunburn. I try to ignore it, but it's like someone's holding a lighter underneath every part of my body simultaneously, bringing it closer and closer by the second.

Lucas looks at me and our eyes lock, his rage all too apparent, and without any hesitation, he draws a long knife from his belt, stabbing one of his mercenaries through the neck.

There's a fountain of blood, and with a surprised look, the man falls to his knees, clutching at the wound, dropping onto his face a moment later.

My vomit takes me entirely by surprise, splashing out onto the stones around me, the bitter acid filling my nose and mouth, and I cough, trying to clear it, blinking tears away from my eyes, momentarily letting the staves go.

I cough again, forcing myself to re-weave the staves despite the godawful taste in my mouth and the godawful smell in my nose, the heat subsiding and then re-igniting as the spell kicks back in.

I don't for a moment think that a brief lapse in concentration was his goal, and as I look up, I see what I've been worried about. A new rift opens right next to Lucas, unzipping a gap in the fabric of reality that sounds like a Banshee's scream as it comes apart. He gestures, surrounding himself in golden light, and I wonder how long we've got before Shamblers or worse come through, and what his plan is for surviving *that* or if he even cares at this point.

The heat gets worse, and I glance around, wondering where the fuck the military are. I can just about see Turner exchanging shots with the remaining bodyguards, Morris crouching behind a large boulder up ahead, but there's at least five of Lucas' goons in the rocky basin.

The pain turns into an excruciating tightness, as if every muscle in my body is cramping at once, like the feeling you get when you're a kid on a plane changing altitude, like screws are being driven into your skull, only everywhere at once. The skin on my hands starts to rise and then blister, and I swear there's wisps of smoke coming from under my fingernails.

I've got to stop. I can't do this. The energy coming into me is making me feel like I could sprint a marathon, but at the same time, the pain is incredible. I try to send more of it over to Woden, but it doesn't work; the energy coming in is exactly the same as the energy coming out.

My vision starts to blur, sweat dripping down my face and back. My armpits are soaked. I can't see properly. The hillside starts to defocus. I can only see shapes and colours, like I've blurred my eyes. I just need to hold on a bit longer. I'm holding the flows, but I can't see Lucas. Am I in cover?

One lucky shot. Surely, someone will get one lucky shot in. Am I weakening Lucas? Would a shot even hurt him? There can't be that many people left.

The pain is excruciating. The hair on my arms is burning off somehow, the stench filling my nostrils. My body doesn't know what to do. The burning is everywhere, all at once.

I hear a rushing sound and I wonder if it's my own blood pounding through my head. It gets louder and louder and it's got a heavy metallic ring to it, like vast sheets of bronze being pounded together. There's a glow approaching in the distance, and I wonder if the sun's rising. Have I been here all night? It gets brighter and brighter, and there's a sudden crash.

I can't do this much longer.

I need to do this a bit longer.

I hear gunfire, but it's muted, like the spatter of rain on a car roof, and then the brightness and heat goes away entirely, replaced only by darkness.

Alice
In the End

I'm not certain if I'll ever relate the specifics of the following events to Ben, but the abridged version is this – we were correct about Raysiel's mind being changed by observing the minutiae of daily life.

As an academic and a researcher, it's important to record the complete sequence of events, and as I understand it, they are as follows.

After our last conversation, Raysiel took up into the air towards King's Lynn from his cave, travelling almost two thousand miles due south. Although all four hundred and fifty-five of the residents of Barentsburg – Svalbard's second-largest settlement – will tell you that a channel was melted in the snow from north to south, there were no fatalities. The fishing trawler operating off the coast of Florø that had its mast singed was content to write it off as a meteor strike after a brief conversation with a government official.

It took Raysiel some time to travel the distance, but

by the time I arrived – Siu-Hing parking the helicopter on the roof of the Marks and Spencer nearby – and dragged Jane down the emergency stairs, the angel had somehow managed to covertly order food from Nando's. It observed humankind for about three hours, according to the CCTV footage. I'm still uncertain as to how he paid, and the cashier who took his order remembered very little of the event.

I leave Jane in the middle of the restaurant, requesting that she informs the owners and keeps an eye out for any other supernatural threats, although we are a reasonable distance from the epicentre of the rifts.

The angel sits in a dark corner by himself, his back against the wall. He's somehow muted his terrible glow, and simply looks like a man in a dark raincoat. On closer inspection, you can see that he looks incredibly striking, like a model, but – at the risk of romanticising this – one glance into his eyes and you feel a wash of fear, like the comfortable rug of reality has been roughly yanked from beneath your feet.

I try not to make eye contact, but he looks at me as I sit down at the next table.

"Human," he says in a low whisper that has my bladder aching to release. "You return."

I nod. This fear is entirely emotional and unreasonable, although I suppose that my life is in a very real danger, so I'm not being completely absurd.

"Raysiel, sir," I say, pleased to not be stammering like

an idiot. "Have you reached a decision?"

The radiant being sighs, looking down at his empty plate.

"Mortal," he intones. "In one day, I have learnt more about the nature of kindness, forgiveness and penance than I have in two thousand years of solitude. I am ashamed."

I have a solitary and ridiculous thought about men, fragile egos and emotional labour, but I banish it quickly.

"It's alright," I say hurriedly. "Everyone makes mistakes."

"I have seen how your adult humans love and nurture their offspring," he says, and I glance around, seeing the restaurant slowly emptying at Jane's behest. "I have seen the kindness of people to each other with no knowledge of each other's natures. A man spent the last of his pension payment to cheer a crying girl, in full knowledge that he would be unable to pay to heat his dwelling. I have seen a handful of such sacrifices, and I must believe that this is the state of humanity, alongside the filth and squalor. I have misjudged your people, Alice, and I must atone. I must ascend to heaven and seek forgiveness."

"Ah," I say, holding out one hand and then jerking it back quickly. He might be safe to touch, but there's no point in taking chances. "Before you do that, I was hoping to ask a favour."

Raysiel growls, a deep, ominous noise that almost has me up and across the room before I know it, but I clutch at the sides of the table to stop myself. Jane, alongside a guy in a Nando's uniform, seem to have evacuated everyone, and is now looking extremely worried, wringing her hands, but trying not to stare directly at the angel.

"In days past," Raysiel rumbles. "I would have reduced you to ash for asking such a thing, but I see now what the Lord meant when He spoke of forgiveness and compassion."

"Well," I say, taking a deep breath. "There's a man who seems to be able to drain energy from the spirits appearing around the country. Two friends of mine are trying to stop him, but their plan ultimately revolves around draining the energy from the enemy and passing it back to the spirit. And Bacchus told me that there's a good chance it'll be fatal to my friend. I told him not to do it, but if you knew these guys, you'd know that they're going to do it anyway."

Raysiel trembles, his whole body vibrating, and in a strange mirror of my gesture, he grips the side of the table, only this time, it starts to melt and smoulder in his hands.

"A travesty of nature," he whispers. "No man was made to hold such a force. The principle of the guardians was put in place to protect humankind, not fuel their rise to godhood. Show me where this thing is happening."

I take out my phone and find Grimspound on Google Maps. Despite his age, and – I assume – lack of hands-on experience with smartphones, Raysiel seems to comprehend it instantly.

"Come," he says. "We will put an end to this."

I slump back in my seat, relieved, feeling damp sweat

on my back.

"Thank you," I manage. "Can I follow you in the helicopter?"

He looks at me and for a moment the vertigo is almost overwhelming as I stare into the deep dark abyss of his eyes.

"That will not be necessary," he says, and reaches out for my hand. I jerk it back, then apologise, horrified that I've offended him.

"Fear not. You can abide my touch for a few moments."

His hand is cool, and almost feels metallic. As he stands, his wings unfold, wrapping around me, and suddenly there's a sensation of incredible motion that lasts for just a moment. And then – at the risk of sounding dramatic – we're somewhere else entirely.

I don't do that ridiculous thing of blinking and wondering if it's all an illusion because it's obviously real. We're stood behind a low rock wall, looking down at a grassy basin. Inside the grassy basin is a pre-historic settlement, perhaps bronze age. I can see the outlines of the dwellings, and a larger area, presumably some kind of store or communal building, maybe a place of worship. Unfortunately, my chances of finding out are rather slim, because not only are there two large helicopters parked on it, but there's a pitched gun battle going on, and a number of what seem to be spectral horsemen sitting on a rise to my left, frozen in place.

I look on in amazement. It's the Wild Hunt. The

front horseman, a rather impressive bearded man that I assume is Woden, is staring directly at a man, a real man, in front of the two helicopters in the basin. This man, who I believe to be Lucas, is gesturing at Woden, but also has a hand outstretched, pointing to my right.

I turn, and see Ben a few metres away from me. His skin has turned an unhealthily bright shade of red, like a deep sunburn, and his flesh is smoking. His face is contorted in a rictus of pain.

Raysiel snaps his fingers and something changes in the air. Ben collapses down onto the grass. Lucas starts to pale, as if energy is being drained from him, and Woden starts to look more substantial.

Lucas gestures at the angel, and there's a hail of gunfire. I duck, but the bullets either miss or – as is perhaps more likely – the angel is impervious to such threats. Raysiel doesn't move, but something shifts in the air, and the men in the centre of the basin are scattered like bowling pins. Lucas manages to keep his balance, but staggers, regaining his footing a moment later.

Raysiel's face becomes darker, firmer, more grimly set, and Lucas falls to his knees. The Wild Hunt's charge resumes, Woden's horse rearing up and then galloping down the hillside towards Lucas and his helicopters, gathering pace. Lucas pales, managing to maintain his gesturing at Woden, but the Hunt seems more substantial than ever, clouds overhead surging forwards with the horses, the hounds and the other horsemen, the sky darkening above us.

Woden's on a direct collision course with Lucas, but as he nears him, there's a flash of bright light and I have to look away.

It's painfully bright and for a few seconds, all I can see are after-images, bright coronae of horses and helicopters in front of my eyes.

When my vision clears, Lucas is gone, a large scorch mark on the ground where he previously stood. Policemen and military are charging in and handcuffing the remaining mercenaries, who are standing around looking stunned. I glance at Raysiel, who seems to have regained his former calm.

"It is done," he says in a bassy rumble. "I took more from your foe than he was taking from the Huntsman, until the contest ended. The rift to the other world is closed. Now I must return to heaven and abide a while. Farewell, human."

I open my mouth to reply but without any preamble, the angel shoots directly upwards into the sky, leaving chevron burn marks on the grass. I stare for a few moments, then run over to Ben, finding him unconscious, his skin hot all over. He's breathing, thankfully, but his pulse is racing. I wave to a nearby policeman, who comes over and starts talking into his walkie-talkie.

It only takes twenty minutes for the remaining military forces to scour the area, establish that all combatants have been neutralised, and for a helicopter – a large chinook – to airlift everyone to Exeter. The mercenaries are shepherded to the rear, searched again, and restrained firmly, while the injured – which seems to be the majority of the force – are gently lifted onto stretchers and benches, being looked at in order of severity. The bodies of the six soldiers and police officers who died in the fight are laid out towards the front of the vehicle and covered with tarpaulins. The bodies of the fallen mercenaries are left on the moorland, and two local police officers stay behind, waiting for additional help so that they can identify them.

Despite my aversion to him, I feel a surge of relief at seeing Matt, Ben's friend, alive and on a stretcher when the large helicopter lands. He sports a large bandage on his leg, and looks rather pale, but greets me cheerfully, and without his usual profanity. He does have to be held back and forced to sit down when Ben is carried in on another stretcher, but calms down once a police officer informs him that his friend is in a stable condition.

I find out, once we arrive at Exeter hospital, that 'stable' covers a multitude of sins, and that Ben has incurred second-degree burns to a large percentage of his body, and that Matt's leg has been impaled by the bladed limb of a Lesser Banshee. Both of them are expected to make a full recovery, which I relate – alongside the events of the day – with Turner, an SAS officer, to Seline in London. Turner has his left arm in a bandage, having taken a glancing blow from a bullet, but he seems in remarkably good spirits for a gunshot victim.

As I finish relaying the news, Seline receives another communication, seemingly from the other Gardeners, who, through some magical back-up plan, had been transported to a site in the New Forest during the missile strike that caused the rifts across London to open. The missiles had impacted the building, killing a number of the First Extraordinary before their magical contingency plans kicked in. Unfortunately, the structural damage to the building had meant that more Gardeners were killed as it partially collapsed, and many more were injured as they tried to dig their way out of the hidden location.

Seline seems both saddened and overjoyed to receive the news, which I understand. In one fell swoop, she's received both reinforcements and news of the loss of many friends and colleagues, but in essence, the supernatural forces of the UK have been substantially increased. She apologises for cutting our conversation short, already giving orders to arrange for air transport to collect the rest of her order.

The police offer to take me to a nearby hotel, but I find myself declining, returning to check on Ben and Matt. We're joined by Chloe and her doctor, who have flown in privately. To my surprise, she seems most concerned by Matt's plight, but I don't remark on it.

I sit with them, unsure of what to do.

"Alice," Ben says. "What happened? We've been told the basics, but you found Raysiel?"

"Look, I know I've been all impaled and shit," Matt

interrupts. "But Chloe, I think you also owe us a bit of an explanation first. I mean, I'm glad you're ok and jealous as fuck as to how you can do the leopard thing, but seriously?"

As much as I dislike the man, I can't disagree with him, and it spares me from telling my story for a moment. Chloe gestures and her doctor leaves us, closing the door behind him.

"As I told Ben," Chloe says, sitting on the side of Matt's bed and crossing her legs neatly. "Many years ago, I was caught in a supernatural event, and a transformation rift opened. I escaped, but it seemed to change me, permanently. As well as heightened mental abilities and longevity, I can transform myself into that creature and back, although it drains me greatly. Somehow, the effects seem stable, although I rather avoid using it unless in dire need. The Gardeners, thankfully, have shielded me from any inquiry, and have told the police that it was a side-effect of Bacchus' presence."

Matt opens his mouth and closes it several times, then looks over at Ben.

"We do magic, Alice found an angel and Chloe's a shapeshifting omniscient with her own cult," Ben croaks, shrugging, although I can tell that speaking is painful for him. "I'm just glad she's on our side."

"Ah, fuck," Matt says. "Me too. Happy to be alive and all that."

"And to have reinforcements," Ben adds, then sinks back into his pillows. "So, Alice?"

Chloe looks visibly relieved, her gaze lingering on Matt for a moment.

I take a breath and start to recount the events to my new friends.

Epilogue
Ben

Alice tells us everything that happened with Raysiel, and despite the protestations of all the medical professionals in Exeter Hospital, we go back to London the next day with Turner to lend what assistance we can. Healing staves, in combination with modern medical care, work wonders.

Seline keeps us on light duty for a couple of days, and we take care of a nest of Shamblers in Cannon Street station, then a couple of Darklings lodged in the District Line tunnels. It's absolutely terrifying, and I wake up in the night, my heart thumping in my chest, covered in a cold sweat, imagining that I'm unable to contain or disperse the Darklings, only to gradually see the ruins of Greenwich Observatory around me.

I'm safe.

I glance at my phone. It's five am and I'm on duty from six. Yawning, I unzip my sleeping bag and get up, quietly pulling on a jacket and shoes, climbing down from the upper floor, heading for the lower balcony where the café operates 24/7. My clothes rub on my burns, but they're a lot better than they were, largely thanks to the staves.

To my great relief, all of my friends and family had made it out of the danger zones in one piece, and I'd even seen Jack, the guy who'd gotten me into all of this in the first place. He'd apologised profusely when I saw him, but I was too busy giving him a massive hug and crying to reply very coherently.

I think he understood that it was all ok.

It wasn't all ok.

Our trainer, Christina, had been found in a ditch not far from the Bracknell facility. She had serious gunshot wounds, and had somehow managed to escape the mercenaries and Shamblers, crawling through the fields nearby. She's in a coma in a nearby hospital, but at least she's alive.

It's made a hell of a difference having Raphael and the other Gardeners back. From the absolute brink of disaster and having a scant handful of functional Gardeners, we've been able to marshal our forces and take a more reasoned approach to the conflict rather than simply clinging on by our fingertips trying to prevent our utter annihilation and the slaughter of thousands.

I must sound so calm. I'm going to have nightmares for weeks and need therapy for months.

The death toll doesn't bear thinking about. It climbs every day as we start to re-take London and the surrounding area, finding more casualties, but we're also closing more and more rifts, and Raphael has appealed to countries around the world to lend us their arms, supernatural and otherwise.

I accept a mug of coffee from the commissary, taking it to the balcony and leaning out, looking north towards the river. The sun starts to rise above the horizon, and I have to turn to avoid the glare, but as I do, there's the now-familiar sound of rotor blades. Suddenly, from the south and the east, the sky is dotted with choppers – our allies, emboldened by the return of the Gardeners from Wild Court, and the assured safety of our skies.

Aid, arms and support – of both the normal and paranormal varieties – are coming to us.

I collapse down onto a metal chair, glancing over and seeing my magical colleagues emerge, their faces pictures of joy and disbelief.

"They came," I manage, and Lincoln, his left hand and arm still heavily bandaged up in a sling, appears next to me, standing and watching the armed forces starting to land in the nearby car park.

"Aye," he says. "Better late than never. We'll flush out the rest of the Shamblers and Ravagers now, you mark my words."

"How many left?" I say, glancing at him.

"Too many," he says tiredly. "But we've got safe spots thanks to the gods, and we'll get it done."

"Some empathy," I snort, gesturing at the helicopters and feeling irrationally pissed off that it took them so long. "Better late than never I guess."

He sighs and takes a sip from a water bottle.

"Ben," he says, yawning. "If it was up to me, I'd go to sleep for a thousand, maybe two thousand years and wait for the human race to be in a better place. My honest opinion? We're a hot mess. We're toddlers. If we're not screaming because we're hungry, we're trying to take someone else's sweets and hitting them. Obviously, there's a few good ones, the exceptions to the rule who somehow manage to drag everyone else along with them from time to time, standing up for progress and equality. But you know what? We're lucky to be here at all, given what a crap, selfish species we've proven ourselves to be."

Given what I've seen of people over the last few weeks, I'm not sure I agree with him. I'm not sure I disagree with him either, but I give him some slack because we'd found out that his friend Tristan had died in a Ravager attack, and his friend Celia is in hospital with severe injuries. Someone calls his name and he limps off without saying another word.

I'm about to go after him, but Matt appears next to me, holding a mug of what smells like unpleasantly strong coffee.

"So, what do you reckon happens now?" I say to him, as he sits awkwardly on another of the metal chairs. He's wearing shorts until his leg heals and uses a crutch, but at least he doesn't have to moisturise every hour on the hour and wear factor fifty sunscreen even on a cloudy day for the next month. Mind you, I'm intensely glad to be alive.

He looks pensive for a moment, watching the

Gardeners down below us greeting the foreign military forces. Raphael, a greying but energetic, smartly-dressed guy, is shaking hands vigorously and no doubt already planning the offensive to re-take the city.

"Well," he says. "You know what Alice was talking about, like, where she found Raysiel?"

I frown for a moment, then understand what he's talking about and have to smother a laugh as I wait for it.

"I could so murder a Nando's," Matt says, and I snort, feeling tears of laughter pricking my eyes.

"Matt, it's still literally the apocalypse," I manage. "Monsters on the streets, ghosts everywhere. We're on duty in an hour, there's gods conjuring beer and getting into fights. We do magic, you fancy a girl who's also a leopard and the country's basically fucked."

"Yeah," he says evenly, looking at me. "But seriously though – whole chicken, extra hot, coleslaw, halloumi, one of those big fucking lagers. Can you imagine? Grilled cheese Ben, grilled cheese and hot sauce."

I stare at him for a full minute. It's not even six am and he's already thinking about having a pint.

"Matt," I say. "Never change."

"So," he says, raising an eyebrow. "Was that a yes?"

I sigh, rolling my eyes, then remember Seline saying something about a shop selling hot sauce on Deptford High Street, and grin at my brother.

"It's not a no."

Printed in Great Britain
by Amazon

22475421R00294